Red Spy in Harbin

Book 1: In the Making

Mark Oulton

马福民

Dedicated to

My wife Yan Yan, my prop in times of strife and my daily ray of sunshine.

To the people of China, whose endurance, sacrifice, and quiet strength carried the nation through its most difficult years. This book is a tribute to their spirit.

Copyright © Mark Oulton 2025

First published in 2025

ISBN: 9798286352432

All rights reserved. No part of this publication may be reproduced, stored in or introduced into a retrieval system, or be transmitted in any form, or by any means (electronic, mechanical, photocopying, recording or otherwise) without the prior written permission of the author or his agent. Any person who carries out any unauthorized act in relation to this publication may be liable to criminal prosecution and civil damage claims.

This novel contains scenes of extreme violence and material of a sexual nature. It is not suitable for minors.

TABLE OF CONTENTS

Introduction ---5

Historical Content --8

Chapter 1: Wuli Tulou, Fujian, China, 1921 ---------------------------11

Chapter 2: Xiamen, China, 1921 --17

Chapter 3: Shanghai, China, 1921 --------------------------------------21

Chapter 4: Batumi, Georgia, Imperial Russia, 1892 onwards --------27

Chapter 5: Wuli Tulou, Fujian Province, China, 1926 ----------------37

Chapter 6: Xiamen (Amoy), China, 1926-------------------------------44

Chapter 7: Xiamen (Amoy), China, 1926-------------------------------53

Chapter 8: Shanghai, China, 1927 --------------------------------------63

Chapter 9: Wuping, Fujian, China, 1927-------------------------------78

Chapter 10: Blagoveshchensk, USSR, 1925---------------------------89

Chapter 11: Xunwu, Jiangxi, China, 1927 -----------------------------99

Chapter 12: Jinggang Mountains, Jiangxi, China, 1927 -------------107

Chapter 13: Suichuan, Jiangxi, China, 1928 --------------------------116

Chapter 14: Yongxin, Jiangxi, China, 1928 --------------------------125

Chapter 15: Quinnatisset Farm, Massachusetts, US, 1928 ----------135

Chapter 16: Lingxian County, Hunan, China, 1928------------------146

Chapter 17: Shanghai, China, 1929 -----------------------------------161

Chapter 18: Tingzhou, Fujian, China, 1929 --------------------------172

Chapter 19: Harbin, Heilongjiang, China, 1929 ---------------------183

Chapter 20: Ningdu, Jiangxi, China, 1931 ---------------------------195

Chapter 21: Ruijin, Jiangxi, China, 1931 --------------------------------208

Chapter 22: Japanese State of Manchukuo, 1932–1934 --------------217

Chapter 23: Ruijin, Jiangxi, China, 1932 --------------------------------224

Chapter 24: Bao'an, Shaanxi Province, China, 1935 --------------------237

Chapter 25: Harbin, Japanese Empire of Manchukuo, 1936 ----------249

Chapter 26: Dataozi, Japanese Empire of Manchukuo, 1936 ---------264

Chapter 27: Harbin, Japanese Empire of Manchukuo, 1936 ----------276

Chapter 28: Moscow, USSR, 1936 --288

Chapter 29: Harbin, Japanese Empire of Manchukuo, 1937 ----------297

Chapter 30: Harbin, Japanese Empire of Manchukuo, 1937 ----------307

Postscript ---317

Supplementary Notes

    Uniform Insignia and Military Rank (1929–37) ------------------318

    Understanding Pinyin Tone Marks ---------------------------------318

    Manzhouli Day and the Neon Swastika---------------------------319

    Others--320

List of Fictitious Characters --321

List of Acronyms --321

Acknowledgements --323

About the Author-- 323

Exclusive Excerpt from Red Spy in Harbin Book Two – The Middle Years --324

Mark Oulton

Introduction

This historical novel tells the story of a spy born in 1911 in Fujian Province, China. He was a Hakka—a member of a distinct subgroup within China's Han ethnic majority. Drawn into the pivotal events of the early twentieth century, he narrowly escaped death on numerous occasions. By the end of that turbulent era, despite his humble origins and youth, he had become one of the most capable communist spies in China.

Many of the characters in this novel are real. Their words—and occasionally their actions—are imagined, yet remain historically plausible. A list of both fictional and historical figures is provided in the appendices. Wherever possible, correct dates and other relevant details have been included. However, during wartime, incidents were seldom recorded at the time, and later recollections—often written years afterwards—are subject to fading memory and shifting perspectives. Some documents remain sealed, censored, or heavily redacted.

Readers may find the appendix relating to the names of Russian fascist parties particularly useful, as these groups frequently changed their names. A separate list of fictitious characters is also provided.

Measurements

3.3 centimetres = 1 Cun (寸)

1 metre = 3 Chi (尺) or 1 Mi (米)

1 kilometre = 2 Li (里)

1 hectare = 15 Mu (亩)

1 kilogramme = 2 Jin (斤)

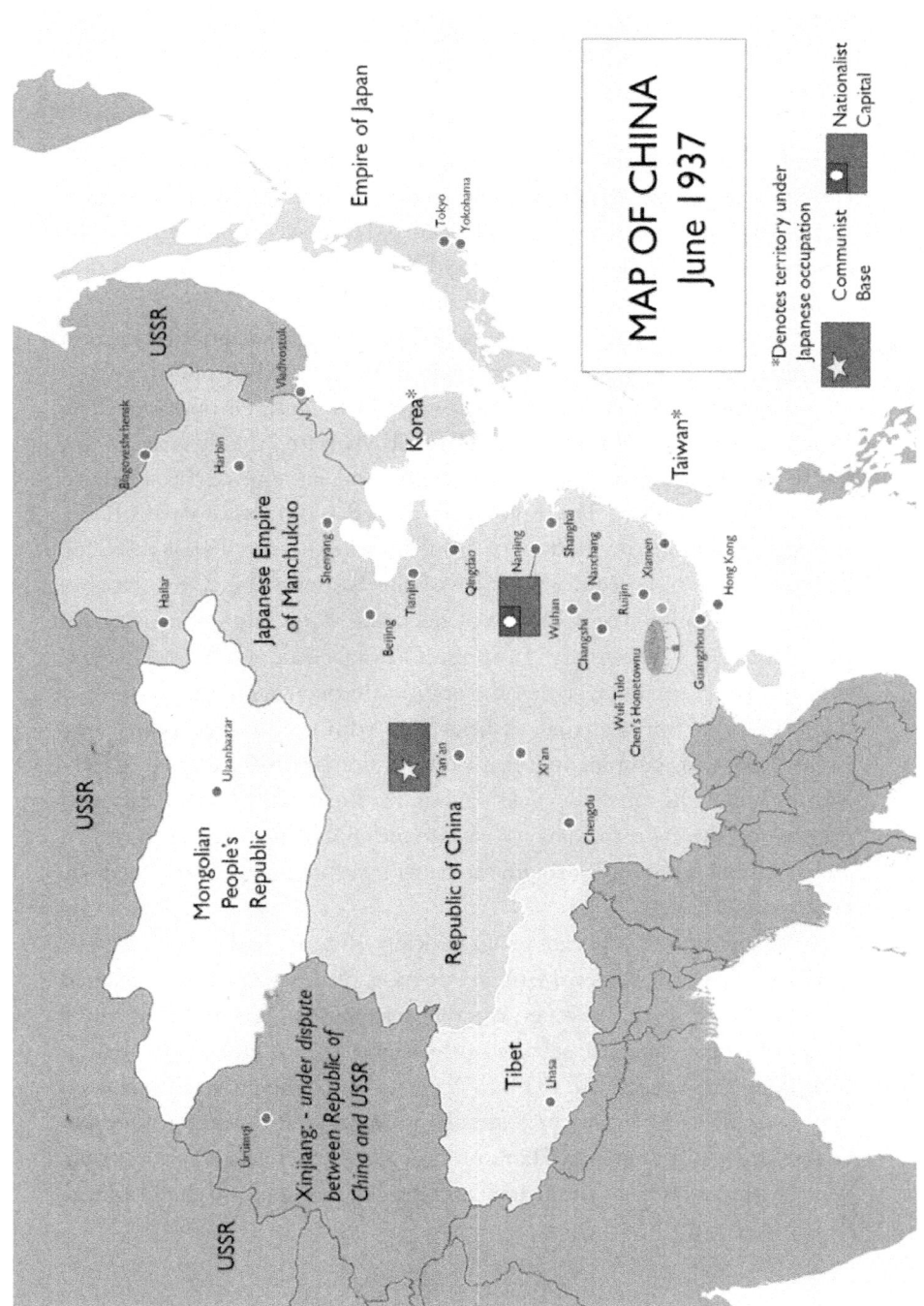

Historical Context

Even by the standards of China's turbulent and often brutal history, the early decades of the twentieth century brought together three extraordinarily violent events that occurred almost simultaneously: the collapse of the Manchu Qing Dynasty in 1911, the outbreak of World War I in 1914, and the Russian Revolution in 1917.

The Qing Dynasty had long failed to prevent foreign intervention in China, including during the two Opium Wars. It had also fallen behind in modernising its military and was wracked by internal uprisings. The Wuchang Uprising of October 1911 finally shattered the dynasty. It was led by the disaffected New Beiyang Army under the powerful northern warlord Yuan Shikai. The revolution gained momentum through the support of various revolutionary groups, including the *Tongmenghui*, led by Sun Yat-sen, the future founder of the Kuomintang. On 1 January 1912, the Republic of China was declared, with Sun as provisional president. On 12 February, Empress Dowager Longyu, regent to six-year-old Emperor Puyi, signed the abdication decree, ending more than 2,000 years of imperial rule. A brief civil conflict between North and South followed, culminating in a political compromise. On 10 March, Sun resigned the presidency in favour of Yuan Shikai, who assumed control of the new Beiyang Government. Following Yuan's death in 1916, China entered a fragmented and volatile era dominated by competing warlords.

World War I, though geographically distant, had significant—if indirect—repercussions for China. For most of the war, China remained neutral. There were, however, notable exceptions—chief among them the joint Anglo-Japanese seizure of the German-held city of Qingdao in Shandong Province in late 1914. In August 1917, China formally declared war on the Central Powers, swiftly reclaiming the former German concessions in Tianjin and Hankou. China's primary contribution to the war effort was human. The British and French recruited 140,000 Chinese labourers, most from impoverished backgrounds. Of these, 100,000 were sent to France under the British Chinese Labour Corps to provide *kǔlì* (苦力—literally 'pain force') labour behind the front lines. Conditions were appalling; deaths from shelling, mustard gas, and disease were common even far from the battlefield. At the Battle of the Somme alone, 840 Chinese workers were killed and buried at the Chinese cemetery in Noyelles-sur-Mer. Simultaneously, 100,000 more Chinese labourers were conscripted by the Tsarist Russians. When the Russian Revolution broke out in 1917, these men were abandoned. With no wages, food, or means to return home, many joined the Red Army.

By early 1919, the political temperature in China had reached boiling point. On 4 May, 4,000 university students marched through Beijing's Tiananmen Square, sparking nationwide protests. Their outrage centred on China's humiliating treatment at the Treaty of Versailles. Most galling was the award of German territorial concessions in Shandong to Japan. Public anger deepened over the earlier 'Twenty-One Demands' made by Japan in 1915—secretly issued to Yuan Shikai's weak Beiyang Government—which would have rendered China effectively a Japanese protectorate. Although international pressure led to some clauses being dropped, the damage was done. One such clause, if ratified, would have given Japan control over policing and financial affairs in Fujian Province—directly impacting the trajectory of this novel's central character.

News that Anhui warlord Duan Qirui had accepted Nishihara loans from Japan in exchange for territorial concessions further inflamed tensions. On the same day, students, merchants, chambers of commerce, and civil organisations united in protest. The Beiyang Government responded by arresting 1,000 students, which only intensified the unrest. In Shanghai, always a cauldron of political activity, students were soon replaced by workers and merchants, and a general strike followed. Among those protesting were several future leaders of the Chinese Communist Party (CCP).

The most consequential development for China's future, however, occurred not within its borders, but to the north in Russia. The October Revolution of 1917 created the first successful communist state. Its ideology, ambition, and military presence loomed over China's northern frontier, separated only by a crumbling line of White Russian resistance. The Beiyang Government even deployed 2,300 troops to Vladivostok to safeguard Chinese nationals and property. In the ensuing chaos, these soldiers found themselves fighting both Bolsheviks and Tsarists—at times simultaneously. The Bolshevik victory reshaped global revolutionary politics and cast a long shadow over China's future.

It is often mistakenly assumed that Mao Zedong led the Chinese Communist Party from its founding in 1921. In truth, his rise to power was far from assured. One of the central themes of this novel, which spans from 1921 to 1937, is how both Mao and Zhou Enlai repeatedly fell in and out of favour—not just with their Chinese peers, but with the Soviet Union and Stalin himself, whose influence over the CCP was profound.

Mao's vision of a peasant-led revolution clashed with the Soviet Union's urban proletarian model, leading to significant friction with Moscow-backed leaders, especially during the 1930s. Mao would not secure undisputed control of the Party until 1943. In the intervening years, both he and Zhou survived through a combination of political cunning, adaptability, strategic realism, and sheer luck. Zhou, in particular, often acted as the conciliator between rival factions. Both men endured mortal threats and purges. They navigated navigating a world of constantly shifting alliances in their struggle to survive.

These events form the backdrop to the life of our protagonist, whose fate intersects with many of the figures and themes introduced here.

Chapter 1: Wuli Tulou, Fujian, China, 1921

Bei Xiansheng—known to all as Mr Bei—was a widower with no children, privately hired as a teacher. He entered the classroom.

In the Hakka tradition of revering education, he insisted on being called 'Mr Bei'—a term he deemed more respectful than the modern *Lǎo Shī* (老师—'old and wise teacher'). He settled into his ornate horseshoe-back chair beneath a statue of Confucius, which stood just over his right shoulder and looked down benevolently over the pupils as they read. He adjusted his conservative camel-coloured long gown and the tanned leather melon cap (*guòpímào* —过皮帽) that covered his short-cropped grey hair. Though it was 1921, he still refused to wear the nationalist Zhongshan suit, with its four pockets representing propriety, justice, honesty, and shame, and its five buttons symbolising the five branches of government.

Life in these Fujian Hakka *tulou* had changed little since the Republic of China was founded fourteen years earlier. After all, a *tulou*—a circular, rammed-earth fortress with a single entrance—was designed to keep out both bandits and alien ideas. Its walls were its strength. Its gun windows on the upper floors served as a warning to intruders. 'Hakka' derives from a term meaning 'guest families' or 'people from another place'—a phrase not always uttered with kindness. This particular *tulou* was large, housing five hundred people and seventy families. Without Mr Bei's extensive reading and his twice-yearly trips to teachers' conclaves in Xiamen—often held at the 'Long-Tongue Teahouse', a well-known centre of gossip—the elders here would have remained blissfully ignorant of the turmoil gripping the nation.

Years of contemplative rubbing had burnished the arms of Mr Bei's chair to a golden hue, a motion he now unconsciously repeated. He looked up and saw Chen Minghe, his most gifted pupil. The boy was ten, enigmatic, and singularly talented. In the old Qing dynasty, he would have been a natural candidate for the Imperial Examinations, with their focus on poetry, writing, and philosophy. But modern schooling now included science and mathematics—subjects in which Chen had no interest.

Life was changing. Even the more conservative *tulou* elders had begun introducing education programmes for girls. But Chen's gift lay elsewhere—and none could have predicted how far they would take him. He spoke fluent Hakka and the local Min-Hokkien dialect, essential for dealings beyond the walls. But it was Mandarin that he excelled in above all.

Mr Bei noticed Chen sitting uncomfortably at his low desk. The boy was growing rapidly: tall, muscular, and striking. He was the only child his age capable of handling a water buffalo on the paddy fields. The girls had begun to notice Chen too, he realised. Once, Mr Bei caught Xiong Hehua gazing at Chen across the room distracted from her work. The sexes were strictly separated, and her inattentiveness earned a sharp crack from Mr Bei's wooden ruler on her desk—enough to make her jump. He had never struck a pupil, preferring to leave discipline to the parents.

The previous winter, he had found Chen and Peng Gangchao, a boy from a rival clan, brawling outside the ground-floor classroom. He summoned Lao Chen, the boy's father, who arrived concerned; Peng's father was well connected among the elders.

'What should I do?' Lao Chen asked,

Mr Bei paused, then said,

'I suspect a whipping isn't the answer—especially if your son can parade the bruises like trophies. Perhaps help him channel that energy instead? He's already a competent pugilist, but there's always room to improve.'

Then, as Lao Chen turned to leave, Mr Bei added,

'And teach him to fire that old musket of yours—Chen may find it useful one day.'

Lao Chen took the advice seriously, intensifying his son's martial arts training in the Hakka Kuen style. Within a year, Chen's triangular footwork and deceptive jamming strikes with the braced elbow had improved so much that he occasionally defeated opponents several years older. Discipline was no longer an issue.

Later, in the presence of father and son, Mr Bei handed Chen a book he deemed too advanced for the rest of the class: *The Art of War* by Master Sun, written 2,500 years ago. Chen was captivated. He devoured *Chapter Three*—'*Attack by Stratagem*'—and marvelled at its warning against prolonged sieges. He saw in the *tulou* itself a testament to that wisdom: a fortress designed to endure, but also to remind attackers of the futility of such a strategy. But it was *Chapter Thirteen*—'*Use Spies*' (*Yòng jiàn*—用間)—that haunted him: a masterclass in intelligence. Five types of spies were described. The fourth—the doomed spy, sent to be captured and feed disinformation before certain death—especially gripped the boy's imagination. He was equally fascinated by double agents.

On New Year's Day, many room doors were left open. Children aged five to fourteen gathered on the ground floor for a grand game of hide and seek, supervised by the ever-watchful Mr Bei. From a lacquered bamboo can—usually reserved for fortune-telling—they drew lots. Each stick bore a red-painted tip and a number. The draw split them into two teams: high and low.

The *tulou* was perfectly suited for the game. Captured players were brought to a roped-off pen in the courtyard, earning a single point. Those who evaded detection and returned at the sound of the local 'walking horse gong' after an hour received two. Once all those in hiding had been found or time elapsed, the teams switched roles. Parents—some already fortified by mother wine, the local rice hooch—chattered amongst themselves and erupted in cheers whenever a new captive emerged.

Chen excelled. Still as a stone and invisible when he wished, he was also mindful of his team's chances. Last year, he'd helped secure victory using a secret trapdoor in the *tulou* roof—accessible only by ladder from the corner of Mr Bei's room. The day before the game, he had stolen the ladder from his father's workshop and stashed it on the fourth floor. Once hidden, he kicked the ladder aside, knowing none of the others would question its presence. At the signal to return, he'd simply opened the hatch, dropped down a metre and a half, and rejoined the crowd with a triumphant grin.

This year, however, his plan failed. The ladder had been chained and locked to the workshop wall. The emergency rope ladders—vital during fire but useless for a stealthy ascent—remained untouched.

Chen did not often see his father. Lao Chen, master carpenter of the *tulou*, was perpetually busy: repairing eaves and railings, staircases and floorboards, well-lifting frames and balcony joints. So when his father suggested a hunting expedition, the boy was elated.

The evening before, his mother and two younger sisters—Fengbao and Yinghui, who adored him—prepared a packed lunch. There were cold noodles with ginger and peanut sauce wrapped in a banana leaf, chicken, sausage, honey maize cakes, and a flask of tea—perfect sustenance for the bamboo- and pine-clad mountains surrounding the *tulou* cluster.

At five the next morning, they set off. Lao Chen slung the musket over his shoulder as they climbed the trails. By dawn, the valley unfolded below: rice terraces, circular and square *tulou*, and the shimmering Nanxi River. It was a magnificent sight. As the mist parted, deeper layers of each *tulou* were revealed—communal courtyards, temples, kitchens, wells, and market stalls—framed by peach-tinted walls and grey-tiled roofs. As they ascended, the pair walked in silence, sometimes halting to absorb the sweeping vista or listen to wildlife scurrying through the undergrowth. There was no need to speak. This was a quiet kind of bonding, and Chen had never been happier.

At a break to catch their breath in a clearing, Chen could no longer hold his tongue. In an excited voice, pitched half an octave higher than usual, he began his stream of questions,

'Dad, Dad, tell me about your gun. What will we shoot and kill?'

'Here in the mountains, there are many things to shoot at. Rabbits are easiest, and the birds—like quail and silver pheasant—are more difficult. This old gun has even killed a few feral pigs and was used to defend our *tulou* from invaders. I've modified and replaced the stock, which still works well.'

'So, this gun shot and killed people?'

'Yes, son. In the Punti War and Red Turban Rebellion against the Cantonese over fifty years ago, our people lost half a million—maybe more.'

Half a million dead was a large number for a ten-year-old to grasp. Sometimes, ten pigs would be rounded up in an enclosure for inspection and selection, and, on that scale, the whole valley floor would be filled with pig enclosures. Chen was in awe—and even more so when the pair reached a clearing and his father set up an old paper lantern as a target.

He unslung the caplock weapon—a long, muzzle-loading gun, heavy in the hand and potentially lethal. As Chen watched, wide-eyed, his father demonstrated each step: pouring powder down the barrel, ramming in the wadding, then the buckshot—small lead pellets used for hunting birds or rabbits.

'This won't kill a man unless he's close,' Lao Chen explained. 'For war, they used musket balls—larger lead rounds, like marbles. One hit could shatter bone or tear through a man's chest.'

He cocked the percussion hammer, showed his son how to align the primitive iron sight, and took aim.

After two direct hits on the target, he strung up a replacement lantern and stepped back.

'Go on. Try it.'

Now it was Chen's turn. He was tense, sweaty, and the recoil was so intense that, even after half an hour of learning, he was still shooting high—his shoulder aching with each attempt.

Lunch was a convivial and rare father-and-son affair, and, by then, the game bag was half full—no thanks to young Chen's erratic shooting. During the break, Chen looked up and asked the question that had been knowing at him.

'Dad, is this the best gun in the world?'

'Not quite, son, but it does the job.'

What was he supposed to say? Lao Chen knew of far more lethal weapons: rifles. However, any that became available were unaffordable and were siphoned off to supply the warlords in Fujian.

At dusk, as they descended the mountain, Chen Junior was once again allowed to take control of the gun, with specific instructions to shoot only at ground-level game. One of the dangers was that an aerial shot could easily spray debris—or even blind an amateur shooter. On a narrow part of the path, Chen saw a bird flickering in the twilight canopy above—and fired.

It was a fluke shot, and a wood pigeon tumbled down. Chen let out a whoop. To him, it was no accident, but the first proof of a future marksman. However, Lao Chen was furious, even though his response was measured.

'Put the bird in the game bag, you fool. That mother likely had five or six chicks. Now they'll all starve because of your thoughtlessness.'

Chen hadn't considered that, and his joy turned instantly to misery. He wondered how long the chicks would survive—whether they would slowly weaken from hunger or be taken by a crow or a weasel.

Nothing more was said between the two during the descent, and tears welled in Chen's eyes at the catastrophe he had caused. He was still a boy. After arriving home, his father made him clean the gun—a task he completed with downcast eyes—before placing it back on the rack. That night, he couldn't sleep. Again and again, he saw the pigeon with its head twisted at a grotesque angle, and in the silence, he imagined the hungry cries of the chicks as they awaited their inevitable fate.

An hour later, Lao Chen crawled into bed and told his wife what had happened. She thought he had been a little harsh on their son. As he snuffed out the candle, he said to her,

'He's learned his lesson: disobedience has consequences. Tomorrow, I will be gentle with him and only show kindness, so that he knows that after a calamity, there is a time to move on.'

It was several months before Chen wanted to go hunting again.

Chapter 2: Xiamen, China, 1921

Mr Bei was no advocate for the declining Qing Dynasty, which had collapsed in 1911. He appreciated the dynasty's discipline and reverence for teachers, but he had always disliked the enforced braided queue and shaved scalp—symbols of subservience to the Manchu court, a source of long-standing resentment among the Han majority, including the Hakka. Most of all, as an academic, he detested how the Qing had stage-managed the press and other cultural outlets.

After the founding of the Republic and the formation of the Beiyang Government in 1912, Mr Bei began to notice a shift in the tone of the newspapers that reached him. He could now read openly about political changes in China and events further afield.

There were reports of White Russians fleeing to the northern Chinese city of Harbin, desperate to escape the Bolshevik Red Army. The Russian Revolution had sent tremors across Asia. Younger teachers at the summer conclave began circulating copies of *New Youth Magazine* (*subtitled La Jeunesse*), founded and edited by Chen Duxiu. A cornerstone of the May Fourth Movement, the magazine became a rallying point for young Chinese intellectuals disillusioned with Confucian orthodoxy. Mr Bei was startled when the May 1918 edition, passed discreetly among participants, was written entirely in the vernacular—*Guóyǔ*—rather than Classical Chinese.

The presentations at the conclave ranged widely in subject. This year, on the second afternoon, three stood out. The first advocated broader access to universal education; the second proposed a model for new-style universities. But it was the third, delivered jointly by two teachers in their mid-twenties, Wang Lisun and Hu Chenggong, that gripped him. Entitled *The Short Story: A New Paradigm*, it sparked intense discussion.

Wang opened with a critique of *One Day*, a short story by Chen Hengzhe about the Boxer Indemnity Scholarship and student life at the University of Chicago. He described it as remarkable not only for its brevity and sparing description, but also for being written by a woman—

a rarity—and, most strikingly, in the vernacular. At a time when most literature remained mired in classical language, Chen Hengzhe's choice marked a quiet revolution.

Hu, an English teacher, followed with a riveting talk on Lu Xun's *A Madman's Diary*, another short story in *Guóyǔ*. Irony laced the tale of a madman haunted by visions of cannibals—traits he perceived in his own family and neighbours. As the story unfolded, the madman retreated into isolation and obsessive reading, discovering references to cannibalism hidden between the lines of Confucian classics. The metaphor was unmistakable: a savage indictment of China's stifling, feudal traditions.

When Teacher Hu concluded and thanked the audience, and the applause rose, Mr Bei, with a wry smile, muttered under his breath, *'Thanking even gnarly old flesh-eaters like me.'*

Mr Bei walked to the teahouse frequented by the teachers, lost in thought and unaware of the sea breeze or the quiet hum of the streets. Inside, the shift in atmosphere was immediate: the rattan ceiling fans stirred the smoky air without cooling it, while streaks of dusty light slipped through carved wooden shutters. The low buzz of conversation was broken by the shouts of *Xiǎo'ér!* (小二 —'Waiter!') and the percussive clatter of porcelain cups. Teachers argued at clustered tables, their voices rising and falling in overlapping waves. Mr Bei spotted Hu in a recessed corner and joined him beside a rack of newspapers, the pages creased and smudged, headlines about the Northern Expedition barely legible beneath ink-stained fingerprints.

He engaged Hu in conversation.
'From your presentation, I can sense your zeal for reform. Dinosaurs like me must either learn new tricks or go extinct. I was young and idealistic once. But promoting democracy and science while the country is carved up by warlords may be a fool's errand. These modernisations require stability—time to take root.'

Hu's tone was calm, even conciliatory.
'I meant no offence, Bei Xiansheng. I agree—this is no real republic. Yuan Shikai usurped the presidency from Doctor Sun Yat-sen. Sun's Kuomintang (KMT) lacked the military strength to resist. Yuan showed

his hand early, declaring himself emperor, almost certainly arranging the murder of the likely future prime minister, Song. He exiled Sun to Japan, and later to London. Yuan knew that once the KMT dominated the National Assembly, he'd be voted out.'

Mr Bei nodded slowly. Even after Yuan's death in 1916, the Republic remained rudderless. No true progress had followed.

'If you're backing the KMT, remember—Sun might be a visionary, but his past is blemished. He failed in two uprisings here and another against the Americans in the Philippines. He wasn't even in China when the Wuchang Uprising succeeded. He nearly got captured by Beiyang spies in London. Had they succeeded, he would have faced certain death. And if he does return, he'll need an army. Doesn't that make him just another warlord?'

'So he failed like Lenin, then?' Hu said. 'Lenin fled after 1905, chased by the Tsar's secret police across Finland, Switzerland, and Paris. But he returned and won in 1917. Sun isn't a warlord. He may need to fight, but the goal is democracy. At least he's back in the country.

Mr Bei saw the logic. He excused himself and found a quiet corner near the washroom. Crouching over a low bench, he pulled out a pen and paper, and wrote: *Sun's family is originally from Meixi, in Guangdong. He is a Hakka. If you need help—within reason—you may ask. Good luck, Teacher Hu.*

Upon returning, he noticed a painted eyebrow bird (*huàméi niǎo*—画眉) in a bamboo cage above him. It offered no trace of its lyrical call, merely cocking its head as though observing him. Preposterous, perhaps—but a timely reminder nonetheless that these were dangerous times, and listening posts were everywhere. He handed Hu the paper and whispered, 'Read it later. Then destroy it.'

Teacher Hu's wish was granted. After returning to China on 10 October, Sun Yat-sen founded the new Nationalist Party of China—the *Zhōngguó Guómíndǎng*—known in most circles as the KMT. He was elected Generalissimo. Rightist nationalists, and later the Chinese Communist Party (CCP), joined the movement to reunify China.

In early 1921, with Chen still under his tutelage, Mr Bei received a parcel from Hu. Inside was a book with a red image on the cover—the inaugural Chinese edition of *The Communist Manifesto* by Karl Marx and Friedrich Engels. Mr Bei immediately grasped its significance. But with his usual eye for detail, he noticed that the character order for '*Communist Party*' was wrong. Retiring to his fourth-floor room, he began reading—and soon found the text riddled with mistranslations and typesetting flaws. There was also a letter from Hu, describing the changing face of urban China and the growth of industry. The industrial working class—the proletariat—had begun to organise, forming fractious trade unions across the country. Mr Bei replied with a balanced, measured letter.

Though usually frugal with paper and ink, and a decisive writer by habit, this response took several attempts. He struggled to find the words that could balance his belief in justice with his fear of revolution. After one failed draft, he crossed out the line, 'Perhaps the proletariat will triumph where the scholars could not.' He acknowledged the pace of industrialisation, but reminded Hu that China remained predominantly agrarian. Without the support of the peasantry, he warned, the struggle would be uphill.

China remained as bitterly divided as ever. For Mr Bei, things only worsened that same year with the publication of *The Geography of the World* in Shanghai. The book, crudely written and ideologically charged, attempted to erase nearly two millennia of historical identity—going so far as to describe the Hakka as non-Chinese. The provocation sparked outrage. In response, over 1,000 delegates from Hakka associations across China and overseas convened in Canton to protest.

Chapter 3: Shanghai, China, 1921

While Chen Minghe was still discovering life, 1921 marked a far more momentous chapter for China itself.

Consul-General André Fournier took pride in the order he maintained in the French Concession, even as China remained in perpetual turbulence. Occasional gunfights and assassinations were primarily the work of the Green Gang—a criminal organisation asserting its authority over any upstarts in their drug, gambling, and prostitution ventures.

He looked down from his bay window onto Avenue Joffre, where London plane trees provided much-needed shade in the sweltering summer heat. Beneath the canopy, he caught glimpses of fashionable women in bright silk qipaos, weaving rickshaws competing with Peugeot cars, stewards removing the last Bastille Day flags, and workers balancing impossibly high bundles on their shoulders. There was no hint of the chaos to come.

His wife, Geraldine, had arranged a magnificent party for the national occasion and had personally overseen the food and drink. The Chinese head chef—trained in France—had, under her supervision, prepared a grand selection of canapés using locally sourced ingredients to accompany the Taittinger champagne: stuffed crab, duck liver pâté, and other delicacies.

All the leaders of the International Settlement had been invited, headed by the senior-ranking delegation—the British—along with consuls from nineteen other countries, including the Americans, Japanese, Spanish, Italians, Portuguese, Peruvians, and Dutch.

To Fournier, Geraldine looked radiant—just as she had when he first met her at a society soirée in Paris. Her manicured blonde bob was framed by a fashionable—and, to him, slightly risqué—powder-blue silk chiffon Deco dress that revealed her long, smooth legs. Complete with a pearl necklace, it made for a dazzling spectacle and belied her years. When the dancing began, she was one of the finest.

The evening concluded with the band moving to the balcony and giving a boisterous rendition of *La Marseillaise,* followed by a firework

display. The inebriated French sang along:
> *Sous nos drapeaux que la victoire*
> *Accoure à tes mâles accents,*
> *Que tes ennemis expirants*
> *Voient ton triomphe et notre gloire!*
> *How lucky I am*, he thought.

There was a knock at the door, and two men were ushered into the boardroom. Vietnamese coffee was served, and the regular security meeting was convened. The first was Pascal Allard, Chief of Police for *La Garde Municipale de la Concession Française*. The second was Raymond Camus, listed as Cultural Attaché but in reality responsible for security and intelligence in the French Concession, as well as liaison with the *Tirailleurs Tonkinois*—the reassuring Indochinese battalion stationed at the garrison.

Fournier began,

'Gentlemen, as you know, we have a long-standing agreement with the Beiyang Government not to allow actions by Bolshevik provocateurs in any of the Concessions—or even the Chinese city at large. And when I say provocateurs, I don't mean the plethora of leftist writers we've accumulated in the city. I believe we should uphold the agreement, even though we have serious doubts about the government's methods and intentions.

'Once again, the Chinese Foreign Ministry has advised us that the possibility of insurrection is intensifying. I'd like to hear your opinions.'

Allard spoke next,

'Our detectives are close to the pulse. We've seen no activity of that nature. What we are seeing is an influx of workers returning from Russia to Shanghai. Some will have fought for the Bolshevik Red Army and either been decommissioned or fled. In my opinion, they are uneducated and too busy finding food and work to concern themselves with fomenting revolution.'

Fournier toyed with his Gallomine silver propelling pencil and glanced at Camus, inviting him to speak.

'I agree with Pascal,' said Camus. 'But another problem has come to light. The Beiyang Government is convinced that a meeting of the Chinese Bolsheviks is imminent—and very possibly in Shanghai. They also believe that one or more Russians will be in attendance.

Pascal has now met with the head of the International Settlement Police, the Chinese Police, and the Shanghai Defence Commissioner outside the Concessions. It was agreed that this must be handled jointly. There is consensus that all Russians in Shanghai will be inspected and monitored, as will all ships arriving from Dalian and Vladivostok.

Chinese military and civil police will also inspect all trains entering Shanghai from Nanjing. The Communications Ministry has been instructed to interrogate any person with a Russian passport—or a Russian with no passport—travelling on the China Eastern Railway from the north. No ticket is to be issued to anyone deemed suspicious. So, reaching Shanghai from the north will be almost impossible through this dragnet.'

Fournier asked,
'That covers the Russians. But what about the Chinese delegates? Do we have a list?'

'Not a full one,' Camus replied. 'But we can make deductions. Chen Duxiu, for certain. He fled here after a jail term. Li Dazhao or Zhang Guotao—if they can slip in from Beijing. Then Li Hanjun and Li Da, both locals. Also Wang Jingmei from Guangzhou. And from Hunan—Mao Zedong or He Shuheng. Possibly Dong Biwu from Hubei. Apart from the Shanghai three, our intelligence is thin.'

'And you trust these reports?'

'Not entirely. They come from Prince Kudashev, the former Russian ambassador. His White Russian bias feeds neatly into the Beiyang narrative.'

There was a knock. A clerk entered with a message for Allard. He read it, scowled, and said,

'Chen Duxiu has slipped his surveillance.'

Fournier exploded,

'Merde, it's true. They are coming here—to Shanghai. Pascal, find out who, when, and how.'

Allard asked not to be disturbed. He needed to think. The obvious Russian would be Grigori Voitinsky—spotted with Chen Duxiu last year. But too high-profile now. Who else?

The Chinese would not meet unless foreign support was guaranteed. Chen might hide in the International Settlement—far easier than the Chinese Old City. He'd ask the British for help, but trusted them little.

The Chinese delegates could blend in easily. Allard ordered his entire network of informants to remain alert. Double pay for whoever found the meeting.

The answer came on 26 July. An informant noticed strange movements at the Bowen Girls' School on Taicang Road. The group inside never went out for food. They didn't behave like teachers. They kept to themselves. Too quiet.

Pairs left each day, always to 106 Rue Wantz. On 30 July, one man slipped in, startled the room, apologised, then returned with two gendarmes. Fifteen people were told to stay where they were.

Allard arrived by car. He knew some faces—Li Hanjun and Li Da. The rest showed dread or defiance. He didn't need to explain. They knew. The air inside the room was heavy with the sour smell of fear.

He turned to Li Da and asked calmly in French,

'How long have you been assembled here?'

'Eight days.'

'Where have you been staying?'

'At the Bowen Girls' School.'

'All of you?'

'Most of us.'

So that was it. Hiding in plain sight. The foreigners likely stayed with sympathisers elsewhere.

He handed Li a notepad.

'List everyone here—in Chinese and English—and their origin.'

Li complied. Allard scanned the room. The two foreigners looked pale. Unfamiliar—but unmistakably Comintern.

. He studied the names. One stood out: *Hendricus Sneevliet, The Netherlands.* Another: *Vladimir Nikolsky, Russia.* Both were intriguing.

Voitinsky replaced. Clever. The Dutchman already in China, the Russian less known. Likely from Siberia. Through the dragnet.

He found Mao, Wang, Dong—just as Camus had said. But no Chen Duxiu.

'Where is Chen Duxiu?' he asked.

'I don't know,' Li answered, expression flat.

Fuck. Neither do we. The bastard had soaked up weeks of work—and vanished. But this time, the seeds were planted. They would take root.

The gendarmes searched the room. No weapons. No papers. But every man carried bundles of crisp cash. Russian donations, almost certainly.

Allard told Li,

'Inform your comrades they are not welcome in Shanghai. They may leave.'

It was a warning. But also a concession. Had the Green Gang come first, there'd have been bodies. His spies had held the line—just.

The next day, the delegates slipped away in two groups, bound for Jiaxing. There, aboard a pleasure boat on Nanhu Lake, they concluded the meeting.

Chen Duxiu—though absent—was elected Secretary and Leader. Li Da became Director of Propaganda. Zhang Guotao was named Director of Organisation. Mao was present. But his time had not yet come.

In September, Mr Bei received a letter and a folded poster. The stamp commemorated twenty-five years of China's postal service. The return address was in Shanghai.

It was from Hu. He had left teaching and taken a post in the Communist Secretariat of the Chinese Labour Congregation. He gave lectures, recruited unionists, and wrote for *Labour Weekly*.

He reported to Li Qihan, but implied that guidance ultimately came from Moscow. Cadres fluent in Russian were returning from The Communist University of the Toilers of the East in Moscow.

The most successful action had just occurred. Flyers posted at British-American Tobacco had triggered a strike. Over 8,000 joined. The company had been forced to make some concessions.

Hu's letter noted expansion. Under Comintern discipline, the Shanghai and Hunan branches had earned praise. Mao excelled at recruitment.

Mr Bei unfolded the poster:

要求厂方实行工厂法 – 第五区卷烟业工会宣传科

(*We demand factories implement the factory law – Propaganda Section of the Cigarette Industry Trade Union, District 5*)

He read it twice, then burned it. He disagreed with Hu. He had no love for revolution. But something in Hu's voice—the certainty, the fire—lingered after the paper turned to ash.

Allard, the Green Gang, and even Huang Jinrong had no idea about the Secretariat—hidden in plain sight on Chengdu Road.

As for the Comintern organiser—Maring—his Chinese name was *Mǎ Lín* (马林). But his Dutch passport said Sneevliet. He had four more. He'd entered Qingdao months earlier on a legal visa. Even the Germans found no cause to stop him.

And Allard never knew the Japanese were watching, too. Their secret services had infiltrated Japan's own Communist cells, which maintained discreet ties to the Chinese networks. Through these links, they learned of the planned meeting in Shanghai—though not the precise location. Some Japanese agents spoke the Shanghai-Wu dialect fluently. They moved among the crowds—unseen, listening, watching.

Chapter 4: Batumi, Georgia, Imperial Russia, 1892 onwards

Chen Minghe now found himself at a crossroads—with some choices of his own, and others imposed upon him. The agreement with the *tulou* elders was to fund male education only up to the age of fourteen. In 1925, Chen's time had run out. As was his habit, Mr Bei invited each departing pupil and their parents to say goodbye, one group at a time. He presented each pupil with a scroll of merit, personally brushed in his fine calligraphy. It was equally a moment of triumph and of sadness.

When it was the turn of Lao Chen, his wife, and Chen Minghe, Mr Bei was crouched on a mat, performing calisthenics to keep his body supple. He sprang up and invited them to sit.

'I hear your son has decided to become your apprentice in the workshop. It's an honourable and necessary occupation. Still, I'm sure he'll be needed in the fields during the busiest times of year, and his physical strength will be appreciated. I had hoped he might become a teacher one day, but we don't have the resources—nor, I'm sure, do you—for education beyond this point, let alone teacher training college. Anyway, it's probably not a good career path in the turbulent times we find ourselves in.'

Lao Chen spoke,

'Bei Xiansheng, we cannot thank you enough for the education you've provided our son. Under your tutelage, he's grown into a considerate and thoughtful young man.'

Mr Bei nodded in appreciation and continued.

'I want to discuss an idea with you. There's no need for your son to give up his education completely. Part of my final lesson to the graduates concerned continuing to learn—self-taught, if necessary—and for life. In your son's case, though, I'd like him to continue studying languages. He has a real aptitude in this area.'

'But... but... what new languages? How would that even be possible?'

'There are, in my view, several languages that will dominate our future world: French, German, English, and Japanese. But the most useful in China may well turn out to be Russian. That has already begun. Several leaders in the newly formed KMT–CCP United Front, along with their National Revolutionary Army (NRA), are already fluent in Russian. Many were educated in what is now the USSR, preparing for their campaign to oust the Beiyang Government.'

'But... but... we don't have a Russian speaker here in the *tulous*.'

Mr Bei smiled.

'As a matter of fact, we do. May I have your consent to organise this?'

All three visitors nodded in unison.

A few days later, in the late afternoon, Mr Bei took Chen Minghe to another *tulou* in the cluster to introduce him to Yao Wenxun, who served an unfamiliar black tea, its deep aroma unlike anything Chen had ever tasted.

'Mr Bei tells me you have a gift for languages and want to learn Russian. I must tell you I haven't spoken it in many years—and I swore I never would again. But the persuasive Mr Bei prevailed upon me to make an exception for you.'

'Sir, I'm honoured by this opportunity and will be a diligent student. I promise.'

'I believe you. I'll just have to swallow a few bitter memories in the process.'

Once Mr Bei had left, Yao continued.

'I need to tell you some of my story. I have a few books in Russian, and even an old Russian–Chinese dictionary somewhere in a chest that you can use. In 1892, we were in a parlous state here in the *tulous*. The never-ending wars—especially the Christian-inspired Taiping Rebellion—which we lost, droughts, and land disputes had left us impoverished.

'As a young man of seventeen, I decided to seek work elsewhere to support my parents and grandparents. I went south to Guangzhou, hoping to find work in a trade I knew well. At that time, it was common for men to leave home for years, often leaving behind wives and children to fend for themselves. Eventually, I found work—but not before my ribs were poking through my skin.

'One day, I visited a tea plantation and factory owned by a man named Liu Junzhou. I was about to leave, disappointed as always, just as the patron arrived at the factory gates. Liu asked his driver to stop and enquired where I was from. I explained I was from Fujian and had experience in tea growing and production. He looked at me, shooed away the guards, and brought me inside the compound.

'First, he ordered food. I scoffed it down like a starving animal. It was congee—rice gruel with a few snippets of pork fat. Anything more, emaciated as I was, would have come straight back up. Then he invited me to his office. It was a thorough interview, but in the end, he knew he'd found the man he needed. He issued me an employment contract. I never looked back and was quickly promoted to Assistant Manager.'

Yao stood up, went to a cupboard, and brought Chen some black-and-white photographs, marked 1892 on the back, of the Guangzhou tea garden and factory.

'We continued to expand production. One day we had an important visitor—a Russian trader named Konstantin Popov, who came to inspect the factory and the garden. He'd first tasted our tea on a visit to Wuhan, at one end of the ancient tea route that stretched to St Petersburg.

'Popov had an idea. He believed tea could be grown in Georgia, then part of the Russian Empire, to meet growing demand and bypass the journey of fifty to one hundred days through Mongolia. It would also undercut the Shufeng Brick Tea Factory, which Russian merchants had founded in the Hankou area nearly thirty years earlier.

'His proposal seemed outrageous at first—but it was potentially backed by millions of *roubles*. He wanted help establishing a garden in Georgia for producing black tea. The Georgians had tried several times and failed, mostly because of their climate worries and lack of expertise.

'In the end, Liu agreed. He selected a team: two translators, ten dual pickers and labourers, and one staff member—me. He purchased one ton of tea seeds and the same again in seedlings. In February 1893, we sailed to Batumi via the South China Sea, the Indian Ocean, the Red Sea, and eventually the Suez Canal into the Black Sea. We established the gardens at Chakvi, just north of Batumi.

'Within four years, we were producing the finest quality black tea on thirty hectares, processed through the factory. The beverage soon became a favourite of the Royal Family and was known across Russia as Liu's Tea. We won several medals—including one from the Tsar in 1909.'

Yao took a slow sip of his tea, as if to savour the memory.

'We were treated well, and the wages were a fortune to us. In the early days, we boarded with local farmers until custom-built cottages could be constructed. Even after that, we continued to eat together in a mess hall, since none of us could cook.

'Before the cottages, the Georgian wives were glad for the extra income. We were shocked to discover how poor the peasant farmers were—many, like us in China, were tenants. We spent the first six months living on *abysta*—a kind of maize porridge—and twenty different walnut recipes: pickled, in sauces, in everything.

'The extra income allowed the introduction of meat into our diet. Once the cottages were ready, Popov sent us a cook who made us *khinkali*—a massive steamed dumpling filled with lamb and chilli flakes—just as good as anything in China. Eventually, he could cook barbecue and rice properly. We were bloated every night.

'As summer came, Batumi grew humid, but not unbearably so, like Guangzhou. At Chakvi, up in the rolling hills, we were always more comfortable. The vegetation was different from home, but with a twist of imagination, it looked familiar to me—apart from the snow-capped mountains in the distance. And the land was perfect for growing tea.'

Chen decided it was time to risk interrupting.

'But you didn't speak Russian?'

'Popov had thought of that. The original plan was to teach the locals how to grow and pick tea, which initially failed—they weren't disciplined enough. So he hired a teacher for us. And because growing tea takes time and patience, he sent us to language classes for three hours each day. At first, I struggled—as did we all. The concept of an alphabet was alien to us. We kept looking at the Russian letters as symbols, as in Chinese. We were all given Russian names, too. I became Egor Konstantin Orlov— named after Saint Egor, the patron of farming. We were also taught a smattering of Georgian, useful in downtown Batumi.'

Yao looked at Chen. Was he still a boy, already a young man, or somewhere in between? He decided on the middle ground—and mostly omitted the seedier parts of life in a large port.

'Once we became more confident in our surroundings and language, we took every opportunity to visit the port town of Batumi—either by a pockmarked, rickety bus, or on company-issued bicycles. Liu never joined us—he was the only married man. On his second trip to China, he brought back his wife and children.

'The return ride by bike, sometimes tipsy, was painful. It was all uphill—mostly pushing, with only the occasional burst of pedalling. There were plenty of bars and many beautiful women in the lively port below. Word soon spread that we had money to burn. But we weren't the only ones—Batumi was booming with oil money. The railway to Tbilisi and the oilfields in Baku had just been completed.

'We avoided the Parisian-style hotels springing up along the promenade—their opulence was a sharp contrast to our rough-and-ready appearance. We didn't have the clothes or the style to blend in. And we stayed clear of the bars full of merchant seamen—if mistaken for Chinese sailors, we could easily end up in a brawl.

'Instead, we preferred a local haunt—*Chacha Bar*—in the old part of town. It was named after the fierce Georgian brandy, even stronger than our Chinese *baijiu*. Its oak-panelled rooms, pink velvet curtains, etched cranberry oil lamps, *chacha* in chilled cabinets, and roaring coal fire in winter made it wonderfully convivial.

'One night, we all set off on bicycles in weather the locals called *"enough to wither the palm trees"*. But we knew tea plants could survive these occasional winter onslaughts. The road was covered in shallow snow and treacherous ice. On one downhill stretch with a bend, we all collided—and several of us, including me, ended up with cuts and bruises.

'We arrived at *Chacha* a little dishevelled, locked our bikes, and waded through foul-smelling Georgian blue tobacco smoke. When we told the locals what had happened, they bought us a round. They remembered we'd tried teaching them mah-jong a few weeks earlier. They'd loved the gambling but couldn't get the hang of it—the tiles ended up scattered in a drunken mosaic across the floor.

'We didn't do much better when it was our turn. They asked us to sing along with a male Georgian folk group—their deep, warbling harmonies made us sound like out-of-tune frogs startled by a snake in their pond.'

Yao chuckled at the memory. Before long, both were laughing at the tale of these migrants—thousands of *li* from home—piled up in a frozen wasteland. Enthralled, Chen begged him to continue.

'At first, I didn't think much of the wound on my head—we were all in high spirits. But by the time we arrived, I realised the gash was worse than I'd thought.

'In one of the darker, more secretive booths sat a group of shady locals—identifiable by their blue and grey suits, open-collared white shirts, gold cufflinks, and overly shiny shoes. Several attractive young women always accompanied them. One of them came over to see if she could help.

'While I was distracted by the scent of her Damask rosewater perfume, she dabbed vodka into my wound—to my horror—then fashioned a bandage from a table napkin. "Don't be a baby," she whispered. Her name was Anna Kvaratskhelia. In my mind, the most beautiful woman I had ever seen—piercing blue eyes, full lips… great…'

Yao suddenly realised he had momentarily forgotten to whom he was speaking. This boy—this adolescent—knew nothing of bars, hoodlums, pimps, racketeers, beautiful women in tight-fitting dresses, red lipstick, or ladies of the night.

'Eventually, I got to know Anna a little better. Once, while she was away from the corner booth, I asked—nervously—if she'd join me for a walk along the promenade. She agreed.

'In the late afternoon light, with the sun from the Black Sea gleaming behind her cascading black hair, she looked even more beautiful than in the bar. She teased me about my terrible Russian pronunciation and said she'd help me. When I asked about her relationship with the men in the bar, she placed her finger over my lips, kissed me on the cheek, and said she worked in a business run by them.

'One night, Anna approached our group and gently pulled me over to the men in the corner—they wanted to talk. She seated herself well away from me, which was unnerving.

'I was offered a seat, introduced to a man called Levan, and handed a glass of *chacha*. With everyone refilled, we downed it in one—as we do in China. Then, without warning, Levan struck me in the ribs. A hard blow—not enough to break them, but sharp. As I gasped in pain, the rest of the group burst into laughter. Anna didn't.

'Levan poured another round of chacha. Again, we downed it. I braced for the next strike, wondering if this was my last night on earth. Surely, next came the alleyway—the knife—the blood?

'Then the strangest thing happened.

'Levan put his arm around my shoulder, pulled a knife, and said,

"I hear you've been seeing Anna. She's different from the others. These girls are our companions, but Anna is special. She's my angel. Do you see this knife? If you ever harm her, I will cut your balls off and make you swallow them."

'He withdrew the knife, and I nodded in agreement. What else could I do?

"You can date Anna. You have my blessing. But now you know what's in store if you cheat on her. Anna is my sister."

'I gulped, then, in my still-evolving Russian, said,

"In ancient times, in China, we also chopped off the balls of our enemies and stuffed them down their throats."

'The assembled crowd collapsed in laughter—even Anna was smiling.

'Anyway, I married Anna in 1897. Even that proved difficult—the Orthodox Church wanted me to convert to Christianity, which I refused. Levan fixed it. A basic marriage licence was issued. I don't know how—perhaps a generous donation, or a threat to burn down a church or two. Levan was unpredictable. Then, in 1901, we had a daughter. Her name was Elene.'

Chen realised huge gaps were appearing in the tale—perhaps painful ones, judging by the skip in the story—but knew better than to press.

'Come on,' Yao said. 'Let's walk down to the river.'

It was an agreeably warm late spring day, and the vista was alluring—

man and nature in harmony. On one side of the gate, blossoming lychee trees displayed a myriad of creamy, star-shaped flowers, drawing warmth from the reflected sunlight of the buildings and attracting nectar-drunk bees, promising an abundant harvest. On the other side were banana and persimmon trees.

Across the flat valley floor stretched a tapestry of miniature plots—mustard, aubergines, potatoes, tomatoes, peppers, and perhaps twenty other crops.

They descended a steep incline and paused at a 15th-century stone bridge. Beneath it, the water gurgled as it twisted around boulders shaded by bamboo. On the opposite bank, they stopped at stones strategically placed by the ancients—known as the Buddha's Hand—and sat down.

It was Chen who spoke first.

'Please, can you continue your story? It's fascinating.'

Yao paused, deciding where to begin.

'Liu started to realise that times were changing around the turn of the century, especially in our region, because of a young Georgian Bolshevik—Josef Vissarionovich Stalin—who was organising worker strikes in Tbilisi.

'In 1901, Stalin came to Batumi and began stirring up unrest. After the leaders—but not the organisers—were arrested, he staged a mass protest. It ended badly: thirteen demonstrators died storming the prison. Their funerals turned into further protests, which I watched from a safe distance. Eventually, Stalin was caught by the Tsar's secret police—the dreaded Okhrana—and exiled to eastern Siberia, likely to die of cold or starvation. But Liu was no fool. He was a competent businessman, but also a master of pragmatism and diplomacy—skills honed in China.

'By 1904, I believe he sensed a new order might be coming.

'One evening, he told me to be ready for an important delegation the next morning. Two cars arrived at the factory, and from the first stepped two men, both in suits and ties, dressed for business. I recognised one immediately—Stalin. The other seemed familiar, but I couldn't place him at first.'

Yao paused momentarily, as if to deliberately make the guessing more of a game.

'Then I realised who it was.'

Chen's eyes widened.

'You saw Stalin?'

'Yes. And then I met him—and finally recognised his even more famous companion.'

'Who was he?'

'Vladimir Ilyich Ulyanov—better known as Lenin.'

Chen was stunned.

'You met Stalin and Lenin? Both at the same time?'

'Indeed. Stalin had escaped from Novaya Uda in Siberia. We gave them a tour of the tea gardens and the factory. They were genuinely interested in our work. The four of us had lunch together, including some Chinese dishes our cook had mastered, washed down with local red wine.

'Then Liu presented a red packet, both thumbs pointed forward in the traditional Chinese way, and said it was a donation—for their political research. Stalin accepted it.

'Later, Liu confided in me—it was fifty thousand *roubles*. A substantial sum. At the time, the rival Mensheviks, led by Julius Martov, were in the ascendancy—even in Georgia. Perhaps Liu had chosen the winning side.'

Above them, the rice terraces rippled beneath the light. Where the terrain had been too rocky to cultivate, cascading forest crept downward. Swifts circled above, swooping for insects in displays of breathtaking aerobatics.

It was a sign dusk was approaching.

Yao suddenly looked tired. Understandable, Chen thought—he had unburdened half a lifetime of memory.

He asked Chen to return in two days to begin his studies, leaving many unanswered questions behind. As they parted, Yao added,

'I'll teach you Russian, young man. But you should know—it will be real Russian. In the Russian East, there's a Chinese ethnic group called the Dungans. Their teachers use the Latin alphabet. The students can't read Cyrillic, can't read most Russian literature, and their accents are—well—appalling. Hardly useful for studying *Anna Karenina*.'

Chen had no idea who this *Anna Karenina* was, but he knew he wanted to find out. More urgently, he wondered—what had become of the other Anna? And of Elene, Yao's daughter?

Chapter 5: Wuli Tulou, Fujian Province, China, 1926

Xiong Hehua, the girl who once stared across the classroom at Chen Minghe, was adjusting to the quiet realities of womanhood. She splashed her face with water drawn at dawn, the cold bracing against her skin. In the polished metal mirror, she studied her reflection.

Her face, she thought, was pleasing. Her skin was soft and pale—smooth as pressed rice flour—distinct from the sun-darkened complexions of the other girls. She had a well-proportioned chin, full lips, and wide, honey-brown eyes. She smiled at the glass. The smile returned.

Her gaze lowered to her breasts—full, round, unmistakably mature. Would Chen find them beautiful? The old taunt whispered again: *Big tits, no brains.* She pushed the voice away.

Lower still, she noted changes more private. A year ago, the hair had been sparse. Now it was dark and soft, unfamiliar and adult. She touched herself lightly, her fingers brushing the sensitive nub of her clitoris. A tremble rose through her, but she stopped—suddenly aware of the mirror still watching.

If only I were taller, she thought. The thought always came, unwelcome and familiar.

Her clothes, at least, were her own. While other girls wore floral tunics with baggy field trousers and headscarves, Hehua stood apart in embroidered silk dresses of her own design. Her reputation had grown. Some days, she was asked to sew ceremonial hats—wide bamboo-rimmed domes with trailing cloth strips. The longer strips at the back shaded the neck; the shorter ones in front had once symbolised modesty. Now, they were practical.

She decorated hats with bright ribbons to mark an unmarried girl, and stitched silver pendants and teardrop charms onto men's festival jackets and women's waistcoats. A single harvest costume could take days—fine needlework, silver accents, meticulous layering. Her hands were nimble, and her eye for symmetry, renowned.

Chen had found a measure of solitude in the carpenter's workshop. Amid sawdust, chisels, and the creak of wood, he split his time between mortises and tenons, roof beams and ladders—and the study of Russian.

It was not easy. The letter *ы*, the tangled verb declensions, the subtle dread of *ш* and *щ*—but the alphabet had only thirty-three characters. Compared to memorising thousands of Chinese symbols, its logic felt almost liberating. He progressed quickly under Teacher Yao's sharp eye.

Hehua began visiting the workshop during her rare afternoons off. If she lingered too long, Lao Chen would gently usher her away. Still, she returned whenever opportunity allowed.

Their conversations were light, drifting from village gossip to personal dreams. Chen imagined a future beyond the valley—perhaps even in Russia. Hehua fantasised about making fruit candy to replace the hard sticks of sugarcane or the rare popcorn from a travelling vendor.

Once, Chen gave her a carved likeness of Lulu, her dog, fashioned from pearwood, complete with six tiny puppies that could nestle along her belly. In return, she embroidered him a fine kerchief to wipe the sweat from his brow.

But mostly, they spoke of travel—of other lands, of places neither had seen.

Gradually, their friendship deepened. Hehua discovered that on Tuesdays, Lao Chen visited a neighbouring *tulou* to stock up on tools and hardware—nails, tacks, hinges, whatever was needed. The forge at home had long been silent—factory goods were now cheaper and more reliable. He was away for hours.

So she rearranged her only afternoon off to coincide. On Tuesdays, Chen would remain in the workshop instead of making repairs. They talked longer. Sometimes, she simply watched him carve, her chin resting in her hand.

Hehua was interested in Chen's Russian books and sometimes invited him to read and translate a passage aloud, although the explanations made little sense to her. The characters ranged from haughty aristocrats, conniving women, devilishly clever tricksters and politicians.

She found him handsome now—grown tall and strong—but uncertain whether he saw her the same way. Romantic entanglements at their age were frowned upon. Marriages were arranged, sometimes years in advance. A bride would one day move into her husband's clan household, her name entered into the ancestral register.

One afternoon, she shared more of her life.

'Did you know that one of my ancient ancestors and two friends, all women, founded this *tulou*?'

Surprised, Chen admitted he did not, and he recognised this as radical compared to the more traditional teachings of Mr Bei.

'Hakka women are strong,' she said. 'We have to be. The men leave for years—sometimes forever. So we plant, cook, raise children, carry water, grind flour... all of it.'

Chen looked at her with quiet respect.

'I didn't know that. What else do you learn?'

'We study four books: household management, virtue, purity, and filial piety. They also encourage us to carry on self-study. As a good Hakka wife, we should arise before dawn, cleanse ourselves, make tea, and then breakfast. First, we fill the storage jars with clean water from the well, also lugging enough to do the laundry. Then we make the pig food and take a short break. Next, we sit down briefly to eat simple food of gruel and pickled radish, appreciating its sustenance, never sad at its meagre contents. Afterwards, we feed the pigs and the water buffalo in the dawn light. Only after we have cleaned the floors with water and vinegar, polished the pots, scoured the oven, and sewn or darned any garments that need it are we ready to go to the fields, frequently not returning until dusk. We use a hoe and cultivate our own fields of vegetables, cut our own bananas, gather grass for the buffaloes, and climb the hills to the terraces to assist with the planting and growing in the communal rice areas. We transport everything on carrying poles, with bamboo wicker baskets attached, up to fifty *jin* at a time. In the evening, we use a grindstone to make flour. We are only relieved of these duties during childbearing and early infancy before handing our offspring over to the family, then returning once more to toil in the fields. We know we should never complain however painful our journey in life is. The only relief is tea-picking. That's when we sing.

She passed on these teachings to less privileged women with no formal education, using a series of songs—*The Ballads of a Hakka Spouse*. She believed these ballads were far more ancient than anything Russia could offer.

Chen was astonished.

'But what about the men? Don't they help?'

She smiled.

'You've seen us in the fields. We plough with buffalo. The only job we can't do is yoke and drive them. You helped us once. You remember?'

He laughed.

'Yes. I also remember the blisters.'

'Teacher Yao travelled too,' she said. 'He was away many years. It's part of being a man, I suppose. But we women—we stay.'

He was curious now.

'And these books—what else is in them?'

'Rules,' she said. 'How to honour your in-laws. How to serve your husband. When to speak. When not to.'

Then, without knowing it, Chen uttered the words that would haunt him for years to come.

'We're lucky. You get to stay, and I don't have to leave. You sew, I carve. We belong here.'

Hehua said nothing. But the silence between them was heavier than it had been before.

It was a Tuesday afternoon. Lao Chen was predictably away, and Chen bent over a high table, carefully sketching a new carpentry design.

Hehua approached quietly and stood on tiptoe, slipping her arms around his waist to steady herself as she peered over his shoulder. Her breath warmed his neck. Her chest pressed against his back.

Something stirred in him—an unfamiliar tension, an energy both physical and emotional. He didn't pull away.

That night, lying awake, he replayed the moment again and again.

When she repeated the gesture the following week, Chen gently held her arms in place, unsure if he had misunderstood her intentions. She leaned in, exhaled softly by his ear, then let one hand slide lower—

resting it deliberately against the bulge in his trousers.

'It's bigger than I thought it would be,' she whispered with a teasing smile.

His face flushed.

'You meant to do that.'

'Of course I did. I wanted to see if what I've read was true.'

'Read?'

She hesitated, then said,

'I'll share something I shouldn't. In secret, we girls have a fifth book—*Mother's Book*. It's never shown to men. Only one copy exists in the tulou. We pass it among ourselves.'

Chen was silent.

'It teaches us what our mothers are too shy to say. It starts with hygiene and virtue, but later… it explains things. About bodies. About men. About how to keep a husband faithful, even from afar.'

'Now that I've told you, you must tell me something in return. Promise me. A secret for a secret.'

He nodded, still a little dazed.

'Come with me. To the stockroom. Just for a moment. I want to see your iron pole.'

His breath caught. But he'd agreed. They walked to the rear room. He closed the door.

Hehua unfastened his belt, lowered his trousers, and touched him. He stiffened quickly. Her eyes widened in amazement, and she examined him with clinical curiosity rather than embarrassment. Then she laughed softly and kissed his cheek.

The next week, she didn't come.

Chen's confusion deepened. Desire and guilt tangled within him. Lao Chen scolded him repeatedly for poor concentration.

When Hehua finally returned, she was cheerful and open.

'I was bleeding. It happens every month,' she said simply. 'It's over now.'

Chen nodded, unsure what to say. But he embraced her. She took his hand and led him again to the stockroom.

This time, she unfastened her dress and let it fall to the floor. Her undergarments followed. She stood before him without shame.

'Touch me,' she whispered. 'But don't put your finger inside—I'm still a virgin, and it might tear.'

Chen's hands trembled as he reached for her. He touched her breasts, watched her nipples harden beneath his fingers. Then, lower—his fingers brushing the warm, wet folds between her legs. Her breath caught.

She reached for him, her hands skilled, coaxing. And then, he came—suddenly, uncontrollably, a white arc spilling across the floor.

She gasped, grabbed his undershirt from the bench, and knelt to mop the mess from the dusty boards.

Then, a creak. The workshop door.

They moved quickly. She wrestled with her dress. Chen wiped the floor again. They had just finished when the stockroom door swung open.

Lao Chen stood in the doorway. He took in the scene—her dress half-fastened, his son red-faced and sweating.

'Xiong, leave. Now. You, boy—you come with me.'

No raised voice. Just cold, absolute fury.

He marched Chen across the fields, far beyond earshot.

'What the hell were you thinking?' he hissed. 'Do you understand what you've done?'

Chen lowered his head.

'If word gets out—if she's pregnant—you'll shame both families. You'll destroy her future, and ours.'

'I didn't... I didn't—'

'Did you go inside her?'

'No. I swear.'

Lao Chen paced in silence, trying to steady himself.

'From now on, you'll not see her alone. Not speak to her unless required. If this is discovered, you'll be thrown out. Or worse.'

Chen nodded.

'And something else. In two years, she's to marry Peng Gangchao. The arrangement is already made.'

The words hit like a hammer. Chen felt winded. Peng—the bully

from school.
'This is our way. There are rules. Obey them. Now let's go.'
They walked back in silence, Chen's eyes burning with unshed tears.

Chapter 6: Xiamen (Amoy), China, 1926

Teacher Yao grew increasingly concerned. Chen, once an eager and gifted pupil, had mastered basic Russian conversation and simple reading within just three months. After a year, he was now proficient and nearing fluency. But now he was withdrawn, inattentive, and noticeably less engaged. Yao, remembering his own youthful mood swings, resolved to uncover the reason for Chen's melancholy.

At the end of a lesson, he confronted Chen in the musty, curtained-off antechamber where they always met.

'Chen, I need to talk to you—not as a teacher, but as a friend. When it comes to languages, you are a formidable talent. But recently, you've changed. You're learning at half the pace you once did.'

Chen remained silent but looked at his teacher.

'Is someone sick in your family? Have you fallen out with your parents?'

Still, nothing.

'Is it... a woman?'

Chen's eyes dropped to the floor.

'Ah, so that's it. It's not my place to pry, but I care about you. When I was a little older than you, I fell for a girl too. It wasn't easy. But talking helped. Will you share what's troubling you?'

'Sir... I can't speak about it.'

Yao was mystified by what Chen might have done—but recognised that his prodigy was distressed.

'Look, I respect your privacy. But I also have the right to try and lift you out from under this cloud. Leave it to me.'

Two days later, Lao Chen spoke to his son. He had received a visit from Mr Bei, who, with earnest expression, requested that Chen be spared from work for two weeks for a special journey. Lao Chen had agreed. Chen would be going to Xiamen (Amoy) with Teacher Yao, who had generously offered to pay for the trip.

Chen looked both surprised and pleased at the prospect.

Although Xiamen lay just two hundred and thirty *li* away as the bird flies, the true journey by road stretched to three hundred and forty. They followed the same route Mr Bei had often taken to the teachers' conclave—a trek of nearly three days.

They set off as the cock crowed, the sky still dim, carrying enough food for the day and bundles of clothing. Yao had insisted Chen bring a right-buttoned tunic, if he owned one.

Beyond the final *tulou*, the road meandered through villages perched along the Nanxi River. Some nestled on farmland, others clung to cliffs, forcing the pair to ascend steep trails before descending once again.

Occasionally, the tracks near the settlements were cobbled, but most of the route was mossy, worn, and treacherous underfoot. Farmers—both Min and Hakka—worked fields they rented from absentee landlords. None of the villages were fortified.

Eventually, they left the river behind, taking winding paths across undulating land. At last, they reached the horse and mule road near Yong Li Si, east of Longyan Zhou, where the route turned towards Xiamen.

By then, they had walked nearly one hundred and twenty *li*, and both had blistered feet. Chen's oiled cloth shoes had fared worse than Yao's leather pair.

At a village guesthouse, they devoured a warm meal with gusto. Afterwards, the landlady brought them a steaming wooden vat infused with herbs, where they took turns soaking their aching feet in the fading autumn light.

The next day, mist-wreathed mountains loomed above them, explaining the circuitous route. The road grew busier: traders, livestock, and carts passed in both directions.

Horses were available for hire, but since Chen couldn't ride, they secured a place in a farmer's cart for a few coins.

By nightfall, they arrived at the Scholar's Inn, nestled along the bustling Six Lanes and Seven Alleys Road in Zhangzhou Longxie.

The final leg was the easiest. By early afternoon, they boarded the train to Xiamen. Chen was mesmerised by the puffing locomotive and its astonishing speed. By midday, they had arrived.

Yao, who had visited this city during his tea-trading days, led the way.

Chen was astonished. The lanes were narrow labyrinths crowded with red-brick buildings painted in vibrant hues. Wooden shutters snapped shut above their heads, while swallow-tail eaves cast criss-crossed shadows on the cobblestones.

Closer to the city centre, homes with courtyards jostled for space with tall shophouses—retail below, living quarters above—many with balconies draped in drying linen.

The streets overflowed with goods: traditional medicine, tea bricks, strange fruits, firewood, second-hand clothes, and hardware. Restaurants spilled aromas of unfamiliar spices and steaming broths into the air.

Nearer the main thoroughfare, Zhongshan Road, construction crews raised a constant haze of dust.

It was chaos. Rickshaws and sedan chairs weaved around dust-choked workers. People hawked and spat thick gobs of phlegm, their throats clogged by the powdery air.

As they approached the Bund, Chen stopped in his tracks.

He wasn't looking at the promenade—he was looking the other way.

Yao, having bumped into him from behind, laughed.

'You've never seen the sea before.'

The inlet shimmered in the morning light, its waters stretching out towards Gulangyu Island. Beyond that: the ocean, and the crossing to Taiwan.

Turning towards the Bund, Chen was equally in awe. A railed seawall lined the waterfront, interrupted by steep ramps too narrow for heavy cargo.

The crowd was thick—what the Chinese called *'a mountain of people, a sea of people.'*

More than a hundred water taxis bobbed along the tide, ferrying goods and people to steamships and anchored junks. Porters swarmed with baskets on shoulder poles, darting like fish when rice balls hit the water.

Then came the noise—louder than Chen's duck-whistle decoy.

An automobile klaxon. A white couple rode past in an open-top car: he wore a high-collared suit; she, a straw hat pinned with flowers.

Missionaries had visited the *tulous* before—but never anyone this elegant.

A second car followed—sleeker, covered, with a fifth wheel mounted on the back. In front, a Chinese chauffeur. In the rear, a suited Chinese man.

Yao guessed he was a businessman—perhaps tied to the customs office or one of the foreign banks along the Bund.

Yao was relieved. There was no sign of the anti-foreign riots that had swept Shanghai the previous year. But today, the city was doing what it did best: making money.

He pointed to the horizon, where a sleek grey vessel sliced through the water.

'That's a British Navy cruiser,' he said. 'Its guns can hit a building from forty *li* away.'

Before heading to the hotel, Yao disappeared into a shop selling colourful bottles and foreign cigarettes. He returned with a parcel wrapped in paper.

From the room behind reception, strange music spilled forth—metallic, fast, with unfamiliar rhythms.

It had the reedy wail of a suona, Chen thought, *though the tones were unlike anything he'd heard before.*

After paying their deposit, they were issued keys and agreed to meet again in thirty minutes for dinner.

The hotel room stunned Chen: a chair, curtains, a bed raised absurdly high off the floor and draped in a mosquito net, and a carpet covering most of the polished boards.

He pressed a switch beside the door.

The room was suddenly bathed in light.

Needing to relieve himself, he opened a second door and found three strange receptacles. One resembled a washbasin. Another—a wide bowl—might have been for bathing. And the third? It was oddly shaped and had a wooden lid.

Should he stand on the lid or seat himself?

He crouched awkwardly over it and relieved himself.

Then he spotted the small hanging chain—and gave it a tug.

A torrent of water erupted beneath him.

Chen leapt backwards, startled, clothing still around his ankles.

They met again in the hotel lobby and returned to the old town for dinner—Yao carrying the paper-wrapped bottle. He insisted they speak only Russian during most of the trip, for practice.

Yao selected the restaurant and ordered an array of unfamiliar dishes. Once seated, he unwrapped the bottle and poured a measure of clear liquid into two glasses. Chen squinted at the red label—Столичная (*Stolichnaya*)—but it meant nothing to him.

Yao encouraged him to taste it. Chen took a cautious sip.

It burned his throat and had little flavour—but within seconds, his face glowed with warmth. Yao showed him how to drink it down in one.

'What is it?' Chen asked.

'Vodka. Russian firewater.'

The *tóng'ān fēng ròu*—a slab of steamed fatty pork in rich gravy—was full of flavour, but it was the seafood that impressed Chen most: ginger-spiced fish and oyster omelettes with creamy peanut sauce.

Towards the end of the meal, with the bottle nearly empty, Chen—who had drunk sparingly—decided to share his hotel toilet experience.

Mid-mouthful, Yao burst out laughing. A spray of omelette shot across the table as he guffawed for nearly two minutes, then managed to explain the flush mechanism.

At breakfast, Yao made a new suggestion.

'Since we spoke Russian yesterday, let's use only Chinese today. We're visiting Gulangyu Island—home to thirteen consulates. Best not to draw attention.'

He explained that many foreigners, especially the British and Americans, suspected the Russians of inciting last year's insurrections. The Japanese, meanwhile, were deeply distrusted—rumoured to harbour ambitions in the region.

Nevertheless, they maintained a strong presence in the old city, even operating their own financial institutions, including the Niitaki Bank.

The two made their way to the Bund and boarded the ferry for the twenty-minute crossing.

Upon arrival, Yao explained he had some business to attend to. The walk was short. Inside a grand stone building, he gestured towards a chair.

'Wait here,' he said, indicating a plush leather seat beside a strange machine with a winding handle.

Chen sat quietly, watching as Yao filled out a form at the counter. Within minutes, he returned.

'Teacher Yao,' Chen asked, 'what is this place?'

'It's where people send urgent messages. I've just sent one to Guangzhou.'

Chen's eyes widened. 'How many days will it take?'

'Not days—less than ten minutes.'

'I don't understand.'

'This is the Great Northern Telegraph Company. That red and white flag is Danish—this building is also the Danish Consulate. The telegraph sends messages through wires. Instantaneously, or nearly so.'

Chen tried to imagine it, still confused.

'But... this is an island. How does the wire cross the water?'

'There's a cable lying on the seabed. And this,' Yao added, pointing to the other machine, 'is a telephone. To invite someone for tea, you wind the handle, the operator connects you, and you speak to them—immediately. No messengers. No waiting.'

Chen was astonished.

'Who did you send your message to?'

Yao smiled. 'That's a secret.'

'Come,' he said. 'While we're here, let me show you around. The island is only four *li* long and two *li* wide.'

They strolled leisurely through Gulangyu's sloping, tranquil streets.

Despite its modest size, the island was lined with towering stone mansions—three or four storeys high. Yao explained that each was home to a single wealthy family and their staff, owned by either rich foreigners or returning Chinese. Although Chen admired the craftsmanship, he was bewildered by the scale; each house occupied more than a fifth of a single *tulou* floor.

The architecture was European, Yao explained—reminiscent of Batumi—but punctuated by occasional Chinese flourishes.

These were the homes of bankers, diplomats, and traders—the lifeblood of Xiamen's commercial world.

Yao explained the use of some public buildings. Chen could appreciate the Gulangyu Public Hall, with its enclosed auditorium for concerts, lectures, and community meetings—so different from the tamped-earth spaces of the *tulous*. He also understood the value of the American Hope Hospital.

Yet the adjoining Union Church puzzled him. Why such a large structure was needed to speak with a higher power remained a mystery.

Then, on a downhill stretch, Yao suddenly pulled Chen aside.

A two-wheeled machine flew past—ridden by a woman in trousers tied at the ankles, her head low against the wind.

Chen's eyes lit up.

'It's a bicycle—just like in Batumi!'

Yao nodded, predicting bicycles would soon be made in China—perfect for bustling cities. He added that this island was a microcosm of European towns: with churches, cemeteries, schools, hospitals, music halls, and theatres.

Two buildings caught Chen's attention.

The first bore the name *Gulangyu Mixed Court*. While they both understood what a court was, neither knew how it functioned here. A uniformed guard explained that the court served Chinese and foreigners who had no consular protection. A Chinese magistrate and foreign assessor presided jointly. Criminal sentencing followed Chinese law—unless the crime was so serious that the accused was sent to Xiamen.

Common offences included theft, brawling, and public drunkenness. Punishments ranged from shackling offenders in a *cangue*—a heavy wooden collar, akin to British stocks, used for public shaming—to up to one hundred bamboo strokes, fourteen days of hard labour, deportation, or fines.

The second building was marked *The Bombay Club*.

Yao explained, 'It's a private club for foreigners, mainly British. There's a bar, a dining room, probably a billiard room with three balls hit across a green table into little baskets, and rooms for cards and conversation. It helps them feel less homesick—and make business connections.'

'So anyone can go in and order a meal?'

'Not at all. It's exclusive. You have to be voted in and pay an annual fee.'

'Are Chinese and women allowed in?'

'Wealthy Chinese, certainly. Women as well—though not in the billiard room. But for businessmen, it's invaluable.'

Chen was impressed by Yao's knowledge and asked where he had learnt all this.

'I never told you,' Yao replied. 'After the Bolshevik Revolution, the British Army held Batumi for nearly two years. One of the first things they built was a club for their officers.'

At the centre of the island was a grassy lawn. White and Indian men played a game dressed in white, wearing different coloured caps. One bowled a red ball towards three upright stumps. Another struck it cleanly. A resounding crack echoed across the green, followed by applause.

Then came a shout that sounded like '*Huzzah!*'—a Russian variant of the word for 'cheers'—and the striker, seemingly out, walked off the pitch.

Chen watched, spellbound. The crowd was applauding too. Some lounged on picnic blankets, others in folding canvas chairs.

Western men wore linen suits and straw boaters; Chinese men, Mandarin-collared shirts with Western jackets and cravats. The women all wore summer dresses—Westerners with hats, Chinese with fans.

To Chen, it was clear that many Chinese were modelling themselves on Western fashion.

He asked Yao about the game. Yao shrugged.

'I have no clue,' he said. 'But it's called cricket.'

As they neared the beach and jetty, Chen asked to paddle with a group of mixed-race boys. Yao agreed but warned him to keep his underpants on. He pointed to a towering man in a blue uniform, with a broad leather belt and waxed moustache beneath a tall striped turban.

'That is a British policeman. He's from India. They're called Sikhs.'

Chen joined the others, earning his first splash of warm seawater to the face during a game.

Back at the hotel, he sat in silence, his mind racing.
What if cables weren't needed in the future? What if conversations travelled invisibly through the air?
Messages. Commands. Perhaps even armies.
No runners. No beacons. No flags.
He was ahead of his time—but only just.
Less than two years earlier, Guglielmo Marconi had successfully transmitted a long-distance, two-way shortwave radio message between Poldhu, Cornwall, and his yacht *Elettra*, moored in Beirut.
Few in China had heard of it.
Fewer still understood what it meant for the future.

Chapter 7: Xiamen (Amoy), China, 1926

The following day was a mixture of practical errands and measured sightseeing. Their first destination was the Hong Kong and Shanghai Bank (HSBC) on the Bund, a striking edifice of colonial authority and fiscal power. Chen remained a few paces behind as Yao approached the cashier with practised confidence and conducted the exchange with quiet discretion—foreign bills or silver, perhaps—for a thick stack of Bank of China *yuan* notes. Even at a distance, Chen could not help noticing how much was being handled. Yao, without comment, requested a rubber band, secured the bundle, and slipped it into his jacket pocket with the ease of someone long accustomed to large sums.

Chen speculated whether this transaction was connected to the previous day's telegram. It was becoming increasingly apparent that Yao was a man of considerable means—though never in *tulou* life had he made the slightest display of ostentation. The opulence of their hotel suite now made perfect sense.

Their second engagement was of a different nature, one that Yao knew would capture Chen's attention: a destination he had, until now, only glimpsed from afar. They stepped through the gates of the University of Amoy, where volunteer students conducted twice-weekly guided tours of the campus.

Their guide, Ms Li, presented a carefully curated image of propriety and intellect. She wore spectacles that lent her a quiet authority, held a parasol with understated grace, and dressed modestly in a floral print dress that reinforced her academic bearing. A notebook and fountain pen were clasped firmly in her hands. She introduced herself as a representative of the Faculty of Science—one of five fully operational faculties—where fourteen professors were currently in residence, including six Chinese scholars who had returned from advanced studies in Europe and the United States. The other faculties—liberal arts, law, business, and education—provided guides on a rotational basis. A sixth division, Chinese Studies, was in the final stages of preparation, and the pride in her voice was unmistakable.

As the group strolled along the campus paths, Chen found himself enchanted by the grounds, which, bathed in the crisp brilliance of autumn light, resembled something from a painting rather than a functioning seat of learning. The gardens formed a tapestry of colour, with flowering annuals arranged in deliberate beds across gently sloping lawns. Towering above were cascading willow trees encircling the perimeter of Lotus Lake—phoenix trees shedding petals the colour of fire—and flame trees blooming in shades of coral and rose. Tall palms flanked the main avenues, their fronds rustling softly in the coastal breeze, while the far edge of campus opened out towards the sea, the scent of salt air blending with cut grass.

Pausing in the shade of a banyan tree, Ms Li provided a brief but illuminating history of the institution. This private university, she explained, had been established in 1921 by the eminent Singaporean businessman and philanthropist Tan Kah Kee, whose ancestral roots lay in Jimei Village, Fujian. Tan had amassed a fortune through his enterprises in canned pineapples and rubber and had devoted significant portions of his wealth to advancing educational initiatives throughout the province—including the founding of numerous schools in Jimei. Amoy University stood as the crowning jewel in his vision.

Gesturing toward the buildings around them, Ms Li explained the architectural blend now known as Jiageng style—a synthesis of Western and Chinese design that local students affectionately referred to as *'wearing a suit with a Chinese hat'*. The structures featured Western-style pillars, arched windows, and grand staircases, yet were crowned by traditional swallowtail roofs with upturned eaves. Tan had personally reviewed the architectural plans submitted by American architect Henry Murphy, insisting upon several modifications. The layout had been reoriented so that the rear of each building faced the wooded hills, while their façades opened towards the sea—a symbolic embrace of modernity and tradition. Though Murphy's proposed plans were ultimately not used, Tan had still paid him in full—1,500 US dollars—as a gesture of professional respect.

The tour eventually moved indoors. Chen glimpsed the impressive expanse of the university's library, several bright lecture halls, and a student dormitory that boasted uninterrupted views of the beach and open water. Their final stop was the refectory, where visitors could purchase a modest student lunch. Yao and Chen each ordered fish ball soup accompanied by plain rice—a meal humble in composition but nourishing. They said little to the others, offering only that they hailed from a remote *tulou* village in the west. One by one, the other visitors drifted away, until only Ms Li, Yao, and Chen remained seated at one of the long communal tables.

Summoning courage, Chen addressed Ms Li in a tone of earnest curiosity,

'Ms Li, are the books in the library written in Chinese?'

She smiled warmly. 'Certainly, many are. But we also hold collections in English, French, German, and Russian.'

'Would it be possible... to see them?'

'Of course. It would be my pleasure.'

They returned to the library, and Chen stood in awe, unable to fathom the vast reservoir of knowledge now laid out before him—rows upon rows of volumes, each offering a gateway to an unfamiliar world. *If only I possessed a fraction of the wisdom contained within these thousands of books*, he thought, *what power I might wield, what understanding I might attain.*

Ms Li asked whether there was a particular section he wished to browse. Before Chen could reply, Yao interjected, his voice calm and certain,

'The Russian section.'

There they stood—shelves lined with Russian literature. Chen selected a slim volume and read the title with care: *Fathers and Sons (Отцы и Дети)* by Ivan Turgenev. He opened the book with reverence, reading aloud a short passage in a careful voice until he stumbled over an unfamiliar word. Yao, without judgement, corrected his pronunciation.

Ms Li looked on, visibly astonished.

Back outside in the early evening air, she hesitated before speaking. Then, with unfeigned curiosity, she asked how such fluency was possible. Yao, with his usual economy of words, offered a brief summary of his years in Batumi.

Her parting words carried a weight that was more than polite concern.

'Only a few weeks ago, the National Revolutionary Army passed through here on its way to Fuzhou. The University has recently welcomed three eminent professors from Beijing—men who had gone unpaid for months. They fled in fear of what may come. Please be cautious.'

By the time Yao and Chen returned to the hotel, dusk had begun to fall. At one point along their route, Yao paused at a narrow side street, peered down its length as if contemplating a change of course, then turned his gaze to Chen—and quietly chose to continue straight ahead.

The side street was dimly lit, its windows smudged with grime. Tattered posters advertising Pirate and Magpie brand cigarettes clung stubbornly to the plaster above first-floor windows. Women in heavy make-up perched on high stools outside houses, singing flirtatiously to passing men. Metal plates affixed above some doors bore official licence numbers, designating the premises as state-recognised brothels. One woman, her expression both weary and rehearsed, crooked her finger at Chen in a manner both inviting and transactional.

For a fleeting moment, Yao considered offering to pay for Chen's initiation—an awkward rite of passage—then dismissed the thought. This was not the healing he had promised Lao Chen and Mr Bei.

'What are these places?' Chen asked, his voice low.

Yao answered quietly, his tone sombre.

'They are brothels. The numbered plaques indicate state licensing. Whether licensed or not, every woman here is selling her body. Some work in comparatively tolerable conditions, with private rooms and dependable clients. Others are treated as chattel—used, drugged, discarded when they are no longer profitable. Most are not here by choice. It is poverty, not desire, that brings them to this.'

Further along the alley, they passed a wooden door bearing the prosperity character—its lacquer faded and peeling. An emaciated man, barely conscious, had been unceremoniously dumped nearby.

'That is an opium den,' Yao said, his voice devoid of emotion.

'I once went into one to observe. It was squalid—filthy mats, overflowing spittoons, men and women lying half-conscious in their own sweat. They rarely ate. They sold everything—their possessions, their dignity, their futures. That man likely exhausted his funds. He will be dead within two days.'

Though shaken, Chen remembered Mr Bei's impassioned lessons on the Opium Wars and the legacy of the Fujian Anti-Opium Society. Clearly, something had gone terribly wrong.

'Teacher Yao,' he asked after a long silence, 'have you ever taken drugs?'

Yao sighed. 'Yes. In Batumi, we occasionally smoked hashish in hookahs. Dreamy, relaxing—not addictive. It bears no comparison to opium.'

'Then why,' Chen asked with genuine puzzlement, 'has the government not outlawed opium entirely?'

'Because it supports entire networks—farmers, traders, even armies. The cost of prohibition is higher than its toleration.'

That evening, Yao outlined the plan for the following day. He promised Chen a day to remember, though he refused to provide further detail.

He had errands to attend to—including collecting a telegram and having his clothes pressed—while Chen, now more confident in navigating the city, was encouraged to explore independently.

Yao handed him some silver coins and instructed him to return by 4.00 p.m.—and to purchase a new pair of shoes.

Chen relished the sense of independence. He soon located the recommended shoe shop, where the assistant, though aloof, eventually helped him select a pair of laced, ankle-high leather boots—sturdy and well-suited to mountain travel once broken in. The alternative—pointed brogues with ornate tooling—seemed wholly impractical.

At the counter, Chen inquired about the price in silver *taels*.

The reply stunned him—it was more than his family could expect to earn over several years.

Before returning to the hotel, he stopped at a newspaper stand. The vendor offered several back issues in addition to the latest edition, which bore the headline:

'Northern Expedition—Warlord Wu Peifu in Retreat as NRA Soldiers Reach Wuchang!'

Chen bought them all. He knew precisely who they were for: Mr Bei.

At the appointed time, Chen waited in the hotel lobby. Yao appeared, visibly flustered, and urged him to hurry—they had only thirty minutes to change into their finest attire.

Chen re-emerged wearing a neat tunic, freshly pressed trousers, and his new boots, feeling faintly self-conscious. Moments later, Yao appeared transformed: clad in a Western-style suit complete with high collar, crisp tie, gold cufflinks, and impeccably polished leather shoes. It was a striking sight, and Chen concluded they must be bound for a significant occasion.

Yao was also carrying a cloth bag, from which the distinct shapes of two bottles could be seen protruding—surely vodka.

They made their way to a berth on the Bund, just as the packet steamer from Guangzhou was arriving. First-class passengers disembarked first. Yao raised a hand in greeting toward one of them.

A short elderly man in a cream suit tipped his Panama hat in return. As he descended the gangway, he and Yao embraced in a silent, heartfelt bear hug. After a long pause, Yao turned and spoke in Russian.

'Chen Minghe, I want you to meet Liu Junzhou, tea master.'

Liu stepped forward and embraced Chen as well—this time more gently.

At last, all the pieces fell into place: the telegrams, the liquor, the formal clothing.

Liu's luggage was sent ahead to the suite Yao had reserved for him at the Foo Sing Hotel. Though the walk was short, they took rickshaws to preserve the freshness of their attire. At Liu's request, a private dining room was booked—suitable for a banquet. He excused himself briefly, asking Yao and Chen to order refreshments and begin choosing dishes.

Yao ordered beer for himself and tea for Chen. He summoned the head chef to discuss possible delicacies.

Soon after, Liu returned. At Yao's suggestion, they continued their conversation in Russian—for Chen's benefit.

Liu began by recounting his journey. Upon receiving Yao's telegram, he had booked passage aboard the packet steamer—the only practical way to reach Xiamen quickly, as the railway from Guangzhou had yet to be constructed. The voyage had taken two and a half days. It had been seven years since Liu and Yao had last seen one another.

'Your return to China in 1919, Junzhou, was timely. You foresaw what was coming.'

'I sent my wife and sons home first. They were in their thirties and needed to marry. When the Bolsheviks annexed Georgia, the entire tea industry was nationalised. I was offered a senior role in the new co-operative—but clashed with bureaucrats who valued quotas over quality. They overused fertilisers, mechanised production—and, of course, the tea suffered.'

'Until?'

'Until Stalin came—one final visit. Lenin was dead. He still reeked of Herzegovina Flor tobacco. He urged me to become a Soviet citizen. I declined—politely. Not long after, I was deported. I wept as I packed. Thirty-three years—gone in an instant. All I carried home were memories and a few salvaged mementoes. I returned wealthy, yes—but weary. Now my sons are married, and I have grandchildren.'

The extravagant dishes began to arrive. The centrepiece was *Buddha Jumps over the Wall*—a thick, fragrant soup of scallops, fish maw, sea cucumber, and yellow chicken, its scent reputedly powerful enough to tempt even vegetarian monks.

Yao uncorked the vodka and poured a round for himself and Liu. The first glass disappeared in one clean motion. This continued throughout the meal, the bottle growing steadily lighter.

At one point, Yao leaned forward and said softly to Liu,

'Please do not speak of Anna—I am not ready.'

Liu nodded respectfully and changed the subject.

'And what of the situation in Guangzhou? The KMT appears to be fracturing—nationalists and communists drifting further apart.'

'Fracturing is putting it mildly. Chiang was waiting for an excuse. The Zhongshan Incident gave him one. Now he commands the NRA, presides over the Whampoa Academy, and governs through martial law.'

Yao turned to Chen and gestured.

'He is our future historian. Perhaps you explain the Zhongshan Incident to us?'

Yao opened the second bottle and poured Chen a modest glass.

'Not tonight. Tonight, we drink and remember.'

And so they did.

The vodka flowed. Laughter came easily. Chen's questions fuelled their memories, which in turn sparked further merriment. Before long, the old friends were singing Georgian folk songs. Their rendition of *Suliko* was passable, given their state. Their attempt at the *Khevsuruli*, however—a fierce warrior's dance—resulted in nothing more than two men staggering and collapsing into helpless laughter as the final bottle rolled away.

Chen supported Yao on the walk home—two silhouettes weaving gently along the Bund beneath the stars.

The next morning, they returned to Liu's suite. Remarkably, both men appeared fresh and untroubled by the excesses of the night before. Chen, however, was concealing a persistent, throbbing headache—one he bore in silence.

Liu pointed towards a suitcase resting by the window.

'Open it, Chen. It is yours.'

Chen lifted the lid and found a sack containing over thirty Russian books. It was an astonishing gift.

He cradled one of the volumes against his chest and closed his eyes—trying to imagine the weight of the ideas, philosophies, and histories within.

Liu watched him quietly before continuing, his tone grave.

'Last night you asked about the Zhongshan Incident. Let me tell you what I know. The *SS Zhongshan* is the most formidable gunboat in the NRA's fleet. In March, it lingered in the harbour at Guangzhou for two days. Its captain was a communist, and a Russian adviser was aboard.

Chiang Kai-shek seized on this as justification for a coup—though some believe it was a false flag operation from the beginning.'

Chen, gently interrupting, asked, 'What is a false flag?'

'It's when one side disguises itself as the enemy to carry out an attack—then blames that enemy to justify retaliation,' Liu explained.

'Chiang cut the city's phone lines, deployed loyalist troops from Whampoa, and disarmed leftist factions, including the Communist Workers' Guard. He placed Wang Jingwei and the Soviet delegation, including Borodin, under house arrest—despite Borodin's long-standing support for Sun Yat-sen. Zhou Enlai was detained. Later, Wang was exiled on a so-called holiday to France. The Communist Party leadership was purged. Zhou returned to Shanghai and began agitating anew.'

Chen looked up, concern etched on his face. 'But does Chiang not still rely on communist troops for his military?'

'He does. And he will not purge the rank and file—only the leadership. He is calculating, pragmatic, and utterly ruthless. Mark my words: one day, he will sever ties with the communists completely. If you are ever caught with these books, Chen, the consequences could be grave.'

Chen nodded solemnly.

'Study them. Learn from them. But never discuss them. Hide them well.'

The following day marked the final chapter of their stay. Liu and Yao excused themselves early—they were heading to Nanputuo Temple, near the university, to offer prayers in gratitude for the blessings in their lives.

Chen, not invited to this act of private reverence, spent the day alone, wandering the city.

That evening, the three men shared a modest farewell meal. Tears were shed. Hugs were exchanged. Parting words were spoken with aching sincerity.

Yao and Chen began their journey back to the *tulou* villages. The final stretch was made longer by the burden of the books, now wrapped in cloth and tied with rope—heavy with meaning as well as weight.

Several days later, Chen encountered Hehua in the courtyard of the *tulou*.

She tilted her head curiously. 'Were you away?'

'I went to Xiamen,' he replied.

She searched his face, noting the quiet change in his eyes—something deeper, quieter, more distant.

'What was it like?'

Chen, recalling the private vow he had made to his father before leaving, offered a single word: 'Exciting'—and turned away without another glance.

Yet the journey had altered him. He had glimpsed a world far beyond the walls of the *tulous*, encountered people and ideas that had expanded his vision, and returned with a burning determination to grow.

He resumed his study of Russian with renewed focus and a deeper hunger for understanding.

And he hid the books well—stacked neatly behind unused timber in the storage room, in a corner so obscure that no one would think to look.

Chapter 8: Shanghai, China, 1927

Consul-General Fournier glanced at his perpetual desk calendar. It was the 14th of April 1927—a date he would never forget.

His frustration with Shanghai, and with the French Concession in particular, had grown unbearable. What had once been a minor irritation—the whispered rumours of the Communist Party's founding meeting in 1921—had evolved into paralysing waves of union-led strikes, rippling through the Chinese city and threatening the security of the foreign zones.

In Paris, the government remained distracted, preoccupied with the rise of communism, fascism, and national socialism across Europe. This was not how matters were supposed to unfold. Two years earlier, Fournier had agreed, albeit reluctantly, to extend his tour of duty. Now, every day, he longed for Neuilly-sur-Seine—for long Sunday lunches with Géraldine and the children, for the calm dignity of a civilised retirement. Sometimes he even allowed himself to dream of an investiture at the Élysée Palace.

Only the day before, his usually unflappable wife had asked about the sharp staccato of gunfire echoing from the Chinese side of the city. And now, today, a *situation délicate*, as diplomats liked to call it, had erupted in full force—one which demanded the emergency meeting he now chaired.

His colleagues filed in quietly: the ever-reliable Raymond Camus, the steady Pascal Allard, and the newly appointed military attaché, Philippe Chastain, a rare fluent Chinese speaker. Fournier wasted no time, opening the meeting with a nod towards Chastain.

'It is not good,' Chastain said. 'Since the Zhili Clique was toppled by insurrectionists led by Chen Duxiu and Zhou Enlai, and their rival administration installed, Shanghai has descended into chaos. On the 9th of April, NRA troops loyal to Chiang Kai-shek entered the city and declared martial law. Now, they have made their next move—Chiang and his commanders have enlisted the Green Gang to do their initial dirty work.'

Fournier turned to Camus.

'Raymond, do your sources confirm this?'

'Indeed,' Camus replied. 'Du Yuesheng, the Green Gang's leader, invited Wang Shouhua, President of the General Labour Union, to dinner. It was an old association—Wang and Du had worked together before—and so the invitation raised no alarm. Our sources believe Du's White Russian bodyguards strangled Wang with piano wire. They dumped his body in the countryside. Beheading was too crude, and gunshots too loud. Shortly after, the army raided the Union's district office and began conducting door-to-door searches for suspected communists.'

Fournier turned next to Allard.

'Pascal, are they taking prisoners?'

'I fear it is worse,' Allard said grimly. 'Some are dragged into the streets and beheaded on the spot. Others are taken away—presumably for interrogation. Yesterday, the unions attempted a mass protest march towards the 2nd Division headquarters of the 26th Army. They were met with machine-gun fire. Hundreds died. The wounded were buried alive alongside the dead. Chiang is now travelling from Wuhan to Nanjing to establish his new seat of power.'

Fournier's knuckles whitened as he gripped the edge of the desk.

'Mon Dieu—what savagery!' he murmured. 'Pascal, have any fled into the concessions?'

'Not yet—but Zhou Enlai may have escaped through the French sector.'

'And Chen Duxiu?'

'His whereabouts are unknown.'

Of course not, Fournier thought bitterly, recalling Chen's vanishing act in 1921.

The man is like a ghost.

Fournier steepled his fingers and spoke slowly, summing up the situation.

'We have never trusted the Beiyang Government nor their warlords, and we lent our cautious support to the Northern Expedition in the hope it would lead to unification. Now, that strategy lies in ruins. The communists and their Russian advisers will surely break away—and ironically, that may weaken Soviet influence. Chiang's camp will not tolerate Bolsheviks indefinitely. We now face three factions—perhaps four, if Wang Jingwei attempts a power grab in Wuhan. *Plus ça change*—everything shifts, yet everything stays the same.'

The room fell silent.

Fournier sighed, pushing the chair back from the desk.

'The meeting is over. I have a most difficult communiqué to write—to Paris, and to the ambassador in Beijing.'

On the 19th of April, Mr Bei received an unexpected visitor.

A fieldworker, breathless and covered in dust, ran into the *tulou*, announcing that a man was waiting at the edge of the woods, asking for Bei by name.

When Mr Bei arrived, he found a dishevelled figure standing among the trees: a man with a welt on his cheek and eyes clouded with fear.

The man stepped forward hesitantly.

'Don't you recognise me?'

'Should I?' Mr Bei asked.

'It's me—Teacher Hu, from the conclave. You once said that if ever I were in danger, I should find you. I came from Shanghai—five days on the road, mostly by bus. I dressed as a peasant and smeared duck fat all over my body. The stench kept the soldiers away—they'd have noticed my smooth hands. It was all I could do not to vomit before I reached a bathhouse.'

Mr Bei looked again, more closely this time. It was indeed Hu.

'What happened?' he asked quietly.

Hu's words came in hurried bursts.

'Chiang's troops arrived. I worked under Wang Shouhua—we were running things, but I was just a clerk. Then they came—gangsters dressed as workers, wearing white armbands with *gōng* (功) for "service". They smashed everything. The army followed and killed without distinction. Wang is missing. I barely escaped.'

Mr Bei shivered. It was even worse than he had imagined.

Chiang had unleashed Du Yuesheng and the Green Gang to do the dirty work before the army moved in.

'Were you followed?'

'A cart passed on the road. The driver waved. That's all.'

'Wait here. I'll return before dusk.'

At the *tulou*, Mr Bei summoned Lao Chen and his son. There was no time to consult the elders—they would buckle under interrogation.

'It is our tradition to treat strangers as honoured guests,' Mr Bei said quietly. 'Tonight, we shelter a man in mortal danger. He is no criminal—merely caught in the crossfire of politics. We must hide him from everyone, including our own.'

Lao Chen glanced at his son.

'That trapdoor in Mr Bei's room you used in your childhood games—it may serve a more serious purpose after all.'

'So that's why you locked up the ladder during the game the year after we won! You thought it gave us an unfair advantage.'

'But at least I found it—by studying your drawings in the workshop.'

'Not quite. You only ever discovered half of what was really there.'

The hidden trapdoor in Mr Bei's ceiling was one of several in the tulou, but the only one entirely concealed. Sanded flush with the timber panelling, it bore no hinges or handle—only a faint bevel, imperceptible except to those who knew where to press.

It opened into a narrow crawlspace tucked just above the eaves, built a decade earlier by Lao Chen at the junction where the firewalls met the cantilevered supports of the overhanging tiled roof. Though lateral access was not impossible, the rear firewall and closely braced structural beams made such movement difficult, noisy, and dangerously exposed—especially under torchlight.

From the courtyard below, the tiling line and deep eaves gave nothing away. Even a sweeping searchlight would reveal no irregularity. The entry point could only be seen from directly beneath—and only when the trapdoor was open. It was the work of a master carpenter.

Inside, the crawlspace narrowed between joists and load-bearing beams, just wide enough to hold a man curled into a foetal ball. The dense timber muted sound; darkness and dust softened each movement.

Only the precisely fitted hatch provided access—and even that was of no use without the bamboo ladder kept in Lao Chen's locked workshop.

Before dusk, Mr Bei returned to Teacher Hu and gave him quiet instructions.

'Once it's dark and the gate is closed, you'll see a blue light on the fourth floor—opposite the main entrance. That's your signal. A rope ladder will be waiting. Climb quickly. Don't hesitate.'

Hu nodded. He said nothing.

Later that evening, the signal flickered. Moving unseen, Hu slipped along the compound's edge, shrouded in deepening shadow. A rope ladder hung from a rear-facing window. He climbed in silence.

Lao Chen was waiting. Without a word, he led Hu to the bamboo ladder inside, which rose to the trapdoor in the ceiling and explained the use of the crawlspace.

'There's no time to talk about Shanghai. You'll be safe—but you must follow instructions precisely,' Lao Chen murmured.

He handed Hu a bucket containing food, drinking water, and a coiled rope.

'Each morning at first light, just after you've relieved yourself, lower it. My son will collect it shortly after—scraps, the water jug, urine, and excrement. Then he will tie up a fresh one.'

He paused.

'There can be no further bowel movements during the day I case there is a lateral search. It's the scent that gives you away—like when you're tracking a boar through underbrush.'

Hu nodded again. He tied the bucket to his waist, climbed the bamboo ladder, and disappeared into the space above.

The trapdoor shut with a soft click.

The rope was coiled and hidden. The ladder returned to the workshop.

There was no further conversation.

Two days later, a detachment of NRA soldiers arrived on foot, led by a Second Lieutenant named Ding, who rode in proud isolation on horseback.

He wore high brown leather boots and tightly fitted breeches, proud of both his uniform and the NRA flag pinned behind his desk—a white sun on a blue sky, bordered in red. His office was set up in a nearby Min village, just beyond sight of the *tulou*—close enough to unsettle, far enough to maintain control.

Ding was not an officer of the Whampoa elite. He had earned his rank the hard way, fighting Sun Chuanfang's warlords during the second phase of the Northern Expedition.

Sun's retaliation had been merciless—beheadings, mass arrests, revenge killings. Though Sun had been defeated, the campaign had left deep scars across the land and even deeper ones across the men who fought it.

Ding knew how the academy officers viewed him: a coarse, brutal man, a product of the ranks. He returned their disdain with contempt of his own, seeing them as fickle creatures who would serve whichever master paid them most handsomely.

That evening, he summoned his sergeant.

'Begin tomorrow,' he ordered. 'Search every *tulou* in this cluster. Arrest anyone suspicious. Start with any teachers. We're waiting on a Hakka translator—find me a fluent Mandarin speaker in the meantime.'

The sergeant saluted.

'Sir, there's a teacher named Bei.'

'Excellent. Begin with him.'

The searches were ruthless.

Mr Bei's quarters were searched first. His modest room was torn apart: books flung across the floor, bedding ripped open, every jar and basket overturned. From this chaos, only one object piqued the soldiers' interest—a slim volume recovered from his bookshelf. It was swiftly tucked into a canvas satchel and carried to Lieutenant Ding.

Every room in the *tulous* was combed through. When it came to Yao's quarters—perhaps due to his age or the greying fringe of his beard—the soldiers conducted only a cursory inspection and found nothing of interest.

Mr Bei was brought before Ding—unshackled, but flanked by guards.

'Who's the best Mandarin speaker here, besides you?' Ding asked without preamble.

'Chen Minghe,' Mr Bei replied. 'A young carpenter.'

'Where is he now?'

'In the workshop—or perhaps on a roof repair.'

Ding leaned forward, his voice low and dangerous.

'There are communists hiding in this settlement. Tell me where.'

Bei met his gaze calmly.

'I wouldn't know. I teach children. That is all.'

'You're educated. You've read their creed.'

'I have discussed it with colleagues—nothing more.'

Without warning, Ding slammed a book onto the desk between them.

'What the fuck is this?'

Mr Bei, frowning slightly, examined it.

'A Chinese translation of Marx's *Communist Manifesto*. It was a gift—from a fellow teacher, many years ago.'

'And what colour is the cover?'

'Well... red, of course.'

Ding's face darkened.

'Liar! This edition is one of the very first—before they changed the cover to blue after a poorly printed run of fewer than a thousand copies. You've been a communist since the beginning.'

Mr Bei turned pale. Some part of him understood—but the rest still clung to the illusion that reason might prevail.

'Give me names—or die.'

Bei said nothing.

There was only one name he could have given—Hu's—but he would go to his grave, if need be, before betraying him.

Sergeant Wu found Chen in the workshop, the air dense with sawdust and the sharp tang of tung oil. The sergeant made a few idle remarks about the carpentry—his father, he said, had once run a timber shop—but Chen sensed immediately that the interest was strategic, not sentimental.

At the workbench, Wu casually opened a notebook and flipped through pages of sketches and measurements, pausing on a schematic for a well hoist. Beneath it was a Russian book Chen had foolishly failed to conceal.

Wu's hand hovered.

'What's this?' he asked.

Chen's pulse quickened.

'Er… a manual on woodwork. In Greek.'

'You read Greek?'

'Not really… I just follow the diagrams.'

Wu's fingers lingered on the cover, thumb pressing against the spine. Chen felt a jolt deep in his gut. His bladder tightened.

'I… I think I'm going to be sick,' he muttered, clutching his stomach and stepping back.

Wu looked at him—a long, unreadable stare—then released the book, his interest fading as quickly as it had come.

He stepped away and barked the order.

'Follow me.'

Lieutenant Ding greeted Chen with a cold, appraising look.

'This book proves Bei is a traitor,' he said. 'He'll probably die for it. Do you have sisters?'

Chen hesitated, then answered quietly, 'Two. Aged eleven and thirteen.'

Ding leaned back in his chair, eyes narrowed.

'Lie to me, and we'll sell them to a Macau brothel. Ten clients a day—until there's nothing left to sell. Do you understand me?'

'Yes, sir.'

Ding raised an eyebrow at the reply.

Chen had seen the prostitutes in Xiamen—faces powdered and blank, perched outside brothels with vacant eyes. He understood exactly what Ding meant. His hands trembled at his sides.

For an instant, he thought of Hehua—how she had once brushed his arm in passing, a touch so light it felt like a whisper.

And he understood something with terrible clarity: even if he betrayed Hu, Ding would kill him anyway. There would be no clemency.

No protection. Not for him, nor his sisters.
If Ding began asking about his parents next—?
He straightened his back.

As long as they did not torture him, he could lie. And in the face of death, lying came easily.

'I know of no communists,' he said. 'I swear it.'

Without waiting for instruction, he dropped to his knees and touched his forehead to the floor in a kowtow.

'Please—I beg you, sir.'

'Stand up, idiot!' Ding barked.

He paused, then added, 'As it happens, I believe you. I've got more people to question today and I need a translator. I am an honourable man. Translate faithfully, and I will spare your family. Betray me, and I will personally behead you.'

The interrogations continued long into the night.

One man had worked years earlier on Soviet fortifications. Another—a boy barely older than Chen—possessed a set of nesting dolls brought from Novosibirsk by an uncle.

Both were detained.

Chen translated each word mechanically, his face blank, his tone neutral. It was far too dangerous to do otherwise.

The following morning, notices appeared across the *tulou* cluster.

All adults were ordered to assemble outside *Wuli Tulou* for a public meeting the next day. Those spared from attending were few. The only exceptions were the elderly, the infirm, and those tending to the youngest children—Hehua among them.

They came without a word, foreboding etched into some faces, while others scanned the scene with unsettling interest.

Chen stood to one side, arms folded, instructed not to speak. Not to translate. Only to watch.

Mr Bei was brought forward first.

He walked unaided, though his wrists were bound tightly behind his back. At the centre of the courtyard, two soldiers took up position, each gripping a length of rope attached to his arms.

With a sudden, practised yank, they pulled forward and down.

The tension drove him hard to his knees, shoulders wrenched back, spine exposed, his head forced low.

Lieutenant Ding drew his Mauser C96—his prized 'box cannon'—with slow, ceremonial precision. He raised it, paused, then fired a single shot into the back of Bei's head.

Mr Bei's body slumped forward into the dust, limbs twitching once before falling still.

There were no cries, no protestations. Only the wind rustling in some nearby trees.

Two more prisoners followed—those already taken: a labourer with past ties to Soviet engineers, and a boy accused over a foreign gift.

The first wept as the ropes hauled him to his knees, babbling pleas for his wife and children. The boy, barely older than Chen, said nothing. He stared ahead, his arms drawn taut, lips sealed in defiance or fear—it was impossible to tell.

Each was executed in turn, the shots loud and final.

Their bodies fell forward into the dust beside Mr Bei.

Deep inside Chen, something cracked—and in its place, something hard and unyielding began to form.

In his heart, he swore revenge.

They buried Mr Bei that same afternoon, on a shaded rise beyond the last ring of vegetable plots. The location had been chosen by an elder who claimed modest skill in *feng shui*.

No priest was summoned.

The rites were plain: a stick of incense, three paper offerings—for money, clothes, and a bed—a bowl of rice placed gently at the head. His *guòpímào* cap and inkstone were tucked between his hands with reverence.

When the moment came, Lao Chen, his son, and two others raised the coffin by rope and lowered it into the earth.

There was no chanting.

Only the soft, final thump of soil returning to soil.

A headstone was added—unmarked, uncarved, for now.

Ding, true to his word, departed two days later.

The soldiers withdrew with their trophies and several captives, leaving behind a fearful, broken community. Doors remained shut. Conversations dropped to whispers. The courtyards, once filled with children's laughter, grew hollow with silence.

Chen kept the *Manifesto*.

It would have been safer to abandon it. Safer still to burn it. But to destroy the book would have been an act of betrayal—not only of Mr Bei's trust, but of everything Chen had begun to understand about the world.

He found a better hiding place.

Not behind a timber pile, but deep within the hollow of the stockroom wall, concealed behind tool racks and sealed with a panel cut to match the grain of the surrounding boards. No casual searcher would ever notice.

Within thirteen days, across seven provinces, nearly 10,000 communists and suspected sympathisers lay dead.

In Moscow, Stalin—enraged by the collapse of the alliance—ordered Borodin to ignite peasant uprisings across China.

In Guangzhou, Wang Jingwei, unwilling to break fully with Chiang Kai-shek, expelled the remaining communists from the KMT.

The uneasy partnership between Nationalists and Communists was over.

China's civil war had truly begun.

When the soldiers left, Hu emerged from the roof cavity where he had hidden for days. His limbs were stiff. His eyes blinked against the light.

At first, he was offered a teaching post in the *tulou*—a gesture of thanks for what he had endured.

But his lessons—laced with veiled political opinion and careful agitprop—soon wore thin. Parents grew wary. The elders exchanged whispers. Murmurs became mutterings. Mutters turned to mistrust.

Chen, already tainted by his role as interpreter, bore the weight of every glance, every hushed accusation. One afternoon, passing by a cluster of women at the grain store, he caught a single word—low, venomous, and unmistakable:

'Traitor.'

It struck him like a stone to the chest.

Three months later, Hu made his decision.

'I have to go,' he told Chen. 'I don't belong here.'

'I'll come with you,' Chen said simply. 'The rumours won't stop. Where will we go?'

'West,' Hu replied. 'Into the mountains. Towards Jiangxi.'

When Chen explained his plan to his parents, they said little. His mother wept in silence. His father placed a hand on his shoulder, wordless.

They packed his bundle with rice cakes, cured sausage, and a flask of water.

Lao Chen, after some hesitation, fetched the old caplock rifle. He handed it to his son along with a pouch of powder, buckshot, and lead balls.

'It might bring down one or two Nationalists,' he muttered, attempting levity. It fell flat.

At least Chen had his new leather boots from Xiamen.

Hu, too, was given what they could spare. He bowed low in thanks, accepting the food and clothes with quiet dignity.

But there was still one matter Chen could not leave unresolved.

Hehua.

He had already informed Teacher Yao of his departure during their last lesson.

Yao, unsurprised, gave his blessing with a slow, sad nod. In his eyes, Chen saw the shadow of something unspoken—perhaps regret, perhaps pride.

That evening, Chen wrote a note and slipped it quietly into Hehua's work basket, tucking it beneath a coil of twine.

'I'm leaving at dawn the day after tomorrow. Meet me to say goodbye—Mr Bei's old rooms at five o'clock tomorrow evening. Leave your reply beneath the rim of

the old herb trough—there's a gap in the stone near the drainage hole.'

By midday the next day, her answer was waiting—folded into a neat triangle and wedged into the crevice beneath the trough.

I'll be there.

No one would suspect a secret meeting in the quarters of a recently executed man. Lao Chen would be working at the front of the compound, keeping an eye on the workshop. The hour was chosen with care.

When she arrived, Chen was already inside.

He opened the door without a word and, once she had stepped inside, eased the wooden bar across. It thudded into place—too loud for comfort.

She was the first to speak, her voice trembling.

'I've missed you so much. You shunned me.'

'I had no choice,' Chen replied. 'After we were caught in the workshop, my father forbade me from seeing you. He said you were already promised to Peng Gangchao. That your marriage had been arranged.'

'It's true,' she whispered. 'I have no choice either. But... you're the one I love. You always have been. And now you're leaving.'

Her words broke on a sob. She leaned into him. He fumbled for the embroidered kerchief she had once given him, dabbing her tears, but she clung to him, unwilling to let go.

When her sobbing eased, she pulled back just enough to whisper,

'Minghe, I want to give you the greatest gift a woman can. My body. So you'll never forget me.'

They both knew what it meant.

They both knew it was strictly forbidden. Yet neither resisted.

Chen hesitated only briefly, glancing instinctively towards Mr Bei's old bed. Then his gaze shifted to the bamboo calisthenics mat, rolled and stored beside the wall.

'Wait,' he said softly.

He unrolled the mat across the floor with a soft rustle and smoothed it with his hands, trying to make it comfortable.

'Come lie beside me,' he whispered.

She obeyed without a word. Her hands moved to lift her dress, just enough to free herself from her undergarments. Chen slipped out of his trousers, heart racing.

From her sleeve, she withdrew several folded cotton cloths and placed them beside the mat.

'My love,' she said, her breath warm against his cheek, 'you must pull out before you… spill. You understand, don't you?'

Chen, though overwhelmed, nodded.

She opened her legs and drew him close. He entered her slowly, carefully, feeling her tense and then relax with quiet determination.

Their union was clumsy, tender, urgent—an aching mixture of youth and yearning.

He moved gently, each motion filled with reverence, as she whispered reassurances into the crook of his neck.

When release finally came, he pulled away just in time, gasping softly, his whole body trembling.

She reached for a cloth and cleaned them both with quiet care, her hands gentle and unhurried.

Then she took his hand and laid it flat over her womb, pressing it there as though to seal something sacred.

They lay like that for a long time, listening to the old walls breathe around them.

At last, Chen whispered,

'I didn't know anything could be so… moving. Magical.'

Then, smiling faintly through the tears he would not allow to fall, he added,

'Explosive, yes. And unforgettable. Hehua, I'll carry this moment with me always. I'm leaving as a man—and I'll always love you.'

She kissed him softly.

'You… got out in time?' she asked, a tremor in her voice.

'I did, my love.'

As he reached for a cloth to fold away, he noticed a small smear of blood.

'You were a virgin?' he asked, startled.

She nodded, her smile small, touched by sadness.

'But what about your wedding night?'

'Don't worry,' she said gently, brushing his fringe aside. 'Sometimes a girl breaks her virginity working in the fields. That's what the *Mother's Book* says. There's a remedy—a vial of chicken blood. No one will ever know.'

They held each other until dusk.

No tears.

No promises.

Nothing remained but silence, as the last light faded through the shutters of a dead man's room.

Chapter 9: Wuping, Fujian, China, 1927

The following day, before dawn, Chen bid a quiet, emotional farewell to his family. As soon as the main gate creaked open, he and Hu vanished into the early morning mist. Before they had covered two *li*, a figure appeared through the haze, running towards them. As it drew nearer, Chen recognised the familiar shape: Peng Gangchao.

He shouted, 'What do you think you are doing?'

'I'm coming with you.'

'No, you're not,' Chen snapped. 'And you're not even equipped for the mountains.'

'Try to stop me.'

It was useless. Like a spectre in the mist, Peng would follow them until they relented—and eventually, they did. Although Chen believed the distance to their first town, Wuping, was around one hundred and sixty *li*, the terrain, with its ravines and progressively larger hills, marked only by ill-defined tracks, would take at least three days to traverse.

In the first village, they stopped to speak with an elder. They requested a carrying pole, some bundling cloth, food, and a blanket to accommodate their new companion. The village seemed poor to Chen: the soil was thin, stony, and unyielding. The Hakka inhabitants refused any payment, as was their custom with guests.

Towards evening, they stopped again—this time in a village seemingly more impoverished than the last. They were given a bowl of rice congee with a few vegetables, which helped preserve their supplies, and were offered a straw bed in an unused pigsty for the night.

As they ate, they questioned the locals about the journey ahead. The villagers advised them on the best trails and warned of two dangers: the infamous Wuping bandits—who had terrorised the area for over 200 years—and Amoy tigers, which could sneak up and bite a man's head in half in a single chomp. Hu looked terrified.

The next day, coming along the trail from the north, were three men on horseback—but had they been spotted? It was Chen who reacted first. They stood in a narrow pass: a sheer drop to the left, a sparse scattering of trees and a cliff face to the right. He told Hu and Peng to pause, pretending to rest, and dived into a shallow hollow, a pine tree giving a little extra cover.

As the three men approached, Chen discerned they were heavily armed with rifles and bandoliers. Each carried a *dàdāo* (大刀), the ubiquitous Chinese sabre—equally suited for hacking through woodland, martial arts, or lopping off heads. These were bandits, without a doubt, and they reined in their horses before the two travellers.

The lead man spoke in Hakka, but with an unfamiliar accent. His tone was hard with suspicion.

'Where have you come from? And where are you going?'

'We come from *Wuli Tulou* and seek work in Wuping.'

'Don't you have crops to tend to?'

'No, sir, we leave that to our women and travel away seeking employment.'

He grunted, eyes narrowing. It seemed plausible enough. Then he pointed at Peng.

'Open your bundle and pockets and lay out the contents.'

Peng hesitated for a moment before obeying, withdrawing from his pocket a few *Mín Guó Tōng Bǎo* (民國通寶), circular coins with a square cut-out in the middle. Fortunately, it was Chen who carried the large purse. The man looked displeased—perhaps because there was so little of value.

'Now you.'

Hu obliged. The bandit looked surprised and reached for his rifle.

'Some of these aren't peasant clothes. They look like those people from the city wear. I don't believe your story. You may not have much money to give me, but you have something of much greater value.'

Hu realised his mistake but dared not ask for an explanation.

'You two are coming with me. I get a bounty from the Nationalists for every one of your type I capture.'

Hu and Peng both realised they faced certain torture and death if handed over.

A sharp crack rang through the pass, followed by the bandit's head bursting—a sickening spray of blood misting the air. It was like the time Chen had dropped a watermelon from the fourth floor of his tulou—except this horror was real. He had used the caplock to take a headshot, and the 0.50 calibre ball at short range had caused devastating consequences.

The other two bandits guessed the shot's direction but hesitation gripped them—they had no way of knowing if the shooter was alone or how long it would take him to reload. They whirled around simultaneously and galloped off, whipping their horses as they went. The third horse, now riderless, bolted after the others.

Then there was silence. It dawned upon Chen that he had killed a person.

Hu and Peng, horrified, doubled over in disgust before vomiting. After a moment, they quickly packed their belongings and secured them to the carrying poles. Chen grabbed the rifle, tore the bandolier off in one swift motion, and handed the caplock to Peng. They stood still, waiting, as the unspoken leader of the group prepared their next move.

'We need to leave this path now. Those bandits will be back in force. According to the villagers, we're nearing the end of this stretch and into the deep forest. They'll think we've retreated south, and if we can hide before they realise, we'll have the advantage. Walking's too slow. We need to trot—and pace ourselves.'

It took one hour to reach the end of this portion of the trail and find a wider road, slowed down by Hu, who had little stamina.

They pushed into the dense foliage, every sense straining, when the sound of hooves reached their ears. They crouched low, holding their breath, as the riders passed southward, unaware of their presence. Then they moved deeper into the forest and to relative safety. It was at that point that Chen whispered:

'We've got about twenty *li* left to Wuping. We wait here for two days, rationing our food and water. After that, we travel only at night—it'll be slow, but it's the only way. We can't risk going into Wuping for provisions, not with the Nationalist barracks there. We'll have to skirt around the edges, again under cover of night. By then, the bandits should have given up.'

They hunkered down, and Chen set to work examining the captured rifle. It was a bolt-action Hanyang 88, a Chinese imitation of the German model. He had never seen a gun like this before, but the mechanics were straightforward enough. After a moment of fumbling, he chambered the first round with ease and guessed the function of the safety flag. But when it came to the spent magazine, he was stumped as to how it came out.

As evening fell, a blood-curdling roar echoed through the forest that could only come from a tiger. Chen gripped the Hanyang tightly, while Peng readied the caplock. Hu leaned in, his voice barely a whisper:

'Do you know how to use that thing?'

'I'm not entirely sure, and I dare not fire it and draw attention to us.'

It was hardly reassuring, but after a while, the tiger's roar faded into the distance, and the men settled down for the first of two sweltering, damp summer nights in the mountains, gnawed by mosquitoes, with no chance of lighting a fire. But at least they were still alive.

On the third day, the group made for Wuping, travelling only from dusk until dawn, stumbling in the darkness and making sluggish progress. As they passed through the eastern outskirts of the town, Chen decided to take a chance. It was breakfast time, and there was a noodle shop. He grabbed their communal food carrier—a lidded receptacle with a top that could double as a mess tin or a cooking pot—and left his compatriots hidden in a deserted back street before stepping inside.

The locals, Hakkas, were friendly and curious, and Chen quickly established that there were no soldiers in the town. He asked which mountain dominated the skyline, marked by a peculiar boulder at one end like a giant wart, and was told it was Mount Liangye, estimated to be three thousand *mi* tall. That made sense to Chen—it was bare rock at the summit, stripped of all visible vegetation.

On his return, while the other two scoffed their first warm food in days, Chen emptied the bandolier and stuffed it, along with the ammunition, into his bundle. He covered the rifle with a blanket, ready to carry. It would only fool people briefly, but no trouble was expected.

Peng kept his caplock in plain sight, and they set off in daylight into the *'land of mountains and waterfalls'*, as the locals had named it. Chen and Peng started to sing and tried to teach Hu the Hakka words, with little success. But with food in their bellies, they were all happy.

They entered an enchanting place and sometimes stopped to rest, absorbing the beauty of their surroundings or remaining aloof from other travellers on the roads and tracks. On one occasion, they observed a striking group of birds, each with a copper-coloured head, black eye stripe, and shimmering blue-green body, attacking and destroying a beehive high in the trees. On another, they gorged themselves on wild strawberries until they were uncomfortably full.

In the final part of the journey, the men left the roads by the rivers and streams, staggering across rugged, steep terrain, the dusty tracks cutting through a sparsely populated landscape. They returned to ill-defined mountainous trails, with a few tarns and brooks offering much-needed water as the weather grew hotter by the day. The kerchief Hehua had given Chen became a sweat-soaked rag.

They followed the trails northeast to the Xiangshui River at Xuposhi. Having crossed into Jiangxi Province, they finally found a larger road leading to Ruijin, arriving on 14 August

When they arrived, they were disappointed. There was no communist army to join—just an unbearably hot, dusty, and sleepy town—but at least it offered the chance to rest. They did, however, encounter two other escapees who had avoided capture in Wuhan. They introduced themselves as Luo and Cai, and the five men traded stories.

Over the next two days, they heard sporadic gunshots in the distance, though it did not sound like much of a military engagement. It was also the first time Chen had the opportunity to fire his rifle. He finally discovered that the magazine ejected automatically, ready for another five kisses of death. After firing five shots, he showed Peng how it worked and encouraged him to try it for himself.

The disappointment did not last long. The following day, a single scout arrived on horseback to reconnoitre for any enemy troop movements—and discovered the five waiting men. He did not have time to interview them thoroughly and took their word that they had come to fight on his side. He announced that the army would be arriving in three to four days.

The newly formed Chinese Red Army arrived, presenting a bewildering sight. It was not a band of rebellious peasants but soldiers—defectors from the NRA. They were distinguished by their attire: some wore red armbands, officers donned hemp rope belts, and other ranks used straw cords, as any red cloth had almost run out.

Severely dehydrated and exhausted, they begged for water, desperate in the oppressive heat. The officers walked alongside their horses, whose flanks were lathered in sweat, making them incapable of bearing riders. Strangely, there were few wounded soldiers to be seen. A long line of porters trailed behind them, ragged, frightened, and even more exhausted than the troops. They carried numerous wooden boxes—hundreds of them.

After helping to provide potable water to the army, the five non-combatants were given red armbands. They were then assigned to an officer who tasked them with watering and feeding the horses. It was Hu who plucked up the courage to speak.

'Comrade, you look exhausted. Where have you come from?'

The officer looked bemused but managed a weak smile.

'I'll get used to it—but that is the first time I've been called "comrade". We came from Nanchang, and on 1 August, around 20,000 of us defected. Some soon abandoned us for the other side. I don't know how many of the enemy were killed—some, for sure—and how many surrendered. It was chaotic.'

Hu invited him to continue.

'We had hoped for more support, particularly from the NRA 4th Army led by Zhang Fakui in Jiujiang to the north. Although he had many communists under his command and seemed sympathetic, he ultimately aligned with Wang Jingwei and Chiang Kai-shek, forcing us to retreat.'

'But this army isn't 20,000 strong. We heard shots, but why were so many killed?'

'Our forces dwindled to around 9,000. The gunfire you heard was our officers firing overhead to motivate the hired porters and prevent them from discarding ammunition to lighten their load. Unfortunately, even our troops have been abandoning their equipment. We began with a million rounds, 5,000 firearms, and those three crates—sufficient to ignite our revolution. Without a proper inventory, I estimate we have about two-thirds remaining. More than 5,000 troops defected to Zhang Fakui; others deserted or succumbed to heatstroke or contaminated water from the rice paddies.'

Chen's attention was drawn to the three crates labelled *ДП-27 ручной пулемет обр тестовая версия* (DP-27 Handheld Machine Gun Model—Test Version). An officer and several soldiers had pried open the boxes and were struggling to assemble the components. Despite an instruction manual and rudimentary illustrations, the Russian text was indecipherable to them.

Chen offered his assistance to the officer, who shrugged and gestured for him to proceed. Together, they attempted to assemble the portable gun with its distinctive circular pan magazine. Translating the Russian manual proved challenging:

Engage the locking lugs into the notches on both sides of the receiver for proper locking and unlocking. This gas-operated machine gun ejects spent cartridges through the bottom of the receiver. The gas port's level is adjustable. Carefully handle the recoil spring and take care to avoid burns from the barrel.

While some instructions were unclear to Chen, they resonated with the military personnel. Within an hour, they had assembled the first gun—and a test firing startled every bird in the vicinity.

Unknown to this army, on 7 August, at a meeting in Wuhan, the already deposed Chen Duxiu, co-founder of the Communist Party, was replaced by Acting Chairman Qu Qiubai, a fluent Russian speaker. He was soon succeeded by a full appointee: Xiang Zhongfa.

Chen Duxiu, apart from any other errors, had been a Trotskyite—another whose influence was in decline as Stalin ascended. Trotsky and his followers still held some sway, but Stalin was tightening his grip, isolating them from key decisions and reshaping the global communist movement to reflect his vision of centralised control and pragmatism over unrelenting revolution.

The more pragmatic Comintern delegate Besso Lominadze soon replaced the less flexible Borodin, the previous representative in China. Mao was initially pleased; Borodin had long dismissed his arguments—particularly those concerning the importance of including peasants, not just urban workers, in the revolutionary struggle. That relief, however, would prove short-lived—Lominadze would soon clash with Mao on entirely different grounds.

With only twenty-two local Chinese members and three Comintern officials present, the Wuhan meeting declared all appointments 'provisional', lacking the quorum for formal ratification. Yet it was significant for another reason: Mao was elected a Politburo member and Hunan Party Secretary. At that same gathering, he clashed openly with Qu and Lominadze.

'*We must be aware that political power grows out of the barrel of a gun,*' Mao warned.

It would become one of the most enduring lines in revolutionary history. He feared that a mass uprising of poorly armed peasants, without military discipline and backing, would end in massacre.

By this stage, many senior leaders were scattered or in the field. After the Nanchang Uprising, communications had collapsed. The importance of these strategic debates would only become clear once contact was restored.

The officer who had observed Chen earlier that day returned just after the first machine gun had been assembled. Looking nervous, he invited Chen to follow. They approached a guarded bivouac. From within came the unmistakable sounds of a furious argument.

Two senior officers stormed out as they arrived. Chen leaned in and whispered a question. His escort identified them as He Long, former commander of the NRA's 20th Army, and Ye Ting, former commander of the 24th Division of the 11th Army.

Inside the bivouac stood two men. Chen's escort saluted. They returned the gesture and dismissed him.

The first spoke. 'I'm Zhou Enlai, Provisional Member of the Communist Politburo's Standing Committee. This is Zhu De, former Deputy Commander of the 9th Army. Li Lisan, Tan Pingshan, and Zhang Guotao are conducting inspections.'

'Where are you from?' Zhou asked.

'*Wuli Tulou*, Fujian Province.'

'You are Hakka, like my colleague here?'

'Yes, sir.'

'We asked because you helped assemble a machine gun earlier today and were instructing the sappers. How do you know about such a weapon?'

'Sir, I don't. But I can read Russian.'

Zhu De, intrigued, switched languages. Chen replied in Russian.

'You can speak it too?'

'Yes, sir. I've been studying it for several years. I had a teacher in the tulous who'd learnt it as a tea grower in Georgia.'

Zhu De glanced at Zhou Enlai.

'Well, he definitely speaks Russian. Even if I'd spent my year at the University of the Toilers in Moscow studying instead of chasing pretty girls, I wouldn't be a fifth as accomplished as this man.'

They laughed, and even Chen managed a smile—a rare moment of levity in grave times.

Zhou Enlai nodded.

'I think you had better tell us the whole story.'

Chen did—briefly. He spoke of Teacher Yao, Hu's escape from Shanghai, a redacted version of the journey to Xiamen, Mr Bei's execution, the bandits near Wuping, and the two other escapees in Ruijin.

He was interrupted twice. The first was to confirm Hu's party membership, which he verified. The second was about his knowledge of telegrams. Chen explained that he believed such messages might one day travel through the air. He added that automobiles could prove essential in warfare.

'The *Manifesto*—may I see it?' Zhou asked. 'Do you think I could keep it safe for you? One day, we should remember Mr Bei and others like him properly.'

Chen almost replied that Mr Bei had never been a communist—but held his tongue. He trusted Zhou Enlai.

'Of course, sir. I will deliver it to your headquarters as soon as I am dismissed.'

'You will join the National Federation of Peasants' Associations Committee with Hu. Learn their ways during your probation for eventual party membership. One more thing: never reveal that you speak Russian to anyone in our Party or Army without consulting me first.'

The escort was summoned again and ordered to issue uniforms and better armbands for all five men. Peng, Luo, and Cai were assigned to that officer's regiment.

After they were dismissed, Zhou remarked,

'It seems we have a young spy in the making—from a most unusual background. Let's test him and see if he's what we need.'

A scout arrived moments later with news that the enemy was massing to the south near Huichang. Orders were issued: prepare to attack at dawn with 2,000 most willing and able men.

It should have been an easy engagement against a small provincial Nationalist force. The machine guns were not to be deployed—they needed further testing and were considered too valuable.

Peng, Luo, and Cai—among the freshest recruits—were chosen. Luo and Cai received a rudimentary crash course on the Beiyang 88 Rifle, their inexperience all too clear.

The battle at Huichang was a disaster. The Nationalist troops were fresh, disciplined, and used their machine guns to devastating effect. Ye Ting's reinforcements arrived too late. He Long's men bore the brunt of the onslaught.

500 were killed. Another 500 wounded.

In the chaos of retreat, the injured were brought to a makeshift field hospital. There was no anaesthetic. Supplies were scarce. But a skilled surgeon and a handful of doctors worked without pause.

Chen raced to the hospital. He questioned a bloodied sergeant, who speculated grimly that Cai and Luo were dead, but Peng might have survived.

He was still asking when Peng was carried in—barely conscious, his left leg gone, the bandage already soaked through.

Chen found him a bed and sought help. Around them, men screamed for mothers, wives, morphine—none of which were coming.

As he knelt by the cot, Peng stirred. His lips parted.

'Promise me… tell Hehua I would have been a good husband. Tell her I love her.'

His eyes glazed. The light inside him went out.

Chen stood motionless, the final words circling in his mind. He had not expected it to hurt this much.

For He Long, Huichang was the final straw. Only days earlier, he had formally joined the Communist Party—witnessed by Zhou Enlai, Li Lisan, and Zhang Guotao. Now he packed his things and returned to his hometown in Hunan—a broken man.

The argument Chen had overheard stemmed from He Long's belief that his troops were unfit for battle. He had warned that no army could march over a thousand *li* in summer heat through Jiangxi and Fujian to reach Shantou. It was hoped they would be resupplied there—from Russia. But now, all that seemed desperately far away.

But He Long would be back.

Chapter 10: Blagoveshchensk, USSR, 1925

On 25 October 1922, Vladivostok fell to the Russian Red Army, marking the final collapse of White resistance in the east. Apart from scattered pockets of holdouts, the Russian Civil War was over. In the border town of Blagoveshchensk, overlooking China across the Amur River, Japanese troops were quietly withdrawing—without ceremony—having backed the White forces in a losing bid to contain Bolshevism and secure their own imperial interests.

Fifteen-year-old Konstantin Vladimirovich Rodzaevsky watched their departure with only mild apprehension. In many respects, he was the ideal student—bright, curious, prone to dreamy abstraction. He had joined the Komsomol and completed the Young Pioneer programme the previous year.

But his family was not in danger. His father, Vladimir Ivanovich, a law graduate from Kyiv University, was a respected small-town lawyer. And the USSR, in its dealings with Imperial Japan, was treading lightly—keen to preserve a demilitarised buffer along the frontier.

Konstantin's childhood had been one of quiet contentment. His mother, Nadezhda Mikhailovna, was gentle and affectionate. His days were spent playing in the garden with his younger brother, Vladimir, and his sisters, Nadezhda Junior and little Nina. But as he grew, the Komsomol's rigid expectations began to stifle him. Smoking, drinking, private expressions of faith—even skipping group sports—were frowned upon as signs of moral weakness.

The final insult came when, despite an excellent academic record and a glowing endorsement from the local Soviet, he was denied university admission. The reference, though positive in tone, was coded with ideological reservations. Several less able candidates, especially of Jewish descent, were admitted instead.

In 1925, at eighteen, Konstantin informed his father—out of his mother's earshot—that he planned to leave. Vladimir Ivanovich pleaded, but his son would not be swayed. At last, he withdrew a modest sum from the bank and asked him to write a letter to be opened only after his departure.

Konstantin closed it with a line for his mother: *'I'm sorry I'll miss the birthday you planned for me.'*

With money in his coat and a soft rain falling, he crossed the Amur into Manchuria and made for Harbin, where he enrolled at the Faculty of Law. More funds would follow, sent discreetly through trusted go-betweens in Vladivostok.

Harbin dazzled him. Its scale, its rhythm, its unmistakably Russian character seized his imagination. Over 120,000 Russians lived there—triple the number of native Chinese. Even they were only marginally more numerous than the city's third largest group: Jews, both Russian and foreign-born.

Most Russians in Harbin were stateless Whites—émigrés who had fled the Bolsheviks. Yet among them moved quieter shadows: Red sympathisers, agents, informants. Harbin's prosperity owed much to the China Eastern Railway (CER), two of whose three main branches intersected in the city. Following the collapse of the Whites, the CER came under joint management between the USSR and Zhang Zuolin, the northeastern warlord known as the Old Marshal. Under this treaty, only Russian and Chinese nationals could work for the CER—though Russians had to retain Soviet passports.

The third branch, seized by Japan in 1906 after the Russo-Japanese War, was now under the protection of the fearsome Japanese Kwantung Army, stationed at Port Arthur.

With term yet to begin and his lodgings secured, Rodzaevsky explored the city. He soon discovered its architectural jewel: Saint Sophia Cathedral. Completed just four years earlier, it towered above everything he had known. The old twin-spired church in Blagoveshchensk—where his parents had wed—seemed quaint in comparison. Saint Sophia's soaring green onion dome loomed like a monument to another age.

Just beyond lay Kitayskaya Ulitsa—Chinese Street—where every building displayed some flavour of European style, built stoutly to endure Manchuria's bitter winters. Harbin was an empire of its own:

Slavic, Han, Jewish, cosmopolitan and volatile.

His stomach rumbled. The scent of smoked sausage drifted through the air. A queue snaked around a stall, and he joined it. While waiting, he bought a Russian-language newspaper. A quarter-page advert announced an upcoming Harbin Symphony concert featuring Tchaikovsky's *Pathétique* and Lyapunov's *Élégie en Mémoire de Liszt*. Beneath that: listings for three cinemas, each screening American films.

At the front of the queue, he found there was only one thing to buy: a hunk of *dalieba* (*далеба*), a dense Russian sourdough, stuffed with smoky barbecued *kolbasa* (*колбаса*) and dusted with paprika and black pepper. It was spicy, greasy, and perfect.

That mellow September afternoon, Chinese Street bustled with shoppers examining Parisian fabrics, Art Deco glassware, and bronze ornaments. Chocolatiers, perfumeries, and ice cream vendors vied for attention beside cafés and restaurants selling stroganoff, samovars of tea, and thick black coffee. A fine double-fronted shop bore the sign *Харбинская книжная лавка*—Harbin Bookstore.

Later, he took a tram to Gogol Street. Like the cathedral, it stirred his imagination. The road was paved with horseshoe-shaped cobbles and flanked by carved marble friezes of Pushkin, Tolstoy, Lermontov. Churin & Co (*Чурин и Ко*), the grand department store founded in 1904, spanned both corners and teemed with shoppers. Jewish, Ukrainian, and Russian stores operated side by side, with only a scattering of Chinese businesses.

There he found another bookshop: Gogol's (*книжный магазин Гоголя*)—far grander than the first. Bookshelves rose like columns. Oil paintings lined the oak-panelled walls. Burgundy leather chairs were arranged beneath crystal chandeliers.

He sat, opened a book, and read without pressure. It was, he thought, the most civilised hour he had enjoyed in years.

Across from him sat a young woman—poised, graceful, absorbed in her book. He spoke first, explaining that he'd just arrived in Harbin and would soon begin studying law.

She smiled.

'This isn't a library, you know. But still, shall we talk elsewhere?'

'Perhaps a drink?'

'Beer? We have the oldest brewery in China.'

'No, thank you. But tea or coffee would be welcome.'

'I know just the place. Excellent coffee—and the best apple charlotte. Do you like apple charlotte?'

He grinned.

'What Russian doesn't?'

They walked to Mamedov Café, run by Lev and his wife, Natasha—an accomplished cook and a friend of Lydia's, as she now introduced herself. Over steaming cups and shared cake, they agreed to use first names. She called him Kostya.

He offered a brief version of his departure from Russia. She described her family's escape from Vladivostok in 1922 and her hope to study at the Harbin Conservatory the following year.

Their conversation flowed. She was cultured, warm, quietly ironic.

She studied him. His hair unruly, his beard still uneven, his posture slightly guarded. But he was intelligent, resolute—and funny.

As dusk settled and the city's gas lamps flickered into life, she asked gently,

'Do you have plans tonight?'

'I was thinking of seeing *The Gold Rush*—an American film.'

'I've heard of it. It's a silent film, so the original intertitles are in English—then someone added Russian and Chinese on top. So yes, technically, it's subtitled three times.'

'Would you come with me?'

'I'd love to. It's rare I get the chance.'

'Why?'

'You're still seeing Harbin's lovely mask—the pearl necklaces and Viennese cafés. But in Nakhalova, it's another world. Stabbings, disappearances, smuggling—everything from opium to diamonds. Russian beggars huddle just streets away. I feel safer with a man beside me.'

She hesitated.

'Are you superstitious?'

'Like most Russians. I never lick food off a knife, nor do I ever give someone an even number of flowers.'

'The Illusion Cinema burned down after screening a film about Jesus. On a Sunday. Some say it's cursed to watch films on Sundays.'

He blinked—then laughed. The tension melted.

The theatre was packed. The Paramount newsreel opened the show: Mussolini in Rome, addressing the nation. Thousands of blackshirts filled the screen. Silent though it was, the footage still crackled on screen. Il Duce thrust his chest forward, chopped the air with his arms, stabbed the air with fingers, clenched fists, wrung his hands—every gesture calibrated. The fascist salute came like a punch.

The intertitles made promises: five million soldiers, a navy, an air force, a new empire.

Then came *The Gold Rush*. The film was captivating, and it was easy to sympathise with the Little Tramp—starving, snowbound, and ever hopeful—as he danced in a frozen cabin and boiled his own shoe for supper. Chaplin's blend of pathos and humour struck a nerve that year. To Lydia, it was without question the best film of 1925—elegant, tragic, utterly human. Kostya simply said there was nothing like it in the USSR. There couldn't be.

As he walked her to the tram, Kostya asked softly,

'May I see you again?'

She nodded.

'I hope you will.'

Back at his apartment, Rodzaevsky stood before the mirror. One by one, he practised Mussolini's gestures. The open hand. The slicing arm. The bent elbow, held aloft like a sword.

The new academic year opened with a formal gathering of 250 first-year students in the main hall. The dean welcomed them, introduced the faculty, and gave a short address.

'This Faculty is founded on diversity, equality, and tolerance. One-third of your study will be devoted to the legislation, history, culture, and languages of China, Mongolia, and beyond.

'You are asked to respect the varied politics, cultures, religions, and ethnicities represented here—over forty languages spoken among you.

'Our foundation rests upon two pillars: the intricate agreements between General Zhang Zuolin's administration and the Soviet Union, and the pivotal financial support provided by the China Eastern Railway. This is symbolised by the five-coloured flag of the Beiyang Government and the Soviet flag that fly proudly above this building. Any acts of communal violence or disrespect towards our sponsors will result in expulsion.'

What the dean omitted was that the hammer-and-sickle banner had been raised at the insistence of the CER; that the Beiyang Government held no real authority in Harbin—Zhang Zuolin did. And though he was firmly anti-communist, even Zhang had been placed under immense pressure by the Soviets to permit such a display. To most of the city's White Russian population, the flag represented not partnership, but exile, subjugation, and loss.

To Rodzaevsky, it all sounded idealistic—naïve, even. The dean's speech had ended in silence: no applause, no whispers, only the creak of chairs. Rodzaevsky scanned the rows. Surely there were Bolshevik sympathisers among them? OGPU informants, perhaps? Maybe even Chinese communists? He didn't yet know who was who, but the lines were already drawn—Reds, subdued and outnumbered; Whites, watchful. The whole place felt like a powder keg, the fuse already smouldering.

He immersed himself in his studies. Three lecturers stood out. Professor Ryazanovski delivered eloquent lectures on Chinese civil law. Deputy Dean Professor Georgy Guins focused on contemporary Western legal systems. But it was Professor Nikolai Nikiforov who truly captivated him.

Nikiforov, like the others, was stateless. But he spoke openly in support of Mussolini's corporatist legal reforms. His admiration for Italy's fascist system was unmistakable.

Students were encouraged to study a second language—Chinese, French, or English. Rodzaevsky chose English.

Not long after, a student named Alexander Pokrovsky approached him. After some subtle vetting to confirm Kostya's White Russian credentials, he extended an invitation to join a breakaway discussion group.

At the first meeting, Rodzaevsky was introduced to the newly formed Russian Fascist Organisation (RFO). Pokrovsky introduced him to two key student members: Evgeny Korablev and Boris Rumiantsev.

Korablev was producing propaganda literature, initially for campus circulation, with broader ambitions. Rumiantsev, fluent in Chinese, was building connections with General Zhang's staff. Pokrovsky focused on recruitment and identifying signs of 'Jewish-Bolshevik' infiltration.

Rodzaevsky was assigned to the Youth National Organisation of Musketeers. On his first visit, he was given a uniform and invited to speak to the assembled boys in black shirts, silver Maltese crosses gleaming on their armbands.

He delivered a theatrical speech in the style of Il Duce, finishing with a high fascist salute. It was returned in unison. The moment was intoxicating.

At the next meeting, a new recruit introduced himself. Calm and composed, Mikhail Matkovsky spoke with quiet authority. He was the son of a Tsarist major-general executed by the Bolsheviks in Omsk. A military academy graduate, he had escaped to Harbin, studied at the Polytechnic, and transferred to the Law Institute.

This time, Professor Nikiforov was present. Any latent dreams Rodzaevsky harboured of leading the movement quickly evaporated. Matkovsky, stocky and neatly moustached, possessed the calm command that Kostya's theatricality lacked.

There was agreement: the RFO would model itself on Italian fascism but also embrace Orthodox Christianity—especially its reverence for tradition and national unity.

Then came the Jewish question.

Pokrovsky spoke first:

'The Jewish scum in Harbin threatens our movement. Their bankers offer worse terms to gentiles, preserving their grip on coal, flour, lumber. They undercut rents for their own shopkeepers and restaurateurs.'

Korablev followed, seething.

'They whisper their poison into every ear. They run four times as many newspapers as the general press. They've opened elite schools to exclude others from higher education, brainwashing their youth with Zionist filth. They charm anyone who'll listen, spinning fantasies of global control.'

It struck a chord with Rodzaevsky—not merely because of Lydia's earlier remarks, but because he too had been denied higher education in Blagoveshchensk. Not for lack of ability, but, as he saw it, because the doors were open to Jews and closed to some Russians like him.

Professor Nikiforov turned to Matkovsky.

'Our organisation is young and vulnerable. Obsessing over the Jews will only isolate us. We must seek allies—Chinese nationalists, Japanese forces, even Bolsheviks if it serves us. And the Zionists? Let them go. Let them be someone else's burden.'

All eyes turned to the Professor.

'On the Jewish question, Europe is divided,' Nikiforov began. 'The Germans, under Hitler, demand exclusion. Mussolini, for now, sees Italian Jews as Italians first. His memoir, *My Autobiography*, may clarify things soon.

Let us not forget—Mussolini was once a socialist, before his expulsion.'

By midwinter, Rodzaevsky and Lydia were seeing each other often. She would arrive with hazel eyes bright from the cold, cheeks flushed pink, and her smile made the cold easier to bear.

They skated on the frozen Songhua River. Watching him glide, Lydia laughed and called him a true Siberian. Afterwards, they warmed themselves in cafés, sipping tea or coffee and sharing cakes.

One afternoon, after her piano lesson, her teacher, Leonid Rabinovich, invited him inside. Lydia played Chopin with poise and passion. Rodzaevsky noted, uneasily, the menorah beside the metronome.

Later, in a quiet café, he spoke,

'Lydia, I've grown very fond of you. Your company brings me joy.

But I must tell you something. Today I learnt your teacher is Jewish.'

'Is that a problem?'

He paused.

'I've joined the Fascist Party. I believe it can reform Harbin—and one day help reclaim our homeland.'

He explained the secrecy, the meetings, and Matkovsky's views.

'I agree. Nothing should divide us.'

Outside, Lydia slipped her arm through his and whispered,

'Kostya, kiss me.'

He leaned in, aiming for her cheek.

She laughed softly.

'Not the cheek, my darling—kiss me properly, on the lips.'

Shortly after Russian New Year, his mother arrived.

She burst into his lecture unannounced. Outside the hall, she clutched him tightly, sobbing into his coat.

Then, wiping her eyes with a mother's quiet strength, she smiled.

'You look dreadful. Are you eating? And that beard—my God. Come on, let's find some proper blinis. I've only three days.'

She brought news from home: gossip, family matters, affection. He avoided politics.

After a pause, he asked,

'Mother, why did you come?'

'To see you. No—truly, I came to bring you home. We miss you.'

He flinched.

'And how did you even get a permit?'

'Your father arranged it.'

His activities had been noticed and probably reported back to the OGPU. God only knows what pressure they had put on his father.

She wept and begged, kneeling beside him, until her voice cracked and her frame trembled.

At last, he said,

'There's only one reason I cannot return. It's not pride or politics. I've fallen in love.'

'What's her name? Is she pretty? From a good family?'

'Lydia Georgievna Malkova. From Vladivostok. A White Russian.'

The following evening, the three dined together. Lydia navigated the evening with elegance and tact. By night's end, his mother relented.

The next morning, they walked her to the station. She waved from the carriage, a pale hand behind the window. He raised his own—then slowly let it fall. He didn't yet know it was the last time he would ever see her.

Years later, he would still remember the shape of her hand behind the fogged glass, the way her mouth formed his name though he could no longer hear it.

Tensions in the city deepened. Kostya and Lydia often lingered at the Mamedov Café, discussing fascist politics over strong, unsweetened coffee.

The following year, the couple abruptly announced they were closing the café and relocating to the safety of the United States. Lydia was aware that Natasha's older brother, Anastase Andreivich Vonsiatsky, had married Marion Ream, a wealthy American divorcée twenty-two years his senior. The couple were to reside on the Ream family estate in New England. The Mamedovs had been offered a new life, a home, and the opportunity to open a restaurant—an offer too compelling to refuse.

This move would, in time, usher in a decade of trouble for Rodzaevsky.

Chapter 11: Xunwu, Jiangxi, China, 1927

After the Battle of Huichang, the Chinese Red Army trudged on for two months, still assuming the Communist political leadership resided in Wuhan. They marched south, against the current of the Gan River—the great artery that splits Jiangxi in two. Wherever they passed, villagers and townsfolk looked on in bewilderment.

It was a strange-looking army, stretched across more than three hundred *li*. In the vanguard, a red flag bearing the hammer and sickle waved above the marchers. In the centre, a smaller group—perhaps fifty unarmed people—carried a second red flag marked with a white plough: the banner of the National Federation of Peasants' Associations (NFPA). Chen and Hu marched among them. At the rear limped injured soldiers and hired porters, alongside a sight even more peculiar: an elderly officer carried in the sweltering heat by four groaning porters. Most officers were young Whampoa men, but a few veterans had chosen to join the Red Army.

There was no time to give Chen—or Hu—formal classroom instruction. Instead, they learned on the move. Assigned to a junior NFPA officer named Wei Haoyu, they joined a group of ten reporting to Yun Daiying, who answered to Zhang Guotao. The latter, one of the Party's founders, had hastily convened a Front Committee to advise on propaganda.

Wei and Hu bonded quickly, though their politics often clashed. Hu, raised among militant urban workers, still admired the Russian model. Wei, a rural idealist, believed that only a mass peasant uprising could save China—a view newly favoured by the Comintern. Hu, deeply scarred by the Shanghai massacre, was forced to set aside his revolutionary idealism. Wei, meanwhile, admitted that the Northern Expedition had come too early, and the alliance between workers, peasants, and the military was now shattered. But he hoped Guangdong still held promise for their movement.

Lacking a printing press, Wei and Hu resorted to hand-painted posters, nailed to village walls, and door-to-door visits offering NFPA membership cards. Crowds came to listen—but mostly to stare. Few joined.

Chen, granted some freedom during his Party apprenticeship, found an old farmer willing to talk. The man invited him to squat on a stool beneath the eaves. His sun-beaten face crinkled into deeper furrows as he squinted into the light.

'You want a revolution?' the man asked. 'We thought we had one when the NRA passed through. Some of us even joined. The wages were decent. They promised a new China.'

He paused, then added,

'A responsible government, no more cruel landlords, a chance for our children. But now? You come here with a tenth of the strength they had. Your ragtag army couldn't stand up to an angry warlord.'

'But Mao Zedong in Hunan has recruited a million peasants. Wu Peifu was routed!'

'If that's true, he used different methods. At first, you paid for what food we had. Then you turned to the landlords. They requisitioned everything—our food, our homes. There's not a single chicken left. No eggs, barely any rice or sweet potato. And the landlords helped you do it. How are we supposed to pay rent, interest, or taxes now? More of our daughters will be sent away—as concubines or servants. Payment in kind, on your behalf.'

Chen said quietly, 'I'm sorry. That was never the plan.'

But inwardly, he was unsettled—ashamed, perhaps—that the revolution had come to rely on the very landlords they claimed to oppose. And yet, armies had to be fed. In war, principle often yields to necessity.

'I believe you're well-intentioned. I even listened to your speeches on self-defence. But with what? Bamboo spears? One speaker promised we'd each get land. When we asked how much—how many *mu*—he said it was still under discussion. That's why no one took your cards.'

The two parted. That evening, Chen returned to camp. Chicken was served, but he had no appetite. Nor did he speak of the old man's words. That day, not a single recruit had joined.

When the army reached the headwaters of the Gan River, it turned east, skirting the edge of Fujian, bound for Shantou on the Guangdong coast. They passed through Xunwu, a sleepy hill town where the peasants watched them with blank, exhausted faces. No recruits stepped forward. After crossing the border into Guangdong, they paused again at Dabu—larger, wealthier, but no more willing to join their cause. From there, the long road to Shantou stretched before them.

Chen realised the route would take him near his family's *tulou* and longed to see them. He approached Wei.

'Is there any chance of a pass to visit home? Just one week.'

Wei hesitated. Such passes were often used to desert. But no one in his unit had ever requested one. He promised to inquire.

Three days later, a despatch rider arrived. He approached Wei's unit and handed Chen a sealed envelope.

Inside was a pass bearing a red stamp and Mao's signature.

Wei glanced at the document, then at Chen.

'Who are you?'

Chen stripped off his uniform, dressed as a Hakka peasant, tucked a pistol into his waistband, and set off. Two days later, he reached *Wuli Tulou*.

The river ran low after the dry summer. Carp flopped in shrinking pools—easy prey for herons and kingfishers. Swallowtails danced around the cork trees, searching for the last flowers. Rice in the terraces swayed, nearing its second harvest. Maize stood tall. In some fields, the oilseed plants had reached their full height, buds just beginning to swell—soon they would burst into golden bloom, with scattered red poppies dotting the landscape.

He entered the gate and found Mama at home. His father and sisters were out. Though strong of spirit, she hugged him and wept. That night, when the family gathered, Chen shared a careful version of his story—leaving out the worst.

Later, Lao Chen took him aside.

'How long can you stay?'

'Two nights. I have a signed military pass. And I've two things to do—visit Teacher Yao, and… tell Hehua and her parents about Peng.

That he died bravely. I'll spare them the details.'

His father paused.

'Yao will be overjoyed. But… Hehua's family is gone. We think they fled to Taiwan. That's become common, these days.'

Chen stood still, absorbing the blow. He had hoped to see her, even if only to say goodbye. Yet, strangely, he felt an odd sense of relief. The task he had dreaded was no longer his.

Yao's reaction was even warmer than expected. He embraced Chen tightly, greeted him in Russian, and brewed tea. Then he asked to hear everything.

Chen spoke. Yao rarely interrupted—only to curse the violence. Later, they reminisced about Xiamen and laughed together. But the laughter faded.

Eventually, Chen asked, 'Teacher… have you ever seen a revolution like this before?'

Yao's face turned pale as he struggled to control his expression. Then he started to weep. He knew it was time to tell Chen about the missing link in his life story. He was sitting opposite a changed and grown-up man.

Eventually, he regained some composure and said,

'I want to tell you Anna's story. As you've observed, there may be winners and losers in revolutions.'

Chen knew this was going to be grim.

'In 1905, Russian peasants rose against the Tsar. Landlords and the rich were attacked. In Georgia, where we lived, the unrest spread quickly. By then, we had a home beside the tea garden. Liu, our friend, lived nearby—his family had joined us from China. His boys often brought Elene little gifts: *tklapi* fruit rolls and straw dolls. My sons were grown— one a grain merchant, the other studying law in Batumi. Anna was happy. Elene, four years old, spoke both Russian and Chinese.

'We didn't think we'd be in danger. The peasants knew us. They had once housed us when we arrived in Chavki. But we were landowners. We sold tea to the aristocracy.

'One evening, Liu and I were drinking wine on his porch, admiring the sea. We saw a group of peasants approaching, carrying tools—pitchforks, shovels. At first, I wasn't worried. Then they turned up our road. My stomach clenched.

'They didn't stop. They reached our house. In minutes, it was ablaze. Liu and I ran towards it, but it was already too late. Anna was still alive—I could hear her desperate cries,

"*Egor, Egor, Egor, save me, for God's sake, save me!*"

'Liu tried to hold me back, but I knew it was impossible. The building quickly became a smouldering heap, with nothing left but the charred remains of my wife and daughter. Then, there was silence. Those desperate screams will haunt me for the rest of my life.'

Liu went to a cupboard and handed Chen a photograph. It showed a woman and a little girl, both dressed for the occasion, smiling into the camera. The child was adorable. The woman—undeniably stunning.

'It was in my wallet,' he said quietly. 'The only thing that survived. The books I gave you were all bought after the fire. Now you understand why.'

As the men parted, Chen wondered if he would ever see Yao again. The army he was re-joining was losing badly. Death felt inevitable. Yao knew it too.

That evening, the family gathered once more. Chen's mother prepared a feast. His sisters tried to cheer him, but the weight of sorrow lingered. Lao Chen assumed it was fear of battle—but it was Yao's story that haunted his son.

The following morning, Chen made his sad farewell. As he crossed the threshold, a terrible possibility gripped him: that the next time he returned, his home might already have been destroyed—burned in a raid, seized by bandits, or taken over by an army.

The Red Army had been incommunicado for over two months. When it reached Shantou on 24 September—unopposed—it had been reduced to 5,000 weary but capable fighters. Only four applicants stepped forward after the Nationalist-leaning police force was summarily dismissed.

They were met by Zhang Tailei, newly arrived from Hong Kong. He presented his credentials as a Politburo member with instructions from the Shanghai leadership. He made no effort to speak in private.

Chen was within earshot when Zhou Enlai, the ranking Party official, asked,

'Shanghai? I thought the leaders were in Wuhan?'

'Not anymore. It became too dangerous—they moved.'

'Tell me your orders, and where they come from.'

'From Qu Qiubai and the Comintern. But first, the Front Committee must be dissolved. Central Command is to resume full authority.'

'Of course,' Zhou replied.

Zhang hesitated, then produced a telegram and began to read, as if needing it as a prop to lend weight to the words.

'Tan Pingshan and Li Lisan have been expelled from the Central Committee and are to return to Shanghai immediately. Zhou Enlai and Zhang Guotao are demoted to reserve members. No new supplies will be sent from the Soviet Union. The army will redeploy to Haifeng.'

There was no disguising the meaning. Supplies were gone. Defeat was assumed. Blame had already been assigned. Even Chen Duxiu had fallen further.

Zhou, humiliated, offered Zhang the Front Committee. Zhang declined.

'I've been appointed Secretary of the Guangdong Regional Committee. If you win at Shantou, you'll need us.'

Zhou sensed the implication—and its loophole.

'Can we engage in the battle before redeploying? I need to fight on the front line.'

Zhang nodded. The understanding suited them both.

Afterwards, Chen sat on the edge of a low stone wall, staring at the lantern glow from nearby shacks. He tried to summon hope—any fragment. But all he saw was the shape of a dying movement: fractured orders, punished leaders, vanishing supplies. The tide had not turned. It had already receded.

Chen returned to his unit. Days later, a messenger arrived. Wei summoned his team.

'Orders have changed. We're to make all haste to Shantou. Every available man is to force-march and join the main army. Our work here is finished. Rifles and ammunition will be issued.'

It was alarming. Party officials with little training were now being rushed to the front. Chen realised how desperate the situation had become. His group reached Tangkeng—one hundred and forty *li* northwest of Shantou—on 24 September. There, they were attached to a depleted company of about 110 men under a young officer named Lin Biao—barely older than Chen himself.

Lin set up targets and ordered each recruit to fire five rounds. Risky, yes, but he refused to send men into battle untested. He needed every body. The next day was worse. They practised bayoneting straw dummies.

The Battle of Tangkeng began on 27 September and lasted three days. On the eve of battle, Lin Biao addressed his troops.

'Men,' he began—then, seeing a female cadre—'and women… Tomorrow, we go into battle against a warlord army. They fight for greed. For a system that leaves farmers half-starved and oppressed. Factory workers suffer just the same. We fight for justice. And that is why we must fight to the last.'

There was scattered applause.

Then he added, his voice rough but clear, 'There will be no conscription this time. The warlords will not absorb you into their ranks. If captured, you will almost certainly be executed. Fight until you can fight no more.'

It was raw. Unpolished. But Chen was moved. The speech had power—especially from a nineteen-year-old standing calmly before men and women about to face slaughter.

That night, Chen was quietly inducted into the Communist Party, witnessed by Lin Biao and Hu. He understood, though no one had said it: they were not expected to survive.

The battle was yet another disaster. Zhu De's forces—fewer than 5,000—faced 15,000 well-entrenched warlord troops, a substitute for the defunct NRA. Chen witnessed artillery for the first time—its impact devastating. The final bayonet charge by the enemy was a bloodbath. Men fell in waves. The survivors fled in two directions.

Ye Ting led his men to Hailufeng, where, with Peng Pai's help, they briefly established a peasant Soviet. Zhu De struck out for Hunan in search of Mao and others in Hubei. Chen and Hu followed the Hunan route with Lin Biao and a small band of survivors.

Meanwhile, the broader revolutionary plan collapsed. In early September, uprisings had been launched in Hubei and Hunan under the codename *Autumn Harvest Uprising*. Hubei had seemed ideal: its capital, Wuhan, had once housed the Communist leadership and boasted a railway to Changsha. Red Spear militia were expected to provide local defence. But the Red Spears proved indifferent—or outright hostile.

Southern Hunan was little better. The strategy had been to raise rural armies, then move on the fortified towns of Puxi and Xianning. Yet the peasants remained apathetic. A small force assembled to attack Puxi, but they had no more than a dozen rifles—the rest carried primitive *suǒ biāo* (梭镖) spears.

They faced artillery and machine guns. It would have been suicide.

Xianning, though smaller, was well-defended. It was never attacked.

By 12 September, the uprisings had collapsed. Survivors fled to the hills near Xikeng, nursing their wounds and shattered hopes.

Only one hope remained in southern China: Mao Zedong's peasant army in Hunan. Could he offer the redemption they so desperately needed?

Chapter 12: Jinggang Mountains, Jiangxi, China, 1927

After the Battle of Tangkeng, Zhu De's forces—now fractured and weary—drifted westward in uncertainty. Lin Biao, Chen, Hu, and a scattering of soldiers followed him into the wilderness, unclear whether Mao Zedong had survived his own failed uprising in Hunan, let alone where he might be found.

It was in mid-October, while studying a map beneath a makeshift canopy, that Zhu De turned to Chen and Hu. Both men had shown tenacity in the past, once finding the Red Army in Ruijin. He tasked them with a similar mission—locate Mao, who, if all had gone to plan, would be somewhere near Changsha.

They were given supplies, a few *yuan* in silver, and a letter sewn into Chen's clothing. They were to pose as travelling tailors. Alongside bolts of fabric, they carried a hand-wound sewing machine slung across Chen's back. Zhu De forbade them from carrying arms—drawing attention in this region could be fatal.

They made their way through Ciping and then towards the convergence of the Guangdong, Jiangxi, and Hunan borders. Soon, they began to hear whispers—rumours of an armed force moving through the nearby Jinggang Mountains. The region held no strategic value. No warlord would want it. It could only be the Red Army. But if so, something had clearly gone wrong—Changsha was still far to the north.

The valley floors were dotted with well-kept fields and walled villages. Some larger homes—those of merchants or landlords—had fortifications of their own. At the village of Huang Aoxiang, they approached a peasant woman sowing winter wheat.

'Have you seen an army?' Chen asked.

She eyed him suspiciously.

'Where are you from?'

'Fujian. A *tulou* village,' he replied.

The woman spat in the dirt and pointed north.

'You'll find your army up there—along with your kind. Thieving Hakka bandits. You're not welcome here.'

The bitterness in her voice was unmistakable.

On 2 November, they entered the lower slopes of the Jinggang Mountains at Taoliao. Steep, winding paths carved into the rock led them past great boulders and ridgelines perfect for ambush. The occasional hut appeared, clinging to the hillside—its occupants malnourished and wary. At one such settlement, Chen called out a greeting in Hakka and received a reply in the same language.

Hu wept at the sight of their poverty. Even Chen, who had seen hardship, was shaken. A few villagers remembered men in red armbands passing through. That lifted their spirits—they were close.

But rounding a bend, they were halted by a band of heavily armed men. The group eyed them with menace, suspicion thick in the air. The leader addressed them in Hakka,

'Who are you, and what are you doing here?'

Chen replied, evenly,

'Travelling tailors. Seeking work in Ciping.'

The bandits weren't buying it. Within moments, their wrists were bound in coarse rope, the sewing machine hoisted cruelly onto Hu's back. Beaten and jeered at, they were prodded along a punishing incline. Hu, barely able to walk, tried pleading in rudimentary Hakka—earning more kicks for his trouble.

At a village perched high in the cliffs, their captors forced them to strip. The bandit leader rummaged through their clothes until he uncovered the sewn-in letter. Then, dressed only in their underclothes, the two prisoners were locked in a dark hut with a dirt floor and no windows.

As the door closed behind them, Chen wondered—was this what Mr Bei had felt, alone in the dark, knowing the end might come at any moment?

Hours passed. It was nightfall when the door finally creaked open. They were marched to a nearby house, where two men waited. One wore military fatigues, the other round glasses and a scholar's jacket. The guards stiffened—the officer was clearly in command.

He stepped beneath a kerosene lamp. His face was deeply pockmarked, the scars casting jagged shadows.

'Tailors, are you?' he asked in Mandarin.

Hu nodded, voice wavering.

'Yes. From Fujian. Seeking work.'

The man gestured for them to assemble the sewing machine. They fumbled with it, hands trembling. Chen cursed silently—there had been no chance to practise.

'Sit down,' said the man.

He took the flywheel, turned it confidently, and stitched a flawless seam. Then he smiled—though not kindly.

'Unfortunate for you. I trained as a tailor once. This machine is familiar. You two are clearly not what you claim to be.'

He pointed to the letter on the table.

'A message from Zhu De. That makes you spies.'

The silence stretched—long enough for them to imagine the worst possible outcome: torture, execution, a bullet in the back of the head. The man said nothing. Only the faint hiss of the kerosene lamp broke the stillness.

Then, suddenly, the man chuckled.

'You've nothing to fear. I'm Wang Zuo. I've allied with Mao Zedong.'

He shook their hands and introduced the younger man as Song Liqiang, a political officer from Jiangsu. Song would escort them to Mao.

Over sweet potato moonshine and bowls of steaming rice, the tension ebbed. Hu soon slumped in drunken silence. Chen, more cautious, asked about the Hakka hostility.

Wang explained,

'It goes back centuries. Guest people like us tried settling here—but were pushed into the mountains.'

His father—a Han, and an opium addict—had died when Wang was eleven. He had turned to tailoring, but when that failed, he'd turned to kidnapping wealthy Han families. Eventually, he made a deal—if he ceased banditry, the local authorities would leave him in peace.

'I met Mao last week,' he added. 'I hosted a pig roast. Then we joined forces and raided Xia Jiabi's Yin clan. We caught them mid-feast.

Xia escaped, but we killed fifty and torched their headquarters.'

He tossed Chen a coin stamped *Hong River*.

'Show that if other bandits stop you.'

The next day, they set off for Mao's encampment in Ninggang County, descending steep trails beneath a pale winter sky. Now accompanied by Song, Chen and Hu felt safer, though the wilderness still evoked a sense of hidden danger.

Along the path, Song recounted what had happened in Mao's ranks, 'Three regiments—it wasn't enough. We thought we could take Changsha, but everything unravelled fast. Lu Deming's 1st Regiment was our strongest—experienced, but too far west to reach Nanchang, a secondary target, in time. They ended up in Xiushui, and desertions hit them hard. They picked up peasants and even bandits to make up the numbers.

'The 2nd Regiment came from miners and railway men. Mao had ties with the Anyuan miners—once disguising himself as a salesman just to visit them. The railway teams were supposed to sabotage the tracks.

'I was with the 3rd Regiment. Purely peasants. Brave, but armed with little more than farm tools. We repelled some Nationalist forces in Tonggu, but it wasn't enough. There was no uprising—only blood.'

Chen glanced at Hu, both sensing an uneasy turn in the conversation. Hu was the first to speak,

'I suppose few peasants joined you—just like in Fujian and Guangdong.'

Song nodded.

'Exactly. Even under the cruellest landlords, most were paralysed by fear. They knew what was expected—kill the landlords, redistribute the land—but reprisals were swift and brutal.'

Hu replied matter-of-factly,

'That aligns with Central Committee policy.'

Song continued,

'All we could muster for Changsha was 7,000. That was our entire attacking force.'

Chen frowned.

'But wasn't there internal support? I thought Changsha had strong communist leanings.'

'Some, yes. But the Nationalists learned of the plan. They imposed a strict curfew. Our attack began on 9 September. We were outnumbered and outgunned. We never reached the city—only the 2nd Regiment made any ground, and even they were quickly driven back. Mao ordered a retreat to Wenjiashi, near the Jiangxi border. We arrived ten days later with just 1,500 men. The Nationalists pursued us relentlessly.'

Chen shook his head.

'You couldn't have been expected to continue an assault with such a depleted force. It would've been suicide.'

'There was a split,' said Song. 'Some at the Front Committee meeting insisted the Central Committee wanted us to press on. But Mao and He Long pushed for retreat. They won—just. We moved towards Sanwan, reaching it on 29 September. But the enemy caught up. Lu Deming and 300 others were lost—including Lu himself.

'Sometimes,' he added, lowering his voice, 'I wish those armchair generals in Shanghai could see what we're up against.'

Hu looked sharply at him.

'Comrade, such thoughts are better kept to yourself.'

'Yes, I know. But retreating saved my life.'

He cleared his throat and pressed on.

'We did win a small victory, though. Passing through Lianhua, we overran a poorly armed Nationalist peace corps. We freed 100 of our comrades and opened the grain stores. Perhaps it will be remembered as our first success—however modest.'

Hu's voice was sharp.

'You exclude all we achieved in the cities—strikes, street fighting, mobilising the urban poor?'

Song replied just as curtly,

'Then why are you here?'

Chen intervened, his voice low but firm,

'Enough. No more bickering.'

The silence that followed was uneasy. It was the first time Chen had truly felt the ideological chasm—between the city-based revolutionaries and the rugged peasants who made up this fledgling rural army.

Eventually, he asked,

'When you reached Sanwan, how many fighting men remained?'

'Barely a thousand,' Song said.

'And what happened then?'

'Mao gathered the remnants and ordered the three regiments merged into one. He Long assumed command. Everyone—soldiers and officers alike—was free to leave. Some officers left, bitter about losing their ranks.

'Then Mao revealed that an envoy from Yuan Wencai had approached him. Yuan led a pro-communist militia in Maoping, here in the Jinggang range. We marched there and arrived on 7 October. Yuan was nervous—he was outnumbered—but agreed to let us in. Mao and Yuan got along well. Yuan had trained at the Peasant Institute, where Mao had once taught.

'Mao asked for two things: a hospital, to care for the wounded and those sick with dysentery, malaria, tuberculosis, and tick fever—and an introduction to Wang Zuo. Both requests were granted.'

Chen raised an eyebrow.

'I assume Yuan wanted something in return?'

'Of course. Rifles, money, and training. The usual currency of bandits. So, we began identifying promising men among the bandits—those who could be educated, turned into Red Army soldiers, and trained as future Party members. They would teach the peasants along the way. There was to be no killing of elites in our base area, and any soldier caught stealing from peasants—even food, hay, or doors—would be punished.'

Hu scoffed.

'Doors?'

'They make good bedboards,' said Song. 'And the hay is used for bedding.'

Hu bristled again.

'It's not the job of half-literate soldiers to teach peasants,' he snapped. 'That's our responsibility—as political cadres. That was always our role. Has that changed too? That's a deviation from policy. The army's task is to support our revolution with force, intimidation, and execution—redistribute the land and eliminate the landlords.'

'Policy has shifted—call it survival. Yesterday you were nearly killed, and today you're back spouting Shanghai doctrine like none of it happened. Look around—do you think urban theorists can just stroll through the mountains and enlighten villagers?'

Hu snapped,

'And who decided we should employ bandits?'

'Mao Zedong did,' said Song bluntly. 'If we attack the Han elites now, they'll summon Nationalist reinforcements and armed thugs. We'd be crushed. And we have no contact with Shanghai—we're isolated.'

Chen saw tempers boiling again and imagined, with absurd clarity, lifting both of them into the dirt. Song's glasses flying, Hu wailing with a twisted ankle. It was almost comical—if it weren't so tense.

It took time to calm them again.

When they reached the camp at Maoping, Song excused himself to report to the local command. The decision was swift: three soldiers would attempt to trace Chen and Hu's original route and fetch Zhu De. But they never found him—he had already departed for southern Hunan.

Upon returning, Song gave his orders. Chen, as a Hakka speaker, would return to Wang Zuo's mountain base, joining the militia and spreading NFPA membership. Hu was to remain in Maoping, teaching the Red Army reserve and accompanying Yuan's troops to recruit villagers during manoeuvres.

New membership cards, bearing a plough emblem, were being hastily printed. While waiting, Song encouraged them to explore the town. It was clear Maoping was poor. A hospital was under construction. The market offered little more than wilted vegetables and ragged chickens. It could never support an army.

On their walk back, Song confirmed as much. Yuan had warned Mao: without expansion beyond the base, starvation and desertion would follow. As a result, Mao crossed into Hunan, heading towards Shaoguan in Guangdong to join Ye Ting's scattered forces.

Meanwhile, Chen Hao, a Whampoa-trained officer, captured

Chaling and declared a People's Committee in December. But a Nationalist counterattack followed. Mao brought in reinforcements from the Jinggang—but it was too late. Chen Hao's battalion veered south, ignoring retreat orders.

Mao caught up and uncovered a betrayal: Chen Hao planned to surrender. He and his fellow plotters were arrested. Back at the Jinggang, in front of the entire Red Army, Chen Hao was executed—his body left on display for a day, as a warning to others.

It was a harsh but unmistakable message: in these mountains, betrayal would not be forgiven.

In late December, Song summoned his two political cadres to a quiet meeting room in Maoping. A brazier smouldered in the corner, offering little warmth. The town lay hushed beneath a grey sky, the frost creeping in beneath the doors.

Song began briskly.

'Report your findings. Hu, you first.'

Hu inhaled deeply before speaking, his voice even but touched by fatigue.

'I've had one success and one failure. On the positive side, we've made real strides within the Red Army. Several soldiers—some even from Yuan Wencai's ranks—have embraced our mission and joined the Party. Through careful instruction and patient engagement, we've begun shaping a cohesive, purposeful force. It isn't yet a true army, but it's beginning to feel like one.'

Song nodded with approval.

'Excellent. And the failure?'

Hu's mouth tightened.

'Recruitment among the Han peasants has proved far more difficult. When we ask them to join the NFPA and commit to land reform, many simply produce membership cards from the so-called Peasants' Improvement Society. They claim they've already received rent and tax concessions.'

'And who organises this Society?'

'The landlords, of course. They use their extended family networks to promote it. It's a smokescreen—effective, but transparent once examined closely.'

Song frowned.

'A clever ruse—but not unexpected.'

He turned to Chen, who sat straighter in his chair. His voice was calm, his delivery crisp.

'My experience has been the inverse of Hu's. From the Red Army, there's been limited gain—some soldiers sent to Maoping have received rudimentary training, but cohesion remains lacking. However, working with Wang Zuo's forces, I've visited almost every Hakka village in his territory. Recruitment has been overwhelming. NFPA chapters are forming in nearly every settlement. The people are destitute, stripped of hope—they join because they have nothing left to lose.'

Song nodded again, this time more thoughtfully.

'Then we're learning something crucial: revolution takes root where the soil is broken enough to receive it. That's the lesson here. You've both made meaningful progress, each in your own sphere. Be prepared—there's a major military manoeuvre planned for next month, and your contributions will be required. But for now, remain embedded with your current units.'

Chen gave a slight nod.

At least he didn't say *bandits*, Chen thought. Not out loud, anyway.

After the meeting ended, Chen stepped out into the cold twilight. The winter air numbed his thoughts. A dog barked down the street—probably a stray still searching for shelter.

He passed a frozen pond where villagers had dumped unwanted things: a broken plough jutting from the ice, icicles hanging from its beam; on the bank, shattered pots and bundles of straw bedding, stiff with frost and long stripped of fleas.

Outside the unfinished hospital, a chorus of coughing broke the silence—harsh, hollow sounds from men wasting away from consumption behind the walls.

We've come to save the people, he thought, *but who will save us from ourselves?*

Chapter 13: Suichuan, Jiangxi, China, 1928

On 10 January 1928, Mao delivered a rousing speech in Maoping—his first address to the entire army. He announced that the next day they would march en masse to Suichuan County, where Xiao Jiabi's militia would be decisively routed. From now on, he declared, the associations would be named the Peasants', Workers', and Soldiers' Associations—fitting for a county with large market towns and some non-agricultural activity. The new government bodies, he said, were to be called Soviets.

Hu was delighted. It might not have been the urban proletariat, but to him, this was a revolution inclusive of the ideal—if only for now.

Xiao Jiabi's militia stood no chance. Four days later, the market town of Caolin fell. Its defenders and elites fled in panic, vowing revenge once the Red Army departed. The barracks were set ablaze, the jail doors flung open, and food distributed—first to the needy and, as always, to the ravenous army.

Song's first task for Chen and Hu was to take an inventory of the town's shops and workshops. Their survey identified 113 establishments, divided into sixteen 'large capitalists', eleven 'medium capitalists', and the remainder as 'small capitalists'. When it came to the final count, the two surveyors chose to report a slightly inflated number. Among the small capitalists, many were heavily indebted to the now-vanished elites.

Hu insisted on drawing up a ranked list of businesses to be appropriated or destroyed, including those whose owners were to be executed. They presented their findings to Song, who told them to return in two hours.

When they did, Song spoke first,

'The largest business owner has been arrested—guilty of numerous heinous acts. He will be executed publicly for his crimes.'

Thinking of his fallen comrades in Shanghai, Hu felt a surge of grim satisfaction. Chen, meanwhile, was more reserved, though he recognised the value of sending a clear message.

'The other large capitalist premises will be handed over to the new committees and managed in public ownership. The medium and small businesses will be allowed to function normally.'

Hu looked disheartened. He wanted to shout, *So this is a revolution?* Instead, he asked,

'And where did these orders come from?'

'From Mao. He doesn't want the town's commercial fabric destroyed. It must continue to function. Now, return to your regular duties.'

By the end of January, it was over. The Communists, following Caolin's model, captured the large county of Ninggang. County Head Chang Kaiyang was seized and dragged to a central square, where ropes were strung together to hang slogans. He was tied to a wooden frame and repeatedly stabbed by *suǒ biāo* in a gruesome, deliberate death, something Chen witnessed.

This part of Jiangxi began to implement Soviet-style management. A calm period followed. Chen returned to his rural work, while Hu, reassigned due to his experience, became a senior member of the Caolin Peasants', Workers', and Soldiers' Committee. He kept his views to himself about what he saw as Mao's leniency towards the petit bourgeoisie.

The calm did not last. In early February, a small detachment of Wang Zuo's former militia—now Red Army regulars—was operating alongside Chen's unit. They encountered eleven young, bedraggled soldiers carrying a white flag. Wang Zuo's men advanced cautiously. The strangers laid down their rifles and raised their hands.

Chen stepped forward.

'Who are you? Where are you from?'

One young man, the only one with a pistol, answered,

'We are from the Guangdong Officers' Training Regiment Cadet Force.'

Wang Zuo's men cocked their rifles. This unit had trained to become Nationalist officers. After the split, it remained part of the Nationalist Army.

'How did you escape and get here?'

'I hid the men. Then I found a peasant about my size and made him strip. Seeing him run nearly naked down the road was quite a sight. I took his clothes and robbed farms at night to feed us. I hoped any Nationalist patrols would blame a local thief.'

Although the Red Army maintained a relatively flat command structure, Chen noted that this senior cadet—who now introduced himself simply as Pan—carried himself with the composure of a future officer.

'Why come here—to your enemy?'

'There was a failed uprising in Guangzhou. Our regiment of 1,500 men had planned to defect to the Communists for months.'

'Who crushed it?'

'A local warlord and Nationalist General Zhang Fakui. He took the city in mid-November and began hunting down members of leftist unions.'

Another cadet, Ma, added that Zhang had seized the moment while Wang Jingwei and General Li Jishen were away in Shanghai. Zhang, already infamous for his part in the Shanghai massacre, had struck again.

'And your commander?'

'Ye Ting. He had been in hiding in Hong Kong. He joined us just hours before the uprising on 11 December.'

'No, I mean the Communist Party leader—who was in charge?'

'You mean Zhang Tailei, Secretary of the Guangdong Committee. He was nowhere to be found in the preparation stages.'

Chen was surprised. Last he'd heard, Zhang Fakui had failed to support the Communists during the Nanchang Uprising. If the reports were true, he was now operating far from northern Jiangxi. And as for Zhang Tailei, Chen had little regard for him since Zhou Enlai's demotion in Shantou.

If Changsha had been a red city, Guangzhou was a red inferno. It had led strikes and boycotts against British and Japanese goods just two years earlier. Suppressing the movement there would have required extreme violence.

Chen recognised the value of this intelligence and changed approach.

'Are you hungry?'

'Starving.'

'We'll give you some cold food. But you must come to our base camp for a full debrief.'

When Chen reached Maoping, he reported to Song. Within the hour, Pan and Ma were brought before Mao, who happened to be at the base. It was the first news from the outside world in months.

A few days later, Song confided in Chen, speaking in hushed tones to avoid harming morale. On paper, there had been 200,000 militant workers in Guangzhou. In truth, barely a tenth of that number took to the streets—fear of repression from Zhang Fakui was too great. The Communists faced 10,000 Nationalist troops, police, and rightist union paramilitaries. It had been a bloodbath. Zhang Tailei arrived to lead the revolt but was killed on the second day. Most who fled went north-west, where Zhu De was rumoured to be organising in southern Hunan. But the cadets had been trapped. Many died.

Chen thought, *Is there no end to the losses?* But at least Zhu De was alive. The scouts had been searching in the wrong place. If the reports were true, Zhu might be just three hundred *li* away.

After the debrief, the base experienced a brief lull. Training resumed. Cadres, peasants, and soldiers prepared for the next stage. During this time, Chen and Song grew close, developing a firm trust and camaraderie.

The lull ended on 5 March with the arrival of Zhou Lu, Head of the Military Branch of the Southern Hunan Special Committee. In Maoping, Mao and senior Party representatives, including Song, met Zhou in a closed session. No army personnel were present. Soon afterwards, reserve members were sent into the field to summon every available soldier and political cadre for a major address on the Maoping parade ground.

Chen was only a day's walk away when he heard the news. He was elated. This could mean Zhu De and Mao might finally unite their forces.

When he arrived, Song's expression was grim. They found a quiet spot, and Chen asked what had happened.

'It began well,' Song said. 'Zhou said he was acting under instructions from Li Weihan of the Central Committee. Mao seemed pleased—Li had been his fellow student. But then it all unravelled. I've never seen such hostility between comrades.'

Chen frowned. 'What changed?'

'Zhou told Mao that it had been too long since they last communicated. He said he had several key updates from the Central Committee. His tone was stiff. Then he announced that Mao had been expelled from the Central Committee in November for multiple deviations.'

Chen was stunned. 'What did Mao say?'

'He asked if Zhang Tailei had returned to Guangzhou and if he had been killed in the uprising. It was clever. Zhou hadn't expected that. If Mao had inside knowledge, perhaps he had deliberately avoided official communication. It also hinted that Zhang might have helped orchestrate Mao's downfall.'

'So what were these so-called deviations?'

'First, that Mao had disobeyed orders by retreating to Jinggang instead of continuing the Changsha offensive. Second, that he had failed to burn landlords' homes, kill them, and redistribute land—unlike Zhu De. Third, that instead of raising a peasant army, he'd allied with bandits.'

'That's absurd.'

'Mao was clearly surprised. But word of his "bandit army" and policy deviations had spread after Caolin. Zhou then delivered the real blow. He told Mao he'd also been expelled from the Party, and that the Front Committee would be abolished. Mao could remain Head of the Army but would now report to the Hunan Special Committee.'

'But if he was expelled from the Party, how could he retain any position?'

'Exactly. It seemed Zhou made it up on the spot.'

'So, Mao was now being ordered about by a superior?'

'Technically, yes. Mao rose and said the meeting was over. Zhou pointed a finger and shouted at him to sit down. Then he ordered Mao to take the entire 1st Army south to support Zhu De's successful campaign, which had already captured Chenzhou and two other towns.'

'And?'

'Mao exploded. "And what if I refuse?" he shouted. Zhou replied coldly, "You'll face the consequences." Mao stormed out, shouting that he'd write to the Comintern—directly to Moscow, not Shanghai.'

Chen shook his head. 'What will he say at the parade ground?'

Song shrugged.

Two days later, Mao addressed the assembled crowd. His high-pitched Hunanese accent rang through the loud hailer. He declared that Zhu De had raised a great peasant army in the south. This, he said, was the beginning of the unified revolution they had all dreamed of. He praised the army's discipline, the Jinggang base, and their humble achievements. Then he raised his fist and cried out three times, 'To Zhongcun—charge!' The crowd erupted, caps flying into the air. He said nothing of his expulsion or his changed status.

On 18 March, the 1st Army reached Zhongcun and awaited further instructions for a rendezvous with Zhu De. Cadres were sent into the countryside to carry out their duties. Ten days passed. Then a member of the Hunan Committee finally arrived.

Chen returned to Zhongcun shortly afterwards. The army had already moved out. Only a few defenders remained. Song, Hu, and newly arrived cadres were gathering the last field units. When they were all back, they would retreat together.

The news was dire. The Hunan uprising had collapsed. Delays in the Northern Expedition had allowed the Nationalists to rally. Mao had divided his forces—Wang Zuo went to assist Zhu De, while the rest fought a rearguard action. Song pulled Chen aside.

'The official told Mao the expulsion was a mistake. He's still a Party member. And Zhou Lu... was killed in the uprising. But this stays between us. Understood?'

Chen nodded, though his mind raced. Had Zhou made a fatal error before he died? Or had the Hunan Committee realised they needed Mao fully onside? Either way, Mao remained politically sidelined.

Later, Song summoned both Chen and Hu.

'I have orders from Zhou Enlai. He remembers you both from Ruijin. Comrade Hu, though we've had our differences, your work here has been recognised. The Central Committee requests your return to

Shanghai. Safe passage will be arranged. I know you were enjoying your post, but your knowledge of the city is urgently needed.

'Comrade Chen, Zhou plans to establish a Communist Intelligence Service. Though it's mainly for cities, he believes you can build a small rural unit of five to ten operatives. I'll help you set it up.

'You've come far together. I hope you'll meet again.'

Hu said goodbye to Chen. Neither man said much. Chen reached for Hu's arm. It was a gesture that said more than words. Both understood: Hu was leaving one danger for a greater one. Chen's path ahead was unclear.

Once all field cadres had returned, they joined Mao's forces. On 27 April, following a successful retreat, Mao and Zhu De were reunited.

Chen could see challenges ahead. Zhu De had 2,000 disciplined Nanchang troops and had raised a 10,000-strong peasant army. Mao's force numbered 1,600. Together, they now commanded nearly 14,000 fighters.

But the problems were immediate. Much of the base area had been recaptured by Nationalists and local warlords. Maoping's reserves had survived by retreating into the highlands, but many cadres and villagers were gone.

Worse, the rugged terrain could not feed so many mouths.

Orders came to march on Yongxin, a market town with fertile land. It fell quickly. Ninggang and Suichuan counties followed. Then came Lianhua. This became the tri-county base.

Mao wisely avoided attacking Ji'an, just two hundred *li* away. Shanghai's doctrine urged peasants to capture cities and set up Party structures. The Nationalists would not tolerate such a threat.

During the victory celebrations in Yongxin, the cadres organised a football match. Why not? China had invented the game 2,000 years ago, albeit in a different form. Soldiers were barred from playing—they were too large and might injure someone. A referee was found: a soldier raised in Hong Kong.

Chen wasn't much of a player, but he had kicked a ball about as a boy in the *tulou*. He was fit, at least. When the teams were posted, he was listed as midfield. Then came the surprise: Mao Zedong, goalkeeper for the opposing side.

Before the match, Chen asked around. Mao had learnt the game at teacher training college and was said to enjoy it.

Thousands turned out. Free drinks had been 'donated', and fireworks promised. Tailors stitched simple shirts overnight—all one size. On the pitch, the *Internationale* rang out. Mao, towering at 1.8 metres, stood tall—his shirt too short for his frame.

Some fans, already drunk and backing Chen's team, thought the referee biased. They chanted, 'British black whistle, black whistle,' accusing him of corruption.

With three minutes left, the score was 2–2. Chen took a pass and darted forward. Mao rushed out. Chen went down. The referee pointed to the spot. A forward converted the penalty. Final score: 2–3.

After the match, Mao stormed over.

'That was a dive, wasn't it?'

'I'm not sure—you came at me fast.'

'Liar. But great deception, comrade. What's your name?'

'Chen Minghe.'

'You're a crafty little bastard—and I'll never forget it.' Then he smiled. 'Let's go and celebrate.'

And that was how Chen met Mao. Everyone drank, sang, and cheered long into the night—though the war was never far behind.

Chen was eager to see what kind of reorganisation would follow. Mao and Zhu De were vastly different. Zhu, a former Sichuan warlord, had strong military credentials and little hesitation in executing his enemies. His Communist cadres often trailed behind the army.

Mao was the opposite. Though less experienced, his army—thanks to cadres like Chen—was disciplined and ideologically grounded. They could even recruit without supervision.

In the end, the two men found common ground. The new combined force would be called the 4th Army. Zhu took command of military operations. Mao was the political authority. As always in the Communist system, the Party outranked the military. Chen Yi, the highest-ranking Party member under Zhu, stepped aside to preserve balance.

On 26 June 1928, Mao's appeal against his expulsion reached Moscow. It coincided with the secret 6th Congress of the Chinese Communist Party in the same city, where Zhou Enlai was present. Moscow backed Mao. The Red Army was too valuable to lose.

No one would argue with the Comintern's decision.

Chapter 14: Yongxin, Jiangxi, China, 1928

It did not take Chen long to realise that his new responsibilities would prove taxing. Song had briefed him on the warfare tactics favoured by Mao and Zhu De. Mao's stated approach was:

'*The enemy advances, we retreat; the enemy camps, we harass; the enemy tires, we attack; the enemy retreats, we pursue.*'

Chen saw that Mao and Zhu De had wisely committed to a guerrilla strategy. Many of these tactics reminded him of Master Sun's *Art of War*—his favourite book as a youth. His intelligence unit would need to stay highly mobile, often ahead of the main force. Infiltrating the Nationalist military at senior level remained too ambitious, at least for now.

He also recognised the need for a secure base of operations—a place to plan discreetly, with no risk of exposure. Recruitment was another priority. Cadres alone would not suffice; he needed soldiers too. And all recruits had to volunteer.

Yet the army was under Zhu De's command, not Mao's. Song resolved the matter by consulting both leaders. They responded with enthusiasm. Song returned with approval for Chen to recruit whomever he needed. What remained unclear was who controlled the new unit—military or political? The initiative had come from Zhou Enlai, but the chain of command still needed clarification.

Chen began compiling a list and presented it to Song verbally.

'I need four people who can pass as peasants. Military service would help, but it's not essential. At least some should be women—they're less likely to draw suspicion. All must speak Mandarin with a local accent and move between towns and cities without attracting attention. I'll also need two cadres. Peasants can't walk into banks or linger at train stations. But they're useful for headcounts and simple observations.'

Hu would have been ideal—but he had returned to Shanghai.

'Understood. I'll handle it—my seniority will help. I have two cadres in mind: Tang Baolin and Ye Jingsheng. Anyone else?'

'Two from the army. They'll provide insight on troop movement and weapons. I'll handle that myself—I know who I want.'

'So, a team of nine, including you?'

'The tenth will be the most difficult.'

'I suppose you want an acrobat to leap over walls?'

Chen smiled.

'No. I need a pigeon fancier.'

'Of course.'

He didn't mention that Russian aristocrats had raced pigeons for generations.

Chen quickly found Senior Cadet Pan, who eagerly volunteered and recommended Cadet Ma. Song secured two willing cadres. The four peasants proved harder to find, but Wang Zuo, using his Han connections, produced two women and two men—with some persuasion. His most valuable addition, however, was the pigeon fancier. He led Chen to a remote village and introduced him to the man, then quietly withdrew.

The man's skin was deeply lined from years in the sun. Slightly stooped, he had lost one eye to cataract. The locals called him 'One-eyed Gu'. His holding—four *mu*—was substantial for the area. Clearly, he had done well.

He first showed Chen a fenced chicken run—necessary in this region. Around it grew vegetables and feed crops. Gu explained that poultry manure made his yields far higher than average.

Then came the two pigeon lofts. The larger held birds raised for meat. These pigeons never left their enclosure. The second loft, smaller and set apart, housed Gu's prized homing pigeons.

Gu gently picked up one of the sleek birds. It sat calmly in his hands, more curious than afraid.

Chen began his questions.

'Are these pigeons the same breed as your meat birds?'

'Yes, but I choose the best ones for homing. Their eyes matter most. If they're deep and alert, the bird has promise.'

'So, if I took this bird to Maoping, it could find its way back here?'

'Easily. This one's made short journeys like that many times.'

'Short?'

'He could return from a thousand *li*, but I've never tested that. It's too far to travel myself. That's about their limit. They can't fly well in darkness.'

Chen saw the value at once. He resolved to add two team members who could travel with the army, carrying pigeons.

'And he'll always return here? What if the loft is moved?'

'Then he's lost. He'd go feral. But there's a method. Take young birds—ones that haven't flown—build a new loft, and give them time to adjust. When they finally fly, they'll treat the new loft as home.'

'How long does that take?'

'Six weeks for fair success. Eight weeks to be certain.'

Chen nodded. If he could establish even two new lofts across the base area, it could save days.

'I plan to mix one homing bird into a cage bound for market. But won't it stand out?'

'A little. Meat birds are fattened and slaughtered at ten weeks. This one's lean—and could live fifteen years. But in a packed cage, no one will notice. We'll remove the leg tag and choose a colour only an expert would spot. Frankly, that's the least of your worries.'

'There's more?'

'Plenty. You'll need a hand cart for the cages, a plucking machine, and a water vat. The path is dense, and you'll need helpers I can train—how to use the machine, how to attach the message. I don't travel far anymore. I sell locally now. But I used to go to Yongxin. People there know me as honest. Still, you'll need to stop buyers picking the homing bird. And how will you release it?'

'I thought I might fake an accident and let it escape.'

'No good. First, the message must be attached in private. Then there's the greatest risk: hawks. They strike as pigeons leave or return. I use whistles and gongs to scare them off.'

'Lao Gu, this plan could change China's future. The Communists are badly outnumbered.'

'Then I'll help. Though I may suffer for it. China needs change.'

'One last thing. You called this pigeon "he". How do you know?'

'Simple. I've seen him mate with his partner. Pigeons pair for life.'
Chen thanked him warmly and took his leave.

The first attack and capture of Yongxin began in mid-May, led by the newly named Zhu–Mao Army. No intelligence was needed. The Nationalists, based in Ji'an, had only one route west—a narrow river valley.

At Chibei, a Red Army scout concealed on the ridge watched as 15,000 troops advanced in five regiments, supported by artillery.

The 4th Red Army had just 8,000 men—Zhu De's 28th and 29th Regiments, Mao's 31st and 32nd. With such odds, they ordered a withdrawal. Yongxin was to be abandoned. The army would fall back to the safety of the Jinggang Mountains.

` Chen had already begun training his team in anticipation. The Nationalists left one regiment to garrison Yongxin and split the rest. One division launched a direct assault on the mountains—a difficult task in such terrain. The other swung south, trying a flank approach. It was intercepted by Mao's two regiments who, though slightly outnumbered, held the advantage in local knowledge and motivation. They drove the enemy back.

During the retreat, the reserve Nationalist regiment in Yongxin moved out to assist—and was nearly wiped out. The survivors fled to Ji'an. Yongxin fell back into Communist hands, and the Red Army gained its first artillery: mountain guns and mortars.

When the news reached Chen, he was elated.

A second attack soon followed. An even larger, well-equipped Nationalist force advanced from Ji'an—five full regiments. Again, the Communists abandoned Yongxin without a fight. Three Red Army regiments took defensive positions in the Jinggang, centred on Ninggang County.

But Mao, with the 31st Regiment, moved west of Yongxin towards the Hunan border, unwilling to concentrate the entire force in one location.

The Nationalists dug in and began resupplying. For the moment, they made no move to press forward.

Then Mao made a near-fatal—but ultimately fortunate—error.

He had long insisted on raiding towns for newspapers, hoping to read between the lines of the Nationalist press—even when he was labelled a warlord or bandit.

In Hengshan County Town, however, he stumbled into a larger and better-organised Hunanese force. They had the element of surprise. He was now isolated—nearly one hundred *li* from Jinggang.

Quickly, he scrawled a message and summoned the soldier responsible for the pigeon post. The bird was released.

Less than an hour later, it landed in Gu's loft. Within another hour, Zhu De's 28th Regiment was descending the mountains on a forced march to rescue Mao.

Their movement did not go unnoticed. From Yongxin, a Nationalist commander observed Zhu's forces racing past—and guessed their purpose.

Chen now activated his second plan: to infiltrate Yongxin. A direct entry was too dangerous.

The cart was disassembled. Crates of chickens and pigeons were packed. The plucking machine and water vat were prepared. Two porters were hired. The agents would be a peasant woman and Senior Cadet Pan, disguised as her mute, simple-minded son.

Though the town was only thirty *li* away, the trail through the mountains to Riguangxiang took all day. There, the cart was rebuilt. At dawn, the two poultry sellers headed for the gate.

A heavy guard watched the entrance, checking goods and travellers alike. But with the army still resupplying, poultry was in demand. The inspection was brief.

They set up their stall in the market square and filled the vat. When it emerged the birds came from Lao Gu, nearby stallholders welcomed them warmly and asked after his health, lamenting his failing eyesight and long absence.

There was no sign of overt military activity. No one suspected they had come from the Communist-held mountains.

A tense moment came when a stallholder tried to talk to Pan. His 'mother' quickly explained that he was mute and slow-minded. The stallholder offered a sympathetic nod. No more questions were asked, and no one paid attention as the lad wandered off.

Meanwhile, his 'mother' overheard something critical.

A lieutenant passed through the market with aides and porters. He was requisitioning supplies—even at inflated prices. Ignoring poultry, he focused on nearby stalls selling maize and rice.

When asked about the quantities, the lieutenant revealed—too freely—that the goods were bound for another unit near Lianhua County Town, thirty *li* west. Grinning, he added that only an officer could be trusted. A junior would have haggled harder and pocketed the difference.

Pan, observing carefully, noticed that half the troops were packing up. He deduced they planned to strike the weakened Jinggang positions, assuming Zhu De was still away.

He toured the town, quietly noting troop strength and layout. Those entering were checked at the gate—but not those leaving. It was possible, though risky, to release the pigeon from inside.

Originally, they had planned to overprice their poultry and stay overnight. But the plucking machine was working well, and they sold out early.

Pan returned with his report. His 'mother' had hidden the homing bird in a cloth purse. With confirmation of the Lianhua deployment, Pan now had all the information he needed.

They announced a final discount, sold the last birds, packed the stall, and left town mid-afternoon.

Once out of sight, Pan wrote a message. They placed it inside a bamboo tube, tied it to the pigeon's back, and released it

The message reached the commander of the 29th Regiment while Mao and Zhu De were still far to the west.

Comrade Pan reporting. Two regiments plan to attack you in the Jinggang and are preparing to depart Yongxin. They are well-equipped with artillery and several machine guns. Two regiments will remain to defend Yongxin. One regiment is stationed near Lianhua, possibly close to Mao and Zhu.

Two orders were issued at once. The first sent scouts by different routes to locate Mao. No one knew if he had survived, or whether Zhu De had reached him. But the intelligence from Yongxin gave the commander confidence: he knew the enemy's position. The greatest risk was a chance encounter with Nationalist scouts.

The second order was to strengthen the mountain defences. An attack was imminent.

The scouts found Mao and Zhu almost at the same time. Both had repelled the enemy. Realising the value of Pan's message, they moved quickly toward Yongxin and halted just short of the regiment near Lianhua.

Due to poor communication between the Hunanese force that had attacked Mao and the Jiangxi regiment, the Nationalist commander near Lianhua underestimated the threat. He expected only a few guerrillas. He believed Mao was far away and Zhu De still in the mountains.

He was wrong.

The Red Army lay in wait. His regiment was destroyed.

The Communists pushed forward. Zhu and Mao's troops marched on Yongxin. Their surprise attack forced the remaining Nationalist forces to retreat towards Ji'an. In two months, Yongxin had changed hands four times.

Now the two Nationalist regiments that had moved into the Jinggang faced a pincer movement. They also withdrew, skirting Yongxin carefully on their way back to Ji'an.

Excitement spread through the base. For a time, they could focus on political work. The Communist zone now included Ninggang, Yongxin, Lianhua, and nearby counties—an area of over 7,200 km², home to more than half a million people.

It was a short respite—from war, at least.

Chen, no longer a cadre, knew that setting up Soviet government structures and redistributing land would be difficult. In truth, he was relieved to avoid it. His focus remained on his growing intelligence network—and a new rocket plan.

Party membership was rising. Mass meetings led by cadres brought many new faces. But Chen had doubts. Some joined only to gain power under their new 'landlords'.

Gu quietly warned him that Wang Zuo and Yuan Wencai were positioning themselves to heavily influence land reform in the region.

On 2 June, Song told Chen that they had been invited to Mao's wedding the next day. The bride was He Zizhen. The guests included Yuan Wencai, Wang Zuo, their families, and close comrades. Yuan's wife had prepared a banquet.

Chen was not surprised. He Zizhen had fought beside them the previous summer, before Mao's arrival. Together, they had briefly captured Yongxin.

At the wedding, Mao gave a short speech. He praised He Zizhen's bravery and joked that she would keep him in line with a gun aimed at each of his balls. The room erupted. That was how she earned the nickname 'The Two-gunned Girl General.'

He spoke of her time as Head of the Women's Committee, recalling how she often translated for him into Hakka, as few could follow his thick Hunanese accent.

He then raised a toast to Yuan and Wang—for their efforts in matchmaking as well as revolution. Wang presented He with a Mauser pistol. Everyone laughed. It was no secret that the two men had schemed for six months to unite the couple and tie Mao more firmly to the region.

If anyone knew Mao was already married—twice—they said nothing. His first marriage, arranged in 1908, had never been consummated. His bride, Luo, was eighteen; Mao was only fourteen. His second wife, Yang Kaihui, had borne him three sons. She loved him—and would eventually die for him.

Later, once the party was in full swing, Mao pulled Chen aside.

'I can't talk long. But what you did in Yongxin—that saved my life. And an entire regiment. It was a brilliant act of intelligence. Tell me—how can I help you?'

'Comrade Mao, I owe our success to an old pigeon keeper—One-eyed Gu. Now, his land is being split seven ways under the new plan.'

Mao winced. He knew men like Gu—rich peasants, not landlords—were vital to the cause. Yet now they were losing land.

'I'll fix it. We'll declare it a restricted military zone. It'll protect your work and his home.'

Chen handed him a small parcel.

'Your wedding gift. Please open it.'

Mao unwrapped the package and looked puzzled.

'What is it?'

'The very tube that carried the message which brought your rescue.'

Mao nodded, visibly moved.

Soon, Mao again found himself in conflict with his superiors.

On 30 June, two envoys from the Hunan Provincial Committee arrived. They ordered him to push into southern Hunan. On 4 July, Mao addressed the Yongxin Joint Conference. He argued for consolidation, not expansion. He sent the envoys back with a letter explaining why he had disobeyed.

Hu Chenggong returned to Shanghai in mid-June. He found the Nationalist Civilian Military Intelligence Group still conducting purges—just as they had a year earlier.

The Party's structure had tightened. Fear shaped its hierarchy.

The cell system came from Russia. Often a cell had only a few members. In China, a cell of twenty was rare. They reported to a Party Branch Executive, who reported to one of seven District Committees.

The system worked. If one cell fell, it exposed only the next link.

Hu knew some Central Committee names—but no addresses. That posed little risk.

He had hoped for a post in the Shanghai City Committee or the Jiangsu Provincial Committee. But that changed after a massacre.

Weeks earlier, District 5 Putou Branch had met in a restaurant's back room. Someone betrayed them. Eleven members, as well as the owner and three servers, were dragged into the street and shot.

This was Hu's old territory. Making him the new District Secretary made sense.

It wasn't all bad. He had contacts. This role came with a meagre salary—enough to live on. Higher posts received better support and safer lodgings. Hu suspected Soviet funds helped fill the gap left by local donations.

Below him were only unpaid volunteers.

District 5, of the seven in Shanghai, was the most valuable for its industry. But it took Hu less than a week to realise the Party was weakening.

On 6 June, the Nationalist 3rd Army captured Beijing. The Beiyang Government collapsed.

In Hebei, the alliance between Fengtian warlord Zhang Zuolin and Zhili warlord Zhang Zongchang still held—but it was crumbling.

Chapter 15: Quinnatisset Farm, Massachusetts, US, 1928

In early 1928, Lydia received a letter from her old friend, Natasha Mamedov. Most of it brimmed with tales of their successful new life in the United States. Natasha's elder brother, Anastase Vonsiatsky, and his wealthy American wife, Marion, had secured them a well-appointed farmhouse near their own at Quinnatisset Farm, Connecticut. With their help, Natasha and her husband, Lev, had opened a restaurant—*The Russian Bear*—which quickly became popular among the affluent locals, drawn to its exotic cuisine.

There followed a detailed account of Count Vonsiatsky—as he liked to be known. Marion's generous allowance afforded him a fleet of sports cars, his own aeroplane, and the means to host lavish parties, some held in a purpose-built gun room and military museum filled with pistols, rifles, and even submachine guns. He played golf, attended college football games at Brown University, and had recently taken a keen interest in politics. He had joined the Brotherhood of Russian Truth—an organisation that swore to restore the monarchy in Russia through violent means.

Rodzaevsky wrote to Lieutenant General Vladimir Dmitrievich Kosmin, the Brotherhood's most celebrated figure, famed for his daring raids into Soviet territory. Kosmin, a supporter of Rodzaevsky's, confirmed that Vonsiatsky had been made chairman of the Harbin branch, though he privately doubted the man's aristocratic pedigree. He also noted that Lev Mamedov had become a member.

That May, Rodzaevsky—now considering himself the de facto leader of the RFO—received a summons from the Disciplinary Committee of the Harbin Law Faculty. It was signed by Chairman Nikolai Ustrialov and Professors Riasanovsky and Nikiforov. He felt no anxiety. Graduation was only days away, and Nikiforov, who had founded the anti-Soviet Union of the National Syndicate of Russian Workers the previous year, was known to be sympathetic.

Ustrialov, a minor concern, had Bolshevik leanings but rarely acted on them. On Rodzaevsky's desk, placed in pride of place, was the Russian translation of *My Autobiography* by Benito Mussolini. A fellow RFO founder, Korablev, had arranged for a translation and had it printed by the local *Izvestia*—a Harbin-based publisher of the same name as the Soviet newspaper in Moscow, though known more for serious academic works. They had collaborated with the RFO the previous year to produce *Theses of Russian Fascism*, complete with a striking lithograph of Mussolini delivering a fascist salute. Bookshops refused to carry it for fear of legal repercussions, but word spread fast and private sales had been brisk.

Rodzaevsky agreed with much of Mussolini's analysis, though he noted key differences. Mussolini aimed to create state capitalism, placing the individual under state supervision. The White Russians, in contrast, sought the return of private property—and often the restoration of both monarchy and church. Mussolini, too, was not fighting the Bolsheviks. And his stance on the Jews, in Rodzaevsky's view, was far too passive.

The RFO had grown quickly. On campus, its membership now stood at seventy-two. The National Organisation of Musketeers was also thriving. Rumiantsev's newspaper, *Our Demands* (*наши требования*), had expanded well beyond the university audience.

Rodzaevsky chose to dress conservatively for the hearing. As he trimmed his beard and straightened his tie, his thoughts turned briefly to Lydia. Though she majored in piano, she had taken violin as a secondary instrument. Already skilled, it was a sensible precaution—pianist roles were scarce, but violinists often found steady work in chamber ensembles and orchestras. Their relationship had blossomed. He now found himself wondering if, once they had both graduated, he should propose.

He arrived at the designated room, knocked, and was shown to a seat. Declining introductions, he waited as Ustrialov opened the proceedings.

'You have been summoned to explain certain actions brought to our attention. We require clarification. I am informed that you are a member of the Russian Fascist Organisation.'

'I am not a mere member,' Rodzaevsky replied. 'I am its leader—just as Mussolini leads the Italian fascists.'

Nikiforov suppressed a wince. *The arrogance! He wasn't even the officially recognised head.*

'And how many members do you claim on campus?' Ustrialov asked.

'We do not disclose that information.'

'I see. Well, it has been alleged that your organisation has instigated clashes with left-wing students.'

'We do not trade in gossip. But yes—we are entitled to defend ourselves from Bolshevik aggression, both verbal and physical.'

Nikiforov gave a slight nod. *At least he was beginning to sound like a lawyer.*

'We have also received complaints from the Soviet Embassy in Novy Gorod. They claim your organisation stages demonstrations outside their gates on the 1st of November and 1st of May—wearing black shirts and referring to the days as Treason Day and Exploitation Day.'

'That is true. But they are peaceful and held off-campus.'

'Secondly, they allege that you have smuggled subversive literature into the Soviet Union.'

'I cannot speak to such an astonishing claim.'

Nikiforov changed tack.

'Your academic record is excellent. You must be looking forward to graduation?'

'Yes, very much. It will be an honour to graduate from this faculty.'

'And do you believe you can contribute meaningfully to Russian society here in Harbin?'

'I do. I have secured a position with a local law firm and intend to do some pro bono work.'

'No further questions.'

Then Riasanovsky, the legal purist, leaned forward.

'Were you observed removing the Soviet flag from the faculty building during the demonstration two days ago?'

Rodzaevsky nodded.

'And what did you do with it?'

'I burned it.'

'Why?'

'Because it represents tyranny. It terrifies the stateless White Russians of this city.'

'Yet you knew it had been raised with the approval of our sponsors?'

'Perhaps—but they can always raise another once I've left.'

With that, he was dismissed to the corridor. Twenty minutes passed. Then thirty. Then forty. What on earth could they be debating?

Finally, he was called back. Ustrialov read the verdict.

'Konstantin Vladimirovich Rodzaevsky, we find that most of your activities do not breach faculty regulations—and evidence is lacking for several allegations. However, removing and burning the flag is a grave offence. It violated an agreement between Marshal Zhang Zuolin, the Soviet government, and our chief sponsor—the railway. You have brought this faculty into disrepute. You are hereby expelled. You will not graduate, nor receive your degree in absentia. Leave this institution—and do not return.'

Rodzaevsky staggered into the corridor and found a bench. He sat for two hours, head in hands. His life lay in ruins. What would he tell Lydia?

She was furious. Her Kostya—impetuous, fanatical, idealistic—how could he have been so reckless? And yet, he was also loving and charming. Sometimes, as he spoke with such conviction, she found the fire in his expression striking—his passion gave him an unexpected allure.

Tearfully, she asked him what he would do. He told her that he would enter politics and would not rest until the Motherland was restored. Her face crumpled. She stammered that if he ever pulled such a stunt again, there would be no forgiveness. He would have to find another woman.

To her relief, none of the other RFO founders planned to practise law. Matkovsky joined the CER, recruiting staff—perhaps also quietly soliciting new RFO membership. The rest, supported by generous donations, rented new offices on Diagonalnaya Street and purchased an upgraded printing press—Korablev's pride and joy. He had plans to send literature to White Russian enclaves as far away as Shanghai. Rumiantsev and Pokrovsky also joined the editorial staff.

At the first meeting in the new premises, held in mid-August, one urgent and dominant issue emerged: the war. The Old Marshal had refused to co-operate with the Japanese, showed no interest in their ambitions, and seemingly did not fear the Kwantung Army. With the nationalists at his throat, he had ordered a retreat from Hebei to Manchuria—but left the allied Shandong Army, commanded by the Zhili clique warlord Zhang Zongchang, in Hebei.

It was a fatal miscalculation. On 4 June, the Japanese planted a bomb beneath a bridge, destroying the Old Marshal's private train as it retreated. He was killed instantly. His son, Zhang Xueliang—the Young Marshal—assumed command.

Rodzaevsky chaired an emergency meeting on 10 June. Every attendee was dressed in full fascist regalia and offered the salute.

'Soratniki—comrade brothers,' he began, carefully choosing the Russian brotherly fascist term. 'An urgent matter has arisen.

'Two days ago, a former soldier—K-6, Lieutenant Colonel Oleg Alekseev—appeared at our front sliding panel. I agreed to receive him upstairs. He had come directly from General Nechaev's White Russian mercenary unit, which had been fighting alongside Zhang Zongchang.'

Everyone present knew of Nechaev and his infamous three-car armoured train—each carriage mounted with artillery and machine guns, packed with 100 ruthless soldiers who terrorised the railway lines without restraint.

Upon his father's death, the Young Marshal had immediately sought peace with the nationalists in Beijing. But Zhang Zongchang had refused to co-operate. On 2 June, with support from the Japanese Kwantung Army, Zhang launched an assault on the Young Marshal, defeating him six days later.

On the penultimate day of the battle, Nechaev assembled his 400 men and offered them a choice: disband and flee, or continue the fight. Those who chose to disband were issued civilian clothing and disarmed.

There was only one direction open to them—towards Harbin.

'Sixty-two men, travelling in small groups, planned to rendezvous outside the Moscow Bazaar, in what they hoped would be relative safety. They were instructed to report directly to our offices and are expected to arrive within two days.'

Pokrovsky looked horrified.

'They can't come here. Technically, they're now enemies of the Young Marshal—and of Japan. How long do you think it will take for the Soviet embassy to hear that dangerous White Russian soldiers are slipping into Harbin?'

Matkovsky interjected,

'I agree the risk is real—but I doubt the Young Marshal cares much about them now. And thanks to Comrade-brother Rumiantsev's connections, our relations with the Chinese authorities remain solid. If they wanted to arrest these men, they could have done so already.

'The question is—how do we keep them away from our premises without turning them away altogether?'

It was Pokrovsky who found the solution.

'We must send Alekseev back to the men. He'll coordinate a plan. We need them off the streets. Schools are closed for summer—dormitories may be available. Families from the Musketeers can help. Between us all, we have contacts. Then, we find them work and help them blend into Harbin life.'

All nodded in agreement. The plan was adopted.

Then Rumiantsev raised a deeper concern.

'Comrade-brothers—another issue. The Soviet Union is our eternal enemy, but who are our friends? The Young Marshal is already reversing Fengtian policy. If he fails to secure peace with Chiang Kai-shek, what stops Chiang from sweeping through Harbin and eliminating us? You saw what he did to the communists. And what of the Japanese? They've been in Manchuria for decades. Dalian is just one enclave—now they're in Qiqihar, Shenyang, and here in Harbin. The Kwantung Army suggests bigger ambitions. Yet we have no communication line with them.'

Rodzaevsky asked simply,

'So—where do we begin?'

'On two fronts,' replied Rumiantsev. 'First, engage the Japanese here in Harbin. A certain Konstantin Ivanovich Nakamura wields influence—he speaks fluent Russian. Comrade-brother Rodzaevsky should make the approach. As for contact with the Kwantung Government—well, the choice is obvious.'

All eyes turned to Rumiantsev, the only fluent Japanese speaker among them. A show of hands followed. Only Pokrovsky dissented, fearing discovery would worsen their position.

Rodzaevsky offered a final idea.

'Alekseev told me there are two other officers with him. Given the risk of Soviet attacks, and since we have funds, I suggest we recruit them—along with a few of their men—as our bodyguards. Eventually, they may serve as our military instructors as well.'

There was unanimous agreement.

On their way out, Rumiantsev pulled Rodzaevsky aside and offered a quiet warning. Nakamura, he said, was under constant police investigation for drug trafficking, child prostitution, and kidnapping. Protected by extraterritoriality, the Japanese consulate refused to act. He was, in short, a dangerous man.

A few days later, Rodzaevsky visited Nakamura's barber shop in Nakhalova. By then, he had hidden Nechaev's men and recruited the bodyguards. The shop had an innocuous exterior—but in China, pink lights implied something more illicit.

Inside, he was greeted by a middle-aged woman with distinctly Russian features, dressed in tight-fitting haute couture.

'Haircut,' she asked, 'or something more… stimulating?'

'Neither,' he replied. 'I'm here for Mr Nakamura. On business.'

'Oh, you mean Kostya.' She led him up a narrow stairwell and opened a door. Nakamura, a portly man with a glistening bald head, stood to greet him. He introduced his wife, Calina, who left them alone.

The room reeked of *papirosy*—Russian hand-rolled cigarettes—and a cabinet-top safe bore opium paraphernalia. Nakamura offered whisky, then cigarettes; both were declined. The two men spoke for an hour.

Rodzaevsky explained his need for high-level contact within the Kwantung Government. Nakamura promised to write a letter of introduction and asked whether Rodzaevsky spoke Japanese. He did not. He would send a colleague: Boris Rumiantsev. Nakamura then inquired whether he had any 'heavies'. Rodzaevsky nodded—disciplined former White Russian fighters, now loyal to him.

Nakamura smiled and led him downstairs to a private parlour behind the shop. The two men sat on a worn sofa. Calina returned.

'I have a gift,' Nakamura announced.

She clapped twice, and two teenage girls appeared—no older than fourteen or fifteen.

'Which one do you prefer?'

Rodzaevsky was appalled. He declined.

Nakamura pressed further.

'Would you prefer a young boy?'

Rodzaevsky recoiled, this time with vehemence. Calina clapped five times. Three striking adult women entered. A refusal now might insult his host. He chose the tallest—a blonde, rare in his hometown. Though not a virgin himself, Lydia had kept their relationship chaste. In a private booth, the woman, eager to please her patron, demonstrated a full sexual repertoire.

As he prepared to leave, Nakamura approached once more.

'Once the city has settled,' he said, 'Rumiantsev should prepare to travel to Dalian. He will meet a man named Yamato Takahama.'

In the interim, catastrophe struck—one of Rodzaevsky's own making.

In early July, one afternoon, the new secretary burst up the stairs, tripping in her haste. Out of breath, she gasped,

'Two men outside—the older one says he's your father.'

Rodzaevsky stepped onto the street—and froze. It was his father and younger brother, Vladimir. The boy was now seventeen, handsome and grown.

He led them inside, up to his office, closed the door—and embraced them, kissing them through tears.

He turned first to his father.

'What has happened?'

'Ten days ago, two OGPU agents came to my law office. They produced a leaflet bearing your name—fascist and anti-Soviet in nature. It had apparently surfaced inside the USSR. They accused me of being complicit. Utter nonsense, of course, but I was terrified. I told them I hadn't seen you in four years.

'Since the Shakhty show trials, where engineers were executed for "wrecking" the railways, the OGPU has become increasingly emboldened. Lawyers might be next. I wasn't arrested—but I knew it was time to flee.

'I paid handsomely to be smuggled across the border in a flour lorry coming from the Soviet side. It was part of a regular delivery route into Harbin. We were hidden among the sacks. There wasn't room for all of us—your mother and sisters will travel tomorrow. The driver said exit checks on the Soviet side are light. With a full load, the right paperwork, and a familiar face, he didn't expect trouble.'

Rodzaevsky arranged hotel accommodation for his father and brother, reserving additional rooms for the women. Early the next morning, the three men went to a quiet road on the outskirts of Harbin.

The driver arrived alone.

The women hadn't appeared at the rendezvous in Blagoveshchensk.

The driver promised to inquire discreetly. It was dangerous even to ask, and they thanked him sincerely. The next evening, he returned, face grave. He had spoken with a neighbour. The night before the scheduled journey, a large, unfamiliar car had pulled up. Three burly men had forced the women inside.

It wasn't the type of vehicle used by local police. The neighbour feared it had been the OGPU—or worse.

The news hit him like a boxer's fist. Rodzaevsky and Vladimir caught their father as he collapsed.

For a moment, the old man stared blankly into space. Rodzaevsky saw, as if conjured, his mother brushing the dust from his coat on a snowy morning long ago—murmuring a lullaby as she fixed a loose button.

Now she was gone.

He knelt beside his father.

'I'm so sorry. I truly am. But we mustn't lose hope. When Russia is free again, we'll find them. I believe that.

'But there's danger here too. This city is crawling with informants, and I can't protect you if we're seen together in public. They might use you against me. That's why I need you to stay out of sight—to blend in. Don't approach me on the street, and don't try to arrange meetings. We'll speak only in private. I'll find you somewhere safe to live, some work—something that keeps you anchored and out of harm's way.'

Within days, a small apartment was secured. A sympathetic law firm hired his father, while Vladimir found work at a local hospital.

In Dalian, something else was already in motion.

Yamato Takahama received Boris Rumiantsev in a private room at a Japanese bank. Impeccably dressed in a bespoke suit, Takahama exuded composure. After a series of formal greetings, he introduced himself as a senior officer in the Kenpeitai—the Japanese Military Police.

Seeing Rumiantsev's puzzled expression, he smiled.

'Yes, we are technically police, but we report directly to the Army.'

Their conversation lasted nearly two hours. Takahama asked about the RFO's membership, goals, and intentions. He interrupted only to clarify, never to criticise. Rumiantsev spoke carefully, offering what he could—evading questions about exact numbers. He sensed Takahama already had a fair idea.

Eventually, Takahama said,

'We have much in common. The Soviet Union threatens us both—directly, and through its support of communists across Asia.

'Do you know that Harbin holds the largest population of Japanese settlers in Manchuria? Like your White Russians, we feel an existential threat. We believe Stalin is preparing to move against us. We must act now. Together.'

'How will Japan respond?'

Takahama didn't answer at once. His expression grew thoughtful.

'Have you heard of *Tenkō*?'

'A change of direction?'

'Yes. Since 1925, we've had the Peace Preservation Law. It demands total loyalty to the Emperor. No other path—no Marxism, no syndicalism—rule by trade unions. Defiance is dealt with… firmly. But many who hesitate at first become our most loyal converts.'

Rumiantsev made a mental note to study recent Japanese legislation. He suspected 'firmly' meant imprisonment, torture, perhaps worse—but refrained from asking.

Takahama continued,

'Of course, we differ from Mussolini. We do not want a corporate state, and we do not persecute minorities. The Emperor remains the head of state. That is non-negotiable. Everything else serves that stability.'

It was a promising beginning.

On 29 December, the Young Marshal formally aligned with the Nationalists. For now, China was mostly unified—except for the communist territories Chiang Kai-shek had yet to reclaim.

As for Rodzaevsky—he became a frequent guest at Nakamura's pleasure palace.

Each visit cost him.

He paid anyway.

Chapter 16: Lingxian County, Hunan, China, 1928

Chen realised that, despite the success of the homing pigeons, they were unreliable for regular use within cities and towns. One mistake, and the Nationalists would uncover the scheme. Every pigeon—whether feral, caged in the markets, or homing—would end up in the pot by suppertime, and any intercepted messages would be read. The birds still had value for transmitting messages to a home base from the field, with minimal risk of detection. However, the further the army advanced, the less useful they became.

Nevertheless, there were successes: all four Red Army regiments now had a trained 'bird man'. Each possessed several pigeons capable of flying to One-eyed Gu's loft, thereby establishing a transfer station within the base area. Chen now needed further innovations. He knew that transmitting messages in times of strife was nothing new. However, methods such as hilltop beacons, mirrors reflecting sunlight, and semaphore flags all had inherent limitations. Some depended on daylight or lacked sufficient range, while others, like fire beacons, were restricted to conveying only the simplest of messages, such as 'beware'. What he required was a significantly more sophisticated system.

The answer came to him as he lay beneath a shade tree on One-eyed Gu's farm, gazing through the leaves at the clear sky above. It would require considerable effort and precise calibration.

When he approached Song with his request, he was met with the usual sarcastic grunts, but by now, Song had grown accustomed to Chen's unorthodox demands. This time, he required several pairs of high-powered binoculars and a visit to a fireworks factory. The first request was straightforward, but the subsequent one posed a challenge, especially since it required ownership by a communist sympathiser. The request would have been impossible if there had not been a lull in the fighting.

The best choice was the Fortune Fireworks Company in Chaling. Chen required accommodation for one night; however, he first visited the factory. He introduced himself to Lei Tianlong, the proprietor, who had been informed of an impending visitor.

'I understand you have a particular request for our factory,' Lei said.

'Indeed, I do, but I need to understand the technology better to determine the most effective approach. I'm seeking the optimal solution for military signalling.'

'Well, that's not new. Gunpowder has existed for over 4,000 years. Initially, it was used in incendiary weapons against enemies, but it wasn't until 1,000 years ago that the Song Dynasty began employing fireworks for signalling. These were basic, displaying only one colour: silver. By the 1600s, a range of colours—probably around ten—had been developed by adding chemical additives to create more meaningful messages.'

'And this technology is still used today?'

'The irony is that such signals reveal your position, and with modern mortars and heavy artillery—developed from the same source, gunpowder—their use is both dangerous and unproductive.'

'And would all the colours be distinguishable from a distance?'

'Probably not. There are about seven colours that are. However, you can achieve more permutations from the dispersal patterns. For example, a chrysanthemum, a waterfall, a fish, or a cross all have very distinct shapes. From a long distance, there might be six or seven such shapes, but four are definitely distinguishable.'

Yes, thought Chen. Sending the army in the wrong direction due to a misunderstanding might not be a wise career move. Better to keep things simple.

'So, how many brief messages could I send with, say, four fireworks strung together with a fuse?'

'How many do you think you need?'

Chen hadn't considered this but suggested that at least fifty might be helpful.

'I think we can do better if you can launch and observe a sequence of four consecutive fireworks to receive the correct linked message. However, the types of fireworks you need aren't normally joined together by fuse strings. You require what we call artillery fireworks. They are placed into a reusable tube, which is weighed down by bricks or another heavy object. It is possible to join them together, but that is complex, so it's better to reload one.'

'And how far, on a clear night, would it be possible to see such messages?'

'You would have to experiment with that, as it will depend on the skill of the observer, whether you have a telescope or binoculars, how high you can launch the firework, the size of the firework, and which colours you choose, as some are brighter than others. It might be as much as fifty *li* in perfect conditions, with a height of six hundred *chi*, but visibility is enormously reduced in daylight, which is why noisy firecrackers are more popular during daytime hours.'

'So, how can I increase the height?'

'There are only two ways: increase the rocket's size to pack more explosives for the launch phase, or add booster stages. Each rocket normally has one fuse to ignite the firework for take-off and a second to detonate and cause it to burst open, creating the dispersion. Adding a booster is possible, but fewer dispersal types work well, and reliability diminishes. For a normal artillery firework, roughly for every three-quarters of a *cun* of the rocket's diameter, the rise will be ninety *chi*, but that tails off rapidly, especially above six hundred *chi*. Then there will be little improvement in observation distance. However, being on elevated ground above the launch point will help.'

The man's knowledge of physics was astounding, but then he asked, 'I still don't understand how I can help you.'

'Suppose there was a celebration with firecrackers and fireworks in a town, perhaps for a festival, the opening of a new establishment, a wedding, a funeral, or just someone setting off fireworks to remember a deceased ancestor. After all, these are common occurrences in China.'

Lei started laughing, then said, 'Now I understand.'

Chen asked, 'When could I have some trial versions?'

'Come back tomorrow, and I will make them this afternoon.'

Chen returned to his guest house, his mind in overdrive throughout the evening. He soon realised he would need some sort of cipher that could be changed depending on the type of information required. He pulled out a piece of paper and started scribbling. The first words were,

I'm not a military commander. Need advice. What would be most important? Total enemy forces, distribution, and types? Maybe weak points to attack?

First firework (Colour)
Purple: Total active regiments: one.
Silver: Total active regiments: two.
Green: Total active regiments: three.
Et cetera.

First firework (Dispersion)
Waterfall: Concentration to the left.
Fish: Concentration in the centre.
Cross: Concentration to the right.
Chrysanthemum: Evenly spread.

Second firework (Colour)
Purple: Town gate at the front heavily fortified; artillery present.
Silver: Town gate at the front heavily fortified; no artillery present.
Waterfall: Town gate at the rear lightly fortified; artillery present.
Fish: Town gate at the rear lightly fortified; no artillery present.
Et cetera.

Third firework (Colour)
Purple: Reinforcements available one day away…

Chen was exhausted and went to bed thinking, *I wish I had paid more attention to mathematics at school.* He woke up in the middle of the night, realising he had the perfect adviser in Senior Cadet Pan, who had been trained in military logistics and undoubtedly had a solid background in mathematics.

Upon returning to the factory in the morning, Chen found the artillery fireworks neatly packed in boxes and stacked on a cart—twenty-eight in total—each marked with its colour and its dispersion type. Lei explained that these were for calibration and that the next delivery, due in a few days, would comprise 112 units, in case the same colour and dispersion were needed four times. There were also three times as many smaller fireworks, similarly labelled, along with several firecrackers.

Intrigued, Chen listened as Lei explained,

'Each shell is timed to burst five seconds after launch. That gives a predictable arc, so the observers can read the sequence clearly.

'Your artillery fireworks are relatively large, so I've made up bundles of smaller ones—like those used at weddings. They're just for show—useful if someone checks your kit or you need the setup to look convincing. You should still practise fusing them—I'll show you how.'

After transporting the fireworks to One-eyed Gu's farm, Chen began calibrating them. Using binoculars and the artillery fireworks, a range of fifty *li* was achievable on a clear night and only slightly reduced on overcast nights, even with light rainfall. However, fog or heavy rain rendered the system ineffective. The smaller fireworks, under optimal conditions, were effective up to twenty *li* in darkness. The artillery fireworks had a similar range in daylight as that of the smaller ones at night. Identifying colour and dispersion types posed no problems. His team also agreed that the smaller fireworks should be set off in tandem but then disregarded to create a more realistic display when using the artillery rockets. This way, the messaging would not resemble distress or location flares.

At the end of June, written orders arrived from the Hunan Central Committee, which had relocated from Xiangtan, near Changsha, to the mining area of Anyuan on the Hunan–Guangxi border—north of the Jinggang Mountains and only a four-day walk away. Anyuan was where Mao had successfully recruited his 2nd Regiment during the failed Hunan Uprising the previous year.

The Committee urged Mao and Zhu De to stop hesitating and march south to form a new peasant army, using force if necessary—particularly against those who had returned home from the Jinggang. They were then to establish a separate base area. Zhu De complied and achieved some successes, including the temporary capture of Leiyang, before he was overwhelmed. At times, extraordinary force was used, and while the violence was primarily directed against landlords, it occasionally spilled over to affect peasants.

Mao, however, took a different approach. On 4 July, he initiated the Yongxin Joint Conference. He declared his intention to continue his political work, recognising that he could not confront such formidable opponents, as they now faced two Nationalist armies, one from Hunan and one from Guangxi. This was alarming because these were two distinct warlord armies, albeit designated as Nationalists. The Hunan Provincial Committee was incandescent, as Mao had yet again disobeyed orders. However, Zhu De's 28th and 29th Regiments continued to follow instructions and moved to Lingxian County, Hunan, while Mao's 31st and 32nd Regiments remained in the local area.

This decision led to disaster. Zhu's 28th Regiment—composed mainly of farmers from Yizhang County in Hunan—realised they were nearly home. They could almost hear their welcoming wives and girlfriends, and smell their uniquely fiery chilli dinners. The prospect of a warm bed and a hot meal proved fatal for most of them. Upon reaching Miandu on the Jiangxi–Hunan border, they found the river impassable and were forced to take a more circuitous route via Chenzhou, where most were massacred. Only 200 men made it back and were incorporated into the 29th Regiment.

There was only one triumph during this period. It came from a defecting Nationalist Eighth Army battalion under Peng Dehuai and an associated scouting and spy corps (xiǎng chéng dié — 响成谍). A violent confrontation broke out on the parade ground as dissenters resisted, leaving Peng with only 800 of his original 2,000 men. After successfully evacuating the Jinggangshan and rebuilding his army, on 22 July, Peng Dehuai—then only twenty-nine years old—launched a successful uprising in Pingjiang, during which the judiciary, military personnel, and over 100 landlords were executed. Peng also declared himself commander of a new Fifth Army to emphasise that he was not under Mao's command.

In mid-August, Mao refused to budge until two pigeons arrived with identical distress messages from Zhu De—one direct, and another via the transfer station, in case Mao had relocated. He had not, and the news from One-eyed Gu's farm reached him first. He immediately ordered a detachment of the 31st Regiment to initiate a rescue. It was the opposite of the previous year, when Zhu De had rescued him from his newspaper raid. This time, Mao was accompanied by several members of Chen's team—and by Chen himself.

Upon arrival, a meeting was held to discuss the next move, with two representatives of the Hunan Central Committee opposing Zhu De, Mao, and Chen Yi, the commissar of the 28th Regiment. The latter group won the day, and the two committee members were dismissed.

Aside from Peng's diversion, these events provided the opportunity the Nationalists had been waiting for. They attacked the base area with vigour, driving the available Communists back to the defensible high Jinggang. Despite a vast disparity in troop numbers, the Communists held out, though the Nationalists seized the entire tri-county area.

Then the carnage began. It was harvest time, and the larger landlords, seething from their exile and humiliation, exacted revenge through their own modest militias. They reclaimed their former land, initiating killings, beatings, arson, debt collection, and back rent demands, although some peasants simply defected to them. The landlords showed little concern if the harvest remained incomplete, as the labour shortage—caused by fleeing or massacred peasants—was of no consequence to them. Many of these peasants were Hakka, specifically targeted as pro-Communist. For those in the high Jinggang, it became evident that a new policy aimed to starve them into submission.

After Mao and Zhu De reconnected, they reorganised and fought their way back into Jiangxi from the south, leaving some troops behind. This manoeuvre forced the Hunan Nationalist Army to retreat from a potential attack from the rear. One of the Red Army's initial targets was the county seat of Suichuan, a town familiar to both them and Chen. Here, walls were unnecessary. Situated on a flat expanse along the Suichuan River, it was a natural fortress with mountains to the rear.

They approached via the southern road, with five other access points: a track from Zhutian to the southwest over hilly terrain; two bridges south of Meijiang, passable before the river swelled; and two northern exits towards Yutian, inaccessible without capturing the town.

Chen dispatched one of his male peasants into the town, where the man had family. The man passed through a checkpoint unchallenged and proceeded to his Great-Uncle Huang's home. He requested that his great-uncle prepare a family-and-friends' feast for the following evening, with instructions to delay if advised. He provided ample funds to cater lavishly for up to fifty guests with meat, fish, and other victuals, then safely returned to the Red Army. Huang was delighted. The funds were sufficient to spit-roast a whole pig, supply premium liquor, and much more.

Chen had already devised the cipher codes, which the team referred to as 'poetry form'—a system that disguised messages in rhythmic or metaphorical language. Since this was a town, not a city, the codes pertained to regiments rather than the larger brigades or divisions.

The next day, as the Red Army approached, he prepared two of his team members: an unutilised male peasant and Senior Cadet Pan. They packed the fireworks along with gifts: a barrel of loquat fruit (*pípá*—枇杷), a stack of wrapped sweet pancakes, and a suitcase for Pan, as both men were to stay for several nights. All items were loaded onto a cart pulled by a mule. The order was given that the attack would occur the next day, and Chen was reassured by the clear skies he needed. By mid-morning, the cart rattled towards the town's outskirts.

The two infiltrators were stopped at a checkpoint. When a guard inquired about their purpose, they explained they were attending the Huang family feast for a celebration. When asked about the contents of the large boxes, the peasant informed the soldier that they contained fireworks. Realising that these were a type of explosive, the soldier waved over a junior officer to discuss his concerns. The officer instructed the peasant to open one box, prodded around inside and then asked,

'Why are there different firework sizes?'

'It will give us a better display for such an auspicious occasion.'

He selected one of the artillery fireworks, pointed at it, and asked how it worked.

'It is fired from a tube straight up in the air and then releases bright colours with a loud bang.'

'Set one up and launch it.'

'Sir, they are expensive. Could you spare us this?'

The officer reconsidered, as the noise from such a large firework might raise alarms in the military camp.

'On second thought, set off one of the smaller ones.'

The peasant did so, and despite it being daylight, it produced a stunning orange chrysanthemum dispersion. The officer seemed satisfied, pointed at Senior Cadet Pan, and asked who he was.

'This is Xiao Huang from our clan, a scholar from Nanjing who has just graduated from university. The feast is in his honour, as he is the first member of our family to achieve such a feat.'

He then asked the guard to pat the men down. On the peasant, he found a tin of snuff and a bag of coins, but on Huang's person, he discovered a book and a wallet.

'What is this?'

'It's a book of my poetry.'

Senior Cadet Pan tried to appear calm, though he could feel the sweat running down his back. The officer flipped it open and began reading a poem titled *Lost Love*. He couldn't make much sense of it. He flipped through again and found one titled *Autumnal Storm*.

Magenta waterfall, with the clack of crickets. Geese from the south, heading towards thunder and lightning. I wonder about their odyssey...

(The first three lines signified: one regiment in the town centre with machine guns and one regiment in each occupied zone; Empty Zone 1 and/or artillery in Zones 3 and/or 4; or alternatively omit this line). Suddenly, he shut the book, handed it back and said,

'Move on. Oh, and congratulations on your academic achievement.'

As they parted, Senior Cadet Pan said,

'Sir, it would be an honour if you would attend my party.'

'I might just do that. Thank you.'

Senior Cadet Pan wandered through the compact town and its environs unhindered. He made a conscious effort to climb as high as possible at the north-eastern end of the town in order to look up the length of the valley floor towards Meijiang. He wished he had binoculars, but there were no signs of reinforcements, nor the dust they might stir up.

By mid-afternoon, the Huang party was in full swing, and the Nationalist officer had arrived, thoroughly enjoying the excellent fare. The plan was to set off the fireworks shortly after dusk, but as the time drew near—much to Pan's dismay—an evening mist began to descend from the mountains, a common occurrence in these parts. He tried to concentrate and realised that the base of the mist cloud might be at about 200 *chi*, but he had no way of knowing about its upper limit. He placed an artillery rocket in its launch tube and asked the officer to light the fuse on some small fireworks, and then launch the first large one. Little did the man know he was potentially signalling his demise. Four artillery fireworks were launched in sequence, followed by a pause—then five more were fired. But by then, the mist had thickened, obscuring the view. However, the crowd could not see them through the mist, and any further launches were restricted to the low-altitude fireworks. As the officer departed, he expressed concern that so many of the large fireworks had been unintentionally left behind and requested that they be removed from the city the following day. Pan agreed.

Before dusk, Cadet Ma and Chen climbed above the valley floor and waited, both worried that their mission was in jeopardy. Then, something magical occurred. Through the mist, a burst of four dazzling fireworks appeared in sequence.

Orange Chrysanthemum, Green Fish, Yellow Chrysanthemum, Blue Fish.

The two observers scrambled down the mountain, and after a gap of perhaps eight minutes, a few other artillery fireworks were visible, but the time interval rendered them meaningless.

They asked for permission to enter a bivouac, which was duly granted, where Mao and Zhu De were poring over a hand-drawn, yet accurate, map. Two boxes containing red and black Chinese chess pieces, which represented regiments, artillery and machine-gun units, had been placed on the table. Some of the pieces had been half covered over with paper. The leaders greeted Chen warmly, as they knew him well. Mao nodded to Chen, signalling him to make his report.

Chen began by explaining how his infiltrators had entered the town and detailed the graduation party. He then proceeded to describe the types of fireworks and the purpose behind the poetry book. He explained that the battlefield had been divided into four zones: Zone 1 in the southwest, Zone 2 at the town centre, and two zones to the northeast, with Zone 4 being the furthest away. He elaborated that the four fireworks had to be seen in the correct sequence, a task that had been accomplished, and then asked if Comrade Ma could place the black pieces on the map, which was readily agreed to.

'The town centre contains two regiments without artillery. To the southwest, there is one regiment with artillery but no machine guns. To the northeast of the town, one regiment is split equally between the two zones. Both of these zones have machine guns but lack artillery.'

Ma then arranged the red pieces in a line, according to their current positions. When he had finished, he stepped back, and the four men observed the completed work, awaiting Zhu De's response.

'I don't suppose you can tell me their commander's name or whether he has a moustache?'

The laughter was hearty and full of vitality.

Zhu De, known for his thoroughness, then continued,

'It's an impressive feat, but I have some questions for Comrade Chen. Comrade Ma, please move the pieces. What would happen to the code if one and a half regiments were in the town centre without artillery or machine guns, one regiment in Zone 1, and one and a half regiments in Zone 3, both with artillery and machine guns, and finally, Zone 4 had no troops defending the more northerly Meijiang Bridge?'

'Then the signal would be *Silver Cross, Yellow Chrysanthemum, Green Chrysanthemum, Red Waterfall*.'

'Are there any situations that you can't cover?'

'Unfortunately, yes. If there are more than one and a half regiments in zones outside the town centre, all you will know is that there is at least that number, along with any present in the other zones.'

'Well, that could be a formidable army—we should head in the opposite direction. Anything else?'

'It is assumed that there is always at least one regiment in the town centre, although up to four can be accounted for.'

'No one would defend a town without troops inside. What if reinforcements are coming, probably from the north?'

'There are two possibilities. If the last dispersion in the sequence of four is a chrysanthemum, it means abort the mission. Alternatively, the launch of a single firework signals an abort and will provide an explanation, including the number of reinforcements, if that is the issue.'

Mao raised a question.

'Why could you not just remember the sequences rather than take the risk with the poetry book?'

'Because the codes are too complex, with many false positives.'

'You mean something remains in a zone until removed later?'

'Yes, or have a falsely empty zone until something is added later.'

'I see. It does sound sophisticated.'

The pieces were moved back to the actual configuration, and Mao looked at Zhu De and asked him how he saw the situation. He replied,

'This looks like the work of a Whampoa graduate. Perhaps I even taught him myself. I would have arranged the disposition of the troops similarly. The machine guns and split regiment in the northeast are to protect the two bridges south of Meijiang. The artillery, alongside the southwest regiment, will be positioned where the road out of town becomes a track. They will be howitzers and cannot be dismantled and moved along paths, unlike our mountain guns. These must be pulled along roads. This regiment can also defend against any attempt to attack from the Zhutian pathways or to head back into town to reinforce the entrenched regiments there. Overall, their disposition is designed primarily to defend the town. I will take the 28th Regiment and two machine gun units, ready to attack from our left, hoping that they will flee down the Zhutian tracks. Our two forces in this zone are evenly balanced, but we have the advantage of surprise, provided we are amongst them before their artillery can inflict much damage.'

Mao could no longer contain his enthusiasm and asked whether this would result in the capture of the howitzers. Zhu De denied this and explained that Nationalist troops had been trained to pack explosives into the gun's breech and render them permanently inoperable in such events. Then he patiently continued,

'Comrade Mao, could you split your forces? Two-thirds are to remain here on the southerly approach road with our remaining machine gun unit and two mountain guns. The remaining troops are to travel tonight with the last mountain gun on the narrow hilly paths to the southernmost of the two bridges and assemble the weapon. However desirable, we dare not send these troops to the furthest bridge because of the risk of them being cut off if the opposing force on the nearest bridge makes an aggressive move. The attack will commence around midday, and this gun will provide the signal.

'There is no plan to assault the bridge, merely to probe and prod. If we are fortunate, we might even catch them eating. Similarly, upon the signal, the two mountain guns here are to open fire on the town centre. These actions are intended to appear as preliminary barrages, while the actual assault will be executed by the 28th Regiment.

'Once the enemy active regiment has fled west, the 28th will circle to the rear at Quanjiang Village and attack the city centre from the rear. Comrade Mao should also advance now. The two regiments in the town centre will flee in the only direction where there is no gunfire—that is, to the west—but if they choose to fight, they will face a simultaneous attack from both front and rear and will suffer heavy casualties. After that, it's simply a matter of eliminating the remaining split regiment and machine guns in the northeast if they do not flee.'

As the two observers were about to leave, Mao, already a renowned poet, turned to Chen and, beaming, said,

'Next time, ask for help with your codes. Your poetry is dreadful.'

Chen laughed—then winced. *Even victors have critics.*

As Zhu De had demonstrated on the map, events unfolded similarly, and the battle of 11 September was over in less than three hours. Even the direction of flight of the vanquished was accurate in every case. However, two machine gun units were too slow to retreat, leading to the capture of two Browning machine guns.

Battle of Suichuan (1928)

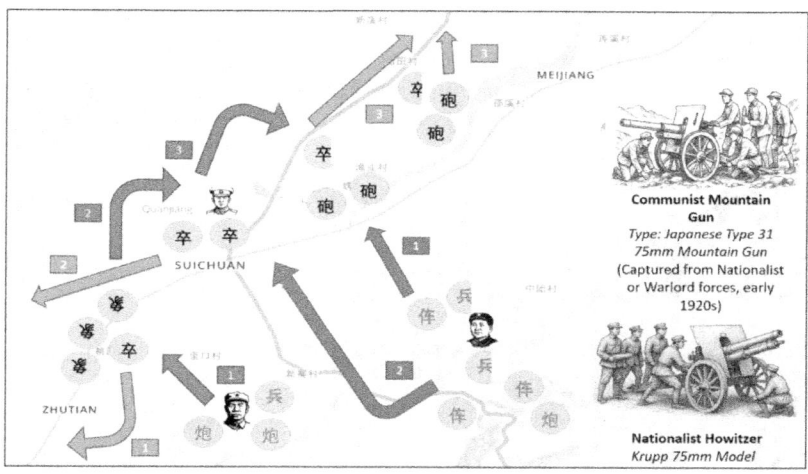

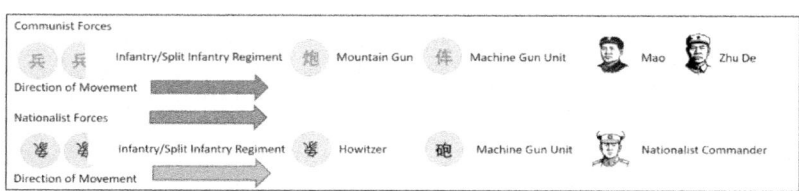

The retaking of Ninggang and Yongxin Counties, along with their towns, was militarily straightforward. On 4 October, Chen became aware that a two-day border-area conference was taking place, and Song, troubled, came to see Chen shortly thereafter. Chen tried to calm him and asked what the issue was.

'I have been expelled from the Party.'
'What? Why?'
'Not just me, but everyone.'

Upon hearing this, Chen found it nonsensical and inquired further, 'Almost every Party member has to appear before a committee to discuss their loyalty, including cadres and army officers, and resubmit their entry.'

'Including me and my Intelligence Corps?'

'No, you and your team are considered exempt and loyal after what you did at Suichuan.'

'So, what is the purpose of this?'

'It is not just Party members. It is to root out and purge those who supported the Nationalist incursion: rich landlords masquerading as middle-class farmers, some peasants, and soldiers who joined the Nationalist Army or who had provided them with aid and became communists of convenience, local fiefs, bandits, and lazy communists seeking a title or influence. Need I go on?'

'No need. But none of these descriptions apply to you.'

'I agree, but honestly, I am scared.'

'And what will happen to those who fail the test?'

'I imagine not all of them will survive.'

Song was quickly readmitted, but the trouble with purges is that they render internecine strife not only possible, but acceptable.

Chapter 17: Shanghai, China, 1929

In late 1927, André Fournier retired, and a new Consul-General, Jean-François Monteux, arrived in Shanghai from Paris. By this time, strikes and demonstrations had become noticeably fewer, with Nationalist military intelligence maintaining a superficially iron grip on the city. The French Concession was generally less affected by any periods of communist unrest, as the number of factories was limited. However, as a haven for fugitives, it held a prime position. Beneath the surface lay a seething mass of espionage, executions, gangsters, terrorists, and various political parties.

Monteux had been born in the early years of the Third French Republic, established in 1871—a period of international expansion and great national pride. By the time he entered government service, France's colonial empire was rapidly growing. Early holdings in Africa had expanded dramatically—stretching across Algeria, Tunisia, and Morocco. Elsewhere, French Indochina, the Levant, and Polynesia were added, creating an urgent demand for diplomats. Previously the preserve of wealthy aristocrats, these roles now provided opportunities for intelligent men like Monteux, who came from a more modest background. The Quai d'Orsay had transformed from a quiet and somewhat neglected foreign ministry into the vibrant centre of a new France. Monteux was regularly promoted during his tours of duty in French Sudan, Chad, and Vietnam. For him, Shanghai was considered a prestigious posting. His wife, Amandine, was thrilled at the prospect and embraced her newfound freedom, as their children were now attending universities in France.

Present at the weekly briefing at the end of May 1929 were Raymond Camus (security and intelligence), Pascal Allard (police), and Philippe Chastain (military). Monteux called the meeting to order and began,
'I've become increasingly concerned by some of your reports of underground activity in our French Concession. It seems Shanghai has gained a reputation as the world's hotspot for sedition and subversion,

and I want to examine where the real threats to our country lie. Let's start at the national level—with the Chinese government. Raymond?'

'The Nanjing government is facing significant challenges, and several warlords, though now under the Nationalist banner, will not relinquish their weapons. Last month, the Guangxi clique—including one member well known to us, Li Zongren—broke off relations with Chiang Kai-shek. As you know, when Li fled here to the French Concession in January, it put us in a difficult diplomatic position, and I think I speak for all of us in saying how pleased we were to see him depart. Feng Yuxiang, with his powerful Northwest Army, has also come out against Chiang.'

'So, is the civil war about to flare up again on a broader scale?'

Camus gave a Gallic shrug, indicating it was possible.

'What about the communists, Philippe?'

'They've successfully taken advantage of the situation and moved their main Zhu–Mao Army out of their Jiangxi base area into Fujian. They were in trouble until the Nationalists needed to divert resources to address this warlord split. They've also gathered in another military group commanded by Peng Dehuai. He tried to hold the Jinggangshan when the Zhu–Mao Army left for Fujian but was overrun—however, he managed to escape with some of his troops intact.'

'And you're sure this information is correct from your contact?'

'Very sure. Peng was a closet communist, and my counterpart was furious about it.'

'And what did we exchange for this information?'

'With Raymond's agreement—our files on the leaders of the Guangxi clique. It's sordid stuff. Would you like to see them?'

'No, thank you—but tell me about the communist strategy.'

'It's clear: expand and create or link as many base areas as possible, where they can attract new army recruits—by conscription if necessary. They're attempting to create a Jiangxi–Fujian Soviet. In the last few days, they've begun advancing on the strategically valuable town of Tingzhou in Fujian. If their momentum continues, they're likely to take it soon. At this rate, they'll soon have 50,000 troops.'

Monteux exhaled.

'Now, I want to discuss another problem—the Russians. Raymond?'

'To my mind, they're a serious threat—and Philippe agrees.'

'The Soviets did have their wings clipped last year, during the final stages of the Beiyang Government. The Old Marshal raided the Soviet Embassy in Beijing, where more than seventy Chinese communists were sheltering in the grounds, and fifteen Soviet officials were imprisoned. Twenty-four of the communists, including Li Dazhao and one young woman, were executed by strangulation. Although most press coverage centred on the violation of diplomatic norms, leaked intelligence suggested that the Soviets understood the Old Marshal's true intent: he had deliberately provoked them to test whether Japan would back him in his ambitions in Manchuria. More interesting to us was that Soviet Foreign Ministry Intelligence Agents—the GRU—were operating in over one hundred Chinese cities. Now, after this setback for the USSR, and with Stalin feeling empowered following Trotsky's expulsion, we can only expect a ratcheting-up of efforts—more money for the communists, and more pressure on them from the Comintern. We can't even be sure Stalin won't invade Manchuria.'

Monteux interjected,

'Invading an embassy is an inviolable intrusion into foreign-recognised territory and a major breach of diplomatic etiquette.'

'They only entered the embassy buildings on the grounds. After all, only last year, the British raided ARCOS—the All-Russian Co-operative Society—in London, which had at least quasi-diplomatic status, and discovered a cache of espionage papers.'

Monteux remembered well the day when a *Top Secret* and *Urgent* message was delivered to him, including instructions to prepare for the possibility that Great Britain might declare war on the USSR.

'The two aren't the same. ARCOS wasn't an embassy or consulate, and the British didn't kill anyone. If the Nationalists breached the French Consulate here in Shanghai—our outer premises or gardens—it would never be considered acceptable diplomatic behaviour. It would be akin to invading a part of France. Anyway, enough. We are adjourning for lunch.'

Allard had hardly said a word, but he quietly wondered whether someone might lend these people a guillotine—to render death less barbaric than by strangulation.

It was an unspoken rule that serious business was not discussed over lunch, a one-and-a-half-hour affair, with the head chef having prepared some delicate dishes, but no pork or shellfish, out of respect for Monteux. They ate vichyssoise, baked mandarin fish in hollandaise sauce, and a chocolate soufflé. Wines were available, but drunk sparingly. The main discussion was about racing dogs.

It was a current theme because the British had banned greyhound racing and wanted the French at their newly opened Canindrome to follow suit. The British grounds for contention were that it attracted illegal gambling, took money from sometimes desperate and impoverished spectators, and drew dubious types, unlike the more upscale casinos. The French were set against it, as it was part of the variety and lucrative way of life in their mostly *laissez-faire* sector, from which they secured tax revenue. It made the French Concession profitable, and the municipal surpluses provided for elegant parks and civic buildings. There had been several interviews with wealthy Chinese race-dog owners in the *Journal de Shanghai* to try and show inclusivity. Shanghai was dubbed the 'Pearl of the Orient', which really meant French Shanghai.

As coffee arrived, Monteux switched to the final topic of the morning session and inquired about the Japanese. They agreed that Japan had expansionist ideas and had become increasingly aggressive, especially in Manchuria. The problem was that neither locally nor through other French secret channels was it clear what the Japanese' intentions were.

Once the meeting returned to the boardroom, Monteux announced that the afternoon session was to focus on local affairs and asked Allard to begin with a report on the Chinese.

'We face no immediate threat from the Nationalists, and Philippe has even publicly parked a couple of tanks at the boundaries to warn of any interference. And, as you have heard, we are communicating sporadically with the new government in Nanjing. However, their pursuit of any communists is still relentless, and any found in the old city are unlikely to survive. If they are discovered in our Concession, the Nationalists will try and use gangsters to capture or eliminate them. I have found the communists naïve and, frankly, brave. They still organise and educate factory workers in their doctrine and sometimes demonstrate or distribute leaflets in the streets. However, they have a tight organisational structure in cells, so it is hard to find their leaders, but some are likely to be here in the French Concession, and we have proof that their mobile printing presses are also here. Tomorrow, Philippe will translate for me as we interview a mid-ranking official whom we caught red-handed and who is in our custody. It should be illuminating.'

Monteux continued questioning:

'So, you are telling me that despite our complete opposition to communism, these people don't threaten our Concession?'

'Not so much in the short term, but there has been a new development. They are fighting back and have allegedly formed something called the Red Squad, which has now attempted to assassinate prominent Nationalists, both in our Concession and the old city. So far, they have had only minor successes and seemingly many bungled attempts.'

'Alright, let's turn to the Russians.'

'We have every reason to think that Shanghai has many Russian agents and financiers using legitimate businesses as a front, as well as the Comintern working with the Communist Central Committee. They remain well hidden, though. What is new is the growing and brazen influence of the White Russians.'

Allard nervously handed around a two-colour broadsheet written in Russian, with a French translation provided. They began to read, and he said he didn't think this was from a local printing press and had probably been produced in Harbin. It had been discovered in the French Concession. It was called *The Motherland* (*Родина*) and was written by B. Rumiantsev and K. Rodzaevsky. Camus confirmed that these were members of the Russian Fascist Party, with the latter likely being the leader. The calls were for the White Russians to return the USSR to a capitalist state and were laced with fascist thoughts.

Monteux had never concealed his Jewish identity. One day, he mentioned that he needed to depart early to attend a Bar Mitzvah at the Ohel Rachel Synagogue on Seymour Road in the International Settlement. Now, as they examined the offensive cartoons and read the abhorrent antisemitic propaganda, reminiscent of Julius Streicher's *Der Stürmer*, they couldn't help but ponder Monteux's thoughts. In contrast to *Streicher's* newspaper, which was never an official Nazi Party publication, this one displayed the emblem of the Russian Fascists: a black swastika on a yellow background, topped with the Russian Imperial coat of arms.

Monteux finally broke the silence:

'Gentlemen, I trust you comprehend that this document is profoundly distressing to me personally. However, I arrived in Shanghai as a devoted representative of our French Republic, a cause I believe in unequivocally, and this will not affect my perspective on our mission here.'

He then rose and proceeded to his office. He had faced antisemitism previously. While studying in Paris, he had witnessed the violent protests in St. Étienne, where crowds demanded a treason conviction and life imprisonment on the infamous Devil's Island penal colony for Captain Alfred Dreyfus, a Jewish officer accused of passing secrets to the Germans. Twelve years later, Dreyfus was eventually pardoned, though not exonerated, by President Loubet, despite the true culprit being identified. Monteux had also observed prominent figures, notably the renowned writer Émile Zola, who was not Jewish, advocating for Dreyfus. However, the invective from the Russian Fascist Party (RFP) that he had read was on a far more severe scale.

The next morning, Allard and Chastain arrived at the jail just as a Citroën *panier à salade*—the French colloquial term for a police van, likened to a metal-wire lettuce spinner on wheels—pulled up.

Several detainees were escorted away. Chastain inquired about their fate and was informed that it depended on whether their cases were political or criminal. A Chinese magistrate, alongside a French assessor, tried the accused. However, in the case of political detainees—mostly suspected communists—they were detained and interrogated for a few days, then released into the old Chinese city at a location that provided a reasonable chance of escape, with instructions not to return to the French Concession.

Perhaps surprisingly, they seldom did—indicating the effectiveness of this method.

They proceeded to an interview room, where they received a thin dossier labelled *Hu Chengong*. Shortly after, the man was escorted in.

Hu had been caught red-handed with a stack of communist propaganda leaflets in a portmanteau, leaving no doubt about his affiliation. It was unfortunate for him, as this part of the city was one he rarely frequented. He might have stood out somehow, leading to his search. Allard spoke, with Chastain translating,

'What is your role within the Communist Party?'

'I am a courier and distribute leaflets to other members.'

'Are you aware that this is illegal?'

Silence.

'We have evidence suggesting that you are more than just a delivery man. Couriers don't typically visit factories and shops, deliver literature, and then linger for hours. This implies you're engaged in other activities—likely overseeing secret meetings. If you persist in refusing to cooperate, the consequences will be far worse than you imagine.'

Hu appeared frightened—perhaps contemplating the nature of French interrogation methods.

'Let's start again. What is your role within the Communist Party?'

'I organise and recruit local members, training them—though seldom in the French Concession due to the scarcity of factories.'

'Well, we will require a comprehensive list of groups, including members' names and locations, both within and outside the French Concession, who have received this training.'

Silence.

'To whom do you report, and how and where do you meet?'

'I report to a leader. We meet in different locations. At each meeting, we agree where to leave the next message—which includes the time and place of the following one.'

'What kinds of places do you hide these messages?'

'All sorts—tucked behind a loose brick or beneath a flowerpot marked by a burnt joss stick, a withered posy, a crushed cigarette packet, or some other piece of debris. The kind of thing no passer-by would notice, but which carries meaning to those who know.'

Allard sighed. It was the Chinese equivalent of the chalk-marked dead-letter box drop. Simple and effective. He knew that if there was no signal, the recipient would have to wait to be contacted again. Perhaps the sometimes-torrential Shanghai rain precluded the method of using chalk.

'What is the name of your superior, and what does he look like?'

'Mr Wang—and I don't know what he looks like, as he always wears a surgical face mask.'

'And what sort of accent does he have?'

'Local. Shanghai or Jiangsu Province.'

Allard was getting nowhere. Wang would be a fake name. It was the classic cell structure, and he said the interview was terminated. Hu asked what would happen to him and was told that there might be some supplementary questions—and then he would be released to the old Chinese part of the city, near his home.

That changed everything.

Hu suddenly launched into an animated and lengthy conversation with Chastain. He appeared to be begging, and Chastain seemed increasingly distressed. Several minutes passed like this, followed by an eerie silence as Chastain considered how to translate what he had heard.

'Pascal, I can hardly believe what I'm hearing. Prepare yourself for a shock. Hu is begging to remain in jail or be released individually in our Concession. The reason is that when we drop off the political offenders late at night, our police are paid a reward and hand them over to the Green Gang—who act as brokers and get a bounty from the Nationalists. On his release, his life expectancy would be a matter of days—if not hours.'

Allard was indeed distraught. He had joined the force to uphold justice—not to facilitate cold-blooded execution under the guise of diplomacy. There is nothing worse for an honest policeman than discovering that some of his colleagues are corrupt.

A lot of it made sense. It explained why so few of those set free reappeared on the streets, and why there sometimes appeared to be a backlog of prisoners. That might have been because some price haggling was going on. He had long suspected his senior Chinese policeman, Huang Jinrong, of making deals with gangsters—but could never prove it, though he was certain Huang would know of this scheme. Still shaking, Hu was reassured that he would remain safe while the investigation unfolded.

Late that night, five political prisoners were released. A plain van was used rather than the *panier à salade*, and Allard and Chastain followed in a borrowed car to the release point—switching off the lights. Fortunately, the moon was bright, and it was not difficult to observe the French police—dressed in black civilian clothes—transferring the captives to another van. One man attempted to resist, and a police officer struck him hard. Allard recognised one of his sergeants, who seemed to be receiving an envelope. He fleetingly thought of trying to rescue the men—but they were outside their jurisdiction, and two service revolvers against a barrage of likely automatic weapons would have been fatal.

The following morning, the first to be brought in was the sergeant—guarded by two soldiers. He broke down when confronted with the evidence that he was complicit in murder and told he could only save himself through his belated honesty. He also admitted that Huang had taken a cut.

Next was Huang, already disarmed and wondering why soldiers were accompanying him. Allard informed him of the discovery and asked Huang if it was true. He did not deny it, and his justification was that this was a regular business practice in China—and that they were communists, enemies of France. He also admitted that more than 200 men and women had been transferred in this manner.

Allard and Chastain, who had witnessed their fair share of

corruption and violence, were disgusted. Chastain, furious, wondered what penalty he would face for flooring this bombast—but then thought better of it.

Instead, they presented two documents requiring signatures in Chinese, with French counter-signatories. Huang read them. The first charged him with multiple counts of accessory to murder and revoked any right to be tried by courts—foreign or otherwise—in China, as he would be sent to France. The second document required Huang to list every police officer involved in the corrupt scheme.

'And what if I don't sign?'

It was Allard who elaborated,

'We have several choices. The first would be to send you to the Communist Red Squad.'

There was no denial of its existence—which was revealing.

'Or we could send you to Du at the Green Gang with a message that we know you've been cheating him for years on various ventures.'

'What happens to me in France?'

'That is a judicial matter—not something we handle here. I imagine they might guillotine you or, if you're lucky, send you to one of our penal colonies to serve hard labour for life.'

'The third…'

Huang signed the two documents and was taken away.

Hu was safely released, on the condition that he wind down any activity in the French Concession slowly—so as not to arouse suspicion—and that factory cells in the old Chinese city would, for now, remain undisturbed. He would be contacted again if needed—and was potentially more valuable to the French *in situ*, so long as his activities were not on their territory. Nobody in the Communist Party learned of Hu's brief absence.

The junior police involved were all dismissed but not prosecuted, as the French were keen to cover up such an embarrassing affair.

Hu, under great duress, did manage to tell the French that the Red Squad was part of a much larger intelligence unit supposedly directed by Zhou Enlai. The French were hoping for more high-quality information.

In fact, in November of the previous year, Zhou Enlai had formed the Special Service—the *Teke* (*Zhōngyāng Tèkē*—中央特科). It initially had four sections: intelligence gathering, protection of senior Party members, assassinations—primarily of defectors—dubbed the Red Squad (headed by Gu Shunzhang), and one for internal communications using codes and ciphers, called the 4th Section (led by Li Qiang). The *Teke* soon developed a web of spies and moles—including in the Nationalist Military Intelligence Group and the Chinese police in Shanghai. It was also supplemented by Zhou Enlai's contacts from his Whampoa days—some of whom, for now, remained sleepers.

Chapter 18: Tingzhou, Fujian, China, 1929

There is an old Chinese saying: 'Misfortunes and serendipity never occur as single events' (*Huò bù dān xíng, fú wú shuāng zhì*—祸不单行，福无双至), and in the case of Zhu De, the first half of 1929 brought him a series of disasters.

After the evacuation from the Jinggang in January 1929, the Nationalists vigorously pursued the Zhu–Mao Army. In one of the first of many harrowing engagements during the retreat, Zhu De's newlywed wife, Wu Ruolan, was captured. Zhu knew immediately what her fate would be, although he never received formal confirmation that General He Jian had ordered her execution. Within two weeks, Mao declared that, for 'operational reasons', he would assume military command of the 4th Army, leaving Zhu De in a difficult position. Without any consultation with Shanghai, Mao had seized control of the Zhu–Mao Army—relying on Peng Dehuai for the leadership of his units. Chen's newly established Intelligence Corps ceased to exist. Every soldier, along with the cadres who did not remain behind, was issued a rifle to assist with the retreat. Chen's four trusted peasant infiltrators had stayed and would hopefully blend back into village life. It was only when Nationalist forces were recalled due to unrest elsewhere in the country that the Red Army seized the opportunity to regroup and plan—culminating in the capture of Tingzhou in Changting County.

Upon arriving in the city, Zhu De learned that his wife had been beheaded, her head displayed on a pole in Changsha. Brigadier Kuo, the local Nationalist commander, was soon captured and executed—his body hung upside down from a tree while Mao delivered a speech. Mao and Zhu each took over a wing of the courtyards of the elegant Xingeng Villa, and shortly after, it was announced as their headquarters. From here, plans were laid to merge at least twenty counties into one contiguous Soviet. Chen was jubilant. To the south lay Shanghang County; beyond that was his home—the *tulous* of Yongding County. Although the Hakka population was widespread across at least seven provinces, Mao had chosen this place—so close to Chen's home—as the epicentre.

One of the immediate advantages of occupying a significant city was the presence of established businesses. A clothing factory that had previously produced Nationalist uniforms was requisitioned. The grey design remained unchanged for expediency, but red lapel insignia were added. At the newly created Red Army Bamboo Rain Hat Factory on Ximen Street, grey caps with red stars were being produced in large quantities. They were urgently needed, as volunteers were joining en masse—though some conscripts were also included.

For the first time, Chen was issued a military uniform. Until then, he had served exclusively as a political cadre. The uniform came with the rank of Lieutenant, denoted by two horizontal bars—marking his formal entry into the Red Army. It was a modest but momentous shift—from ideological educator to junior officer.

He realised this was one of the first steps towards building a more professional army. Such ranks, though still controversial among veteran revolutionaries, were becoming necessary—especially when integrating defecting Nationalist units, whose structures were rigidly hierarchical.

He put on the uniform, buckled his leather belt, stepped out to get a haircut—and noticed several young women giggling behind covered mouths, casting admiring glances at the nineteen-year-old officer.

The atmosphere of excitement and newfound pride did not last. It changed abruptly with the arrival of Liu Angong, a military adviser recently returned from training in the USSR, who had travelled from Shanghai. There was no longer any way to conceal Mao's takeover of the army, which lay well outside his formal remit.

On 12 June, Chen requested a two-week pass to return home, accompanied by Comrades Pan and Ma—both recently integrated into the Red Army. Pan had been granted the rank of Second Lieutenant, marked by a single collar bar. Junior Officer Ma, though holding no insignia, was nonetheless recognised as such: his authority derived from official orders, his association with Chen, and the sidearm he now carried.

They were issued horses and armed with pistols for the journey. No trouble was anticipated, as all the counties en route were considered securely under communist control. Mao signed the pass. The only condition was that Chen submit a report upon his return about the morale and condition of the peasantry. He had to learn to ride along the way—Pan and Ma were accomplished horsemen from their Whampoa days—but they were generous in teaching their equine-novice leader.

The three men, well provisioned, spent an agreeable three days travelling together. Neither of the two ex-Whampoa men had seen terrain like it. Pan was from Jiangsu with its flatlands, and Ma from Xi'an, having spent most of his life in an urban environment. They marvelled at the lushness of the pine and bamboo forests. At one point, they stopped to observe a troop of monkeys screeching indignantly at the intrusion into their territory. In one village, they encountered a large group of locals in a field using marker stakes to surround a member of the Land Allocation Committee. The villagers were all shouting at him and at each other—jockeying for the most fertile plots. The beleaguered official was relieved to see three Red Army soldiers arrive. After that, the land division took place without further protest.

They approached Chen's *tulou* cluster and slowed their pace to avoid causing alarm. The walking horse gong rang out, signalling assembly, and a runner was dispatched to fetch the most senior local communist—the commissar—and the *tulou* elders. By the time they reached the gate of Chen's *tulou*, a substantial crowd had gathered. A young woman stepped forward and handed Ma a red flag.

As they dismounted, Chen's mother, father, and sisters—who had not seen him for two years—rushed to the front and embraced him, their faces alight with joy. The hot water stoves roared to life, and each soldier was offered a bath and a shave. Chen, however, excused himself—there were matters to attend to. His two subordinates, Pan and Ma, were left to soak up the atmosphere. Several young women vied to assist the pair of dashing young men, both under twenty.

An interpreter was found for them from the Bei School, named after its most illustrious former teacher. They were offered plates of fresh fruit and sweetmeats. It was explained that the young women with coloured ribbons in their hats were unmarried and eligible—though it was quickly understood that this did not necessarily mean 'available'.

Chen was obliged to observe traditional formalities. That evening, he dined with the commissar, the elders, and his father—however much he longed to be with his family and friends. The Hakka in the local *tulous* had willingly accepted the communists. There was much discussion about what it all meant for the future. Within the *tulous*, there was little land to redistribute, as plots were either communal rice paddies or small, roughly evenly divided areas. But in the world beyond, the landlords had fled, and both Hakka and some Min farmers now had a chance to make a better—if still modest—living from their land. This time, they felt they had nothing to lose.

Later, Chen privately visited Teacher Yao, now over sixty. He was saddened to see that the past two years had not been kind to the old man. His skin was sallow, and the whites of his eyes had taken on a yellowish hue. Still, Yao had lost none of his humour. They spent several pleasurable hours conversing in Russian. Afterwards, Chen returned to spend time with his family, and the following evening, Pan and Ma were invited to the family dinner. They marvelled at the culinary talents of Chen's mother and gorged themselves on a dozen dishes, including salt-baked chicken and tender pork belly with mustard greens. Chen asked the ever-creative Ma to recount the tale of the fireworks and the attack on Suichuan. He did so with characteristic flair—adding a few embellishments to make the story both fascinating and amusing. Nobody went to bed before 3.00 a.m., and the goodbyes the next morning were exchanged through bleary eyes.

On his return, a man was waiting for Chen. He also learned from Song that, at a meeting on 22 June, both Party cadres and army representatives had voted to reinstate Zhu De—and that Mao had disappeared to consider his position. Song admitted, somewhat nervously, that he had voted against Mao. After the earlier request for a pigeon fancier, Song had merely shrugged when Chen asked next for a forger. But that was precisely what this man was.

He called himself Lao Shu (老鼠—the rat), and he refused to reveal his real name. He admitted he had once been imprisoned by the Nationalists and had secured his release by producing perfect copies of works by famous Chinese watercolourists. The verbal contract had been honoured.

Shanghai and the Comintern saw matters differently regarding Mao. In August, they issued dispatches declaring that Mao was in overall command of both Party and army affairs, and that Liu Angong was to return to Shanghai. However, Mao did not immediately return to the fold, and it was only at the Gutian Conference in December 1929 that he formally reintroduced himself as the Comintern-backed political commissar. He had vanished for weeks. Now, he returned with a title, a smile, and a telegram from Moscow. No one dared ask what had changed.

By May 1930, there were three Red Armies in existence. The Zhu–Mao Army was the largest, with around 16,000 soldiers, but Peng Dehuai's independent Fifth Army had mushroomed to approximately 12,000. The third was a separate Red Army—the Hubei Group under He Long and Duan Dechang—numbering around 10,000, with other scattered forces elsewhere.

Now, Shanghai was ready to flex its muscles. When Zhou Enlai left for the USSR in March, his temporary stand-in—the militarily aggressive and ambitious Li Lisan—decided to attack two provincial capitals: Nanchang in Jiangxi by the Zhu–Mao Army, and Changsha in Hunan by Peng Dehuai. The two cities formed the base of a triangle, with the ultimate objective being to march on Wuhan at the apex in the north. By the end of June, plans were ready to be implemented.

Chen deployed two team members to each of the two armies and arranged for couriers to travel between them, as pigeons would be useless. Mao instructed him to join the army attacking Nanchang. Chen selected Junior Officer Ma and a trained cadre member to go to Changsha, and Second Lieutenant Pan with cadre member Tang Baolin to accompany him to Nanchang. They began refining their cover stories.

Chen considered his options. Nanchang was too large to employ fireworks, and with an established road network, provisions were brought into the city by lorry—using local village traders as intermediaries. He noted that the team, including himself, should learn to drive—but that would have to wait for another opportunity. With a significantly larger Red Army now in the field, security would be tight. It was time to rely on conventional espionage.

The railway and the river were the two main entry points into both cities. Chen judged that the passenger boat terminal would be under less surveillance than the railway station. Pan and Tang boarded a boat departing from Wuhan at Hukou, travelled along the shores of Poyang Lake, and entered Nanchang. Pan wore a business suit and carried a briefcase with a combination lock, secured to his wrist by a chain and handcuffs. He had also been given the names of two communist sympathisers in the city that could be used if help was required. The first owned a bicycle repair workshop; the second was a locksmith. Tang wore the more traditional clothing of a travelling salesman.

As the boat was making its docking manoeuvres, Pan received his first piece of bad news. Moored were two river gunboats, the *USS Luzon* and the *USS Oahu*, flying American flags.

The two spies split up in the predictable inspection line, with Pan in front and Tang four people behind him. At the exit were plainclothes men inspecting paperwork and four armed soldiers. When it was Pan's turn, one of the men inspected his two pieces of paperwork. The first was a Wuhan identity document with a unique stamp for approved work, and the second was a letter from a board member of the Bank of Communications, stressing the importance of the work of this courier and demanding that he be allowed to pass without let or hindrance.

'Where are you going?'
'To our main bank branch here in Nanchang.'
'And in the briefcase?'
'Confidential papers.'
'Open it.'
'I will not; it is designed so the bank knows it has been tampered

with.'

'So, what if I were a thief, and at gunpoint demanded the combination?'

'I wouldn't give it up. Even if you shot me, you'd still need to chop off my arm to get to the briefcase unopened.'

The interrogator looked irritated by this bravery and stupidity.

'Then give me the key to the handcuffs, and I will have the briefcase opened and returned to the bank.'

'I can't. The bank has the key and will unlock the handcuffs when I arrive.'

'Either you open it, or you will accompany me, and we will forcefully open it. I will give you my phone number so the bank can verify that I prised it open.'

Pan felt he had little choice and dialled in the combination. The interrogator was amazed and wondered if he had exceeded his authority. There was a change of shirt and underwear; the other article was a stack of crisp new high-denomination railway bonds worth millions. He gave Pan his phone number and told him to move on. All the documents and bonds were the work of master forger Lao Shu.

Although Pan and Tang had no plan to recognise each other, Pan dawdled briefly and was within earshot to observe his comrade pass by.

'Where are you going?'

'To Dai's shop to take sales orders for vanilla, rose essence, and powdered egg.'

'Yes, his cakes are among the best and have become popular throughout the city. Are you going to the shop on Shiyao Street or Yunfei Street?'

Tang looked puzzled. The interrogator seemed pleasant enough, or perhaps he had a sweet tooth.

'I'm glad you like them. I'm going to Yunfei Street.'

It happened in seconds.

'Guard, arrest this man.'

A soldier unslung his rifle and stepped forward. Something had gone wrong, and a panicked Tang began running back towards the river. Simultaneously, the interrogator screamed,

'Don't kill him,' and a shot rang out.

Tang dropped to the ground, and Pan flinched—his throat tightening with guilt. He turned away, afraid to look again, worried it might unravel him before the mission was complete. The interrogator's furious reaction, shouting at the soldier, made it clear that Tang was dead.

There was no cake shop on either Shiyao Street or Yunfei Street.

Tang had been given the correct address but had not used it. It would be an agonisingly slow recovery from the guilt for Chen and Pan.

Feeling chastened and frightened, Pan took a rickshaw to the Bank of Communications and then blended into the crowds. He removed his suit jacket and draped it over his arm—a natural gesture on such a hot summer day—ensuring the fabric hung down to conceal the top of his briefcase and the handcuffs. He then proceeded to the friendly bicycle repair workshop, where he was taken to a backroom and had the handcuffs removed with a hacksaw. The alternative locksmith was a last resort; had a search been carried out for Chen, that profession would have been the first to be investigated.

Next, Pan proceeded according to the plan. It would have been desirable to dispose of the railway bonds, but since he intended to stay for two nights, there was always a slight risk they could be found and someone might attempt to cash them. He headed to the City of God Temple and approached the funeral urns, where people gathered to burn high-denomination paper money, known as 'ghost money,' as it is believed that the deceased might need cash in the afterlife. Only an elderly woman, hunched and oblivious, stood nearby, paying no attention as Pan fed the railway bonds to the flames.

Later that day, a senior employee from the Bank of Communications called to verify that the interrogator had compelled their courier to disclose the combination—an act typically forbidden without prior authorisation.

It soon became clear to Pan that the Nationalists had gathered enough intelligence to transform Nanchang into a defensive bastion. Although the city walls had been removed in 1926 and 1927 under the orders of Beiyang Commander Sun Chuanfang, Nanchang remained a formidable challenge for invaders. Surrounded by water on three sides, it was naturally defended. Heavy artillery batteries had been positioned behind lakes and rivers, rendering a direct assault impossible, while other strategic locations bristled with machine guns and mortars. Troops scurried in all directions. From the opposite side of the street at the railway station, Pan observed long carriages disgorging fresh forces. With two US gunboats stationed nearby, a direct assault on Nanchang would be suicidal.

Pan observed a few weaker points in the defences, but they were only relative. On the third morning, as more troops arrived from the opposite direction, Pan decided to purchase a railway ticket to Wuhan. He was searched—including an inspection of his briefcase—before leaving the city and disembarking at the first station outside Nanchang.

Upon returning to the Red Army, Pan found Chen, who immediately took him to Mao and Zhu for his report. It was a sombre assessment, but both leaders began to contribute ideas. By prodding the defences of Nanchang and making it appear the focus of an attack, they might improve Peng Dehuai's chances in Changsha. Chen, having lost the first member of his team, spent time with a distraught Pan, who, upon parting, said bitterly,

'All he needed to do was provide the address we had given him.'

Chen promised to provide additional training and explained the difficulty of being a perfect spy, admitting he was still learning. Song then continued,

'Had he been captured alive, he would have faced an excruciating death. Do you know how many lives you've saved through your courageous actions?'

Ultimately, the Zhu–Mao Army in Nanchang conducted provocative raids at the weakest points identified by Pan, hoping to divert attention from Peng Dehuai's attack on Changsha—a Red Army trademark: a two-pronged assault with ambiguity about the main thrust.

On the way to Changsha, Peng's army encountered a hostile force—

not Chinese but American—part of the Yangtze Patrol Force, initially created to ward off aggressive warlords. On the Yangtze, Xiang, and Gan rivers there were six American shallow-draught river gunboats to protect their citizens, who had spread out from Shanghai into treaty ports to trade along the Yangtze River basin. Peng's troops engaged the *USS Guam* as it made threatening manoeuvres. They opened fire, killing a seaman—Samuel Elkin of Brooklyn, New York—on 4 July, Independence Day, of all days. The report the following day in *The New York Times* made it clear that these 'bandits' needed to be crushed. This development was certainly not going to help Peng as he advanced on Changsha along the Xiang River, as the United States had put him on notice that these vessels, with their guns and small detachments of marines, would attack his forces.

By mid-July, Peng's troops had positioned themselves for an assault on Changsha, although he did not deploy Chen's two spies, deeming it too dangerous for them. On 25 July, Peng's highly motivated and professional force took the city and defeated a much larger Nationalist force and their commander, General He Jian. This served as some revenge for the murder of Zhu De's wife, and a message was sent to Mao and the Nanchang attackers. If there was any doubt about the power of the American gunboats, five days later, the *USS Palos* arrived in the city, opened fire with its two six-pound guns, and killed fifty Red Army soldiers. With a firing range of eight kilometres, this posed a severe threat. The Nationalists managed to regroup, and on 6 August, Peng sent a message to Mao, stating that he had been forced to retreat. Then, on 19 August, the Nanchang attack was called off, and the two armies marched and met at Yonghe on 23 August.

Mao merged the two armies under a single command, appointing Zhu De as commander and Peng Dehuai as his deputy. Chen heard through Song that there was considerable grumbling among Peng's officers about their final loss of independence. It made a little more sense when Chen was finally briefed that Mao had decided the entire army—under a single chain of command to himself—would attempt to retake Changsha a second time. Chen kept his thoughts to himself but considered it folly. There would be no element of surprise this time, and after the first attack on Changsha, it would likely be impossible for his spies to infiltrate the city. Military reinforcements in Changsha were also inevitable.

The second attack on Changsha was a disaster for the communists, and after three weeks of heavy losses, they gave up. As a result, Mao also suffered a personal loss as his ex-wife, Yang Kaihui, and their eldest of three sons, eight-year-old Anying, were taken into custody on 24 October. Until this point, Nationalist General He Jian had ignored Mao's family in his hometown of Changsha, considering them non-combatants, but he now took revenge. Yang was offered her life if she denounced Mao. She refused. After being paraded through the city, she was executed by firing squad on 14 November, leaving orphans behind, as Mao was in no position to look after three children. It was the second time in a year that He Jian had ordered the death of a communist's wife. First Wu Ruolan. Now Yang Kaihui. There would surely be more to follow. Their only crime had been to love the wrong men. He Jian became the most reviled man on the Nationalist side.

It was not the army that was blamed for this failed adventure but Li Lisan, and in October, he was summoned to Moscow for several personal dressing-downs by Stalin. Mao attempted to appoint himself the head of a field-based China Revolutionary Committee, but the Central Committee and Moscow were having none of it. However, on 20 September, Mao was finally restored to the Central Committee as a reserve.

Chapter 19: Harbin, Heilongjiang, China, 1929

In the spring of 1929, Konstantin Rodzaevsky married Lydia Malkova at St Nicholas's Cathedral in Novy Gorod. It was to be a two-day society wedding, lavishly funded through private donations. On the first morning, Kostya arrived at Lydia's family home accompanied by Rumiantsev—his witness, impeccably dressed in a blue sash—and Korablev, bearing chocolates, flowers, and envelopes of money. All were attired in full Fascist regalia, ready for the playful indignities arranged by the bridesmaids.

They were met at the door by one of Lydia's parents' friends, who refused to release the bride until a cash 'ransom' had been paid. A linen napkin imprinted with lipstick marks from the bride and her bridesmaids was then handed to Kostya, with the demand that he identify Lydia's kiss. He failed to pick it out, and with much laughter, the other gifts he had brought were promptly confiscated. Suitably fleeced, and the fee handed over, he was finally permitted to see Lydia. She was radiant: her dress adorned with shoulder pieces of white silk roses in bloom, a matching posy, and a full-length pearl necklace with earrings to match.

At the cathedral, members of Musketeers—Rodzaevsky's ceremonial honour guard—stood to attention. A priest met them at the entrance with candles and recited a brief prayer to complete the betrothal. The building was packed. Many of the guests wore black uniforms. Kostya's father, younger brother, and Lydia's immediate family sat in the front row.

Three notable figures attended the ceremony. The first, recently arrived from Dalian, was General Nechaev—a White Russian mercenary famed for his armoured train and recently employed by the Chinese Nationalists. The second was Lieutenant General Kosmin of the Brotherhood of Russian Truth. The third was Ataman Grigory Mikhaylovich Semenov, leader of the Transbaikal White Russian Cossacks. Though still based in Harbin, Semenov maintained a loyal network—primarily farmers and ex-soldiers from the Far Eastern Army—many of whom had turned to banditry and cross-border raids in the aftermath of Soviet reprisals. His connections with the conventional Japanese military remained strong.

Kostya harboured many reservations about Semenov, finding him old-fashioned and unreliable. Yet these dignitaries conferred legitimacy and grandeur on the event. Semenov arrived in full White Russian uniform, resplendent with a high-winged collar, cascading gold-braided epaulettes, and an impressive display of Tsarist medals. For Kostya, it was the perfect symbolic trio: Church, Fascist Party, and the former Monarchy—though he had no intention of allowing the latter to rule Russia again.

The bride and groom were led to the centre of the cathedral and stood upon a rose-coloured cloth wrapped around a small podium. The bishop placed crowns upon their heads, offered them wine from a silver chalice, and led them three times around the platform. Rings were exchanged. A benediction was given, and they were declared husband and wife. As they left the cathedral, Lydia asked for two crystal glasses to be smashed—the more shards, the happier the marriage. Both the bishop and Kostya refused.

A four-car motorcade had been arranged, each vehicle with armed bodyguards riding on the running boards. These men, and others like them, had been recruited into the Fascist Special Department. The bride and groom rode in the first car; immediate family and General Semenov followed in the next two. The final car carried a few of Kostya's RFO colleagues.

It was a warm, agreeable Saturday, and Kitayskaya Ulitsa teemed with life—its crowds now swelled further by curious onlookers. As the motorcade swept through the street, Kostya rose from his seat, his hand raised in a sequence of sharp Fascist salutes—many of them returned with fervour.

If the wedding had brought personal fulfilment, this moment delivered something altogether different: a surge of raw power. He could almost feel what *Il Duce* must have felt, standing before tens of thousands.

The reception was held the following day at the Grand Hotel, beginning after the Sunday Church service. Once again, no expense was spared. Several Jewish guests, who had not attended the Orthodox ceremony, were present—at Lydia's insistence. She had wanted some of her orchestral and conservatoire friends to attend, though several had politely declined. Kostya made it clear that he expected flawless conduct towards the visibly nervous attendees. The dress code was strict: white tie, with no military uniforms permitted.

The feast included a gelatine swan stuffed with poultry, generous helpings of caviar, champagne, and a traditional bread-and-salt loaf for the couple to share—symbols of faithfulness and prosperity. A small live orchestra played wedding favourites and popular dance pieces. At the appointed time, every guest was handed a glass of iced vodka to signal the first kiss between bride and groom—the longer the kiss, the longer the marriage, so the tradition went. Coins were thrown to the floor. Then came the inevitable cry of 'bitter!' (*Gorko!*—*Горько!*), prompting the couple to kiss again to offset the vodka's bite.

Before too many guests had departed—and most were already inebriated—a table of Jewish musicians from the symphony orchestra asked if they might borrow the house band's instruments. A balalaika was also produced. They launched into a rousing rendition of *Kalinka* (*Калинка*). Guests began to sing. Some took to the dance floor. As the tempo rose, several men attempted high kicks and twirling steps. It was not elegant, but it was joyous—raucous laughter rang out. For a fleeting moment, fascists, gentiles, and Jews danced together as Russians. It was a scene never again to be repeated in Harbin.

The Rodzaevskys rented a modest apartment in Pristan District, close to the Sungari River, in a handsome stone building. It was cramped—but it was theirs. Just a month later, Lydia told Kostya she was pregnant. On her doctor's advice, she decided to retire from her musical career and become a homemaker. Kostya was thrilled on both counts. For the first time since childhood, he felt the future might truly belong to him.

The uneasy cooperation between the USSR and Zhang Xueliang, the Young Marshal, over control of the CER began to unravel in mid-1929. For years, the Russians had dominated the staffing of both management and labour—and with the full support of the Soviet authorities, the arrangement could no longer be seen as a partnership.

On 27 May 1929, Zhang's police raided the Soviet Consulate in Harbin and arrested thirty-nine Soviet citizens. Moscow was furious. In a blistering front-page article in *Izvestia*—the Moscow edition—dated 8 June, the Soviets denounced the illegality of the raid, accused Zhang's police of planting crude forgeries—written in outdated Soviet typescript—and vehemently denied claims by Zhang's forces that a Comintern meeting had been taking place in the building's basement. Worse still, they claimed, was the same-day arrest in Mukden of Soviet Consul-General Kuznetsov. The article criticised Western news agencies for their silence, save for British Reuters, which the author suggested would print anything anti-Soviet and still smarted from the ARCOS raid.

Further measures soon followed. On 11 July, the Chinese authorities dismissed the Russian General Manager, his deputy, and the entire Russian department of the CER. These actions continued until China held full control of the railway.

Rodzaevsky was ecstatic. He had never forgiven the Bolsheviks for his expulsion from the Harbin Law Faculty the previous year. He had, however, ultimately secured his degree—reportedly through some rather forceful persuasion at the institution. The Harbin fascist press erupted, demanding the arrest of Soviet Consul-General Melnikov, the expulsion of all Bolsheviks and Jews from the city, and the mobilisation of patriotic White Russian military forces. Zhang, eager to bolster his own army, agreed to arm approximately 3,000 new recruits—many of them members of the RFO. Rumiantsev facilitated the arrangement.

Diplomatic relations were severed on 19 July. On 17 August, the first clash occurred, when Soviet forces attacked Chalainor and suffered heavy casualties. But subsequent operations saw Soviet victories, owing to their superior naval strength, modern weaponry, targeted propaganda among Manchurian Chinese, and strategic use of radio communications.

The conflict ended swiftly. Several thousand Chinese citizens detained inside the USSR were imprisoned, tortured, and sent to forced labour. On 13 December 1929, the Chinese Nationalists signed the Treaty of Khabarovsk. It permitted their nationals to return home and effectively restored the status quo.

Nechaev was forced into retirement shortly after and later emerged as a respected figure in community development. The only conspicuous absence in this equation was the Japanese. They controlled their portion of the railway and possessed a standing army—but said nothing. The RFO maintained its two lines of communication: Nakamura's barber's shop and Rumiantsev's secret meetings with Takahama.

During the first half of 1930, RFO membership continued to grow, partly due to widespread rumours that Stalin harboured growing ambitions in China, fuelling fear among the White Russians. However, actual membership numbers remained modest—just a few hundred—the figures kept secret from all but the leadership. The RFO had assumed it enjoyed broader support across the émigré community.

At this time, Rodzaevsky became aware of a second Japanese group: the Tokumu Kikan Special Service (TK), briefly mentioned by Rumiantsev during his regular meetings with Nakamura. On one visit to the barber's shop, Rodzaevsky finally raised the subject.

'My trusted friend, whom do you fear more: the TK or the Kenpeitai?'

'A difficult question. If you're a spy or a saboteur, then it's the TK. They report directly to military command in Tokyo, not just local headquarters. One of my clients once criticised Japanese intentions—and the TK took him.

'What happened to him?'

'He never reappeared. I imagine he's in a heavy cage at the bottom of a lake.'

'And the Kenpeitai?'

'Ruthless, too. Their interrogation methods are infamous—but they'll make accommodations if interests align.'

'You mean smuggling, drugs, prostitution, and kidnapping?'

'You may say that—I couldn't possibly comment.'

It seemed Takahama, urbane and idealistic, was either unaware of the Kenpeitai's criminal links—or chose to ignore them.

'So how do we contact the TK?'

'You don't. If they want to talk to you, they'll find you.'

'But they have no authority over me.'

'Then you can explain that—while strapped to a chair in some basement.'

'Do the two agencies ever work together?'

'Only when they must. You're making me nervous. Let's change the subject. Would you like some relaxation with one of my best girls?'

Uncharacteristically, Rodzaevsky declined. Nakamura had seen it before—young, recently married men hoping to start a more honourable life, especially when their wives were pregnant, as Lydia was. Some returned. Many did not.

A few days later, Rodzaevsky's first child—a son—died during childbirth and was never christened.

In 1930, Rumiantsev continued to foster relations with Takahama and gained further insight into Japan's global strategy. In April, as always, they discussed the Soviet threat.

'Last year,' Rumiantsev asked, 'when the USSR dealt such a blow to the Young Marshal, why didn't you act?'

'Because we are patient,' Takahama replied. 'We don't rush into battle without careful planning or a high certainty of success. The Soviet action allowed us to observe both their military methods and the Chinese Nationalists' poor performance. Also, we're still recovering from the 1927 Shōwa Financial Disaster. Like your Western Depression, it nearly bankrupted us. We need time to rebuild.'

'Still, the Soviets might have turned on the Kwantung Army.'

'Unlikely.'

'Why?'

Takahama merely smiled and declined to answer. But the hint was clear: some back channel may have existed between the two adversaries.

'So, you'll take Manchuria when it suits you,' Rumiantsev continued, 'but I still don't understand why you want it. It'll drain your resources and risk war with China—or worse, provoke the USSR.'

'We want coal, steel, aluminium, oil, gas—and agriculture. Japan lacks all these. But oil is key. Geological work by a Russian, B. P.

Torgashev, soon to be published, shows promising formations. We believe there are abundant shale reserves.'

Rumiantsev listened, humbled again. The RFO existed in a bubble.

'Our domestic oil reserves are insufficient,' Takahama added. 'Korea helps, but not enough. Even with Manchuria, we'll still need American oil. Relations with the U.S. are strained, especially since their ban on Japanese immigration.'

When talk turned to White Russian support, Takahama sought reassurance.

'You still have our support,' Rumiantsev replied. 'But there's a problem. Since the CER crisis, the Young Marshal confiscated all remaining weapons from our forces.'

'Understandable,' Takahama admitted. 'He wouldn't want you keeping thousands of rifles that might one day be turned against him.'

'True. But it leaves us exposed.'

'That must be addressed.'

In February 1931, Rumiantsev brought news to Takahama: the RFO was evolving. A date had been chosen—26 May—for the First Congress of a pan-Asian political movement: the Russian Fascist Party (RFP). When Takahama asked if assistance was needed, Rumiantsev requested funding.

The money was delivered in cash to Nakamura's shop, avoiding the scrutiny of Harbin's banks. The sum surprised even Nakamura. Delegates from distant provinces, including two covertly from Japan, were issued stipends.

Fifty-two assembled at Fisher's Building on Diagonalnaya Street, not far from Rodzaevsky's flat. Rumiantsev had secured non-intervention from Zhang's government—on condition that no fascist insignia be worn and delegates arrived in business attire.

All founders of the RFO attended, along with Matkovsky.

The first order of business: electing a Party Chairman. Lieutenant-General Vladimir Kosmin won—appeasing monarchist factions. Rodzaevsky, however, claimed the post of General Secretary. It was the true seat of power.

The manifesto fused Italian Fascist economics—corporatism, syndicalism, decentralised unions—with Russian orthodoxy. Religion, particularly the Orthodox Church, stood at its core. Private property and wealth were permitted. Ethnic minorities were granted protected rights—except Jews.

The RFP declared itself the sole force capable of saving Russia from communism.

Rodzaevsky would remember 11 August for the rest of his life. Lydia had requested a romantic dinner—just the two of them.

After ordering, she reached across the table.

'Happy birthday, my love,' she whispered. 'I have two presents for you—both of which I'm carrying with me.'

Kostya raised an eyebrow. 'A riddle?'

She handed him a large envelope. Inside was a musical score, complete with lyrics beneath the staves.

'What is this?'

'A rousing anthem for your new party. Full orchestration. I composed it—and wrote the words.'

Kostya, drawn as always to classical music, examined the score in silence. It was superb—he knew it instantly.

Finally, he looked up.

'It's magnificent. I'm so proud of you, Lydia.' He reached for her hand. 'And the second?'

She smiled.

'I'm pregnant again.'

On 2 September, Rumiantsev met Takahama once more. But something was different. The Japanese officer was solemn, his manner unusually reserved.

Concerned, Rumiantsev asked,

'Are you unwell?'

'I am in good health. But I called this meeting because I have something important to tell you—something that must remain absolutely confidential. Before the month is out, we will invade Manchuria.'

Rumiantsev was not entirely surprised. Tokyo had undergone a regime change—one widely viewed as hawkish.

'Can you tell me when?'

'Of course not. But I will say this: the Japanese community in Harbin—and in other cities—may face reprisals. White and even Red Russians may suffer if public opinion sees us all as collaborators. I doubt you care much for the latter. I don't either.

'Reaching Harbin will take time, depending on resistance and strategy.'

'But the White Russians are unarmed. They'll be slaughtered. I've said this before.'

'And I listened. Arrangements have been made.'

'What arrangements?'

Takahama exhaled slowly, folding his hands.

'Once hostilities begin, I won't be able to meet you again. I'll be reassigned. But you and your General Secretary will soon be contacted by Major Kenzō Miyake of the TK. He's based here in Harbin and speaks excellent Russian. Miyake supports the invasion—as do I. But many oppose it. This is, in truth, is an act of insubordination in Manchuria.'

The men stood, bowed formally, and shook hands. Their paths had crossed; each recognised the other's competence. It was a farewell of gravity—marking a shift in everything that had come before.

Shortly after, Major Miyake contacted the RFP and requested a meeting at Nakamura's shop. Rodzaevsky and Rumiantsev climbed the familiar staircase and entered to find a slight man seated in Nakamura's chair. The barber stood rigid in the corner, perspiring—his close ties to the Kenpeitai now a liability.

Miyake gestured for them to sit. He wasted no time on pleasantries. In crisp, deliberate Russian, he began:

'Everyone here knows that the Empire of Japan is about to go to war with China.'

He turned to them.

'That you know this is a regrettable indiscretion by Takahama. The TK reports directly to Tokyo. Takahama, you understand, holds only regional authority. If you wish to work with us, I expect obedience.

'Your first task is this: Mr Rumiantsev must sever all ties with the Chinese government. Do I have your assurance?'

Rumiantsev nodded. He recognised Miyake for what he was—dangerous, informed, and well placed. The Japanese were clearly not united in their plans.

Rodzaevsky was furious—how dare this man speak to him that way?—but he kept his face composed and gave his assent.

The three descended to a waiting car and were driven to a warehouse in Pristan District, owned by Nakamura. Inside were crates of liquor, beer, and cigarettes—typical Yakuza contraband. In one corner, however, stood unmarked wooden boxes. Nakamura prised two open. One contained pistols. The other, Austrian Steyr-Solothurn MP34 submachine guns with spare magazines. Miyake handed Rodzaevsky a list.

Nakamura's men would distribute the weapons to the White Russian population once hostilities commenced. In the meantime, the RFP was tasked with going door to door, using supplied factory and residence registries to direct citizens to Japanese-designated 'safe' zones.

Miyake believed the connection between the RFP and Japan would soon be exposed—if it wasn't already. The backlash, he warned, would be severe.

On 18 September 1931, the Kwantung Army staged a false-flag operation. Without Tokyo's approval, they placed a small charge beside the South Manchuria Railway near Mukden. The explosion caused no real damage, but the Japanese accused the Chinese of sabotage—and launched their invasion.

Following a brief artillery barrage, 500 Japanese soldiers attacked the local garrison of 7,000 and the adjacent airfield. By late afternoon, it was over. Mukden was occupied. Five hundred Chinese soldiers and two Japanese lay dead.

The Young Marshal lost his air force and his Renault tanks—strategic assets. He offered only token resistance, retreating from Manchuria and never returning.

The invasion violated a pact signed in April with Chiang Kai-shek, a rare agreement promising joint resistance to foreign incursions.

Japanese reinforcements arrived from Korea. Apart from skirmishes in Jilin and some resistance from the Heilongjiang Provincial Army, the Japanese faced little difficulty. They moved city to city, portraying the campaign as a liberation. Public atrocities were avoided.

In Harbin, Major Miyake had expected chaos. He anticipated mass flight by Russians. Some fled—but not many. The city's Chinese population did not rise against the heavily armed Japanese civilians or the lightly armed White Russians. The Harbin Municipal Police—mostly Chinese—carried on as normal. Blame was directed not at the invaders, but at the Young Marshal's retreat.

Miyake needed gratitude. He needed submission. He summoned Rodzaevsky.

His order was clear: the RFP must supply plainclothes members—some of them women—who would be attacked by Japanese agents disguised as Chinese protestors. This was not a request.

The directive caused uproar. Senior RFP members were horrified. Were they partners—or puppets?

Pokrovsky stormed out and resigned. Korablev opposed it, but stayed. Pokrovsky would never see his comrades again—save at Korablev's funeral. Korablev died of tuberculosis in 1932.

Live rounds and explosives were used for realism. Bullet holes were made available for carefully selected journalists. Corpses were doused in blood. Photographs were released to the White Russian press. The scenes were cleaned before independent reporters arrived.

Rodzaevsky took part in this event. He was terrified. Bullets—supposedly missing him—whistled close.

The ruse worked. The White Russians moved willingly into Japanese zones.

The Kwantung Army marched into Harbin on Friday, 5 February 1932. The Rising Sun flag appeared in many top-floor windows. It was a bitter winter. Young women threw confetti and paper flowers. Some kissed the soldiers.

That evening, Kostya and Lydia joined 10,000 White Russians outside the Japanese Consulate. They shouted their thanks.

The Americans protested—but imposed no oil embargo.

The USSR watched—silent, and increasingly concerned.

Rodzaevsky, for the first time, believed the world would let Japan take everything.

Chapter 20: Ningdu, Jiangxi, China, 1931

Historically, cadets at the Whampoa Military Academy studied the fate of Napoleon's *Grande Armée* in 1812 shortly after enrolment. The Russian scorched-earth policy, the brutal winter, unfamiliar terrain, overconfidence, and the defenders' resolve had all contributed to the French catastrophe. By this time, Mao had already recruited more than 30,000 peasant irregulars into his three newly designed 'Route Armies'—regional Red Army units created specifically to carry out a scorched-earth strategy. Any advancing Nationalist force was soon brought to the brink of starvation.

Contemporary military doctrine considered a minimum attacker-to-defender ratio of three to one, essential for overwhelming a smaller force. The Nationalists, believing they faced a disorganised guerrilla rabble, neglected the fundamentals of warfare—and received no adequate intelligence beforehand.

The strategy devised by Chiang Kai-shek and his senior officers became known as the Encirclement Campaigns. The Communists referred to their response as Counter-Encirclements. The Nationalists aimed to surround a landlocked pseudo-state with overwhelming numbers, like squeezing an orange—extract all the juice and discard the dry, useless pith. The Communists, unable to receive arms from the USSR by sea, Mongolia, or even distant Xinjiang, remained isolated.

Although other bases—such as the Shaanxi–Gansu and Honghu Soviets—were also targeted, the Jiangxi Soviet remained the central focus.

The First Encirclement Campaign proved disastrous for the Nationalists. Their 6th, 9th, and 19th Route Armies assembled 100,000 troops under Lu Diping, with reinforcements held in Hunan. They faced 40,000 motivated Communists who, though short on arms, held the advantage of terrain. The Nationalists were insufficient in number. The Communist 4th Army, now designated the 1st Front Army, along with local militias, crossed the Gan River and held the line. The Nationalists, attempting a westward crossing, became overstretched.

Confusion reigned. Two Nationalist divisions mistakenly opened fire on one another in heavy fog before pushing into Soviet territory towards Ningdu. On 30 December 1930, the 18th Division was destroyed in a well-executed pincer movement. More brigades were annihilated at Dongshao on 30 January 1931. The Nationalists suffered 9,000 dead or captured, and 6,000 wounded. The Communists seized 12,000 rifles and several artillery pieces. Any illusion that the Nationalists were fighting a disjointed peasant rebellion was now shattered.

At the same time, the Party hierarchy was undergoing a reshuffle. A pivotal figure was Wang Ming, one of the 'Twenty-Eight Bolsheviks' educated in Moscow. In 1929, he returned to China alongside Comintern emissary Pavel Mif, who had been tasked with suppressing deviationism within the Party. Targets included Xiang Zhongfa, Li Lisan, Mao, and Zhu De. Mif swiftly engineered Wang Ming's rise, reducing Xiang—the second General Secretary and Chen Duxiu's successor—to a powerless figurehead. Xiang attempted to resign, but this was refused.

On 15 January 1931, Wang Ming dispatched another of the Twenty-Eight, Xiang Ying, to Jiangxi to establish the Central Bureau of the Soviet Area. Xiang was appointed Acting Secretary and Chairman of the Central Military Commission. The return of Moscow-trained cadres was met with hostility but had already shifted power dynamics in Shanghai. As the new structure took shape, Mao was demoted to commissar of the 1st Front Army. Zhu De was reduced to Red Army Commander.

It was at this point that Chen was summoned to report to Zeng Xisheng, head of the 1st Front Army's Signals Intelligence (SIGINT) unit, headquartered in Ningdu. His first impression was of a bespectacled man in his late twenties, dressed in civilian clothes, with thinning hair and intense eyes—the eyes of a zealot. A blanket concealed something large in the corner of the spartan room. Zeng reminded him that the meeting was top secret. Any divulgence, he warned, would bring immediate and severe consequences. Chen believed him.

Zeng began by asking about Zhou Enlai's reasons for the meeting, probing the firework protocols and other intelligence activities. He then outlined his own background and the work of the *Teke*. His superior in Shanghai, Li Kenong, had infiltrated the Nationalist Military Intelligence Bureau in 1929 and specialised in codes and wireless transmissions. So skilled was he that Chiang Kai-shek had eventually promoted him to Head of Section. It was Li who had personally recommended Zeng for promotion, citing his early work on wireless protocols and his reliability during sensitive courier and encryption assignments.

Zeng instructed Chen to change shirts. His pulse quickened. It wasn't the insignia that startled him—but what it meant. He had just been promoted to Captain, making him one of the youngest commissioned officers in the Red Army. Until now, he had served as a Lieutenant, following his formal induction after the recent capture of Tingzhou.

Before that, he had belonged to the political cadre, working under figures such as Zhou Enlai and Song Liqiang, though he was consistently entrusted with military responsibilities—supporting Mao and Zhu De in field operations. His role had always been atypical: a trusted agent of the political command, embedded within the military structure yet never fully part of it.

This appointment—authorised by Li Kenong and conveyed through Zeng—marked a decisive shift. For the first time, he held direct military command within a specialist unit—one critical to SIGINT operations, though still under political oversight. Beneath the insignia was a second badge: a lightning bolt. Chen was now in charge of the army's SIGINT unit at Ningdu.

The compound would now serve as the Red Army's central SIGINT base. Zeng would return to Shanghai. Then he stepped over to the concealed object, drew back the blanket, and revealed a radio transmitter and receiver—standard military equipment modified for field use. Chen recognised it immediately. Just as he had predicted five years earlier in Xiamen: voices could now travel invisibly through the air.

The receiver was under repair, but training would begin immediately. Did Chen have questions?

He had two.

'May I bring in members of my former team—Comrades Pan and

Ma? Pan is especially skilled in codes. And how will we learn to use the equipment?'

Zeng picked up the telephone and summoned a man named Wang.

Lieutenant Wang Zheng entered—a man roughly Chen's age. He was a Whampoa graduate and, to Chen's astonishment, a former officer of the Nationalist 18th Division. It now became clear why Chen had been promoted to Captain: Wang would report to him. He had also studied at the Nanjing Military Communications Technical School. Captured in January along with ten colleagues, all had since defected. These defectors were now tasked with training the Red Army in radio interception, signal classification, and cipher analysis.

Pan and Ma would join the unit, Zeng assured him. For now, he excused himself, instructing his subordinates to reconvene the following morning. Before leaving, he gestured to the lightning bolt badge.

'It represents radio transmission,' he said. 'From today, you are not merely part of the army. You are now the Radio and Intelligence Communications Group—*Wúxiàndiàn qíngbào hé tōngxìn xiǎozǔ* (无线电情报和通信小组). Most will probably just call you the "Pigeons"—*Gēzi* (鸽子).'

Over a generous breakfast—better than standard army rations, including a boiled egg each—Chen received a briefing on the broader SIGINT network. Wang described how a network of communist wireless operators had been established, primarily in Shanghai's Old City, with some also located in the French Concession. These included recent graduates from the Leningrad Frunze Military Communications School.

The returning Russian-trained operators were now training new recruits in both sophisticated decryption and radio communications. The latter remained particularly dangerous, as the Nationalists, the French, and the British all possessed Marconi–Bellini–Tosi direction-finding systems capable of locating a signal source quickly.

At Ningdu, neither the trainers nor their pupils were tasked with advanced cryptography. However, intercepted messages in the field often required immediate decoding, so operators were expected to handle basic ciphers or relay the material to more specialised personnel. For now, their role was strictly limited to interception and monitoring.

The second function of the Ningdu base was internal: to manage secure communications with Shanghai as needed for message transmission and monitoring.

Two additional sources in Shanghai had contributed to early success. The first was Zhang Shenchuan. By remarkable Nationalist oversight, he had enrolled in a radio school that shared a building with the Nationalist 6th Army's communications centre. There, he secured a night-relief position and was able to copy codes, frequencies, and call signs.

The second source was Li Qiang, head of the 4th Section. He had studied at the Nanyang Road Mining School, where all instruction was in English. This proved helpful, as Li was spearheading the development of a home-grown wireless capability. He sourced parts from the grey market, most of which came with instruction manuals in English. These were translated into Chinese by Hu Chenggong—a former English teacher and one of Chen's comrades. Wang admitted that, upon defecting, he had been astonished by the scale and sophistication of the communist network in Shanghai.

Chen was intrigued.

'So, over what distance can our clandestine operators in Shanghai send and receive messages?'

The answer shocked him.

'They can communicate directly with Moscow through a covert shortwave relay station in Hong Kong—manned by Russians. It's fitted with the most advanced equipment available.'

'So from Ningdu, we can link up with Shanghai and even Moscow via the Hong Kong station?'

'Not yet. We're using captured Nationalist radio sets—short-range, line-of-sight devices best suited to tactical field use. Even if range were improved, transmissions could still be intercepted, and mountain terrain severely degrades signal clarity. The best we can do is transmit encrypted messages step-by-step to a relay station near Shanghai. From there, a trained courier physically carries the message in and out of the city.'

'And enemy detection systems?'

'Also a concern. The Nationalists and their allies do have signal-tracking equipment—especially in and around major cities like Shanghai. Even outside the cities, they've deployed mobile teams and fixed stations in key locations. We can't assume we're safe, even out here. We reduce the risk by frequently changing frequencies during transmission—manually, for now. It buys us a few extra minutes.'

Chen's next question concerned priorities.

'There are several,' Wang replied, 'but in my view, two stand out. First—we cannot run a functioning SIGINT programme with just ten operators, three radios, and two in repair. The next assault will be far larger. We must recruit and train.'

'The second issue,' said Wang, 'is that relying on captured codebooks is dangerous. If the codes are strengthened and we have no officers in place to crack them, we're blind.'

Chen could only partially address that concern. They also discussed the risk of transmitting in the field instead of merely intercepting—a giveaway of position, and of the existence of a mobile network. Chen requested twenty-four hours to consider a response.

The following morning, they met again—but only after Chen had outlined his ideas to Zeng. Zeng, in turn, shared a directive from Zhou Enlai that had arrived the previous week. It called for the training of new SIGINT recruits and the assembly of radios using domestically sourced parts. For Ningdu, Zhou wanted capable, politically conscious operators—men and women, drawn from the ranks of workers and peasants—who could carry both a rifle and an ideology.

'We should focus where we're strongest,' Chen said. 'Can you design an aptitude test—for army personnel or youth with at least secondary school education?'

'I can.'

'Good. You'll also be assisted by trusted Party cadres—teachers, professionals, loyal and respected. They'll help identify your top trainees. How long to train the first batch?'

'Three to four months.'

'For the code-breaking unit, I'll assign you Second Lieutenant

Pan—a Whampoa cadet with a gift for cryptography. But when it comes to avoiding detection—I have no solution.'

'That's not urgent—for now. We'll train using simulated radio traffic: dummy transmissions, nothing real. In the field, we'll only listen and relay intelligence up the chain. But once we go live, the Nationalists will find us—and when they do, they'll strike hard. Spotters, snipers, artillery. We'll have seconds to tear down the gear and disappear—or die with it.'

As the first recruits arrived in Ningdu, Chen was astonished. Half of the dozen entrants were women. The youngest—a girl of fourteen—had scored highest in the aptitude test. On two of the five parts, of a three-hour examination, she had a near perfect score:

SECTION A: MENTAL ARITHMETIC & PATTERN RECOGNITION (30 MINUTES)
Objective: Test thinking speed and accuracy under pressure—similar to what may be needed in the field.

20 quick-fire calculations
- Work out how far a vehicle can travel with a given amount of fuel.
- Use two compass readings to estimate a hidden radio signal's location.
- Decide how far to stand from a damaged transmitter to stay safe.
- Choose how to divide supplies fairly between teams, depending on the terrain and level of danger.

10 pattern-based problems
- Spot hidden number codes in market receipts.
- Rebuild broken picture sequences from training booklets.
- Notice unusual signals buried in background noise.

5 memory tasks
- Remember five-digit codes after waiting three or six minutes.
- Recall passwords seen only briefly.
- Spot a small change in two sets of nearly-matching coordinates.

SECTION B: READING & INTELLIGENCE ANALYSIS (30 MINUTES)
Objective: Understand and explain messages quickly and clearly under time pressure.

Interpret a sample enemy message
- Say what the message means, how urgent it is, and any hidden clues.
- Suggest how we should reply or mislead the enemy.

Find unusual patterns in short messages
- Notice if the same harmless words (like 'parcel' or 'uncle') keep appearing.
- Point out if the writing style suddenly changes, which could mean danger.

Write a short explanation (essay)
- What might happen if someone misses a planned message handover?
- What signs could show someone is pretending to be another agent?

No uniform fit her. She was emaciated, her arms and ankles as delicate as dry reeds. The team pooled their spare garments and stitched together something serviceable.

Wang's forward testing unit had returned to assist with training. One of his men knelt beside the girl and offered her a stick of sugarcane.

'Little sister, would you like a treat?'

To everyone's delight, she gave a small salute.

That evening, the team assembled in the mess hall. The girl sat beside the man who had given her the sugarcane. Dinner was served—steaming rice, vegetables, slivers of pork, and a touch of hot sauce. Her new comrade asked if she knew what it was. She nodded, then admitted she had eaten meat only once a year—during the Lunar Festival.

She devoured the meal, running her tongue along the bowl's edge to catch every last drop.

'Would you like some more?' he asked.

Her face crumpled. She burst into tears. She had just received more meat than in the past two years—and more rice than she had seen in four days.

Chen scratched the back of his neck, thoughtful. Even if the *Gēzi* were restricted to signal monitoring, he had no intention of putting this frail girl near the front. Her contribution would come later.

Despite disliking the restrictions he imposed—especially those limiting movement—he deemed them necessary. All team members were confined to barracks, allowed outside only once a week under armed escort. Meals were communal. Officers had individual rooms—Chen's slightly larger, with a desk, bed, bookcase, and a rack for clothing. Lower-ranking members slept in single-sex dormitories.

Security was essential. Chen tasked Pan and Ma with developing a new communist cipher system while continuing to crack Nationalist codes. It was a gilded cage—but a necessary one.

One new operator caught Chen's eye the moment she arrived—Ruan Daxia. She was two years his junior, a native of Shanghai, and striking. Tall and willowy, with flawless skin and a disarming smile, she stood out—even in uniform. She, too, had noticed her superior: broad-shouldered, confident, striking. During meals and brief outdoor gatherings, the two often found themselves in quiet conversation.

With more recruits arriving, Pan and Ma made rapid progress. Despite improvements in Nationalist encryption, intelligence from scouts and intercepts provided fragments. Captured codebooks added structure.

The Nationalists used a form of Morse adapted for Chinese—numeric telegraphic codes. Each character was assigned a four-digit number. For example, 'attack' (*gōngjī*, 攻击) might be written as 攻 (6342), 击 (7810). Translated into Morse:

6342 became: -....   ...--   ....-   ..---   --...   ---..   .----   -----

The method's security relied entirely on the integrity of the codebooks.

The Communists, meanwhile, were developing an advanced encryption method: one-time cipher pads—pages of random numbers, each used once and then discarded. If generated properly, this method rendered a message unbreakable. The difficulty lay in ensuring the randomness of the numbers. Even so, the resulting security far surpassed that of the Nationalist system.

While Ningdu advanced, Shanghai unravelled. On 26 April, Chen received an urgent summons to Zeng's office. The older man looked exhausted.

'Sit down,' he said. 'We've suffered a serious blow in Shanghai. This is highly confidential—even within your unit. Gu Shunzhang has defected.'

Chen froze. Gu—the head of the Red Squad. Soviet-trained. Ruthless.

'Two days ago, in Wuhan, he was recognised from a photograph and arrested. He pleaded for an audience with Chiang Kai-shek and, in exchange for his life, revealed everything: names, addresses, activities—our entire Shanghai apparatus. Miraculously, most of our top leadership survived.'

In one of the most astonishing operations in CCP history, Qian Zhuangfei—a Communist mole embedded within Nationalist Section

20—had intercepted the report. He had secretly copied Xu Enzeng's personal cipher code and used it to read a transmission from Wuhan to Nanjing detailing Gu's arrest. Emergency alerts were sent to Zhou Enlai, prompting a mass flight to new safe houses—many inside the French Concession, beyond Gu's knowledge.

Lower-level cadres were unlikely to receive word in time. Zeng remained hopeful that Hu Chenggong, Chen's old comrade, had been warned. As for the *Gēzi*, Zeng doubted Gu even knew of their existence. But he could not be certain.

Not long after, Wang Ming departed for the USSR, citing medical reasons. He positioned himself close to Moscow's leadership and left Zhou Enlai in effective command, aided by trusted proxies such as Bo Gu and Kang Sheng. By October, Wang had seemingly taken permanent residence in Moscow—as the CCP's official representative to the Comintern.

The Second Encirclement Campaign began on 1 April 1931. Chiang Kai-shek deployed 200,000 troops—enough, in theory, to annihilate the Communists. This triggered a tense confrontation within the Military Commission between Wang Ming's acolytes and senior army commanders. The latter narrowly prevailed.

The Communists could not defend every corner of their territory. The agreed strategy called for withdrawal from exposed areas like Futian and Guangchang, while repositioning in Longgang and Donggu to avoid encirclement. This bought time to conscript new forces and identify weaknesses in the Nationalist advance. The Red Army correctly anticipated that the 5th Route Army would lead the first attack near Donggu.

Lieutenant Wang and his first cohort of radio graduates were prepared. On 12 May, they intercepted a coded transmission from the 5th Route Army's 28th Division in Futian to the 43rd Division in Ji'an. It detailed an imminent dawn assault and follow-up objectives.

Wang immediately dispatched a scout to Zhu De and Mao, who repositioned their troops under cover of darkness. At daybreak, both

Nationalist units were destroyed. Unaware, the 27th Division moved in to assist—and met the same fate.

On 22 May, the Red Army retook Guangchang, inflicting major losses on the 5th Division. On 31 May, they attacked Jianning and annihilated a brigade of the 56th Division. The campaign was over. The *Gēzi* had played a decisive role. It appeared Gu Shunzhang had not betrayed them.

In Ningdu, the mood was jubilant. Central Command now regarded the *Gēzi* as elite and indispensable.

Hu Chenggong had received timely warning of Gu's defection, along with the address of a safe house in the French Concession but he chose a different path.

He visited a local ironmonger, claiming to act on behalf of his landlady to solve a rat infestation—a familiar issue in Shanghai's seedier districts. The price of strychnine, he complained, was exorbitant. The vendor merely shrugged. The poison was in high demand: wanted Communists, jilted lovers, contract killers, and addicts all sought it.

Hu, an occasional drinker, stopped at another shop for a bottle of *baijiu*. At home, he poured a generous cup, lacking even a shot glass. The first sip made him gag, shivering violently. He sat at his desk and reached for pen and paper—but the words would not come.

Fifteen minutes passed. Another cup. The second was more bearable. After a third, his mind began to drift, and the tormenting questions returned.

How have I reached thirty and failed at everything? I've never had a woman. They all think I'm ugly. I tried to be a good Communist—and failed. I can't go to the French Concession. I broke my promise to those big-nosed foreigners. They'll recognise me. Capture me.

A man's head, split open, oozing blood. The Wuping Bandits wanted to trade me. The corrupt French police wanted to sell me. Is that what I am—a commodity for torture and execution? Even pigs aren't tortured before slaughter. I'm pathetic. A useless virgin.

Maybe I should find a whore. But I'm drunk. What if I can't get it up? Final humiliation.

He poured another drink. The room spun like a top wound with string. His thoughts unravelled.

How many have I seen die—for nothing more than a few coins or a square meal? They weren't believers. They didn't understand our higher ideals. I told the French about the sale of prisoners—to save them.

No. You did it to save yourself.

You betrayed your comrades. Loyal workers. Not a miserable traitor like you. The Party will find out. They'll force a confession out of you. Days of agony in the tiger chair. But this way—this way, I remain undiscovered. Maybe they'll remember me as loyal.

Mr Bei was a brave hero. He died for me. I am loathsome.

The bottle was three-quarters empty. Images turned violent. Thoughts more fractured.

The Nationalists didn't catch me in 1921. But now they know. I'll cheat them in death. Their secret police will roast my flesh. The Green Gang will use a rat-in-a-tube—just like the Cheka's method. The trapped rat will gnaw into my stomach. Then they'll bury me alive.

Liberté, égalité, fraternité. The French have forgotten its meaning. But we haven't. Save the peasants. Save the workers. Save China.

He began a letter: *Dear Baba, Mama, and Little Sister…* He stopped.

He could not explain this life. This failure.

He poured more *baijiu*, stirred in the powder, and drank. The taste was worse than the foulest Chinese medicine.

At first, only nausea. Then his jaw locked. A violent spasm gripped his spine.

Agonising convulsions followed—his limbs jerking, back arching against the chair, foam spilling from his lips.

The pain was excruciating—every muscle lit by misfiring nerves, clenched tight as if wired to a live current.

Fully conscious, he endured each wave as his body seized again and again.

After nearly twenty minutes, his lungs gave out. He died twisted in the chair, beside the shattered cup.

The highest-ranking casualty of Gu's betrayal was Xiang Zhongfa.

Many in the Party already viewed him as politically unreliable. Disillusioned, he had drifted into a life of comfort and indulgence. On 21 June, he was arrested at a jewellery shop in the French Concession, accompanied by his mistress—a cabaret dancer. Under interrogation, he confessed readily. Though Chiang Kai-shek issued a pardon, it arrived too late. Xiang had already been executed.

Another high-priority target was Li Kenong—a man who would one day shape Chen's destiny. Unmasked as the mole who had infiltrated Nationalist military intelligence in 1929, Li fled for his life and reached the Jiangxi base in August 1931. There, he was appointed Executive Director of the Central State Political Bureau before being seconded to the 1st Front Army as Director of the Political Security Bureau.

Chapter 21: Ruijin, Jiangxi, China, 1931

On 26 October 1931, Chen instructed his *Gēzi* to start packing several of their radio sets. Then, on 30 October, he announced that the following day they would attend a special event in Ruijin, leaving behind only a skeleton radio crew. They were to travel one hundred kilometres southeast of Ningdu, and the following morning they set off on foot, as the road between the two was still incomplete. Soldiers accompanied them to help carry the radio equipment. They spent the first night at Xiajie and the second at Luofang.

They had still only covered half the distance when, the next morning, they were met by three almost-new Minsheng 75 trucks: two for the *Gēzi* and one for the soldiers and radio gear. Some soldiers were instructed to carry the most sensitive components in their hands to prevent damage. As the tailgates were lowered, a wave of excited chatter broke out—none of Chen's team had ever ridden in a motor vehicle. Daxia managed to secure a place on a bench seat next to Chen.

The ride was alarming at first. The truck bounced violently over the uneven earthen road, with only brief relief on short stretches of crushed limestone. The passengers clung to one another as if their lives depended on it. Chen found himself clutching a laughing, screaming Daxia. It was their first physical contact.

As they arrived in the town centre, they saw Ruijin was bustling with activity. Several more trucks were parked nearby, alongside a menacing Vickers Mark VI machine gun carrier and trailer. Chen told Daxia he believed it had been captured from the Nationalists. He informed his team that volunteers would show them to their quarters and that, for the next few days, they were free to explore. Before leaving, he asked Daxia to meet him in three hours beside a large, partially completed building. One of the volunteers then led Chen to a substantial structure in Yeping Village, reserved for officers, where he was given a simple but private room.

At the rendezvous, the building's purpose became clear—it was to be a central bank. To one side stood a roped-off display, with a long queue waiting to peer into glass cabinets. While they waited, Chen told Daxia he had visited Ruijin in 1927, though he spoke only briefly of the failed Nanchang Uprising. She could see that even the memory unsettled him.

Eventually, they reached the front. Inside the first cabinet was a sign: '*Proposed New Currency*'. It was no ordinary bank—it had its own mint. Rumours had long circulated, but here was tangible proof. Three types of currency were on display: a brownish paper note bearing Lenin's portrait, printed with '*Chinese Soviet Republic National Bank*', and copper coins marked the same way. But the third type was the most intriguing: a pile of silver dollars, similar to Mexican *pesos*, with no communist markings.

'These are meant for circulation in Nationalist areas,' Chen said. Daxia was impressed.

In the next cabinet, a series of proposed new postage stamps were displayed. Chen's eyes lit up—he might be able to send letters to his family inside the Soviet.

As they wandered through streets adorned with red flags and banners, they passed communal food pots and wall verses declaring Party slogans. It became clear this was more than a celebration—it was a grand, strategic statement. New roads radiated out from the town, one of which now connected to Tingzhou, opening access to the Tingjiang River and the world beyond. Chen suspected the USSR had made a significant donation.

They walked to another section of Yeping Village and found the completed Delegates' Assembly Hall. Its steps led up to a broad entrance, crowned by a red star with a globe at its centre. Yellow hammer-and-sickle emblems flanked the doorway, and two more red stars stood on either side. They stood in silence, absorbing the gravity of what lay ahead.

As they turned to leave, three men emerged from the building. Chen immediately recognised one—Song Liqiang, his former political mentor, now one of the 610 chosen delegates. They embraced, spoke rapidly, and almost forgot their manners until Song asked to be introduced to Daxia.

'I am pleased to meet you, Ms Ruan, and delighted that my old friend Chen has found such a beautiful young girlfriend.'

She blushed, which only made her more beautiful. Realising his presumption, Song added quickly,

'I hope we can speak again when I'm not burdened with delegate duties.'

They agreed. Song expected the congress to last at least two weeks, during which a constitution would be drafted and new laws enacted. He had been assigned to the section outlining that all ethnic minorities had the right to choose whether to join the Republic. Chen was not surprised—Song was suited to such work.

As they parted, Song said gently,

'I was sorry to hear about Hu Chenggong—such a tragic end.'

Chen bowed his head and nodded.

As the sun faded, red lanterns were lit, food scents filled the air, and the streets grew crowded. No alcohol was served—discipline in the Red Army was paramount. Chen and Daxia found a quiet corner. He lit a cigarette, and she asked,

'Chen, don't you want me to be your girlfriend?'

He looked uneasy, still rattled by Song's comment. Then he met her eyes.

'Daxia, you're the most beautiful and intelligent woman I've ever met. I worry I'm not good enough for you.'

'Well, Minghe, why don't you kiss me and find out?'

Chen leaned in. But just before their lips met, she pulled away.

'That smell of cigarette smoke is disgusting.'

They continued walking. Chen was enthralled by her. Later, she asked about Hu, but all he said was,

'He was a hero who died for our revolution. There will be many more like him.'

The mood darkened. Daxia sensed she had pushed too far but also recognised the depth of Chen's thoughts. It drew her in. As they parted, she said,

'Minghe, let's meet tomorrow after work. You're gentle and brilliant—and handsome too. But please, clean your teeth so I can kiss you properly.'

It was the last cigarette Chen smoked for many years.

The *Gezi* were tasked with establishing a secure radio station to monitor Nationalist transmissions during the celebrations. The work was completed in a day, with nine operators assigned rotating shifts. Electricity was supplied by a 24-hour generator. Chen visited daily but had time to himself.

That evening, Chen invited Daxia to his quarters. He wasn't sure if it was permitted but no one challenged them. They sat on the bed and spoke quietly. Chen told her what little he knew of Hu's death. Daxia moved closer, relieved to find no trace of tobacco. They kissed. For Chen, in that moment, the world narrowed to the softness of her mouth and the sense that something rare was being offered. Then she asked if he wanted to see her naked, and invited him to do the same.

She laid a small packet on the bed as she undressed. In the flickering lamplight, her body looked even more beautiful than Chen had imagined—small, perfect breasts, long legs, and a neat triangle of hair.

She admired Chen's erection and began to rub it, then reached for the packet.

'Do you know what this is?' she asked. 'Have you ever used one?'

He hadn't. The label was in Russian: *Barishnikov Product No. 2 – Medium Size Condom* (Баришников. Изделие №2 — презерватив среднего размера). He didn't mention he could read it. She helped him roll it on. It was thick rubber, dry, dusted with foul-smelling talc. It didn't matter—she was ready, and he entered her easily. Though the condom dulled sensation, they both climaxed with satisfaction. Chen knew she had experience; it showed in the way she handled the situation—swift, sure, without hesitation.

They lay in silence, holding each other. Then Daxia said,

'I didn't know you'd be so big, Minghe. Next time, I'll order a larger one. This was the medium size in the Product Number Two range.'

'Did I hurt you?'

'Not at all. You were wonderful.'

He smiled. 'Perhaps we should investigate products one, three, four, and five?'

She started giggling.

'What's so funny?'

'Product one is a rubber gas mask. I dread to think what the others might be.'

It was late, and Daxia had to return before anyone in her dormitory noticed her absence.

The following day, they wandered hand in hand through Ruijin, careful not to draw attention. That afternoon, they returned to Chen's quarters and made love twice more. The second time, Daxia aroused him again by running her tongue along his scrotum and the base of his shaft before mounting him, her smooth legs curled around him. Despite the wrong-sized Barishnikov, Chen did not last long.

At one point, he asked her gently why she had chosen to make love so soon.

Her answer was both candid and profound.

'First, I needed it—especially from such a handsome man. But when you told me Hu's story, I realised something else. If we're risking our lives for a future that may never come, we should at least know what happiness feels like—before they ask us to die for it.'

They followed this pattern every night, save for one: the night of the parade.

On 7 November, a new country—the Chinese Soviet Republic—was born, covering nearly 30,000 km². Mao was appointed Chairman of the Central Executive Committee and Chairman of the Council of the People's Commissars. Zhu De became Chairman of the Central Revolutionary Military Committee, with Mao as a member. Yet Chen understood where true power now lay: with Zhou Enlai, who had secured the chairmanship of the Central Committee in absentia while remaining in Shanghai.

Though Mao was the public face of the revolution, he had lost control of the Party and the army. Still, in Moscow, the newspapers were filled with pictures of President Mao. The civil administration was to be based in Ruijin, while the military headquarters would remain in Ningdu.

That night, a spectacular parade was held. 10,000 troops marched past a podium where the seven most senior appointees stood, waving and clapping. If Mao felt wounded by his diminished role, he did not show it. Strings of electric lights powered by a generator illuminated the scene, though plans for microphones and loudspeakers had failed—such devices would never have reached a crowd this size anyway.

The soldiers marched in tight formation, carrying torches and lanterns decorated with red stars, hammers, and sickles. Once the march ended and the fireworks exploded overhead, there was enough food—and this time, alcohol—for all. Minghe and Daxia kissed, holding each other close until around 3.00 a.m. As Chen staggered back to his quarters, he could not help but wonder how Chiang Kai-shek would respond. Whatever came next, it would surely be extremely violent.

Three days later, the *Gēzi* returned to Ningdu by the same route and the same mixture of walking and riding. Though the mountain air was sharp, their padded jackets kept them warm. Chen was mostly left in peace with his new companion, keeping well out of earshot as they talked in low voices.

Daxia had grown up in Shanghai, the daughter of a surgeon at Renji Hospital. Her family was moderately wealthy and deeply traditional. She had shown great promise, particularly in mathematics, and there was no doubt she would pursue higher education. In her first year at St John's University in Shanghai, she met a young man who introduced her—gently at first—to Marxist ideas. Over time, once she was convinced, he encouraged her to join the communist cause and train as a radio operator—part of the future, he said. She excelled. But when her father discovered her secret, she was cast out and never finished her studies. The young man had been her first lover, but once her training began, he left her.

She had come to Ruijin to begin a new life, and was quickly recruited by the SIGINT unit—she already had experience.

For balance, Chen told her a brief, honest account of his past with Hehua.

The problem upon returning to Ningdu was the lack of privacy. They had little time off together, and Chen's room was part of his office. She had no access. After a month of frustration and strict regulations, Daxia suggested a solution.

Chen requested a meeting with Zeng for 7 December. Though Zeng was now based in Ruijin, he continued to visit Ningdu regularly. During the meeting, Chen announced his intention to marry. Zeng showed no surprise—neither at the name of the bride nor her role on Chen's staff. These marriages were common in times like these—some for love, others for security.

Zeng had spoken with Daxia several times and liked her. He had already been considering married quarters and noted that couples within the *Gezi* posed far less risk. Before the meeting ended, he added,

'I need you to bring to my immediate attention any further signals from Shanghai regarding the gold shipment.'

A message had arrived the previous day. A shipment of twelve gold bars sent from Ruijin a month earlier had not yet reached its destination. The journey had been broken into six stages. At each stage, a trusted leader was given a locked box containing a puzzle piece—about the size of a draughts piece—with the word *kuài* (swift—快) engraved upon it. Each leader received a code to unlock the box and was told to retain the piece until a Ruijin courier collected it. The transfer was only complete when all seven pieces were returned.

The gold was urgently needed to fund safe houses, food, and rent for Party operatives in Shanghai. Over the following days, four more increasingly anxious transmissions arrived. Finally, on 22 December, the six pieces were assembled—only to discover the final one missing. The shipment had been stolen. The sixth courier had vanished.

Chen knew what this meant. Without that gold, comrades in Shanghai would soon be abandoned. Deaths would follow. Then rumours. Then fractures.

Chen and Ruan Daxia's wedding was set for three weeks later. A quiet celebration with close colleagues was planned, after which they would visit his family *tulou*. But on the day itself, Zeng quietly withdrew as witness—an unexpected guest had arrived.

A short, slim man appeared, wearing a red Chinese opera mask—the fierce face of Guan Yu. A porter followed with a basket: pork belly, chicken, beer, yellow wine, and *baijiu*. The masked man removed his disguise.

It was Zhou Enlai.

He smiled broadly and gave a short, warm speech, praising the couple's loyalty and diligence. Then the celebration began.

Later, Zhou picked up a bottle of *baijiu* and two glasses and approached Daxia with a twinkle in his eye.

'May I borrow your husband for a moment?'

They walked to Chen's office. Zhou murmured a quiet toast in Russian, raising his glass.

'You never gave away our secret, did you?'

'No. Not even Daxia knows.'

Chen then told him about the Barishnikov condoms. The room trembled with laughter, quickly rising to a full-throated roar.

Once they caught their breath, Zhou leaned closer.

'As you've probably seen in the transmissions, governing is as hard as commanding an army. Since my arrival, I've found too many signs of behaviour that contradict Party discipline. Factions are forming—especially between the army and the administration.'

Chen nodded. He knew Mao had made many enemies within the military ranks, despite stepping back from his command.

'If you intercept any messages suggesting these cracks are widening into a schism, make sure they reach me and me alone. I'm arranging a motorcycle and sidecar for you, in case you ever need to reach me in Ruijin quickly.'

Chen agreed. Zhou clapped him on the back.

'What a wonderful wedding!'

Chapter 22: Japanese State of Manchukuo, 1932–1934

Towards the end of 1932, two events created serious problems for Rodzaevsky.

In September, he returned home to find Lydia reading a letter from Natasha Mamedov, filled with vivid descriptions of émigré life in a verdant corner of the United States. But for Rodzaevsky, the most striking revelation was that Vonsiatsky and Lev Mamedov had resigned from the Brotherhood of Russian Truth. Fortuitously, their departure had come just before a Soviet sting operation targeting the Brotherhood's plot to sabotage oil pipelines. The organisation promptly collapsed.

Now, the two men were contemplating the creation of a new fascist political movement. Rodzaevsky was uncertain. Neither had followers or real experience—but if properly guided, they might yet be moulded into his global operations, with himself, of course, as supreme leader.

Relations with the *Tokumu Kikan* had marginally improved. They were beginning to see some utility in the RFP. Out of curiosity more than necessity, Rodzaevsky contacted Miyake—now more accessible—and asked whether Japanese intelligence had any information on Vonsiatsky. A month later, they met discreetly. Miyake brought a slim file—seven pages at most—containing a few American press clippings. Rodzaevsky caught his first glimpse of the man in question, albeit upside down. The pages were in Japanese, with pencilled highlights and a rudimentary flowchart. Rodzaevsky braced for a verbal summary, knowing parts would inevitably be withheld.

Miyake began,

'Your man is of little importance to us.'

Seven pages—not hundreds. That told Rodzaevsky everything.

'He's something of a fraud—playboy, exhibitionist—but his provenance is not entirely without merit. His grandfather, a minor aristocrat, was decorated by Tsar Alexander II in 1863. His father led the Russian police forces in Warsaw but was assassinated in 1910. I have records showing the son at the Moscow Military Preparatory School. He graduated in 1916, and then joined a Hussar regiment. After the

Revolution, he vanished, then re-emerged penniless, wounded in early 1920. A family named Muromsky took him in. Their daughter, Lyuba, nursed him back to health. There was a shotgun wedding—a Russian Orthodox ceremony held within a month. But there was a complication. Lyuba is Jewish.'

Rodzaevsky exploded,

'Что ты говоришь? Это абсолютно незаконно в православной церкви!'
(*What are you saying? That is absolutely illegal in the Orthodox Church!*)
Miyake coughed discreetly.
'Shall I continue?'
Po-faced, Rodzaevsky nodded.
'We have discharge records from Gallipoli. He then turns up in France—without his wife. He meets the extremely wealthy American, Marion Ream, in a Paris jazz club. By then, he's working backstage at the Folies-Bergère. Though still legally married, he appears to have bigamously wed Ream in February 1922 and later gained American citizenship. She was over twenty years his senior, which raised eyebrows even in Paris. Some speculated it was a transaction—wealth and a passport in exchange for youth and novelty.'

Miyake handed over a *New York Times* clipping dated 23 November 1922. The Russian Orthodox ecclesiastical court in New York had ruled the marriage to Lyuba invalid—though the Japanese believed a substantial bribe had made the matter quietly disappear. For Miyake, and most Japanese officers, bigamy was a serious cultural taboo.

None of it brought Rodzaevsky any comfort. Still, he had the presence of mind to ask,

'So—where does that leave our relations? You surely can't support two fascist parties?'

Miyake looked coldly at him.

'I'm not sure. My superiors in Tokyo will decide. Besides, there is a new man on the world stage—very different from the *Il Duce* you seem to admire.'

'Adolf Hitler?'

'Yes.'

'Hitler is antisemitic, like you. But he also considers you a Slav—sub-human scum.'

That hurt.

The struggle between the two fascist leaders had begun. Rodzaevsky was better known, particularly across Asia. He had credibility. Vonsiatsky, as an American citizen, enjoyed free speech—and seemingly limitless funds.

The first blows were struck in the press. In October 1933, Rodzaevsky launched *Nash Put* (*Our Way* – *наш Путь*) from Harbin, with global RFP ambitions. At Lydia's suggestion, he also penned a private letter inviting Vonsiatsky to Harbin. But his rival had already acted. *The Fascist* (*фашистская*), launched in August from Thompson, Connecticut, was already in circulation. It served as the flagship publication of the All-Russian Fascist Organisation (VFO), the new party Vonsiatsky had founded in the United States. Lavishly funded, it was distributed internationally alongside other VFO propaganda. Its pages carried reports of sabotage and uprisings inside the USSR, allegedly from embedded correspondents. The tone was cautious, not overtly antisemitic—but by then, U.S. authorities had taken notice.

The Japanese, seeking unity, proposed a merger of the two factions. Rodzaevsky was appalled. In his view, there could be only one true defender of White Russia.

In early March 1934, Miyake made a rare personal visit to RFP headquarters. Tokyo had brokered a summit between the rival leaders—scheduled to take place at the RFP offices in the Japanese capital. Rodzaevsky and Matkovsky were to accompany him. But Rodzaevsky looked so dishevelled that Miyake handed him a wad of high-denomination Manchukuo notes and instructed him to buy two suits and several shirts.

The three men departed on 19 March. The journey was unforgettable: five days from Harbin to Dalian by train, followed by a steamship crossing to Yokohama. Miyake had arranged private cabins and a room for strategic discussion. Though not warm, the atmosphere was businesslike. It became clear that neither side trusted Vonsiatsky. Neither wanted a 'Russian Yankee'—a decadent dandy—representing global Russian fascism. They also agreed that Ataman Semenov, while politically archaic, must be kept close. His Cossacks could still prove useful in any future assault on Soviet territory.

Rodzaevsky and Matkovsky pressed for greater intelligence-sharing—on the USSR, on Germany, and on Japanese strategy. They argued they had already demonstrated loyalty and discretion. Miyake agreed, and disclosed further details on Vonsiatsky. One topic, however, remained untouched: funding.

Vonsiatsky had announced in *The Fascist* that he, Marion, and Kunle, a trusted associate from Central Asia, were embarking on a global tour. Kobe would be their first port of call. Mamedov remained in Connecticut to manage affairs. After a grand send-off in New York, the VFO team headed west.

Upon arrival in Kobe, Vonsiatsky delivered a flamboyant speech, claiming to command 150,000 stormtroopers, saboteurs, and agents ready to support Japan against the USSR. The Japanese delegates exchanged glances—expressionless but unconvinced.

The summit began on 24 March and lasted nine days. Miyake departed early to report to his superiors, while Marion went shopping—purchasing several crates of exquisite Meiji-period *objets d'art* to ship back to the United States. The Harbin delegation needn't have worried. They found Vonsiatsky, frequently hungover, and Kunle both pliable—especially the former, who only fully engaged when his ego was flattered. In the final week of March, as negotiations dragged on, the Americans displayed genuine interest only when the conversation turned to an attack on the USSR. When asked about drafting a party constitution, they seemed indifferent.

The *Harbinskii* secured all but two of their key demands. Vonsiatsky was appointed Chairman of the Executive Committee of the newly unified All-Russian Fascist Party (VFP). Rodzaevsky, however, would serve as General Secretary—retaining real power. Harbin was to become the new global headquarters.

Two issues remained unresolved. First, Vonsiatsky adamantly refused to deal with Semenov, at one point shouting that he was 'an uneducated bandit and train robber'. Eventually, he grudgingly agreed to tolerate him—from a distance. Second, there was Rodzaevsky's virulent antisemitism, which Vonsiatsky found abhorrent—and which even Matkovsky disliked. The matter was shelved.

Vonsiatsky also pledged a vast personal donation: at least $500,000 to the new party. For Rodzaevsky, it meant improved living conditions and the possibility of establishing a modest fund for little Yuri's future.

Following a formal celebration and the ceremonial introduction of the new constitution at the New Grand Hotel in Yokohama, the Harbin delegation returned via the Korean rail network, stopping briefly in Dalian.

Upon arrival in Harbin, Rodzaevsky delivered an impassioned speech at the station, thanking the Japanese for their unwavering support in the struggle against communism.

Originally, the plan had been for the VFP Executive to travel together to Harbin—but at the last moment, the Manchukuo Ministry of Foreign Affairs refused the Americans' visa applications. It was a humiliating blow—especially for Miyake—and yet another sign that Manchukuo was beginning to act independently of Tokyo. Miyake had no authority over the ministry.

On 7 April, the Americans changed their plans and sailed for Shanghai.

Only one man could resolve the matter. Reluctantly, Rodzaevsky turned to Semenov, who pulled strings through old contacts. Ironically, the 'uneducated bandit and train robber' proved the most effective fixer.

After weeks of delays and uncertainty, the Americans finally disembarked in Dalian on 22 April. Vonsiatsky gave a speech, then continued to the capital, Xinjing, before finally arriving in Harbin on 26 April 1934.

What awaited them exceeded all expectations.

Blackshirts in full regalia stood in formation beside the Musketeers and fascist youth and women's groups. Semenov had sent a ceremonial detachment of Cossacks in their winter uniforms—green coats trimmed with yellow piping, yellow-striped trousers, fur hats, and sabres glinting at their sides. Municipal police were deployed across the square in case of unrest. Several thousand White Russians surged behind the cordon, straining to glimpse the new *Amerikanskii* leader. Alongside them stood curious Chinese—and, hidden in the crowd were a Red Russian agent, an American intelligence officer, and a Chinese communist operative.

The American government's concern was understandable. On 16 November the previous year, after Roosevelt's victory over Hoover, the United States had formally recognised the USSR. Meanwhile, Vonsiatsky's antics had become increasingly provocative. After a series of choreographed dinners, patriotic speeches, and staged parades, the Americans left Harbin on 8 May to continue their tour—Germany, Italy, France and Eastern Europe.

Later that summer, in Berlin, Vonsiatsky delivered a well-attended address. But the Nazis were unimpressed. By then, they were already considering banning the VFP entirely.

Rodzaevsky had reached the summit of his political career—but something was beginning to unravel. Vonsiatsky's looming shadow, the stifling air of home with a screaming infant, Lydia's increasing distance, and the creeping sense that he was a mere pawn of the Japanese—all of it began to sour his mood. Lydia, too, withdrew.

One evening, Kostya returned home to find she had made a stew. The mutton was greasy, gelatinous, reeking faintly of rancid fat. The potatoes—half-rotten—were puckered and tangled with sprouting shoots. The bread, days old, had the texture of adulterated flour—stretched, perhaps, with sawdust by some crooked baker. He stared at the meal, nausea rising.

He shoved the plate aside with a snarl, barely able to meet her eyes.

'What is this filth? Are you trying to poison me?'

He stormed out, leaving Lydia in tears. The truth was, she had done her best. The meagre allowance he provided made anything better impossible.

Another night, his temper flared again. Lydia was playing Max

Bruch's *Kol Nidrei* on the violin—its mournful tones drifting through the cramped flat. It was too much.

'Stop that Jewish music!' he shouted.

Lydia flinched, but did not move. She lowered the bow slowly, her fingers still resting on the strings. She felt the silence settle into her bones, as if her body itself had given up.

Then came the final blow.

Kostya was home when Lydia noticed Yuri's rising temperature. The boy's forehead burned. Still, he reached up from his cot and whimpered,

'Baba... baba.'

They rushed him to the hospital, where he was admitted immediately. A senior doctor—an admirer of the newly formed VFP—entered the examination room solemnly.

'I'm afraid it's typhoid. The child's lack of responsiveness is especially troubling.'

Lydia's voice shook. 'What are his chances?'

'Not good, not for one so young.'

'Is there any medicine?'

'There are experimental drugs—but they're not available here.'

'Where can they be found?'

'In the United States.'

That was when Kostya snapped. He seized the doctor by the throat and slammed him against the wall.

'Then have them flown in—immediately—or you won't survive. Do you understand?'

Lydia had never seen her husband so violent. The medicine was shipped from San Francisco—but it arrived too late.

Yuri Rodzaevsky died on 23 June 1934.

It did not happen all at once. But as Lydia wept beside the cot, and Kostya stood frozen—his fists still clenched—they both knew it in their bones.

It was not the end—but it was the moment they began to live apart in the same room.

Chapter 23: Ruijin, Jiangxi, China, 1932

By the end of 1932, Chen graduated from an unusual institution just before the Nationalists launched a new attack. After arriving at the Jiangxi base in August, one of Li Kenong's key legacies was the establishment of a spy school during his tenure as Executive Director of the Central State Political Bureau in Ningdu. The school was headed by Qian Zhuangfei, another escapee from Shanghai who had fled just in time. Most delegates attended course modules that fit around their other duties. Entry was selective: preference was given to those who were unmarried or not in a serious relationship, due to the high risks involved. Other desirable traits included logical reasoning, composure under pressure, and quick thinking.

Chen was both an instructor and a pupil, frequently teaching radio communications and coded transmissions. With his experience infiltrating Chiang Kai-shek's operations, Qian taught the essential skills for infiltration and intelligence gathering. The curriculum also included the use of an Arsenal-Kyiv miniature camera, driving, and lectures on political geography and history. The most gruelling exercise was a two-day simulated interrogation, designed by Li Kenong, who had conducted many real ones. Trainees were slapped but not tortured, although their mental health often suffered temporarily.

The second part of the course involved specialised break-out modules. One focused on language skills in either Russian or English. Fluency was not the aim—rather, the lessons were practical, covering how to buy a railway ticket or read a street sign. Naturally, Chen chose English and excelled. He also topped the class in self-defence, which centred on *gong fu*, a discipline he had mastered as a child. He was equally proficient at shooting.

During the English course, he encountered a female trainee from a separate, ultra-secret group—one so clandestine that even Chen had not heard of it. His discovery of its purpose, through charm and strategic leverage of his rank, demonstrated his growing skill as a spy. The woman was swiftly expelled and deemed unreliable. Chen learned that she had been attending courses at similar to those nicknamed *Sparrow School* in

Russia—a reference to State School 4 in Kazan, near Moscow. Among participants, the Chinese programme was jokingly referred to as the *Mata Hari School of Economics*.

This covert training took place in a separate house away from the main military compound. Its director had recruited a minor Shanghai film actress who had embraced the communist cause and now taught the arts of seduction and espionage. Curious—and slightly embarrassed—Chen enquired further. He discovered that trainees practised initiating contact in bars and other public places, honing their seduction techniques on one another. There was even a bedroom section where they rehearsed sexual encounters, with female participants trained to simulate orgasm—each session filmed for later analysis to refine technique. A few volunteers explored same-sex seduction, revealing homosexuality as a powerful tool for coercion—an area explored in detail.

Within a month, this controversial section was shut down. Li Kenong, upon discovering its true nature, swiftly reported it. One of his superior's red lines had been crossed. Zhou Enlai had always been resolute: Communist Party members must never serve as sparrows and were to remain chaste and virtuous—unlike the Russians, who harboured no such moral constraints.

By October 1932, the Nationalists had obliterated most of the outlying Communist bases in Hunan and western Hubei, as well as a major stronghold at the junction of Anhui, Henan, and Hubei, forcing Zhang Guotao and his 84,000-strong army into Sichuan. When attention turned to Jiangxi, Mao, serving as Army Commissar, hesitated, believing he was outgunned—an understandable caution that clashed with prevailing Comintern doctrine. Mao had never been doctrinaire like Wang Ming; he preferred to poke, prod, and depend on guerrilla warfare—tactics that, while controversial at the time, would later prove prescient.

Matters came to a head at a meeting in Ningdu on 5 October. With Zhou Enlai in the chair, political and military leaders present, and with Bo Gu's consent from Shanghai, Mao was unanimously dismissed. He made two desperate attempts to send messages to Moscow from Ningdu. Zhou read them locally, while Comintern representative Arthur Ewert received them in Shanghai and chose to forward them to Moscow via a painfully slow courier. It was a rare display of local defiance. Zhou Enlai was appointed to replace Mao. On 12 October, Mao left Ruijin for medical treatment in Tingzhou and did not return until February 1933.

In January 1933, Bo Gu and German Comintern adviser Otto Braun (*Lǐ Dé*—李德) arrived in Ruijin from Shanghai, forming a new triumvirate with Zhou Enlai, who had been based there since late 1931. Zhou retained political leadership of the Red Army as commissar, with Zhu De remaining its commander-in-chief. Bo, following Comintern instructions, was tasked with repairing ties with Mao — still sidelined in Tingzhou, his return to frontline leadership uncertain.

The Fourth Encirclement Campaign against the Chinese Soviet Republic in Jiangxi was a Pyrrhic victory. Though the Communists repelled the Nationalists, the enemy's strategy had changed. In January 1933, 500,000 Nationalist troops advanced on the 70,000-strong 1st Front Army. This time, when Nationalists captured a town, they left behind garrisons and refrained from pursuing the Red Army into open terrain.

In one of the earliest battles, the Communists attempted to take Nanfeng in the Fu River region but failed. On 22 February, they staged a feint at Xingfengjie, regrouped, and set a trap. On 26 February, they annihilated two Nationalist divisions, capturing both commanders. On 21 March, the Red Army surprised and destroyed the Nationalist 11th Division, then mauled the 9th Division in a follow-up attack. Altogether, the Communists killed 20,000 and captured 10,000—but what followed was ominous.

The Nationalists retreated only far enough to construct blockhouses—permanent armed structures. From then on, the Red Army hurled itself repeatedly at these fortifications with no effect and suffered mounting losses.

The Fifth Encirclement Campaign was a disaster. This time, there would be no counter-encirclement.

On 7 October 1934, Chen was in Ningdu when an urgent message arrived: a beggar in Ruijin was demanding to see Zhou Enlai, claiming to have vital secret information. Chen summoned the dispatch rider with a sidecar, and they set off at once. The engine howled as they bounced over rough tracks south of the town, only gaining speed once they reached the start of a made-up road.

Despite the conditions, they made it to Ruijin in just under three hours. Chen's legs were numb by the time he climbed out, his coat streaked with dust and grit.

Uncertain how to proceed, the local police had searched the man for weapons, found none, and placed him in a cell. He was brought to an interview room, with a guard posted outside. The beggar was filthy, his mouth bleeding and his face swollen from apparent injury. Chen began to question him.

'What's your name?' he asked.

'Xiang Yunian,' the beggar replied.

'Where have you come from?'

'De'an.'

'That's near Kuling—Chiang Kai-shek's headquarters?'

'That is correct.'

'And how did you manage to get here with this supposed information?'

'I walked.'

'You crossed the mountains alone?'

'That's right—no food and little water.'

It seemed unlikely to Chen. The mountains were mosquito-ridden and tiger-infested, with no paths and, in places, treacherous drops into roaring rivers below.

'And when you reached the Nationalist checkpoints, how did you get through?'

'I pretended to be a teacher. I hid important information inside four dictionaries in my bundle, with a toothbrush, powder, a cup, and a few clothes placed on top.'

'And were you stopped at the checkpoint and asked questions?'

'I was—by Second Lieutenant Bai Jun. His first question was whether I spoke Hakka. I told him I did, and that I was from Liancheng. That made things easier, and I was allowed to pass.'

Chen was surprised by this. The Liancheng *tulous*, located just north of his own, were familiar to him. He switched to Fujian Hakka, and the supposed teacher replied in the same dialect.

'Was the information in the dictionaries?'

'Yes. But there were so many Nationalist troops beyond the checkpoint that I took cover and threw them away. Then, I took a rock, smashed my front teeth in, and made myself look as dishevelled as possible. Whenever I was stopped, I explained that I was just a poor man who had met robbers on the road, who had beaten me up and taken what few coins I had. I received mostly sympathetic looks.'

'And what was in the dictionaries?'

'That information is for Zhou Enlai only.'

'You must give me something to get you before him.'

'Please tell him that the information comes from Mo Xiong.'

Chen had never heard of him but summoned a runner to explain the situation to Zhou. Within twenty minutes, the runner was back, breathless, and said,

'You must both come with me at once. It is extremely urgent.'

Chen and Xiang were ushered into Zhou's office. Zhou offered them seats, though he chose to remain standing. Chen summarised the events so far. Then Zhou asked,

'How did you get the information from Mo Xiong into the dictionaries?'

'My *Teke* cell, consisting of four people, worked night and day to copy all the documents marked with the blue "*Top Secret*" stamp that Mo Xiong gave us.'

'So the information is all lost?'

'Not entirely. I made a summary on fine rice paper.'

Xiang took off his left shoe, and in the sole was a piece of paper, which he handed to Zhou. As Zhou read it, his bushy eyebrows quivered, and his face paled. When Chen asked whether he should leave, Zhou told him to remain seated and, with a cracked voice and tears in his eyes, said,

'Comrade Xiang, your bravery is astounding. You are a true hero of our revolution and have saved countless lives. I cannot thank you enough.'

Zhou then called for an orderly to escort Xiang to the hospital and turned his attention to Chen.

'Mo Xiong is my most important informant. He is Commander-in-Chief of the Fourth District in Jiangxi and has managed to place several spies close to Chiang Kai-shek. He was a rare and genuine "walk-in"— he approached us. He wanted to join the Communist Party, but I insisted he was safer working from the outside. You had better read this.'

Operation Iron Barrel: Conceived by the German military adviser to Chiang Kai-shek, von Seeckt. We will encircle the enemy and advance 1.7 li daily to reduce their occupied area gradually. A wire mesh will be placed every li, and for every ten li, a new line of blockhouses will be constructed, close enough to interconnect by covering fire. Advances should total at least 50 li each month until Ruijin is captured within six months. At that point, 300 barbed-wire fences and 30 bunker lines will surround the town. Mines will be laid between each blockhouse for those not killed in the crossfire. If the enemy attempts to break out, we will deploy our rapid reaction force using 1,000 new American military trucks to stifle any such effort.

No wonder Zhou looked disturbed. The gravity of the situation was beginning to dawn on him. Chen absorbed the text and asked quietly,

Is this the end?'

'Perhaps. I'm not sure. But we must evacuate quickly. You are not to speak of this to anyone.'

'Shouldn't we inform Chairman Mao?'

'Under no circumstances. I do not need interference at this critical moment.'

The structure of the Red Army had changed little since 1930, still comprising three armies: the 1st Front Army (Jiangxi Soviet), the 2nd under He Long (Hunan–Hebei), and the 4th under Zhang Guotao (Sichuan–Shaanxi). Thus began what would later be called The Long March. But who should go, and who should stay?

Zhou Enlai devised the evacuation in strict secrecy. Even Chen was privy only to its broadest outlines. Though he still encountered Zhou occasionally, it was his immediate superior, Zeng, who summoned him on 5 October. The conversation was harrowing.

'Comrade Chen, you are one of the few aware that we will evacuate our Soviet base. Certain preparations must be made. We cannot take the larger radio sets—the batteries and spares are too heavy. You must take a small group—perhaps seven people, including Daxia. When the time comes, I will need volunteers to remain behind and destroy the large equipment. We will only take the smaller sets. Wang, Pan, and Ma are obvious candidates, but I will leave the final decision to you. Do we still have contact with the 2nd and 4th Route Armies by radio?'

'I have radio operators in both. We can reach Zhang Guotao's 4th Route Army, but we've had no signal from He Long's 2nd Route Army for three months. I don't know why, though an expeditionary force has been dispatched to locate him.'

'That is concerning. In any case, we plan a diversion—several thousand troops will feign a breakout to the north. Can you generate interceptable radio signals to support the ruse?'

'We can try, though it goes everything we've taught. They may not believe it.'

'You must also brief your staff on the rules.'

'The rules?'

'Restrictions will apply to the clothing that may be carried and to the manner in which it must be packed. Children under the age of thirteen must be entrusted to relatives or foster families. Older children shall depart with their parents. Efforts are being made to secure funding to assist with these arrangements. No exceptions will be permitted—not even for the children of Chairman Mao. I should not be telling you this, but your path is obvious. All spies and former sparrows will disperse—

they are of no use in conventional combat, though at least they have the skills to vanish.'

Chen shivered. Once again, the horrors of war loomed. What was he going to tell Daxia?

When Chen returned home, Daxia was feeding Weidong congee sweetened with rock sugar. The child sat in an intricately crafted highchair—one of Chen's own creations. He asked Daxia to put Weidong to bed as soon as possible. Once their child was asleep, Chen relayed Zeng's instructions.

At first, Daxia screamed, then collapsed into sobs. Zeng had been right—there was only one course. The next day, they departed for *Wuli Tulou* to leave Weidong with Chen's parents.

Since their marriage, the couple had visited the *tulou* only three times: just after their wedding in 1932, during Chinese New Year in 1933, and earlier this year, when Weidong was one and a half. Their sudden appearance could only mean trouble. The moment Chen's parents saw them, they knew something was wrong.

Chen's younger sisters, Fengbao and Yinghui, offered to take in Weidong—until warned that the entire family could face execution if their link to him were discovered. The final arrangement placed Weidong with a twenty-three-year-old married woman, with Mrs Chen assuming the role of a distant grandmother. Chen offered his meagre funds for the fostering, but as per Hakka tradition, the offer was politely refused.

They ate together that evening. Chen was surprised by how sparse the food was and asked his mother about it. She explained that most supplies were given to support the Soviet and the army, and that the encirclements had caused severe shortages. He also learned that Teacher Yao had recently passed away from cancer.

The farewell was solemn. No one wept—there was no room for sentiment. Chen and Daxia had no way of knowing if they would ever see their son again. As they walked away, Chen glanced back once. He thought he saw movement in the *tulou* doorway—but it vanished. He said nothing to Daxia.

The withdrawal from the Jiangxi Soviet began on 16 October 1934, near Yudu. The force numbered 86,000 soldiers—almost three-quarters of them Hakka—mainly from the hills of southern Jiangxi and western Fujian—along with some 40,000 cadres, civilians, and porters. A small rearguard, composed mainly of the sick and wounded, remained behind. The porters carried printing presses, a cumbersome X-ray machine, ammunition, artillery, and even sewing machines.

Unknown to Chen, Zhou Enlai had secured a covert agreement with Cantonese Hakka warlord Chen Jitang, permitting them to pass through three lines of blockhouses. Though loosely aligned with the Nationalists, Chen Jitang preferred to avoid direct conflict with such a massive force.

The central leadership group, numbering around 5,000, was protected by Lin Biao's 1st Corps to the left and Peng Dehuai's 3rd Corps on the right. The column stretched over fifty kilometres. Chen's radio team relayed constant updates to front-line commanders as they marched westward, often by night. Desertions mounted, particularly among the porters, who were ill-equipped for the relentless autumn rains.

There were three potential escape routes to avoid the looming trap at the Xiang River. The first was uncovered by Chen through intercepted messages on 17 November, after dividing his team into interception and signal operations. Part of the final blockade was held by the prestigious, predominantly Muslim Gui Army under Bai Chongxi—a trusted Nationalist general from the Northern Expedition. A minor Communist attack at Longhu Pass convinced Bai that the Red Army's main force was there. The intercepted message revealed Bai had been granted permission to retreat.

Chen relayed this to Zeng but was dismayed when no change in course followed. A second chance to evade the trap lay to the north, near Lingling, where viable paths still existed. Yet this option, too, was dismissed—by Mao and Zhou themselves.

The fourth line of blockhouses and the Xiang River crossings in Hunan proved disastrous. This time, they faced the regular army of 300,000 under General He Jian.

By 1 December, only half the Red Army—about 40,000—had

crossed to the river's western bank, including Chen and Daxia. A pontoon bridge was being frantically assembled to supplement the ferries, but time was against them.

The third and final possibility was to retreat swiftly to the ferry between Quanzhou and Xing'an and cross at once. This would mean abandoning all heavy equipment. A desperate radio message from the western bank commanders urged this—but the option was rejected by Bo Gu, whose inexperience was glaring, and by Otto Braun, who had originally been sent to Shanghai to advise on urban warfare, not campaigns of this magnitude.

Chen heard the approaching planes but had no idea what was about to unfold. The bombs first obliterated the pontoon bridge the retreating army had hastily constructed. The pilots then turned their attention to the soldiers—most of whom had never endured an aerial assault. The Red Army was mercilessly bombarded, defenceless without anti-aircraft weaponry. Coupled with a massed assault that pinned half the army on the eastern bank, the result was carnage.

Chen's *Gezi* unit managed to transmit frantic radio signals and orders across the river, helping coordinate a desperate rear-guard action at Xinxu. Through the static, Chen and Daxia barked new frequencies and call signs. Every second gained might save a life—or cost one. Still, it was not enough. In a single, devastating battle, the army lost more than half its fighting force. With the wounded accounted for, fewer than 30,000 combatants remained—but Chen and his beloved wife had survived.

Among the fallen were two men dear to Chen: Qian Zhuangfei, who had taught him the art of espionage, and his first political mentor, Song Liqiang, a guiding figure since their meeting in the Jinggang Mountains in 1927. Chen told Daxia of Song's death. His voice was steady, but the sorrow was unmistakable in his eyes. He reserved his grief for solitude, when he could finally mourn his mentor in private.

On 15 January 1935, the 1st Front Army seized the town of Zunyi in western Guizhou, prompting a two-day emergency conference.

Without Song to provide intelligence, Chen had been forced to rely on inference. He was appalled by communications that exposed the catastrophic strategic blunders of Bo Gu and Braun.

Chen was summoned to a meeting with his immediate superior.

Zeng, characteristically terse, offered only what was necessary to keep SIGINT operations functioning.

'Braun has been removed from military command. Mao has been appointed Chairman of the Military Commission.'

He paused, his expression tightening.

'It was the final straw with that foreigner. He found fault in everything—maps, orders, even the weather. But you, Chen—' his gaze sharpened—'you followed orders without question. That is why we are still here.'

Chen held his stare.

'What are your orders?'

'New directives. We are to march north, toward Sichuan, to link with Zhang Guotao's 4th Route Army. You are to relay this without delay.'

Although Chen welcomed what he saw as more reliable leadership, one concern remained. When this battered army met Zhang Guotao's forces, a power struggle was inevitable.

Relying on intelligence reports, Chiang Kai-shek's forces prepared an ambush near Tucheng. On 29 January, Mao decided to retreat, crossing the Chishui River and heading west. Though the river was at its seasonal low, the crossing was anything but easy. Soldiers waded through the icy current, rifles held high above their heads, their limbs numbed by the water. The riverbed was slick with silt and loose stones. The muddy banks offered little grip, threatening to drag them back into the flow.

By then, radio intercepts confirmed their plight: the Red Army was encircled—Liu Xiang's forces to the north, others to the west and east, and the main Nationalist army closing from behind. The Nationalists also had the option of deploying the Hunan and Guangxi armies, stationed nearby.

The army veered south into a remote corner of Yunnan, reaching

Weixin. There was a pause for a meeting at Bijie on 5 February. Following Braun's dismissal, Bo Gu was also removed. Zhang Wentian (*Luò Fú*, 一洛甫), another of the 'Twenty-Eight Bolsheviks', became Party Chairman.

The army moved east again, crossing the Chishui at Taiping Ferry on 21 February, then turning west to confront the Nationalist main force at Loushan Pass—before again retreating south through Zunyi and recrossing the river at Maotai on 16 March. They were trapped. The Western Army was closing in.

On 17 March, Daxia intercepted and decrypted a radio message. The Nationalists feared the Red Army might push north towards Chongqing, attempt a crossing of the Yangtze, and unite with Zhang Guotao's 4th Army in Sichuan—a move that could turn the tide of the war.

In response, Mao deployed a regiment to simulate a northern advance. On 22 March, the army crossed the Chishui for the final time at Taiping Ferry and advanced towards Guiyang, the provincial capital—then sparsely defended.

Nationalist radio networks erupted into chaos—no decryption was needed. The *Gēzi* team discovered that Chiang Kai-shek himself was in Guiyang and overheard frantic orders for his evacuation. They also intercepted instructions for General Sun Du's Guizhou–Yunnan army to defend the city, inadvertently opening a gap through which the Red Army escaped.

Had Chiang not been in Guiyang, events might have taken a very different turn.

Yet the 1st Front Army had been reduced to only 24,000 men. Ahead lay snow-laden peaks, treacherous ravines, rope bridges that swayed in the wind, bitter cold, and almost no food. Though he said nothing to Daxia, Chen could not shake the fear that neither of them would survive.

Central command typically travelled in the middle of the column—protected from surprise attacks on the vanguard and distant from skirmishes at the rear. The army moved in staggered waves across narrow mountain tracks, often spread out over dozens of kilometres. Chen and Daxia marched near the core communication units, close enough to relay decrypted intelligence but far enough behind the front to pass the stone cairns and carved names left by those who had gone before.

He wondered whether Weidong would one day read his father's name carved in bark, high in a mountain forest no one remembered.

Chapter 24: Bao'an, Shaanxi Province, China, 1935

The 1st Front Army and the 4th Front Army finally linked up at Lianghekou on 21 June 1935, with the former reduced to a mere 10,000 troops. It would be another three days before their commanders formally met—ample time for Chen and Daxia to observe and converse with the officers and soldiers of the 4th. This was a vast army, 84,000 strong, swollen further by several thousand non-combatants. Many showed visible signs of malnutrition.

On the second evening, Chen and Daxia found a quiet moment by a fire, far from the others' hearing. Daxia, eyes alight with a mixture of excitement and disbelief, spoke first.
'Minghe, did you know there were only thirty-six women on our journey? I could never speak to them—our paths didn't cross, and they were mostly the wives of senior commanders. But for the past two days, I've seen something extraordinary. I spoke with one of the women's regiment leaders in the 4th Army. It's unlike anything I've known. These women fight with their babies strapped to their backs, while their husbands follow—because staying behind meant certain death at the hands of the Nationalists. The unmarried ones are heavily protected from molestation. Every woman knows that if captured, she'll likely be raped and killed. So they fight like wild animals.'
'I've never heard of a family-based combat unit where husband and wife fight side by side.'
'It's not quite that. The husbands are weak fighters—most of them addicted to opium. It's the younger boys who are kept busy. They feed the horses, carry messages, play bugles, even mind the babies.'
'I wonder how effective this whole army can be.'
'Integrating two forces this different will be hard. Commissar Zhang Guotao and General Chen Changhao command an army eight times the size of ours—they won't be looking to play second fiddle.'
They turned in soon after, though sleep was a matter of sheer exhaustion. Daxia had long refused intimacy, fearful of pregnancy. She had heard of He Zizhen, Mao's wife, giving birth that February—only to

abandon the infant with a local family. That knowledge weighed heavily on her.

On 9 September, Zeng summoned Chen to a meeting. By then, leadership changes were no longer unexpected. Zhang Guotao had forced the replacement of Zhou Enlai with Chen Changhao as Red Army commissar. Zhang himself had taken Zhu De's place on the Military Commission—both moves enacted by 18 July. Zeng explained there was a split: Mao insisted on marching north to Shaanxi, while Zhang favoured a push south and west, to found a new base area. The armies would part ways. Zeng had also sent Chen Yun to Moscow, requesting new one-time cipher pads, which by then were in regular use by the *Gezi*.

Most of the 1st Front Army pushed northward through treacherous mountains, often crossing vast chasms on precarious rope bridges. But the deadliest stretch came during an eight-day slog through the fetid swamp south of Banyou. The army suffered relentless warlord attacks, wretched terrain, and unspeakable deprivation. With rations exhausted, they chewed on belts, carcasses, and weeds. Dysentery spread rapidly. Though Chen and Daxia were spared the illness, there was no way to sleep except crouched together, clutching one another for warmth. Each night, more bodies were left behind. Though they survived, the horror never left them.

On 18 October 1935, just 7,200 survivors reached Soviet-held Shaanxi at Bao'an, where they were welcomed by Liu Zhidan's local communist leadership—a separate base area established earlier in the decade, centred on the northern Shaanxi–Gansu border. Meanwhile, the courier's arrival in Moscow three days earlier triggered two key developments. Two weeks later, *Pravda* published a front-page editorial recognising Mao Zedong as the undisputed leader of the Chinese Communist movement. Then, in November, a trader arrived from Russian Mongolia bearing the new cipher pads—re-establishing communication with the Comintern.

The Long March's toll on individuals only emerged as survivors reconnected or news reached Bao'an. In Ruijin, many were executed for staying behind, including Qu Qiubai and Mao's youngest brother, Mao Zetan, who died in April 1935.

Mao Anlong, the child Mao had with He Zizhen, had been entrusted to her sister, who was married to Mao Zetan. During the collapse of the Republic, he had moved the boy to a secret location. When he died, he took the hiding place with him. He Zizhen never saw her son again. To Chen, though, the greatest heartbreak was learning that none of his radio operators had survived.

After He Long's retreat from the Hunan–Hebei base, the Nationalists executed his entire family—including his brother and three sisters.

Between 1930 and 1933, the Ma Clique—a Hui Muslim force under Ma Bufang allied with the Nationalists—had inflicted a severe defeat on the Dalai Lama's Tibetan Army. Despite British munitions aid to the Tibetans and a belated diplomatic protest from London, the fighting remained one-sided. Two years later, Zhang Guotao's decision to challenge this same force proved disastrous. Ma's experienced troops crushed the Fourth Front Army in Qinghai and southern Gansu, reducing it from 84,000 to just 21,800. Only a fraction would ever reach Bao'an. The human cost was immense. Only around 2,000 members of the 4th Army reached Bao'an in October 1936. Though a founding member of the Communist Party in 1921, Zhang Guotao never recovered from the failure. In 1938, he defected to the Nationalists.

He Long's Second Front Army departed the Hunan–Hubei–Sichuan–Guizhou base area on 19 November 1935. Another 2,000 soldiers from the First Front Army formed the Sixth Corps under Xiao Ke, who had been sent months earlier to locate He Long. Upon finding him, they learned the radios had been destroyed in a mortar strike, and the operators killed.

With 18,000 men, this force was driven far west, deep into Yunnan, and forced to traverse the 5,000-metre-high Jade Dragon Snow Mountain and the treacherous Tibetan plateau. Over 10,000 soldiers perished. Children were not abandoned quite as often as they had been in the First Front Army, though many were still left behind. He Long brought his wife, Jian Xianren, and their newborn daughter, He Jiesheng. Starvation stalked them through the barren grasslands. Tibetan communities, though destitute, adopted some children, and the soldiers were able to fish—an option not used by Tibetans due to religious beliefs. Further north, by confiscating food from the rich and presenting the Long March as a patriotic campaign against Japan, He Long managed to keep his numbers intact. His wife and child survived. The baby girl would be the youngest known survivor of the Long March.

No one can say how many died during the Long March. The Red Armies recruited even as others died or deserted, but the best estimates suggest a total loss near 200,000. Over twenty thousand *li* were traversed in a journey marked by grief, hunger, and unrelenting hardship. By a blend of courage, cunning, and luck, Chinese communism had survived—though only barely.

The Red Army was unable to press on to Yan'an which was under Nationalist control and settled instead in Zhidan County, near Bao'an. To Chen, the landscape seemed monotonous—an endless palette of yellow. The skies were a pale blue almost daily, and the rivers, impregnated with loess, shimmered a dull mustard hue. But there were compensations.

Daxia chose a *yáodòng* (窑洞) for them—one of many cave homes carved neatly into the hillside. Chen was assigned a similar one as his office. Their quarters were designated for senior military officers and Party cadres, and they were close to the homes of Mao and Zhou Enlai. Occasionally, the two leaders and their wives would wave from their courtyards, three terraces below.

The valley yielded wheat and beans but little meat. Still, the simple and consistent diet left Chen and Daxia noticeably healthier within weeks. A purpose-built training centre was quickly established to replace the radio operators lost after Jiangxi, while maintaining constant links with Moscow.

Daxia noticed that parcels were regularly delivered to her

husband—always bulging with papers. She once asked what they contained. His silence was answer enough, and she chose not to press him. Instead, they made time for long walks, spoke of their future, and grew still closer. To Chen, Daxia seemed more beautiful than ever—more radiant and compelling in those quiet moments than in all the years before. They counted themselves lucky. Only when they spoke of their son, Weidong, did sorrow return.

In late June 1936, Chen was summoned to a meeting that would change the course of his life forever. As dusk settled over the yellow loess hills, he stepped into a candlelit cave. Inside, Zhou Enlai introduced him to Li Kenong, Head of Intelligence, who had replaced Deng Fa on the Long March. Though Chen had never met Li, he knew of him well—Li had founded the spy school in Ruijin, where Chen had trained. Zhou assured Chen that he could speak freely on any subject, including his proficiency in Russian. Li began by commending Chen for the *Gezi's* contributions to the Long March before proceeding with his questions.

'Comrade Chen, I would like to begin with your assessment of the current global situation. Let us start with Chiang Kai-shek. Do you believe he will attack our new base in Shaanxi?'

'It is possible, but he has more pressing matters to attend to and might be better advised to focus his attention on potential Japanese or Russian aggression. After the Nationalists re-established diplomatic relations with the USSR in 1932, when I was still in spy school, this became a subject of heated debate—who would benefit most from it?'

'And which side of the argument did you take?'

'At first, I thought it was unhelpful to our cause because I couldn't see how Stalin could support us while also maintaining friendly relations with our enemy.'

'I didn't immediately grasp the bigger picture, but later, I changed my mind.'

'Why?'

'Because in November 1933, after the United States and the USSR established diplomatic relations, I realised Stalin must have been seeking allies wherever he could find them. I believe he is terrified of a Japanese attack on the USSR, coordinated with one from Nazi Germany, stretching his forces from coast to coast. And I imagine he saw an arrangement in which both the Nationalists and Communists were prepared to fight Japan together as a useful counterbalance.'

'So, you trust the motives of the USSR and consider them reliable allies?'

Chen was taken aback by the question and had to think quickly.

'They have supported our revolution in every way. The radio signals we recently sent out were to coordinate USSR supplies through Mongolia and ensure we remain well equipped. That seems like the act of an ally.'

'And Stalin has no interest in Japan attacking China—including us?'

Chen was shocked. This was a level of strategic thinking beyond what he was used to.

'It would be highly advantageous for the USSR, as Japan probably couldn't sustain a war on two fronts.'

Zhou smiled and interjected,

'Well put, Chen. But do you think all this diplomatic activity is above board? Surely the Americans will use it to plant spies in Moscow, just as the USSR will do the same in Washington—embedding so-called military attachés in Nanjing? Shouldn't we do the same?'

'I suppose we should seek out sympathetic or cooperative foreigners, as we stand out too much as Chinese. Although we are not yet a communist country, we should attempt to plant spies and moles in Japan, the United States, and, if possible, even Germany.'

'And the USSR?'

'You mean we need spies and moles in Moscow, our so-called benefactor?'

'Precisely. We already have them—and they are not Chinese, for the reasons you mentioned. If Stalin falls or plays us, we have no idea who might replace him, so we see it as an insurance policy.'

It was a bombshell.

An orderly served a hearty meal: steaming chicken broth with jujube fruit, wide wheat noodles, and the fiery sauce they were growing accustomed to—its sharp, vinegar-laced heat a far cry from the fragrant chilli oils and rice-based dishes of the south. A flagon of *baijiu* accompanied the meal. There was no attempt at small talk. Each man at the table had endured too much to entertain idle conversation.

Zhou continued the conversation,

'Chen, have you been reading the newspapers we sent you—especially the Russian ones from Harbin?'

'I have. They have given me a better understanding of the world after being deprived of information, and they have also been useful for language practice. But I am curious—why did you go to such trouble to acquire them for me?'

'You didn't show them to Daxia?'

'No, of course not. I keep them under lock and key in my private work area.'

Zhou looked grave.

'We have a problem. While we are in a strong position to uncover the intentions of the Nationalists, their warlord allies—especially the Young Marshal—as well as the USSR, and have even had some success in Germany, we have failed to penetrate Japanese intelligence or uncover their true intentions. Remember, although we have not engaged in direct combat, the Communist Party declared war on Japan in early 1932. Since then, they have been watching us closely. Every time we attempt to infiltrate, they capture, interrogate, and execute our operatives in Manchuria and Tokyo.'

Chen was intrigued.

'I… I am not sure I can help you with that.'

'Have you heard of a man called Rodzaevsky?'

'I have read a little about him. He is the leader of the Russian Fascist Party based in Harbin.'

'That's correct, and he is working with the Japanese, so if they decide to invade the USSR, he can supply men to fight on the Japanese side and gather intelligence inside the USSR. It would have been useful to have penetrated his organisation and discovered more of his and, even more importantly, the Japanese plans. We've tried repeatedly to infiltrate Rodzaevsky's circle, but the only viable method is by working with Red Russians. Our counterintelligence team suspects that the enemy has obtained lists of our potential infiltrators — or that there are leaks within the Russian Communist ranks. Either way, our agents are too easily identified by Rodzaevsky's Head of Security or the Japanese agencies. There are plenty of Russian-speaking Chinese in Harbin, but they have no espionage experience. We did manage to get a relief cook into the Fascist Party offices, but he was never seen again, so I imagine he was either rumbled or caught eavesdropping; none of our men ever returned.'

Chen knew what was coming next, and it terrified him.

'We would like you to go to Harbin and find a way to solve our dilemma. You have all the right credentials. You are from the south of China, don't appear to understand a word of Russian, and are a trained spy. And this is to be a Chinese-only operation just in case there are leaks, as I discussed.'

Or—in case the USSR and communist China move apart in the future— thought Chen.

'Do we have any resources in Harbin?'

Zhou looked at Li, who expounded on this aspect,

'We do indeed. We have a *Teke* cell of five men and one woman—one of our oldest units in China. They were formed in 1929 and were originally established to provide intelligence to us and the USSR to help the Soviets when they attacked the Young Marshal Zhang's forces over the Chinese Eastern Railway. Four of the six-person group form a Red Squad, who have successfully assassinated some medium-level employees of Zhang who betrayed us. The fifth member, who is the leader, is from the *Teke* intelligence-gathering wing. The final member is from the 4th Section—she will be able to assist you with codes and ciphers and getting information to us and only us. She has a radio and has been Russian-trained in its use because the Japanese are highly adept at transmission location finding. They have only used it once and were nearly caught. It is only to be used in the direst of circumstances.'

That sounded more promising to Chen, but he remained frightened. Then Zhou said,

'Chen, you must hand over your *Gezi* command to Second Lieutenant Wang Zheng, who has thrived under your leadership.'

So, I'm not a volunteer for this mission, thought Chen. *Telling Daxia would*

be horrendous.

Zhou continued,

'We both know this mission will be difficult. You have my assurance that, in the event of an… unfortunate outcome, I will personally ensure Daxia is protected, and we will do everything possible to return your son to her eventually. I will know you are thriving if messages continue to come, and when possible, I will convey that to her.'

There was nothing left to say. Chen got ready to go, and on the way out, Zhou said,

'Don't forget to burn the newspapers.'

When he had gone, Zhou looked at Li.

'I have known this fine young man since shortly after the Nanchang Uprising, when I interviewed him with Zhu De and even attended his wedding. Now, I have likely sent him to his death.'

Daxia was horrified and furious, and the pitch and volume of her screams grew higher with Chen's evasiveness.

'So, what is this special mission you must undertake?'

'It's a secret. I can't discuss it, even with you.'

'Is it something to do with those parcels you've been receiving?'

'That's part of it. I can't say.'

'How long will you be away?'

'Truthfully, I don't know.'

'Is this a SIGINT project or something you learned about at spy school?'

Chen lied smoothly.

'Some of both.'

'And is it dangerous?'

'It carries some risks, as always in our lives.'

He knew he wasn't being believed. She screamed louder, and Chen thought she was about to hit him.

'Chen Minghe, if you don't start answering, you won't have a wife to return to. Where were you tonight?'

'At a meeting.'

'You mean you've been carrying on behind my back, haven't you?'

'No, I love you and would never do such a thing. You know it.'
'So, who was your meeting with? Don't lie to me.'
'Zhou Enlai and Li Kenong.'

That had to be true. Even Chen couldn't make that up. The silence was a relief for Chen, and finally, Daxia spoke in her usual tone and pitch,

'Can you tell me anything? Is this vital to our survival?'
'Yes.'
'And how will I know you're safe?'
'Because Zhou Enlai has promised to inform you personally. He will know because of the messages I send.'
'At least tell me where you're going and how long you'll be gone.'
'How long, I can't say, but I'm going to Harbin.'
'Harbin!'

That was indiscreet.

Chen was expecting another explosive outburst—it didn't happen. Daxia was tearful and said,

'Get on the *kàng* now, you brave, stupid man, and make love to me as you've never done before,' she said, referring to the raised, heated brick bed used in the north.'

Their lovemaking was frantic, a mix of desperation and passion. Afterwards, Daxia suddenly sank her teeth into his arm in a horse bite. It hurt. There would be a purple welt for months—a deliberate marker to ward off any wayward northern girls.

Chen became aware of a foreign man with peculiar habits as he made arrangements to leave for Harbin. He was tall; Chen guessed about the same height as Chairman Mao, with swept-back black hair and wearing a long jacket with four pockets on the front—like a drawing Chen had once seen in a book, showing clothing typically worn by foreigners for tiger hunting. Underneath, he wore a shirt but no tie. Curiously, he only seemed to rise after 10.00 a.m., and one sleepless night, Chen saw him return at 3.00 a.m. There was only one person, as was his habit, awake at that hour: Chairman Mao. On enquiring, Chen discovered there was no secret about this man; he was free to wander almost wherever he chose, but not within the SIGINT building. His name was Edgar Snow, an American journalist interviewing Mao. Few probably realised, but Chen certainly did, that Snow would have needed to cross the Young Marshal's enemy territory, allied with Chiang Kai-shek, and would have stood out. For some reason, he had been allowed to pass through. Chen couldn't figure out why, though.

Exiting the base area and joining the Xi'an–Beijing railway at Taiyuan, completed the year before, proved easy for Chen. He had a third-class ticket and had to sleep as best he could in his threadbare summer clothes on hard wooden benches, occasionally buying snacks from hawkers at stations along the way. Dry and dusty Shaanxi, with its camels, turned into lush pastures with horses, ochre-coloured cows, and fields growing various crops in fertile soil—of which Chen recognised only a few, such as peanuts, wheat, maize, and mustard. A man from Beijing sitting next to him tried to engage in conversation, and Chen had to admit he was not a local and struggled with the man's accent, which sounded as though someone had stuffed a cotton wad in his mouth. The man helped describe the other crops: tobacco, cotton not yet ready to disgorge its white fruiting fibre from the bolls, leafy sugar beets, and rows of mounded potatoes. At a station near Shijiazhuang, the man suggested that Chen buy some local produce, so he chose steamed buns and a clay pot of yoghurt infused with honey—both new tastes that he found very much to his liking.

In the evening, as the train approached the outskirts of Beijing, Chen observed the mayhem in the streets and the throat-tickling fog, which was irritating even from within the confines of the railway carriage. It soon became clear where the source of the acrid smoke originated. Arrow alleyways (*hùtòng*—胡同), with courtyard homes, were preparing summer dinners on charcoal braziers, polluting the air and mingling with Gobi Desert sand from a summer windstorm. Chen could only imagine what this place would be like in winter when coal would be used to keep warm. There were bicycles and rickshaws piled high with everything from fruit and vegetables to furniture. There were open spaces with temples, markets, and even a grazing area for the camels that had been taken to the city. Chen slept in one of the cheap hotels that proliferated around the station, too tired to explore his surroundings.

The next part of the journey, from Beijing to Harbin, was far more perilous, although Chen was well-prepared. As he reached the border with Manchuria, the sight of the Japanese flag flying prominently signalled that he was entering another country. Each class of railway passenger was herded into lines for approval, with a Chinese-speaking Japanese official carrying out the questioning. The third-class passengers were largely ignored, but when it came to Chen, he was asked about the purpose of his visit to Harbin. He explained that he had come from Xiamen to visit his aunt, who needed assistance with her bakery after breaking her leg. He proffered a letter from his aunt, but the official simply waved him through. He then went to the money-changing stall to convert his remaining cash into Manchurian *yuan*.

By the time he arrived in Harbin, Chen was exhausted. The journey had taken four days and nights. His 'aunt', with her plaster cast, met him at the railway station and took him to her bakery.

Chapter 25: Harbin, Japanese Empire of Manchukuo, 1936

Shortly after arriving in Harbin, Chen attended his first meeting of the Communist cell to which he had been assigned. It took place in a family-run restaurant with a private room, operated by a sympathiser in the Chinese quarter, Fuchiatien. Even there, a teenage boy crouched near the threshold, peeling vegetables and watching the street. Their leader, Bai, began by introducing Chen under his pseudonym, Feng Shaogong, explaining that he had been sent on a vital mission by the leadership in Bao'an.

Chen sensed the unease in the room. His arrival had unsettled them. Apart from Bai, there were four men and one woman—each seemingly older than him, each with the air of hard-won survival. Bai explained that none used their real names and introduced the men first. Chen had expected the *Teke* Red Squad assassins to be fierce-looking killers, but the first two, Xu and Li, were short and bookish. Li wore glasses. Bai read Chen's expression and clarified: neither engaged in killings—they performed support duties. Xu, for instance, had recruited a reluctant collaborator—Detective Yuan of the Harbin Municipal Police—who had grown disgusted by the overt anti-Jewish and anti-communist zealotry of his superior, Inspector Nikolai Martinov.

Then came the Wang brothers—brawny, sinister, unmistakable in their purpose. The elder bore a deep scar running from ear to jaw and wore his hair tied back in a rough ponytail. Their role needed no explanation. At the far end of the table sat a woman with a tight bob and eyes that gleamed with energy. She might have been thirty. Though her appearance was plain, her intensity was not.

'And I suppose you are *nǚ wáng* (女王)?' Chen asked.

The room erupted with laughter. Wang was the most common surname in China; *nǚ wáng* meant 'queen'. Her codename was Liu. Chen already suspected she would be his most valuable asset. Ms Liu would be his contact with Bao'an.

Dinner was served. The food was saltier than anything Chen had eaten before, setting off an unrelenting thirst. Bai, proudly, introduced the Harbin Beer—China's oldest. Its chill and sharpness offered momentary relief, but only deepened the craving, trapping him in a cycle of salt and beer, each mouthful driving the next.

As they ate, Chen began asking questions and outlined the purpose of his mission.

'How much do you know about the leader of the Russian Fascist Party?'

Xu answered first.

'You can't miss Rodzaevsky and his Blackshirts. They strut around Harbin, holding noisy parades. He's also a senior member of BREM, the Bureau of Russian Émigré Affairs, and heads the education and cultural affairs department.'

'What does BREM do?'

'Officially, it represents all foreigners in Manchuria except Soviets. In practice, it's a puppet. The Japanese pull the strings. Each department's run by a VFP member or someone close to them. The most powerful here is Matkovsky—he runs administration and planning. His office controls passports, work permits, residency papers—no one moves, leaves, or works without him.'

'Does Rodzaevsky have a security detail?'

'Usually. A man—probably called Bolotov—organises his guards. They're armed, but the Japanese limit how many weapons can be carried publicly. Kidnapping or killing Rodzaevsky would be difficult.'

'Have you followed him? To see if he's ever alone?'

'No. We focus on Marshal Zhang's men—recruiting or eliminating them. Rodzaevsky's not been a priority, and none of us speaks Russian. We leave that to our Russian comrades—but none has succeeded in infiltrating his circle.'

'So, you share information with them?'

'Only when it serves our mutual interests.'

The elder Wang leaned forward.

'You want us to assassinate Rodzaevsky?' he asked, his tone edged with disbelief.

'No. I intend to infiltrate his organisation.'

'But how? We don't speak Russian. We rarely enter their districts.

We're expected to stay in our quarter—though it's not always enforced.'

Chen held their gaze.

'I speak and read Russian.'

A silence fell. Every eye locked on him. A Chinese man from Xiamen—or was it somewhere else?—fluent in Russian? The mystery deepened. Chen offered no explanation.

He outlined his plan. The cell's Russian contacts were to remain unaware of him. No one questioned it. In their world, you destroyed your enemy—and trusted no one, not even friends, unless it was absolutely necessary.

Before the meeting ended, Chen reviewed their resources. A safe house lay hidden within a traditional medicine shop, with living quarters above. Ms Liu excelled at disguise. Li could drive. Bai had a knack for identifying secure restaurants and houses. Ms Liu had also collected Chen's miniature camera—hidden in a magnetic box—as it had been too risky to bring on the train.

Chen's first task was reconnaissance. Though the team claimed competence, they had received little real training. In Harbin, killings could easily be staged to resemble gangster feuds with minimal preparation; careful reconnaissance, however, demanded an entirely different discipline—one they had scarcely begun to master.

For a week, Chen explored the Russian quarter on foot. He carried no map. With his aunt's bakery starting at 3.00 a.m., his afternoons and evenings were his own. He took light duties to manage his sleep. He located Rodzaevsky's residence and the VFP offices. He did not linger or approach. He remained detached, testing for surveillance. There was none. One night, he heard gunfire outside a bar and turned away without hesitation. On another day, he observed a well-attended VFP rally. It was his first glimpse of the man: Rodzaevsky shouting fascist slogans, fervently received by a loyal crowd. Bolotov, presumably, was the one inspecting the guards. Chen listened, understanding both their language and their intent. As he walked the streets, he observed the city's peculiarities—what each group wore, how Chinese chauffeurs served foreign masters.

Chen mentally mapped out a test route, beginning along Friendship Road, and split the cell into two teams. Each was given enough money to purchase suitable props or other items within reason. They had forty-eight hours to prepare. The trial would take place on a crowded weekend, amid shoppers and revellers. Each team's objective was to approach him closely enough to take a pistol shot—no easy task. Other simple tracking exercises would follow in due course.

The first surveillance team comprised the Wang Brothers and Xu. Chen, in his usual baker's delivery garb, reached the starting point with a basket of bread. He had walked less than half a *li* before spotting all three. At the corner of Friendship Road and Chinese Street, the Wang Brothers loitered at Novikov's newsstand, each pretending to read a Chinese newspaper. Yet the Chinese newspapers they held were not among Novikov's stock, which consisted mainly of Russian, French, and English titles, along with a single local Chinese paper.

Xu had fared marginally better—dressed in a traditional bowl cap, long gown, and coat, carrying what looked like a document tube. Still, the clientele in this part of the city expected Chinese professionals to wear Western clothing. All three tailed Chen from behind, unaware that he had slipped unnoticed into a Russian café—one of two on that stretch—where he frequently delivered bread. The counter wasn't visible from the street. Handing over some loaves as a gift from his aunt, he lingered in small talk with the owner, who spoke passable Chinese. Five minutes later, Chen emerged back onto Chinese Street—his would-be assailants now ahead of him. A glance over his shoulder confirmed he was not being followed.

The following day, the second team—Bai, Li, and Ms Liu—posed a far greater challenge.

Chen entered the assigned section of Friendship Road. No tail—at first. He varied his pace. A man behind matched it perfectly.

He slipped into a storefront doorway and watched. The man paused, pretending to admire a shop window. Chen recognised him. Li—draped in cassocks, a novice priest of the Russian Orthodox Mission, silver cross swinging gently on his chest. Clever.

He turned down Chinese Street, ducked behind a parked car, then slipped into a recessed doorway. He looked back. Li had stopped—calm, hands folded. That meant the others were ahead.

Two possibles stood out: a tall Russian in a cream suit, boater on his head, beside a Chinese nanny and pram; and a traffic officer—off-duty or pretending.

Chen crossed the street and entered the only canteen that served Chinese patrons in this part of town.

He ordered from the wall menu and handed over his basket—*dalieba* and *kalach*—asking an assistant to keep it under the counter. Then he spoke briefly to the server, a man he had previously recruited and discreetly rewarded. The man gave a nod and slipped into the male lavatory. A minute later, Chen followed.

Soon after, the nanny entered. She retrieved a cloth bag from the pram parked outside and walked into the female lavatory. Inside, she changed—headscarf, dress, shoes—and exited through the rear alley.

Chen emerged five minutes later, hair dusted with building grit, clothes shapeless and dirty. He slurped noodles from a deep bowl that covered half his face. Across the street, the Russian lingered beside the pram. The nanny was no longer there. Perhaps she had an errand to run or needed a rest break.

Chen retrieved his basket and slipped out the back. Further up the alley, a woman in pale-blue workwear—gloves, headscarf—was stacking boxes into a rubbish bin. Her face was hidden.

Minutes later, he looked back and saw Li running towards him down the alley.

Chen tried the back doors on either side. All locked. Proprietors had learned the hard way to protect what was theirs. He picked up speed and approached the next road-and-alley intersection.

Chen's breath caught—not from fear, but calculation. He had seconds to choose.

Seven options. None good.

Turn right onto a side street, then double back up Chinese Street. Or cross to the opposite pavement, and similarly head up Chinese Street again. He could turn left onto the cross street, but that ran open for blocks with no more alleys. Straight ahead meant a long run, exposed to Li chasing him. He could go right, cross Chinese Street, and either go down the adjacent alley or backtrack up it. His final choice after turning right was to continue straight along the cross street—but again, no alleys.

He crossed and slipped into the downward alley, at least temporarily out of Li's sight. Luckily, there were more bins here to hide behind, and he watched Li continue along the side street before moving on down the alley.

At the next junction, Bai was waiting—shirtless, glistening, digging a drainage trench. A gift of chance placement. Before Chen could process it, Bai approached, smiled, and mimed a pistol with two fingers.

Ms Liu appeared behind him. Li would follow shortly—search exhausted.

Chen turned to her.

'The man with the nanny?'

'A tall Chinese friend. Disguised as a Russian. He knew nothing. Just a prop. The baby? I pinched her. One cry was enough. We guessed you'd choose the canteen. But the shops all have locked back doors.'

'If I'd left through the front?'

'I was watching and kept the back door ajar. If you'd walked down the street, I'd have gone to the front door and signalled from the middle of the road in Chinese Street. A white handkerchief. That would cue Li—he'd shout in bad Russian: "In the name of God, let me pass; I need to attend to a dying man." The crowd would part—always on the far side from you. With that advantage, Li moves faster than you. Once he and I joined, we'd shadow whichever way you turned. If you backtracked, I'd signal green. He'd intercept and close. If you chose the rear alley—as you did—I'd signal blue. Li chased. I followed after he had overtaken me.'

'And if I turned left at the cross street?'

'You'd only have me behind you. Li was instructed always to go right and continue along the cross street if he couldn't see you. Bai—by then—would realise you weren't coming his way. He'd sprint up the next alley and join me. You'd be bracketed either way.'

'So even if I turned right and continued along the cross street?'

'Li would reset. The religious charade again—and get ahead of you and wait for you to walk into him. Once he was confident he was ahead, he'd stall and watch for any shop dives. They've no back exits.'

Chen nodded.

'So, I was flanked no matter what.'

'Almost. Your best chances? After crossing Chinese Street, turn right up the alley, double back, spot Li behind you early, and hope he gave up. But even then—maybe not. You still had no idea where the other two chasing you were. If you crossed and went back up Chinese Street, he could still outpace you. The other option? Immediately turn back up Chinese Street without crossing and blend in—because there is a short gap where you are out of Li's sight, and he had instructions to go straight if he couldn't see you. But again—where are we? You could also have dashed up the middle of any of the roads and hoped you wouldn't be hit by a vehicle. But we believed a spy's instinct was to blend into the crowd. The only other variable was if I got run over while trying to signal with a handkerchief.'

Chen turned to Bai.

'How were you so convincing?'

Bai grinned.

'I joined the road gang yesterday. Took a lower rate. Told them I was frail. Every muscle's sore.'

Chen nodded, half-smiling.

'At least I spotted Li.'

'No,' said Ms Liu. 'He revealed himself on purpose. It was part of the plan.'

Chen accepted the rebuke. In a real scenario, he'd be dead.

The exercise had proven something crucial. A crowded street was no longer a sanctuary.

Still, he had his team. Li, Bai, Ms Liu—and probably Xu—were all reliable.

The Wang Brothers, muttering, were relegated to night watch on Rodzaevsky's apartment.

Rodzaevsky was easy to follow on foot, but he often travelled by car. Xu arranged for Detective Yuan to watch for registration plates 1621 and 1767—used by the VFP. Other vehicles came and went, but these were consistent. The Maybach Zeppelin, plate 1621, was decadent—three passengers in both front and rear, guards on running boards. Chen doubted the VFP owned it; more likely, it was on loan from wealthy émigrés. The Packard 845 De Luxe, plate 1767, was quieter and far more discreet.

As Yuan pursued his leads, Chen worked with Ms Liu. She showed him a high-frequency radio hidden in a loft. She still had active one-time cipher pads. Together, they developed a network of message drop sites. After the Long March, Ms Liu had created a courier system to contact Bao'an. She would not reveal its workings. Messages took five days each way.

Their first dead-drop was a grocer—a fussy friend of Chen's 'aunt'. She insisted her vegetables be displayed perfectly. Even in winter, her stall always had carrots, potatoes, and mushrooms. If a carrot faced the wrong way—tapered end up—it signalled a message was ready. It would be hidden behind a loose brick in a nearby alley. The grocer knew nothing more.

At the next cell meeting, surveillance gave way to strategy. Chen, now the undisputed leader, began.

'Comrades, our surveillance has revealed Rodzaevsky's patterns. Wang Senior—summarise.'

'He walks to work with a briefcase, escorted by two guards—one armed with a pistol, one with a submachine gun. Sundays, he walks to church with the same detail. After church, he lunches with his wife. Once a month, they buy flowers and visit their son Yuri's grave. No briefcase. His wife has one guard when shopping or performing in concerts.'

The Wang Brothers suggested methods of assassination, but Chen dismissed them. Xu spoke next.

'The Maybach is used mostly for ceremonies. On Saturdays, they visit the Russian Railway Club in Novy Gorod, have lunch, walk in the park near Novotorgovaya Ulitsa.'

'What do they do at the club?' Chen asked.

'They play bridge—a modern version of *Biritch (бирич)*.'

'*Biritch* requires skill,' Chen noted.

'He often wins—especially when the others drink. The smaller car—1767—is used without his wife. The roll-top is usually up. He doesn't want to be seen.'

'And where does he go?'

'Two places. First, the Cabaret Fantasia, with only a driver. Second, the outskirts of Nakhalova—still with only a driver. No guards, either way.'

Chen's brow furrowed.

'Nakhalova?'

Bai answered,

'The worst place in Harbin. Past the crumbling shops lie hovels of cardboard and timber. No heat. No sewage. Each winter, people die—disease, cold, or both. Gangs rule it. Traffickers, beggars, thieves. Some Chinese, but they live elsewhere. Children are sent to beg in richer districts. Young girls—ten or eleven—learn to please men for a few *yuan*. If Rodzaevsky enters that world, someone powerful keeps him safe.'

Chen fell silent. The list of questions in his mind had grown longer, not shorter. Why would the Russian Fascist leader venture into such a place? Who was he seeing? Was it business, blackmail—or something darker still?

Whatever the reason, Chen knew one thing with certainty: to get close to Rodzaevsky, he would have to go deeper into Harbin's shadows than he had ever gone before.

And he would have to do it soon.

Chen knew he had the perfect team to investigate. The Wang Brothers would easily blend in. He instructed them to carry out both day and night surveillance in Nakhalova, rather than at Rodzaevsky's residence, in light of the new information and to gain a clearer understanding of his peculiar behaviour. They were delighted. Keeping watch over Rodzaevsky's home at night had been tedious and unrewarding.

Next, Chen inquired about the music hall, a place he had passed several times.

'And what do we know about Cabaret Fantasia?'

This time, it was Li who responded:

'Quite a bit. I've a friend—very attractive—who worked there as a cocktail waitress. All the waitresses are Chinese. The place is modelled on Shanghai venues. They put on burlesque shows with scantily clad girls, troupes playing nostalgic Russian folk songs, comedy acts, magicians. But it's most famous for jazz. When Sergei Ermoll and his six-piece swing band are billed, the tickets sell out instantly.'

Ms Liu arched an eyebrow.

'It seems the devil's music has seduced our comrade. I wonder—does he own a phonograph?'

Li blushed furiously. The others burst into laughter at his expense.

But Chen said nothing. The detail mattered. A man's leisure revealed as much as his politics. Harbin's jazz halls, where identities blurred in sound and smoke, were loud enough to make private conversations possible.

It didn't take long for the Wang Brothers to uncover what Rodzaevsky was doing in Nakhalova. Most traffic there consisted of hand-pulled rickshaws and the occasional horse-drawn cart. On the third evening, just after dusk, they spotted his car. The driver parked one block from the destination. There was no visible security. Rodzaevsky stepped out, dressed in plain clothes, a briefcase in hand. Two men, pistols drawn, escorted him down the street to a building with a pink light in the window. A sign above bore characters in Japanese and Russian. Recognising the Japanese characters—visually similar to Chinese—the brothers deduced it was a barbershop. Later, they confirmed the proprietor was Nakamura, a man the *Teke* cell knew by reputation.

Rodzaevsky stayed inside for just over an hour before returning to his car. As the night wore on, more clients arrived—some by car, others on foot. Judging by appearance and dress, they included Russians and Japanese. By 2.00 a.m., the flow had slowed to a trickle. By 3.00 a.m., the street was empty. Then a rickshaw arrived with what appeared to be pre-packed food—likely for the prostitutes. None emerged. It seemed they slept on site.

Chen assigned Wang Junior to night surveillance and Wang Senior to the day shift. His instructions were clear.

Each day, Wang Senior observed Nakamura's women emerge around noon. They seemed free to wander and choose their own meals—mostly Russian, Korean, Japanese, or Chinese. Only three were Chinese. Over three days, he confirmed that no guards followed them, but escape would be impossible. Nakamura's control was unspoken, but total.

He waited for one of the Chinese women to separate from the others.

It happened soon enough. Two went into a pharmacy selling cheap cosmetics. The third stood outside, shielding herself with a parasol. Wang approached, flicked open a switchblade, and pressed it gently against her lower back—just above the kidney, careful not to break the skin. He warned her not to scream. Her eyes widened, but she said nothing. He told her they would take a short walk.

In a quieter alley, he leaned against a wall and motioned for her to face him. Up close, she looked older—perhaps in her early forties—with a slight roll of belly fat beneath her tight dress. Her eyes flickered with panic, and her lips trembled. The hand holding the parasol was stiff and white with tension.

Wang folded the knife and slipped it into his pocket.

'I'm not going to hurt you. Unless you try to run. I'll pay you for your answers.'

He handed over a few banknotes. She tucked them into a concealed pocket—women here never carried purses; they'd be stolen.

Then he showed her a newspaper clipping with a photograph.

'Do you know this man?'

'Yes. A Russian. Kostya.'
'He comes for sex?'
She looked puzzled by the question, then understood.
'Sometimes. But before that, he often visits the boss upstairs.'
'Alone?'
She hesitated.
Wang gave her more money.
'Not always. Sometimes with a Japanese man. I've heard him speak the language with Nakamura. He wears a stiff-collared suit. A few weeks ago, when it was hot, he carried his jacket. Madam Calina asked me to hang it up. I felt something under the lapel. I lifted it. There was a gold chrysanthemum, embroidered—just like on army uniforms.'

Wang recognised the symbol. Kenpeitai. Rodzaevsky's link to Japan's secret police was confirmed.

'Does the Japanese man go with the women?'
'Never.'
'What about Kostya? What kind of women does he prefer?'
'Only us Chinese. One in particular.'
'Her name?'
'Number Three. I'm Number Two.'
'Why Chinese?'
She gave a tight, knowing smile.
'Because we work hard to please. The Japanese girls? They'll use their mouths, but they don't like to be touched below. No fingers. No nothing. They say it's dirty—or maybe they're just scared. Kostya prefers us. We don't argue. We get it done.'
'And Number Three is his favourite?'
'Yes. Once, when she was sick, he came to me. I made him spill his seed twice. He even tipped me. Want to know how?'
'No.'
'He's hairy. A massive beard. Hair all over. Naked, he looks like a monkey. It was disgusting.'

They parted. She told him to come back if he wanted more—for a price.

It was time to take stock. Chen and his team had gathered valuable intelligence on Rodzaevsky, but placing someone close to him remained a challenge. The *Teke* team agreed: eavesdropping was not enough. They needed a longer-term strategy.

The most promising option was to place a Chinese operative as a chauffeur for the VFP. The Wang Brothers had confirmed that the Rodzaevskys didn't employ a maid—or perhaps couldn't afford one. It was a gamble, but as Li noted, many White Russians, Jews, Poles, foreign diplomats, and Japanese officials used Chinese drivers. They were considered discreet, reliable—and knew the city's peculiar layout. In Harbin, some districts drove on the left, others on the right, depending on which foreign power had last claimed authority. A Chinese driver could navigate that chaos without drawing attention.

But how to make Rodzaevsky accept such a driver? No White Russian or Japanese agent had ever been turned, and any Red Russian posing as an insider would be swiftly exposed. Hiring a gangster might work for kidnapping or murder—but not for infiltration.

Then Bai spoke, more from irritation than inspiration.

'Kaspé.'

Chen looked up.

'What is Kaspé?'

'Not what—who.'

'Josef Kaspé was one of Harbin's wealthiest Jews, owner of the city's finest emporiums and entertainment venues, including the Hotel Moderne. The hotel includes a private wing, a luxury cinema, a theatre seating over a thousand, and an in-house jewellery shop. His wealth was legendary—his Fabergé collection, unmatched. Despite his background, Kaspé could operate freely. Rodzaevsky spent years vilifying him in his writings—calling him a Red Jewish Comintern agent. Ridiculous, but potentially useful.'

'Go on.'

'Kaspé had two sons—Simeon and Vladimir. They lived in France and took over the Moderne. Simeon was a concert pianist—Paris Conservatoire, class of 1933. When he arrived in Harbin on tour, his father raised the French flag over the hotel. As a French citizen, Simeon thought he was safe.'

Chen frowned. 'I still don't see the connection.'

'Because on 24 August 1933, Simeon was kidnapped. The key suspects were Inspector Martinov, Nakamura, and Rodzaevsky. Our source—Yuan—says Nakamura provided the safe house. Kaspé refused to pay the ransom. The gang panicked. They cut off Simeon's ears and sent them to his father. Still, he wouldn't pay. In December, the boy's body was found in a shallow grave near Xiaolin.'

Chen stiffened. 'That was two and a half years ago.'

'Yes. The trial ended last month—quietly, and under a municipal court. Four men were sentenced to death, including Martinov.'

'Were they executed?'

'No. Two days later, the Japanese arrested the judge. The verdict was voided. Martinov is expected to return to his post.'

Chen fell silent. The weight of it settled slowly.

'So, Josef Kaspé has every reason to take revenge?'

'He does. But he's never been violent. After burying his son, he left for Paris.'

Chen nodded slowly.

'Then maybe we do it for him.'

The meeting ended, but Chen asked Wang Senior to stay behind.

'I need your contacts again. I'm looking for a Chinese flower girl (*huā gūniang*— 花姑娘)—young, attractive, clever. She must speak some Russian, ideally a little English. And she must be exceptionally good in bed.'

'That won't be easy. Who's paying?'

'I am. She'll earn more from the target. She'll also be placed as a cocktail waitress.'

Chen named the fee.

Wang whistled. 'That much?'

'She'll be under contract. No other clients. If she wants to leave, she must ask. She'll be given a safe exit route.'

'And if she bolts?'

'Tell her we'll find her and terminate her.'

'Anything else?'

Chen hesitated. He remembered Zhou Enlai's rule about sparrows. 'Yes. She must not be a Party member.'

Wang grinned. 'That's hardly likely. I'll start looking.'

Chen wasn't sure if he was breaking a rule—but he'd face the consequences later, if he lived.

Chapter 26: Dataozi, Japanese Empire of Manchukuo, 1936

Chen had planned a training exercise for his team on the outskirts of Harbin, selecting a location near Dataozi, across the Songhua River. The area, unlike the surrounding flatlands given over to arable farming, was forested—birch trees and scattered glades offered just enough cover. Yet the plan had to be postponed with the arrival of a newcomer.

Her name was Tao Baoqi, and Chen—accompanied by Ms Liu—was the first to meet her. She wore an orange *qipao* tailored to accentuate her curves, with a thigh-high slit revealing her delicate, doll-like legs. The prim Ms Liu was unimpressed; in private, she muttered that the girl looked like a strumpet. Securing her a position among the ever-changing roster of cocktail waitresses at Cabaret Fantasia would be easy; drunken groping and backside-slapping by White Russians regularly drove the others away. Chen dismissed Ms Liu before addressing Baoqi.

'Has Mr Wang explained my requirements clearly?'

'Yes, you want me to seduce this Rod... zer?'

'Yes—and his name is Rodzaevsky.'

'You're paying me well. Are you hoping I'll get him talking?'

Chen was impressed. She was sharp enough to guess he might be a spy.

'No. Just stay close to him—keep him content in any way you can. It's a dangerous task. You may be questioned about your relationship with him.'

'So, if I let him have his way and I'm pulled in for questioning, as long as I never mention this meeting, I'll be in the clear—and you can carry on with whatever business you have with him. That way, we both survive?'

'Something like that.'

She studied him for a moment, then darted forward and threw her arms around him.

'You're the bravest man I've ever met, Mr Feng—though I doubt that's your real name. Now hug me—but hands off.'

'I'm happily married.'

'You dear man, that's what they all say.'

In her first week at Cabaret Fantasia, Baoqi proceeded cautiously, but the manager quickly recognised her value. She served drinks with elegance and warmth, easily charming the clientele. Her target was easy to spot—always seated at his usual corner table—though her own serving area was some distance away. She thought she'd caught him looking at her, but nothing more came of it.

The following week, however, the manager asked her to attend that very table. An important guest—a politician—was present. Five men sat there, all in suits and ties. The manager introduced her in Russian to Messrs Rodzaevsky, Pokrovsky, Balykov, Dolov, and their guest of honour, Mr Matkovsky.

Matkovsky switched to fluent Mandarin, complimented her beauty and her exquisite silk *qipao*, and asked if she spoke any other languages. She replied that she spoke a little Russian and some English. He translated for the others. While she was at the bar, the manager approached and whispered,

'Pay special attention to Matkovsky and Rodzaevsky—especially the former.'

The drinks flowed, the entertainment progressed, and at one point the men began singing an old Russian gipsy tune. They grew increasingly drunk—except for Rodzaevsky, who sipped champagne. It was Dolov who noticed Rodzaevsky's fixed gaze on Baoqi and muttered,

'So, you like a bit of Chinese, huh?'

Rodzaevsky shrugged. Later, on his way to the restroom, he paused and quietly asked Baoqi if she could serve his table on his regular Thursday visits. Her reply, delivered in halting Russian with a suggestive undertone and a wagging finger, made her meaning clear: she preferred gentlemen who kept their hands to themselves, and his companions would need to behave. He awkwardly offered,

'We could go dancing one day—'

He immediately reconsidered. Where could someone of his public stature take a woman like her? He wasn't even particularly attractive. But her response was unexpectedly warm:

'I would like that very much, sir.'

At the end of the night, he left a tip that—for a notorious skinflint—was almost generous.

A few days later, the Teke team set off on foot for Dataozi, walking for two hours. None of them knew what Chen had in mind, and he refused to explain. He had instructed the Wang Brothers to bring three semi-automatic pistols with ample ammunition, a bundle of farm tools—including two axes and a knife—a coil of rope, a tape measure, and a basic hoist with tackle. He had also asked Li to bring an old shirt and jacket, a basket of bread, and four of the smallest, firmest watermelons he could find.

They stopped at a village on the outskirts, where Chen collected a pre-arranged horse-drawn cart. Inside was a crate containing a pig, three five-metre wooden planks, and a vat of water. He rejoined the others, and they continued with the cart—just large enough to carry the team—for another hour until they reached a clearing in the forest. There they dismounted and unloaded the pig, while Chen took out the tape measure and recorded several dimensions of the cart's base and wheels.

He then told the group to rest—except for the Wang Brothers, whom he instructed to chop four logs, each sixty centimetres long. These were to be positioned upright—two on each side of the cart—twenty centimetres in from the rims of the wheels. The brothers then straddled the logs with two of the planks, creating makeshift running boards.

Once the preparations were complete, Chen instructed Bai to prop the third plank upright against a tree and fasten one of the watermelons at a height of around one and a half metres. A strip torn from the shirt was tied lower down on the board to represent a second target. He handed out the pistols—loaded—and paced six metres back.

'This is a dummy target,' he said. 'Walk three metres backwards, advance, turn, and fire once at the head, once at the heart.'

Each brother followed the instructions. Bai examined the results and confirmed both had hit their marks. Chen nodded, satisfied. Then he had them step back to eight metres and repeat the exercise—without advancing.

This time, Wang Senior missed the head, and Wang Junior missed both targets. Chen took up position at the eight-metre mark. Raising his pistol, he fired twice.

'Both direct hits,' Bai confirmed.

Wang Junior stared.

'You're firing as well?'

'Yes. In the real event—at your brother.'

They both gaped. Wang Senior, turning pale, muttered,

'With shooting like that, you'll kill me.'

'No, I won't—but I will come close.'

Then, it was time for the pig. Chen ordered Wang Junior to cut some rope and secure the animal's legs. Using the hoist, they slung the line over a low branch and, with effort, raised the pig by its hind legs until its head dangled downward, swaying gently. Its terrified porcine squeals echoed through the trees. Even Bai turned away, jaw clenched.

Chen instructed Li to fetch the old shirt and jacket. He tore them into strips and wrapped them around the pig's front legs—two layers each. Then came the knives. He directed Wang Senior to make the first incision—halfway up the humerus—deep enough to cut through the cloth and create a wound of moderate depth.

Wang Senior obliged with enthusiasm. The pig screamed. Chen leaned in and saw bone glistening. Too deep.

'Again,' he said.

The second attempt was no better. Wang protested.

'Shouldn't we just kill it first?'

'No. I need to see how much blood it loses.'

He handed the task to Wang Junior. On his second and third attempts, he achieved the desired wound—a jagged but not fatal gash.

Chen nodded.

'Good, because the next time you do this for real, it will be on my arm.'

Then he gave the final order.

'Slit its throat.'

There was a pause. A moment later, silence fell, broken only by a faint, wet gurgle.

If there had been any doubt among the *Teke* team, there was none now: Chen had a plan and was firmly in control. He placed two logs on either side of the cart, then laid the planks across them. Ms Liu was the first to understand—it was a mock-up of the Maybach. Chen responded,

'Not quite, the running boards are longer and are set at double the height of the Maybach to account for the fact the cart wheels are larger in diameter. Please keep that in mind when we get to the real event.'

One final component remained. Chen reached into his pocket and produced a pack of ten ileostomy bags and a roll of heavy-duty sticky tape.

Ms Liu, ever knowledgeable, explained, 'They're bags for collecting excrement when someone can't pass it normally.'

'Correct,' Chen said. 'When full, each pouch holds around a litre of liquid. This clip releases the contents slowly. On the day, the pouches will be filled with pig's blood.'

He demonstrated by filling one with water from the vat and taping it to Wang Senior's abdomen. Then, he arranged the team.

Li took the driver's seat, Xu became Rodzaevsky, and Ms Liu sat beside him in the role of his wife. Chen and Bai climbed onto the running boards. The Wang Brothers were stationed a short distance from either side of the cart.

Now Chen explained the plan and that he would play dual roles, switching to a second one once his role as a guard was complete and he was 'dead'.

This was to be an attempted kidnapping. If Rodzaevsky were to die, the mission would be a failure. In such a case, any survivors were to retreat to a getaway car.

'The operation will take place on a level stretch of Kitayskaya Ulitsa. The car will be moving south. The street is nine metres wide—enough for parked cars on both sides and a single moving lane in each direction. Vehicular traffic is usually light, though the pavements are always crowded with people. Wang Junior, you'll attack from the near pavement. Your brother will cross the road and strike from the far pavement. That's why, during the shooting drill, you both stepped forward before firing—pavements are crowded. Shoppers may jostle or obstruct you, but the shooter must remain stationary to hit a moving target. If both move, the difficulty increases dramatically.'

Then he addressed the issue of the guards.

'You'll notice that Bai and I, standing on the running boards, are almost the same height as Rodzaevsky and his wife seated inside the car. Therefore, the shots must be fired just after the car passes. Each guard must be hit twice—in the back and in the back of the head. Otherwise, we risk killing Rodzaevsky, though based on your shooting so far, that risk is low. Still, until they're dead, we're outgunned four to two. The driver does not carry a holstered weapon, but he keeps a gun in the glovebox. Rodzaevsky wears one in a shoulder holster.'

Turning to Wang Senior, Chen said,

'You'll then jump onto the running board—Rodzaevsky always sits opposite the driver—and point your pistol close to his head. You will say: '*Если ты дотянешься до своего пистолета, я убью тебя*'—"If you reach for your pistol, I will kill you." I'll teach you the phrase later. It's tricky, with odd pronunciation. For now, use Mandarin—but remember, you won't be dressed in Chinese clothing.'

He turned to Wang Junior.

'Next, you'll shoot the driver. Aim for the head.'

'Why the head?'

'Because only a brain shot shuts down all motor function—no spasm, no reflex. If he's hit in the body but not killed, he might recover, reach for the pistol in the glove compartment, or even drive off. Don't shoot too soon, though. Give him a second or two to hit the brake. Of course, a trained professional would instinctively accelerate the moment the guards go down—and if that happens, we fall back.'

Chen looked at both men.

'Once the driver is down, Wang Junior will drag him clear and will attempt to climb into the seat. It will be difficult—dead weight, pistol in hand, and the need to stay balanced, composed, and fast.'

Wang Senior gave a knowing nod. He had done something like this before.

'At that moment,' Chen said, 'a man will drop a breadbasket on the near pavement, rush towards Wang Junior and twist his wrist to the breaking point, seize his weapon, and stay behind him—out of Wang Senior's firing line. Wang Senior will try to circle the back of the car to help, but the bakery delivery man will fire at him—he will miss. Wang Senior will shout at his brother to run, and both will flee across the road.'

'And then?' asked Wang Junior.

'I'll try to take the driver's seat but temporarily won't be able to fire my pistol. You'll draw your knife, slash my left arm and run. This time, pretend. Then I'll recover, fire three shots: the first two will narrowly miss your brother; the third will go high and wide—into a chimney flue or the crumbling stone cornice above the awnings. I've already identified several of them. That bullet will fragment or vanish completely. On that third shot, Wang Senior falls, clutching his stomach, and the pouch on his abdomen releases its contents. You'll tuck your pistol into your waistband and drag him by the shoulders. Both of you retreat to the getaway car, which heads south, navigating around the bloody scene. Meanwhile, Ms Liu will drop a swatch of clothing near the pool of blood.'

Chen took a breath. 'Any questions?'

'What about hitting bystanders?' Li asked.

'Don't worry. Harbiners know how to run at the sound of gunfire. They'll scatter —and I won't hit any of the stragglers.'

'Why slash your arm?' asked Bai. 'A leg would be safer.'

'I'll be wearing a traditional gown. The legs are hidden—it's hard to slash accurately.'

'And what will we be wearing?' asked Wang Senior.

'Suits, ties, and boaters—or summer hats.'

'How do we escape?'

'In a stolen getaway car. Li will drive. Bai will be armed and ride with him. I've already picked the vehicle. Wang Junior will break into it.'

Had Chen considered every angle? Not quite—but he wasn't saying.

He never said more than necessary. What mattered was control—the plan, the team, the theatre of violence they were about to perform. But even he could feel the faint tremor beneath it all. One twitch of a finger, one moment too late, and it would all unravel.

They spent the rest of the day rehearsing—first in slow motion, then at full speed. By the fifth attempt, Chen was satisfied. To an outsider, it might have sounded like a hunting expedition—wild boar or pheasants, perhaps—given the gunfire.

They buried the dead pig, and the cart, vat, and planks were returned to the farmer. They walked home late in the afternoon. Along the way, Chen had Wang Senior practise his Russian line again and again, ensuring he understood that pistol was *pistoyl*. He also asked if anyone could dog-whistle. They tried. Only the Wang Brothers and Xu succeeded.

Xu was appointed lookout. He would whistle to signal to abort, should anything go awry.

Chen couldn't force the sound from his lips. Bai remarked drily, 'They don't teach you that at spy school?'

The attempt was scheduled for one week later. The final preparations began the night before. At the safe house, Ms Liu arrived with a large paper shopping bag printed with the name *Mordecai Berenson and Son, Tailors*. Inside were the outfits she had purchased, along with suitable shoes.

She also brought a wicker box. Opening it, she pulled out two hinged drawers filled with cosmetics. She began with Wang Senior, snipping off his ponytail and giving him a fresh cut. Wang Junior's hair was already short. She dyed both heads brown and waved them with heat. Next, she applied adhesive to smooth their upper eyelids, eliminating creases. Then came foundation and tints, transforming their skin from wheat to olive—concealing Wang Senior's scar.

She painted deep brown eyeliner above and below each eye, white along the waterline, and curled their lashes. For the final touch, she glued on a false beard and moustache for Wang Senior, trimming it carefully.

The men changed into their tailored clothes. Ms Liu used shears to cut a swatch from the inner pocket of Wang Senior's beige summer suit and frayed it.

Ms Liu stood back, eyeing her work with the quiet satisfaction of a painter finishing a canvas. She said nothing—but the glint in her eye spoke of pride.

Everything would require touching up in the morning—but the transformation was complete. By morning, the Wang Brothers no longer looked like operatives at all—they were Russian gentlemen, right down to their shoes.

The pig's blood was delivered early that morning to a rendezvous point near Dataozi. The farmer who supplied it had been paid well—and though curious about the loss of a hog and the mysterious demands for pig's blood, he knew better than to ask questions.

The attempted kidnapping took place the following Saturday. Rodzaevsky, dressed in a suit and tie, and his wife, wearing a silk headscarf and sunglasses, set off to play bridge. They followed their usual route along *Kitayskaya Ulitsa* and across the railway bridge—the only practical access to *Novy Gorod* and the Railway Club.

Wang Senior broke into the getaway car, hotwired it, and drove to the safe house, where the Wang Brothers, already disguised from the night before, made final adjustments before collecting Bai and Li. False number plates were affixed over the originals. The heat inside the vehicle was stifling, but the makeup did not run.

By 9.30 a.m., they were in position, with Xu stationed further up the street as lookout, and the getaway car parked just north of the site of the attack. At 9.50 a.m., a loud whistle rang out—the signal that Rodzaevsky was approaching the interdiction team. At 9.56 a.m., the operation began.

Shots cracked through the air. Two security guards collapsed onto the road. The driver, having stalled the car while braking, was dragged—

already dead—onto the pavement. There seemed to be some sort of altercation between one of the attackers and a man who had interfered with the new driver. Ms Liu screamed at the already panicking crowd to flee, dropped the cloth swatch, and began to run. As the Wang Brothers retreated, Chen—bleeding and in considerable pain—had a clear line of sight. He fired at the man still holding a gun. Chen restarted the engine, accelerated, and stopped one kilometre further down the road.

Turning to a pale Rodzaevsky, he handed him his empty pistol—stock first, gripping the tepid barrel—in case he hadn't yet realised he'd saved them.

Rodzaevsky slowly unholstered his own pistol. Only then did the couple begin to grasp the truth. This man had saved their lives.

Lydia turned to her husband.

'Do you have a handkerchief?'

He was too stunned to reply. She unwound her scarf and pressed it gently to the bleeding wound on Chen's arm.

For the first time that day, Chen closed his eyes. The pain had settled into a dull throb, but it wasn't the blood loss that concerned him—it was the margin for error. Until now, he had always sent others into the field. One of them, Comrade Tang, had died. Now, for the first time, he understood the razor-thin divide between success and failure—between life and death.

The critical part of the operation had lasted less than five minutes.

The Municipal Police were first to arrive. They dragged Chen from the vehicle at gunpoint as Lydia tried desperately to explain what had occurred. Two Kenpeitai officers arrived shortly afterwards. One spoke Russian and, having listened to Lydia's account, defused the situation. He took Rodzaevsky's two pistols and asked whether there were any other weapons. With trembling fingers, Rodzaevsky pointed to the glove compartment, from which another pistol was retrieved.

By then, Lydia had lost her composure.

'Are you blind?' she cried. 'This man saved our lives!' Then, steadying her voice, she added, 'Please. He needs help.'

Chen was driven to the Guard Forces Hospital. The Rodzaevskys were escorted home and informed that they would be interviewed later that day. Once the scene was secured and the bodies removed, Major Kenzou Miyake arrived. He made it clear that he was taking charge. No one dared to argue.

The interviews were completed by 3.00 p.m. Lydia told her husband she was going to the hospital and had arranged for a Russian friend from the orchestra—who spoke Chinese—to act as translator. She wanted to meet the young man who had saved them.

Kostya declined.

'A Jewish hospital,' he muttered, though the staff came from various backgrounds.

Lydia asked her friend what gifts might be appropriate. She had not cried. Not when she saw the bodies, nor when she saw the blood. But once home, something shifted. The urge to do something—anything—kind rose to the surface.

They began by preparing a nutritious soup with rice, packed it into a traditional Chinese stacking lunch thermos, then stopped to buy tinned peaches and pastries.

At the hospital, the doctor assured them the patient was recovering well and would be discharged in the morning. While his wounds were mild by local standards, he joked that the hospital might not possess a suitable implement to open exotic canned fruit—but promised to find a way.

They were granted half an hour with the patient. Chen, mildly sedated and already interrogated, greeted them with quiet modesty.

Through the translator, he explained that his instincts had been shaped by previous work as a chauffeur and guard. With his aunt now out of her plaster cast, he planned to return to Xiamen. He worried that his former employer had already replaced him, and with the economic downturn he'd heard of, finding work would be difficult.

What followed, understood by Chen in both Chinese and Russian, changed everything.

'Mr Feng,' Lydia said, 'once you've recovered—if I can arrange it—

would you consider driving for my husband and me? I've never felt as safe with anyone. You risked your life for us. I wouldn't trust anyone else.'

Chen was silent a moment before replying to the translator.

'I would very much like such a position. I believe I can quickly learn the Russian for "left", "right", and "straight on"—and how to point at a street map.

When Lydia returned home and relayed what had occurred, she was surprised to find that Kostya did not object.

'It's common to have Chinese drivers nowadays. This man would be an asset. I've lost three good men. In different circumstances, we might both have been killed. I'll need to get him clearance from Bolotov first.'

Chen was exactly the man Rodzaevsky needed—though for a different purpose.

That evening, Chen received one final visitor: the manager of Bomele, the local cake and bread shop. She explained that all the bread dropped during the incident had been gathered and sold. A sign had gone up in the window: *Proceeds in honour of the Heroes of the White Revolution.* The public responded generously. Politics, it seemed, touched everything—even bread.

Without a word, she handed Chen a bulging envelope. The transaction said more than any slogan could.

Chapter 27: Harbin, Japanese Empire of Manchukuo, 1936

At the next meeting on the Rodzaevsky case, held the day after the attempted kidnapping, Miyake assembled his team, consisting of the heads of forensics, ballistics, and a senior intelligence officer. He could hardly hide his irritation that the head of the Russian Fascists had been attacked and that the incident had made the morning editions of several newspapers. He began to ask questions of the others who had gathered.

'I have read the report and have already spoken to Rodzaevsky and his wife, both of whom are still in shock. I do not believe this was a murder attempt, as the attackers had ample opportunity to kill them both. I want to start with the ballistics. It seems that five shots were fired in quick succession at the guards and driver?'

'That's correct. All found their intended targets—fired from the rear, striking both the head and heart of the guards, and the head of the driver.'

'And then it appears that matters went wrong—and this Chinese man, Feng Shaogong, intervened?'

'He did, and wrestled the gun from an assailant, firing a shot at his partner but missing as he was able to take cover behind the car. That man then attempted to flee. Feng then tried to get into the driver's seat, but the assailant—whom Feng had disarmed—slashed his arm with a knife before running off.'

'Then Feng fired three more shots, and, according to eyewitnesses, the third shot struck the attacker. We have already interviewed Feng at the hospital, where he is recovering from the knife wound, and he told us he simply emptied the magazine.'

'So, did we recover all the bullets and spent casings?'

'Yes, all the spent casings—and all but one bullet, the one with which Feng scored a hit.'

'And the weapon that Feng handed over to Rodzaevsky?'

'A FÉG Model 37M with a registration number, but untraceable to the owner from that.'

'Hungarian?'

'Correct—and a weapon of choice for a professional. Seven bullets per clip.'

'And the weapon that killed the second guard with two shots—was it Japanese?'

'No. It was 9×17mm and could be one of many. Perhaps a Beretta. Our standard issue, as you know, is always 8×22mm. Not a Japanese-issue round.'

That was something of a relief.

'But if we recover the other pistol, you could match it to the recovered bullets and casings?'

'Likely. Barrel striations on the bullet, firing pin and extractor marks on the casing—they're as unique as fingerprints. If it hasn't been scrubbed, we'll know.'

'And the fingerprints on the FÉG?'

'Scrambled. The gun has been handled many times.'

'Let's discuss the wounded assailant. What do we know?'

'Quite a lot. Eyewitnesses agreed that the third shot struck him somewhere in the abdomen, and he started to bleed profusely. He was screaming in agony, consistent with one of the most painful wounds possible, to the stomach or nearby. Although the blood had already begun congealing in the warm weather, I estimate he lost one and a half litres before being bundled into the escape car.'

'And the blood—definitely human? Could it have been faked?'

'We can only confirm it wasn't a concoction designed to look like human blood. I suppose it could have come from an animal, but the other evidence doesn't support that, so we can't be certain. However, we did find a small piece of blood-stained cloth—perhaps from trousers or a jacket—ripped off the wounded man as he was dragged along the street.'

'How long could someone survive such a wound without treatment?'

'A few hours at most. It would require immediate surgery, and even then, survival would be unlikely if he lost three litres or more.'

Miyake turned to his intelligence officer.

'Has anyone shown up at the hospital in this state?'

'No one has.'

'And who is this man, Feng Shaogong?'

'We sent the Municipal Police to investigate. He is temporarily working in a bakery owned by his aunt, who slipped on some oil and broke her leg. They searched his room and found nothing of interest—he has few possessions. He has three regular friends of a similar age; one man and two women, with whom he sometimes dines at a restaurant. He seems genuinely popular with the locals and the vendors whom he visits on his bread delivery rounds. He is from Xiamen, where he previously worked as a chauffeur for a wealthy Singaporean businessman who had sent him on a protection training course, including firearms training. We are in the process of verifying that information.'

'What about the car?'

'Black, almost certainly a Ford, with false plates. It was stolen earlier in the day, and the owner didn't even realise it was missing for four hours. We still haven't found it.'

'And the kidnappers' clothing and appearance?'

'Fashionable—Russian styles, olive skin, and one with a beard. One wore a blazer and tie, sporting a boater. The other, who was shot, wore a beige suit, a tie, and a white flat cap.'

'I'll tell you in a moment where I think you'll find the car, but first—when I spoke to Rodzaevsky, he was clear that the man who held the gun to his head used the word "pistoyl", whereas the correct word in Russian is "pistolet".'

'Is that significant?'

'Highly. Rodzaevsky recognised the word—it's Yiddish. Almost all White Russians in Harbin can't speak the language. There is a slight possibility they're Red Russian Bolsheviks—more likely, they're from out of town. If I'm right, you'll find an abandoned car, maybe a dead body, and even a tailor working with the same suit cloth near Artilleriyskaya Ulitsa, the central Jewish area. For now, we can rule out a gang from Nakhalova or the communist Chinese. This was a professional job,' he said slowly. 'Even though it went wrong. I think we've been fed a line. Someone else is steering this.'

Within the day, the Municipal Police, with Kenpeitai support—since the TK lacked the resources for such an extensive search—had found the getaway car, parked in a side street close to where Miyake had predicted, its interior bloodstained. A local Jewish tailor confirmed that the cloth and colour were commonly used by tailors in the area, but no injured or dead man had been found. When the three men reconvened, Miyake was even more convinced of his analysis.

'Gentlemen, professional assassins and kidnappers rarely make mistakes. Yet, we have a man speaking the wrong language, clothing linked to Jewish tailors, and a car found in the Jewish area. We have one used weapon: the Hungarian FÉG 37M, which is not commonly found in Harbin. Many people want to see Rodzaevsky dead, but this doesn't feel right, especially since there was no effort to kill him. However, there is one person with both the resources and the strongest motive.'

'Kaspé?'

'Yes, Kaspé—even if he's in Paris.'

'But why wouldn't Kaspé have Rodzaevsky killed?'

'I don't know, but there is an old Jewish saying—"an eye for an eye, a tooth for a tooth"—and perhaps the old man felt Rodzaevsky was only peripheral to his son's murder.'

Two days later, Mr Kyaw-Yap Ng received a call at home from a man claiming to be a detective with the Xiamen Police. Mr Ng confirmed that Feng Shaogong had originally been employed as a gardener and, upon his chauffeur's retirement, had requested to be trained as his replacement. He had been sent to driving school and instructed in both security and self-defence, just as his predecessor had been. The following day, Mr Ng received another visitor—this time a Russian diplomat—who asked nearly identical questions. The interviewee expressed surprise, having been asked almost the same questions the day before.

Bolotov told Rodzaevsky that he wanted another Russian driver but was overruled and instructed to interview Chen to ensure he was not an impostor. When Chen arrived at VFP headquarters, he was ushered upstairs to a room with a translator. Bolotov—whom Chen immediately recognised—sat at a table, and Chen was shown to a chair.

Bolotov began noting down the basics: name and marital status—

Feng Shaogong, twenty-five, single. Reason for coming to Harbin—his aunt had broken her leg. Political affiliations or military experience—none. And so on.

His interviewer had wild eyes and a slight nervous tic, frequently pausing to sniff and blow into a handkerchief. Chen suspected the man was a cocaine user. Then Bolotov focused on Chen's background as a driver and security guard, informing him that he had already contacted his former employer, Mr Kyaw-Yap Chew.

Chen replied that there must be a mistake—the surname should be Ng. He was then asked to recount the attempted kidnapping from his perspective, which he did.

However, when it came to his motive for assisting Rodzaevsky, Bolotov grew angry and challenged the explanation of such an instinctive reaction.

Next came questions about languages. Did Chen speak any? Only Mandarin and a local Fujian dialect, though he had spent the past few days trying to learn a few basic Russian phrases for the job he hoped to secure. He was asked to provide an example.

'Отвези меня на вокзал.' (Take me to the railway station.)

It was barely intelligible.

Suddenly, Bolotov stood up, walked round to Chen's chair, grabbed him by his injured left arm, squeezed it hard, barking at the translator to be accurate.'

'You are a lying piece of shit. Who are you working for? Are you a communist?'

Rodzaevsky heard the screams of pain along the corridor, ran to the interview room, saw what was happening, and angrily told Bolotov to let go and sit down.

Chen gingerly held his arm and listened to an incredible conversation, keeping his face as blank as possible while the translator cowered.

'What the fucking hell do you think you are doing?'

'My job is sifting out any security risks.'

'By torturing a man who saved me?'

'I considered that, and yet, he still has all his fingernails intact.'
'Well, I want him as my new driver.'
'I will not let that happen.'
'You will do as you are told, you insolent prick. Because of your incompetence and the lack of training in your team, I have three dead men and their widows to speak to.'
'If you had thought about the dangers of posing in public, it might not have happened.'
'So, you are accusing me of being responsible for their deaths?'
'Partly. But anyway, I won't allow you to take on this man.'
'Yes, you will, and you will fucking well obey my orders, you drug-crazed lowlife.'
'And if I don't?'
'I will arrange with Matkovsky to deport you to the USSR tomorrow.'

Chen was hired and given servant's quarters in Pristan. The day before he started his new job, Lydia brought him an impeccable uniform, including a white chauffeur's cap with a black rim and white gloves. He thanked her profusely, clasping his hands together to show it. Rodzaevsky arranged a private meeting with a translator on his first day of employment to explain his terms and conditions. He was promised one day off per week, more than decent wages, and was required to be available at antisocial hours and remain confidential about his movements, with the understanding that Bolotov might try to find some dirt on him. Chen had one request: he didn't want to drive to any Japanese offices due to his fear of them, so it had been agreed that a relief driver would be assigned for such tasks. More importantly, Chen didn't want any questions to be asked about his job or to be recognised by an officer involved in investigating the attempted kidnapping. It might happen anyway, but there was no need to invite trouble. Chen proved to be a model driver—always safe, considerate, and dependable. By now, he also knew that the Japanese had not found the high and wide bullet from the kidnapping attempt, as he had not been questioned again.

Rodzaevsky did not go to Cabaret Fantasia for two weeks. Besides the shock of nearly being kidnapped, he was also dealing with growing problems involving Vonsiatsky in the United States. After an acrimonious year, the two men irreconcilably split following the Third Congress of All Russian Fascists, which ended on 7 July 1935. With Vonsiatsky boycotting the event, he was stripped of all titles and expelled from the VFP. It was hardly surprising. The perspectives of the two men were fundamentally different. Rodzaevsky wanted a pan-National organisation, as antisemitic as possible, and sought to establish ties with Mussolini and Hitler. Only a fraction of the $500,000 promised by Vonsiatsky at the VFP's founding in Tokyo had ever materialised. Vonsiatsky, infuriated, had started using his well-funded publication, *The Fascist*, which was mailed out globally from the US. He used it to advocate for direct action within the USSR and even fabricated reports of loyal White Russian raids. Worse still, the same newspaper had hinted that Bolotov was involved in the Kaspé affair and continued attacking Ataman Semenov as a Cossack thug. In contrast, the Japanese considered Semenov integral to their plans, and the conference had endorsed cooperation between the Cossacks and the VFP. There were issues with the suave Matkovsky as well, who had formed a more moderate—and not antisemitic—faction within the party.

Rodzaevsky had made discreet inquiries and discovered an exclusive, members-only club that suited his needs. He visited, and the Russian owner explained that it was a venue where ladies and gentlemen could meet privately for lunch or dinner in secluded rooms, each escorted in and out separately to preserve discretion. Even the menus were divided—those given to the men listed prices; the ones for the ladies did not.

Rodzaevsky requested the men's menu and struggled to suppress a cough as he absorbed the exorbitant prices. To enhance discretion, a narrow slit was cut into the door, allowing guests to insert colour-coded cards visible from the outside: red signalled that service was required, blue indicated a request to visit the restroom—unobserved of course—yellow meant 'do not disturb', and green signified readiness to depart.

The annual membership fee was steep, with monthly invoices discreetly sent to his office marked *'Private'*—or, if preferred, payment could be made in cash. He told the owner he would think about it. He did not have the funds to support such a lifestyle—and could think of only one way to obtain them.

During Chen's first time driving him to Nakamura's, Rodzaevsky gave simple directions in Russian. Chen parked while his employer, flanked by two minders, disappeared inside carrying his briefcase. He remained inside for fifteen minutes. From the length of time, Chen deduced that his employer hadn't been with Number Three. He also noticed that the briefcase was now bulging. Chen could only guess, but he suspected this was how the VFP received its funding from the Japanese. He then drove across town to Rodzaevsky's home, opened the car door, saluted in the conventional manner, and left. That evening, once Lydia was asleep, Rodzaevsky pocketed a portion of the donation and secured it in his desk. He doubted he would be caught because the sum varied each time as no effort was made to reconcile the accounts. A flicker of guilt crossed his mind at the thought of stealing from his benefactors, but he justified it by reminding himself of his personal needs.

The next day—Thursday—he spent the evening in raucous company before inviting Baoqi to lunch the following Monday. She accepted, and he handed her a card with the address in Chinese. Chen drove his employer straight from the office. Rodzaevsky left his briefcase on the back seat without a word and disappeared inside.

Their first lunch together was a resounding success. With autumn setting in, Baoqi arrived in a fashionable yet modest coat and a Garbo hat, both of which were hung on a rack in the corner. They were seated opposite each other—positioned so she could not glimpse the prices on Rodzaevsky's menu—and were left undisturbed. Baoqi looked exquisite, donning the only other *qipao* she owned. Her hair was parted to the left, with added volume at the back, falling to neck length and secured with a stick pin. Her features were perfectly proportioned, with full lips accentuated by red lipstick, striking hazel eyes, and elegantly sculpted cheekbones. Unlike in the dim cabaret, her silky skin glowed, completing the image of an entirely captivating young woman. She was, moreover, charming and effortlessly witty.

The menu was printed in Russian and French. She slid her chair around to Kostya's side. As she moved, he caught a faint scent of jasmine perfume. Smiling, he turned over his own menu and began translating hers. He carefully enunciated the correct Russian pronunciation. She made a valiant attempt, but her delivery was a garbled mess. They burst into laughter and the awkwardness between them dissolved. Settling on a sumptuous selection of dishes and a half-bottle of Taittinger, Kostya signalled for service by placing the red card in the slit in the door. Almost immediately, a waiter appeared to take their order.

As they waited, he explained the purpose of the coloured cards. As a waitress, Baoqi was already familiar with the words for 'order', 'depart', and 'lavatory' in both Russian and English, but she puzzled over the yellow card. Kostya attempted to clarify its meaning until she suddenly asked, 'It's for kissing?' Her playful guess caught him off guard, and they both laughed again.

The waiter returned, poured the champagne, and placed the bottle into an ice bucket. Kostya raised his glass to toast Baoqi, but after the first sip he set it aside, untouched. She watched as he hesitated, and then learned his first words in Chinese for 'I don't like it': *Wǒ bù xǐhuan*—我不喜欢. Over lunch, they navigated each other's worlds through their stilted, patchwork conversations.

Baoqi attempted to share details about herself—her age, just twenty-five, and her hometown, a poor farming village near Dalian. She illustrated this by mimicking the sounds of farm animals. When Kostya spoke of his work, she struggled to grasp his role. From what she could gather, he was a soldier of some kind. What she understood with certainty, however, was that he was married.

As their time together drew to an end, Baoqi took the yellow card and placed it into the slit in the door. Returning to Kostya, she gestured for him to stand. Rising onto her tiptoes, she pressed lightly against his chest and placed a soft kiss on his cheek. She had never kissed a man with a beard before, but to her surprise, it wasn't as unpleasant as she had imagined. She replaced the yellow card with the green one. They stepped out together, parting with an unspoken understanding that they would meet here again soon.

Kostya brought a gift to their next lunch and asked Baoqi to open it. She beamed at the contents: an Art Deco white gold and enamel bracelet of exquisite quality. She asked him to fasten it around her slender wrist. They continued their mixed-language conversation, which was much improved this time as Baoqi had brought along a Chinese–Russian dictionary.

After they had eaten, she placed the yellow card in the door slit. Kostya grinned as she returned and sat beside him. This time, she kissed him on the lips and flicked her tongue inside his mouth. It was erotic because Lydia never did this, and Number Three wouldn't allow it. He placed his hand on the open side of her *qipao* and ran it upwards towards her thigh. She didn't pull away, and their breaths became more rapid. Then she removed his hand and said, 'Need big bed.' The green card replaced the yellow one.

Rodzaevsky returned to the club alone and spoke with the owner, who had dealt with this type of request on several previous occasions and handed him two keys. It was for a nearby basement apartment, accessed from the outside, which he described as quite luxurious. The cost would be added to Rodzaevsky's monthly bill for as long as he used it. The owner also mentioned they could deliver cold cuts and wine. The price was commensurately high.

 For Rodzaevsky, stealing had started as a habit—but now, it was becoming an addiction.

At the Cabaret Fantasia, Baoqi was careful to be a model waitress with her Russian clientele, not favouring any one man. Still, Rodzaevsky managed to slip her an envelope containing a key, date, and time, and from a brief nod, he knew she would be there.

On the agreed day, Baoqi made sure to arrive first to ensure the room was warm, closed the curtains, and filled and placed a circular rubber hot water bottle in the double bed. She wanted to make tea and found a powder that smelled familiar, placed next to a metal urn. She had seen such an object in Dalian—a samovar—but she had no idea how it worked. She would need to ask Kostya about it.

It was late afternoon. Rodzaevsky, impeccably dressed with a trimmed beard and carrying his briefcase, asked Chen to collect him from the office and informed him of their destination. Chen, watching in the rear-view mirror, noticed Rodzaevsky carefully placed the case at a peculiar angle, not aligned with the leather seat stitching.

Kostya returned Baoqi's warm greeting. There was no doubt about what was about to unfold. She showed him to the warm bed, gestured for him to undress, and went to the bathroom. A few minutes later, she returned, standing before him naked, and Kostya gasped. She possessed the most captivating figure. Her breasts were smaller than he had imagined, and he wondered whether her *qipao* had padding to accentuate them. They were perfectly formed, and her nipples were already erect. Her pubic hair was dense, much more than he had seen on any other woman.

She asked him in Chinese if he liked what he saw, and he replied, also in Chinese, that he did.

She lowered herself onto the bed. They briefly explored each other's bodies, but he was so aroused that she realised this was not the time for extensive foreplay. He was erect, grunting with excitement. She suddenly sat up, moved down the bed, turned over, and got onto all fours, allowing him to see her tender buttocks and tightly puckered anus. She used one hand seductively to open her most intimate parts, inviting him to come closer, and asked him in Chinese to join her.

Kostya had never seen anything like this and, without hesitation, penetrated her. He lasted less than three minutes but was delighted to discover that she also had an orgasm. Unaware at the time, he only later realised that no condom had been used and resolved to discuss it with her.

They spent the next two hours continuing to explore each other's bodies. Kostya was fascinated by Baoqi's lush thicket, while she used all the tricks she knew to please him. After that, she pointed to the samovar, and he showed her how to make Russian tea. They then made love again, this time in a more conventional position, which was equally satisfying. They tried talking for a while, then dressed, hugged, and parted.

Kostya wondered whether he should offer her money but felt it might be demeaning, and she did not ask for any. He felt overwhelmed.

Baoqi walked to the bus stop while Chen drove to Rodzaevsky's residence. As they set off, Chen watched through the mirror, noting how his employer glanced at the exact position of the briefcase—just as he had left it. Chen hadn't touched it. Upon arrival, Chen opened the car door and gave a respectful salute. He had used his waiting time effectively, secretly attaching a concealed magnetic box with a camera to the underside of the car.

Chapter 28: Moscow, USSR, 1936

Josef Stalin had spent much of his life chasing shadows. He systematically eliminated perceived enemies—Trotskyites, dissenters, and anyone whose loyalty he doubted. In March 1936, Hitler violated the Treaty of Versailles. He reoccupied the demilitarised Rhineland and sent troops to Spain to support Franco.

Fortunately for Stalin, talks for an Anti-Comintern Pact—initiated by Germany—were only approved by Japan. Great Britain, China, Italy, and Poland refused to sign, weakening the pact's impact. Still, these were ominous signs of a growing axis of power attempting to isolate the USSR.

Under mounting pressure, Stalin finally snapped and initiated the Great Purge—a brutal campaign that would last over two years. The dragnet spread far and wide, leading to the execution of perhaps 750,000 people, with over a million more sent to the gulags. His intelligence services were also gutted. Although the Chinese communists had conducted purges—particularly against Nationalists within the Red Army—Stalin's were of a different magnitude: indiscriminate, absolute.

In April 1935, he dismissed Jan Berzin, head of the GRU for over a decade, and replaced him with Semyon Uritsky. Berzin was sent to Asia, where he managed one of the USSR's most valuable assets: the German-born spy Richard Sorge. Having joined the Nazi Party as part of his cover, Sorge worked as the Japan correspondent for the *Frankfurter Zeitung*. In 1934, he visited Manchukuo, and by 1936, had begun forming a Tokyo-based spy ring. Despite Sorge's reports indicating that Japan would likely attack China rather than the USSR, Stalin refused to believe it.

Meanwhile, other intelligence intercepts suggested that Germany, Italy, and Japan were secretly negotiating a new pact—potentially one that would further encircle the USSR. Stalin pressed his Comintern Chief, Georgi Dimitrov, to facilitate cooperation between the Chinese communists and Chiang Kai-shek.

Zhou Enlai had discussed these international developments with Chen, though only in part. Zhou never revealed the full scope of his operations, which ran through many layers. Since November 1935, he had been quietly conducting secret talks with Chen Lifu, head of the Nationalist Investigation Section. These talks focused on forming a united anti-Japanese front—an idea Mao had endorsed during his interviews with Edgar Snow.

By the summer of 1936, the talks had broken down. There was simply too much bad blood between the parties. Chiang's refusal to prioritise the Japanese threat over his war on the communists proved immovable.

Yet some progress was made elsewhere, in secret meetings between Zhou and two of Chiang's allied commanders: the Young Marshal Zhang Xueliang of the Northeast Army, and General Yang Hucheng of the Northwest Army. Zhou and Zhang got on well. Both commanders favoured a united front and the formation of a new National Revolutionary Army (NRA) against the Japanese. Chiang flatly rejected the proposal.

Then, on 25 November 1936, Germany and Japan signed the Anti-Comintern Pact. Italy had not yet joined. Stalin's paranoia, once derided, now seemed fully justified. He also foresaw repercussions in China. Chiang's attempt to modernise the Nationalist Army had been built on German loans and weapons—many sourced directly from the Nazi regime. That arrangement, already precarious, now stood in jeopardy.

Rodzaevsky maintained his predictable routine, visiting Baoqi at least twice a week. In addition to gifts, he insisted on giving her money. In January, she requested enough to cover a month's rent for an apartment. Within a week, she secured a more discreet, affordable flat on the edge of Pristan District and relinquished her existing tenancy in the Chinese quarter. She began remaking the new space into their love nest—and studying a little more Russian.

Kostya had fallen deeply in love with her. They seldom dined at the private members' club anymore. Rodzaevsky had briefly considered whether she might be a spy, but she asked little about his work. Her spoken Russian was improving, yet she could read only a few words. Winter descended, and with it came the end of the open-top parades.

He still made regular visits to Nakamura, who had noticed the change in routine. Why Rodzaevsky no longer asked after Number Three puzzled him. He concluded that either the marriage had recovered—or someone new had taken Lydia's place.

Chen still hadn't dared to touch the briefcase. He had bought a penlight and placed it in the glove compartment alongside his pistol. A basic repair kit, including spanners and screwdrivers, was stored in the boot.

His first break came on 9 December, when the Packard was assigned to transport Rodzaevsky and five colleagues to Harbin Riverside Park for the second anniversary of Manzhouli Day. In that city, the fascists had erected a giant neon-lit swastika above their offices, three kilometres from the Russian border. It remained illuminated day and night.

They arranged for the drivers of three horse-drawn sledges to stage a race across the frozen Songhua River. As the men returned to the car, Chen overheard the tail-end of a conversation:

'His days are surely numbered, and our position will be much stronger once he is dead.'

'But is that possible? Perhaps it's a trap?'

'Miyake didn't think so—and he chose to inform us, in case of backlash from the local Chinese population. They might not have the support of an army, but there is a festering resentment against the Japanese and, by implication, against us in many places.'

'It's a curious situation. The Japanese merely have to sit back and watch the situation unfold.'

'As do we. Let's return to the office and discuss the necessary preparations.'

After work, Chen returned to his quarters, turning the fragment of conversation over in his mind. He couldn't make sense of it. It was only the following morning that he glimpsed a Russian newspaper left in the office waiting area. He dared not pick it up, but the headline froze him:

Chiang Kai-shek in Xi'an... No progress in peace talks with Marshal Zhang who will address angry students

From earlier reports, Chen inferred that Chiang was in Xi'an attempting to assert control over the Northeast Army after their humiliating defeat at Zhilou Town on 22 November. It now seemed clear that 'his days are surely numbered' referred to Chiang.

This was urgent. Chen had to contact Ms Liu immediately and relay a radio message to Bao'an. For emergencies, he relied on a word-of-mouth chain. For routine communication, he used dead-drop procedures.

The emergency protocol required him to stop at a corner shop during his short walk to work from his servant's quarters. It sold Russian cigarettes, sweets, and assorted Chinese and Western medicines. Its clientele was diverse. On this occasion, the intermediary was a young Chinese shop assistant.

It was easy enough to palm the message—but dangerous. Chen needed more time to be sure he wasn't being followed. If observed, this contact could cost both him and the runner their lives.

The message reached Ms Liu. She retrieved the codebooks and headed to the loft. Though Chen had kept it brief, she had to transmit the message twice before receiving the acknowledgement. A Japanese SIGINT unit intercepted the signal, but could only trace it to a general sector of Harbin's Chinese quarter.

In Bao'an, a faint signal surfaced on a long-defunct frequency—forgotten by most, but not by a vigilant assistant to Daxia. She intercepted and recorded it. Protocol required a confirmation of receipt. Then the frequency went silent again, and Daxia's heart pounded. Surely, this had something to do with her husband?

She rushed to the newly built decoding room. When a cryptologist appeared, he demanded to know Mao's whereabouts. She waited, heart racing, as Party leaders were summoned.

From inside Mao's compound came shouts, laughter, and toasts. The celebration lasted for an hour—until all those summoned had gathered.

Suddenly, the noise from within the compound died down. Though

Daxia could no longer hear it, Mao had turned to Zhou Enlai and asked him to speak.

'Comrades, if this is true, we may celebrate a great—perhaps unexpected—victory tonight. There is no man at this table, including myself, who has not lost family, friends, and comrades to Chiang, a ruthless butcher. Such is the nature of war.'

All eight men around the table nodded, some bowing their heads to conceal their tears—Mao among them, who had previously appeared gleeful but now sensed there was more to come.

'In the old days, we bent the rules at times when confronted with Comintern demands to hurl ourselves into suicidal battles. But we always remembered who provided for us. This is different. If we do not send this information to Moscow immediately, we risk a confrontation—not with the Comintern, but with Stalin himself. And when Stalin discovers we have withheld this message—and he will—our relationship with the USSR will be seriously damaged.'

Then Mao spoke,

'And if we do send it, Stalin will immediately inform Chiang. Stalin's agenda is to secure Chinese national unity to counter Japan and prevent an attack on the USSR. Stalin knows Japan could not take on both China and the USSR and might even decide to do neither. If Chiang is killed and Marshal Zhang attempts to seize control of the country, we may enter a civil war—one that would significantly strengthen our position.'

Another posed a question,

'How did we get this information?'

Zhou and Li Kenong were about to offer a vague response, but Mao interjected,

'Comrades Zhou and Li never disclose their sources, not even to me.'

The debate raged for hours. In the end, a mixture of hatred for Chiang, frustration with the Northeast Army's continued attacks, and the recognition that Chiang would never permit communist inclusion in a united front led to a fragile consensus: to do nothing and wait.

Zhou was curious how the Japanese had acquired the intelligence and made a mental note to warn Zhang he had an infiltrator—though the opportunity never came. Events moved too quickly. Zhou, however, was thrilled with the work of his spy, Chen Minghe, as was Li Kenong, his direct handler.

Chiang Kai-shek arrived in Xi'an on 4 December with a light security detail. He took up residence at Huaqing Pond, with Mount Li looming in the background. Between 7 and 10 December, Zhang visited three times to discuss national unity.

It soon became clear that Chiang had no interest in collaboration. His focus remained squarely on the Northeast Army's failure to suppress the communists. He was also irritated by Zhang's speech to the students on 9 December, in which he had called for unity. Chiang informed him that he would be replaced in the Northeast Army by Jiang Dingwen.

At approximately 5.00 a.m. on 12 December, 400 soldiers from the Northwest and Northeast Armies stormed Chiang's compound. A fierce gunfight broke out, and Chiang's guards suffered heavy casualties.

When Sun Mingjiu of the Northeast 2nd Battalion entered Chiang's bedroom, he found it empty—except for the untouched hat and coat. Moments later, Chiang was discovered in his nightshirt, hiding in a nearby field.

Ten senior advisers were also rounded up and imprisoned, among them General Chen Cheng and former ambassador to Tokyo, General Zhang Zuobin. Many officers wanted Chiang executed immediately, but Zhang held back. He sent a telegram to Nanjing outlining key demands, including communist participation in negotiations.

The Nanjing response was swift. He Yingqin, Head of the Military Affairs Commission, drew up plans to bomb Xi'an and retake Tongguan. Once more, China stood on the edge of internal war.

Calmer voices ultimately prevailed. Soong Mei-ling, the wife of Chiang Kai-shek, and Vice-Premier H. H. Kung flew to Xi'an to negotiate.

Stalin was irate. He did not shout; instead, he became quieter—the more dangerous version of himself. He called Georgi Dimitrov at the

Comintern and ordered contact with Wang Ming, instructing him to urge CCP delegates to prioritise a united front. He also demanded to know whether the Communists had prior knowledge of Chiang's abduction.

When the reply came, Stalin fell deeper into silence. Radio contact with Bao'an had been severely disrupted on 10 and 11 December. Such lapses were not unprecedented—but the timing was suspicious. Then Dimitrov added,

'I'm afraid there's another problem. Wang Ming showed me a draft telegram to Mao suggesting Chiang's execution.'

'You realise those are the opposite of my orders?'

'Yes. But Wang swears he didn't write it.'

'Then who did?'

'Artur Artuzov. Deputy Head of the GRU.'

'And you believe that?'

'Frankly, yes. Wang's not brave enough to do something like this on his own.'

Stalin hung up. He felt betrayed on all sides. Artuzov was still useful—for now. His infiltration of the Nazi Party and work supplying arms to the Spanish Republicans were invaluable. But his time would come.

Stalin considered how the CCP might have obtained the intelligence. Zhang was unlikely to have shared it directly—he remained, at least formally, their enemy. Perhaps it had come from the Japanese. If so, how had Zhou acquired it? Had someone in Harbin or Tokyo passed the information through a third party? That would imply Zhou had access to a network deeper than Sorge's—and that the Soviets had been deliberately bypassed. He could not prove it. But he could feel it.

Stalin's assistant liaised with the editors of *Izvestia* and *Pravda*. In their 14 December editions, it was suggested that Zhang was collaborating with Japan. Stalin sent a second message to the CCP urging peaceful resolution. In a separate message to Chiang Kai-shek, as a goodwill gesture, he was prepared to release Chiang's son, Chiang Ching-kuo—still being held in a Soviet steel mill after eleven years.

Negotiations resumed. On 16 December, Zhou Enlai and Lin Boqu arrived in Xi'an aboard Zhang's plane. A ceasefire was declared. Chiang refused to speak with them directly.

Zhou was in a precarious position. He did not need Stalin to tell him national unity was essential. The Communists were exhausted. An earlier attempt by three Red Armies to break through Suiyuan and link with Soviet weapon supply had failed catastrophically. Zhang Guotao's forces had been annihilated.

On 22 December, Madame Chiang arrived in Xi'an. By then, it was clear: without agreement, Chiang would not leave alive. On 24 December, he finally met Zhou and, reluctantly, accepted the terms. What followed was unexpected. On Christmas Day, Marshal Zhang met Chiang, offered a formal holiday greeting, and voluntarily placed himself under house arrest as a guarantor. Together, they returned to Nanjing.

True to his word—and perhaps out of humiliation—Chiang confined Zhang to house arrest for the rest of his life.

It was an act of conviction. Stalin was pleased. Mao was pleased. The CCP was now formally recognised. The Japanese and Russian fascists, though passive observers, welcomed the disintegration of the Northeast Army's power. Stalin believed he could arm China—on his terms.

To Chen Minghe, however, the entire affair felt like a failure. He knew his message had reached Bao'an. He was certain Stalin had been informed. Yet somehow, Chiang had walked away alive.

One small benefit of the new alliance was family reunification. Prisoners were released. Postal routes reopened. The CCP was granted territory and funding to sustain nearly 50,000 troops in Yan'an.

Some weeks later, Daxia received a letter—and a photograph of Weidong, now three years and three months old. Her eyes filled with tears, though she had no way to reach Chen.

The boy had been brought to Yan'an by Chen's father, now grey and worn at fifty. Their first meeting went badly. Weidong threw a tantrum, shouting,

'You aren't my mother! Don't hug me like that!'

Desperate, Daxia requested a meeting with Li Kenong. He was, as ever, buried in reports and transmissions, but she was granted an audience. Her request had been too unusual—and too urgent—to ignore.

When she entered, she hesitated. What she was about to say could endanger her—and worse, it could expose Chen. He had told her something he should never have shared.

'I believe my husband is alive,' she said quietly.

Li looked up, unmoved.

'I believe he sent the message we received from Harbin.'

He paused. The room seemed to narrow.

'He told you he was going to Harbin?'

She nodded, once. 'Before he left. He shouldn't have. I didn't tell anyone. I want him to have this photograph.'

There was a long silence.

'No,' said Li at last. 'He shouldn't have. I don't know when we will be in contact again. It could be months. Sending this photograph may endanger him—and others.'

'But surely it would give him hope—and a reason to go on?'

Li looked at the photo, then at her tear-streaked face. 'I'll see what I can do.'

He believed Chen might think he had failed. The photo, if it could be delivered, would say otherwise.

Chapter 29: Harbin, Japanese Empire of Manchukuo, 1937

The original drop-off point—located near the grocery store by Chen's aunt's bakery—risked causing a week's delay. Many other, more convenient sites Chen had visited with Rodzaevsky were deemed unsafe and rejected. This included Nakamura's, where exiting the car might arouse suspicion, and any location near his lodgings or office, in case he was under surveillance.

One distinctive feature of Harbin was its dark green, slatted roadside benches, all facing inwards. Since Rodzaevsky had relocated for his trysts, Chen's priority was to establish a new drop-off point and discreetly inform Ms Liu of its whereabouts via the grocery store and the loose brick in the alleyway. He could park near the chosen location—close to Rodzaevsky's new love nest—and, with a flick of the wrist, affix a sticky envelope—or one day, perhaps, a miniature film canister—to the underside of one of the benches.

The benches were cleared each morning of dirt, rainwater, and snow, yet their undersides remained untouched. Using a screwdriver from his car repair kit, he could adjust a holding screw on the designated bench—left, right, or not at all—signalling a *Teke* 'maintenance' operative to inspect it later. A left turn of the screw signified a message was ready for collection or delivery; a right turn meant the drop-off had been discovered or compromised. Leaving the screw untouched maintained the default setting. Messages could be exchanged twice a week—sometimes more.

With each passing week, Rodzaevsky grew more trusting of his new driver. Chen decided the time had come to inspect the contents of the briefcase. Though several opportunities presented themselves, he judged that daytime was safest: a penlight in a parked car at night might attract attention, and night-time photography risked grainy results.

After Rodzaevsky departed for his rendezvous with Baoqi, Chen donned his chauffeur's gloves, chalked the briefcase's original position, and placed it on the front seat. He inspected it carefully for hair strands or tape, but found none. The contents were, at first glance, mundane:

minutes from several BREM meetings and a few newspapers. There was no need to retrieve the camera from the car's underside. In the margins of the minutes, Rodzaevsky had pencilled several notes. Chen returned the briefcase precisely to its marked position and wiped away the chalk.

It was not until the third attempt that he found something unusual—a Japanese military document, translated into Russian, and classified as Top Secret. It originated from Surgeon General Shirō Ishii at Kenpeitai Headquarters, Changchun. The heading read:

Kwantung Army Epidemic Prevention and Water Purification Department—Unit 731 (Pingfang/Harbin)

Chemical Weapons Section—Unit 516 (Qiqihar)

Chen could only skim through the twelve pages.

'...*The two-part programme is now prepared to replace operations at Zhongma Fortress*...'

Part 1: Human Experimentation

Codename: Maruta (Бревно)

Initial delivery requirement: 500 logs per month to the lumber mill, with a long-term target of 250 monthly...

'...*Components include:*

(6) Amputation and live vivisection.

(7) Effects of untreated syphilis and gonorrhoea, including forced impregnation...'

Chen's hand trembled slightly. He forced himself to breathe evenly. Time did not permit a full reading of the experiments and their grotesque procedures.

'...*The Kenpeitai will be responsible for collecting logs from the Chinese sector of Harbin. Selection must include a broad range of ethnicities, physical conditions, both sexes, and children. With Kenpeitai support, Nakamura will select suitable logs. Rodzaevsky and presumably Bolotov will advise on subjects from the Russian, Korean, and other communities*...'

In the margin, Rodzaevsky had scribbled: *Jews and communists in Nakhalova.*

Part 2: Chemical and Biological Research

'...*Delivery requirements for this unit remain under assessment*...

>*…Components include:*
>>*(3) Efficacy of chemicals, including:*
>>>*(c) Adamsite*
>>>*(d) Phosgene Gas*
>>
>>*(4) Efficacy of diseases, including:*
>>>*(a) Bubonic plague via aerial dispersal (fleas or rats)*
>>>*(b) Typhoid variants via water contamination*
>>>*(c) Anthrax…'*

'*…Plans underway for aircraft dispersal of agents near the village of Anta. Transport of prisoners for testing is being finalised…'*

He forced himself to read one final line—then recoiled in horror.

'*…No processed logs are expected to survive. Incineration will be required…'*

Retrieving the hidden camera, Chen photographed each page, extracted the film, sealed it in a plastic envelope, and secured it beneath the designated bench. Then, returning the camera to its hiding place, he retrieved his screwdriver and turned the signal notch to the left.

For weeks, sleep eluded him. The horrors he had uncovered refused to fade.

Two days later, a brief inspection confirmed the screw had been reset to its neutral position.

Once developed in Yan'an, the film was delivered directly to Zhou Enlai and Li Kenong, who met twice to deliberate. The first meeting focused on redacting identifiers that might expose Chen in the Russian version—including Nakamura's name—and ensuring the text was accurately rendered in Chinese. The second addressed strategic response. A full reading revealed atrocities even worse than Chen had grasped.

Their immediate priority was to transmit the intelligence to the USSR. As radio transmission was too risky for the full report, only a short summary was sent. A courier was readied to deliver the documents in person. With a government of national unity on the horizon, they anticipated swift coordination. An addendum proposed sharing the intelligence with Chiang Kai-shek's Nationalists—a recommendation they expected would be approved.

Days later, Stalin convened a Kremlin session with senior intelligence and military figures, including GRU Head Uritsky and Chief of the General Staff Aleksandr Yegorov—both already marked for removal by Lavrentiy Beria, head of the NKVD. Beria did not attend. Instead, he sent assistants—few of whom would survive his purges.

Also present was Aleksandr Loktionov, Commander of the Soviet Air Force, whom Stalin had begun to distrust. The meeting room was filled with officers, doctors, and scientists. On one wall hung a large map featuring two concentric circles: one labelled *Mitsubishi Ki-15*, centred on an aircraft carrier; the other, *Nakajima B5N*, drawn from the Manchukuo–Mongolia–USSR border.

Stalin, by now, was convinced that a Chinese Communist had infiltrated the Japanese high command—possibly the Kwantung Army or Tokyo's inner circle. He opened the meeting by condemning Japan's blatant violation of the 1928 Geneva Protocol against chemical and biological weapons—a treaty to which Japan was a signatory. Unsurprisingly, Manchukuo had been chosen as the testing ground—remote and free from oversight.

He demanded an assessment and gestured to Loktionov.

'The map indicates two likely aircraft for dispersing plague: both within estimated range,' Loktionov began.

Stalin interrupted.

'So you've no idea of their range at all?'

Silence.

Of course you bloody well don't, Stalin thought. *What use is intelligence without data? Loktionov may soon find himself Beria's next plaything.*

'A high-altitude drop would lack precision,' Loktionov continued, 'but in urban areas, wide dispersal would occur. Fleas would spread the plague, and airborne pathogens would blanket entire neighbourhoods. Our western cities—Vladivostok, Khabarovsk, Chita, Irkutsk, Blagoveshchensk, and Magadan—are all vulnerable, whether targeted from airfields or carriers.'

'And during war,' Stalin asked, 'would we shoot these planes down before they reached us?'

'Not all of them. Carrier groups with Nakajima aircraft might breach our air defences. The Mitsubishi is fast and operates at high altitudes—up to 9,000 metres. A greater risk arises if our own western airfields were seized.'

Stalin pondered grimly. It seemed Japanese aviation was outpacing theirs.

'But surely fleas—or bacteria—would be destroyed by the blast?'

'Not necessarily. Some bombs use ceramic or plastic casings with detonator fuses for dispersal. Contaminated clothing could also be dropped. We already possess similar technologies.'

He turned to the land forces and invited Yegorov to speak.

'Our situation is more complex. While we are familiar with mustard gas and certain other compounds, many of these new chemicals—if effective in the field—appear significantly more lethal. The report suggests the Japanese intend to test them on a simulated battlefield. Respirators, masks, and protective clothing might mitigate the effects.'

Yegorov glanced at the scientists. They nodded, then hesitated, looking uncomfortable.

'But we lack such protective equipment in sufficient quantity.'

'Why not?'

'We assumed the Geneva Accords would be honoured and prioritised field armaments instead.'

'So you trusted the Japanese?'

There was no reply.

Stalin's mistrust of doctors and scientists was well known, yet he turned next to someone he respected: his recently appointed Surgeon-General, Nicolay Burdenko—a battlefield physician with experience in epidemics and trauma.

Stalin asked,

'I want to begin with the aerial dispersion of fleas in the cities we discussed. Do we have any preventive measures against plague?'

Burdenko replied,

'Yes. We developed them following the 1911 pneumonic plague outbreak in Manchuria, which killed 60,000, as well as for the bubonic variant. But prevention is key. In such a scenario, many would already be infected before we could deploy insecticides. Treatment is limited. Mortality could exceed fifty percent. Quarantine must be absolute, even for troops.'

'If Vladivostok were struck in such a way, what would be the expected death toll?'

'Our models estimate around thirty-five per cent—approximately 150,000 souls, including in outlying districts.'

Stalin nodded grimly.

'And contamination of food and water?'

'That could be achieved with dispersal bombs targeting potable water—reservoirs, for instance—using typhoid or anthrax. Unlike fleas, the infected area could span an entire water catchment.'

'Tens of thousands dead?'

'At least.'

Stalin stood.

'That is enough.'

Everyone rose with him. As he turned to leave, he cast one last question to Loktionov.

'What would happen if such an attack were launched from southern Manchuria—against China?'

'The results would be catastrophic. Northeast China is densely populated. Beijing would be within range—and even Nanjing could suffer.'

'We must notify our Chinese allies. This development plan would take time—years, perhaps. That, at least, is today's one piece of good news.'

A clever remark. It revealed nothing of the information source.

Stalin exited.

The remaining officers and scientists debated for over two hours the value of such depraved research. Some of the horrors had already been reviewed by Chen, but others included flamethrower testing on prisoners, lethal dose experiments with ricin and puffer fish venom, water deprivation trials, and hyperthermia tests on infants. One account described a low-pressure chamber in which victims' eyes burst before death; another, human crush tests.

Many military officers turned pale. The scientists, by contrast, remained disturbingly clinical.

Later, the military and NKVD convened privately. They understood the political consequences of an intelligence failure. They agreed to conduct a sabotage assessment of Unit 731, using local Russian Red Cells based in Harbin. Three NKVD agents, protected by diplomatic immunity, would oversee operations on the ground.

Two weeks later, while inspecting the benches, Chen noticed a screw had been turned to the left. Inside the designated compartment, he found a small package and reset the screw. Within the envelope was a standard seven-by-five-centimetre black-and-white photograph of a smiling young boy, wrapped in a winter coat.

Chen stared at the image for twenty minutes. Then, with deliberate care, he tore it into strips and pocketed them for later disposal.

For the next month, Rodzaevsky's briefcase contained little of intelligence value. One file documented a minor piece of correspondence between Rodzaevsky and his Berlin contact, Averkiev, concerning the relocation of the VFP office—approved by the Gestapo. They also lamented Mussolini's refusal to recognise Manchukuo or support their cause in Rome.

Another document concerned membership figures: officially 18,000, though it was implied the true number was closer to 36,000. None of it warranted risking Chen's network.

Then came something new.

Chen had learned at spy school that White Russian incursions across the Soviet border had occurred since 1917—first against the Russian Soviet Federative Socialist Republic (RSFSR), then the USSR. Some served as banditry, others propaganda or sabotage. In the 1920s, these raids were carried out by Kosmin's forces, later by Ataman Semenov's Cossacks. Neither had advanced the dream of restoring the Motherland. But with the Japanese arrival in Harbin, that began to change.

The TK saw potential in the angry, rootless youth of the Russian diaspora. With Rodzaevsky's encouragement, they began selecting the most promising to train as professionals. Others, outside the VFP, volunteered willingly. Successes were few: NKVD border controls were ruthless. But there were always more willing volunteers.

In October, the TK had approached Rodzaevsky to supply fifty recruits for insurgency training. In early November, some of these men attempted to infiltrate the USSR, timing their operation to coincide with the 7 November Revolution holiday. One group reached Chita and distributed anti-Soviet leaflets among the crowds. Within minutes, NKVD officers arrested anyone caught holding one. Miraculously, the team escaped and returned to Harbin.

Rodzaevsky capitalised on the story.

On Chen's next inspection of the briefcase, he found a short memorandum addressed from Rodzaevsky to his Head of the Organisational Department, Lev Okhotin. It was entitled *Recruitment*.

The document proposed the formation of a permanent, professional White Russian unit within the Kwantung–Manchukuo Army—named the *Asano Brigade*. Its initial strength was to be 250 soldiers, rising to 3,500. It would serve under Japanese command.

The priority was to appoint a commander. Two candidates were shortlisted: Gurgen Nagolyan and Dmitri Smirnov.

Rodzaevsky favoured Smirnov and intended to lobby both the TK and Matkovsky to secure his appointment. He distrusted Nagolyan—an Armenian who had dropped out of the Harbin Institute before completing his railway studies and later joined the Manchukuo Imperial Army in 1932.

Chen photographed the memo and sent the film through the usual channel. In Yan'an, it was redacted to remove any reference to the VFP, then summarised and transmitted to Moscow.

Stalin was already convinced that Zhou Enlai's mole was within the Kwantung Army—not Tokyo.

It was not the size of the Asano Brigade that alarmed Stalin. The MIA already numbered 125,000. Rather, it was the fact that a unit was being formed specifically to attack the USSR.

Doubts returned. Would Japan strike north before finishing a war with China? The Chinese Communists, reading the same intelligence, came to a similarly unclear conclusion.

Weeks later, Stalin raised the issue with Beria in private. Had there been any local intelligence?

Beria confirmed—and added that Dmitri Smirnov had suffered an unfortunate accident three days earlier in Changchun. He had fallen from a fourth-floor window.

Stalin raised an eyebrow.

'You arranged it?'

Beria nodded.

'And why?'

'Rodzaevsky's distrust wasn't justified. Gurgen Nagolyan is one of ours—an NKVD officer.'

Stalin's lips curled. It had been some time since he had smiled that broadly.

In April, Rodzaevsky received an unexpected invitation to TK Headquarters from Kenzō Miyake. As usual, Chen was not driving him that day.

Miyake greeted him with uncharacteristic warmth—a sharp contrast to his usual sternness.

The reason became clear quickly. He slid a copy of the *Russky Avangard*, the Shanghai-based paper edited by Konstantin Steklov, across the desk.

'You appear to have competition. Vonsiatsky's All-Russian National Revolutionary Party is attacking you—quite entertainingly, I must say. But I imagine these personal attacks must sting.'

Miyake read aloud. One article implicated Bolotov in the murder of Simeon Kaspé, claiming he acted on Rodzaevsky's orders. Other articles made equally damaging accusations. Rodzaevsky squirmed.

'Why bring this to me?'

'Because I can make it stop. But I'll need something in return.'

Free cheese is only found in a mousetrap, Rodzaevsky thought—a

Russian proverb that felt uncomfortably apt.

'Have you heard of Dai Li? He serves Chiang Kai-shek directly.'

'Should I have?'

'Not necessarily. Dai Li—or Dai Chunfeng—is Chiang's spymaster. He heads the Bureau of Investigation and Statistics and leads the Blue Shirts—a clandestine Fascist group, but virulently anti-Japanese. We suspect he has penetrated Mao's circle. He trained at Whampoa and speaks fluent Russian—his staff, too.'

Rodzaevsky began taking notes—an old habit Miyake had failed to break.

The Japanese still lacked accurate intelligence on events in Yan'an. That was the subtext.

'We want you to approach Dai Li. Present yourself as a fellow Fascist—unhappy with our treatment of you—and offer intelligence on Japan's plans in China. We'll provide credible material to support your role.'

Rodzaevsky was aghast. They were asking him to become a double agent—a suicidal task.

'The risk is too great for a petty personal gain. I can live with Steklov's nonsense.'

Miyake paused, then coughed discreetly.

'You know, we've always wondered how you escaped the OGPU in 1925. Perhaps you are a Soviet agent. Perhaps we should investigate. I imagine we'd get a confession soon enough.'

They'd find out about Baoqi. About the embezzlement. I'd be finished.

He composed himself.

'It seems I have no choice.'

'No. You don't.'

When the film reached Yan'an, it triggered a storm. Mao and Zhou were alarmed by Rodzaevsky's private notes on his meeting with Miyake—specifically the claim that Dai Li had infiltrated their ranks through a Russian-speaking Whampoa graduate. A re-examination of all such graduates was ordered—if necessary, by coercion.

The intelligence was not shared with Moscow.

Chapter 30: Harbin, Japanese Empire of Manchukuo, 1937

In 1937, the perception of the Chinese Communist Party among the broader populace improved significantly as a result of the United Front. The Communists, though junior partners, were portrayed as disciplined allies in a unified military effort. This was aided by Chiang Kai-shek's decision to allow his brilliant head of propaganda, Shao Lizi, to assist the Communists in developing materials to promote the impending alliance. It was a shrewd move—Shao was well known to them.

Suddenly, Chinese newspapers were filled with glowing accounts of Mao Zedong. There were even discussions of a future biography, edited by Shao himself and loosely based on interviews with the American journalist Chen had observed before leaving Bao'an: Edgar Snow, who was preparing his own work, *Red Star Over China*.

By late spring 1937, Chen had grown melancholic. Rodzaevsky's briefcase had yielded nothing of value in weeks. He was still only twenty-six years old, had not seen his wife, Daxia, in nearly a year, and could only recall his son as an infant. No extraction timetable had been communicated.

With little to occupy him outside work, his thoughts darkened. He realised that his training had provided no preparation for psychological endurance. What had been taught as 'psychology' had focused solely on resisting interrogation and torture. Loneliness, isolation, and the constant threat of exposure gnawed at him. The waiting was worst of all.

His lodgings had begun to take on a sense of permanence. With his wages, he had bought a few Chinese books and some small ornaments. One of the waitresses at the restaurant near his aunt's bakery noticed his low spirits and invited him on a date. She was young, pleasant, and eager to settle down—but the evening ended in disappointment. She spoke earnestly of her desire for marriage and family. Chen knew she could not build a life with a man who appeared once a week at most—and who was already married.

The nights were hardest. He turned to alcohol in the hope of inducing sleep, but it only made the mornings worse. A spy with a clouded mind was a danger to himself and others. Yet the sweat-drenched dreams kept coming. He saw the execution of Mr Bei. He relived Peng's death, Hu's suicide, the hunger of the Long March—men gnawing on their shoes for nourishment, knowing they would not survive the next mountain pass without them.

Sometimes, his dreams softened. Daxia would appear—tender and forgiving—but then her features would change, morphing into those of his childhood sweetheart, Xiong Hehua, or even Baoqi. When awake, he drifted into bleak introspection. Since his idyllic childhood, all he had known was cruelty, upheaval, and death. In his better moments, he believed that only Daxia could heal that wound.

In May 1937, Rodzaevsky and Matkovsky received an unexpected summons to a secret meeting with Miyake. It did not take place at his offices but at a secluded Japanese safe house. Upon arrival, the two men were each handed a lengthy document. Miyake informed them he would return in half an hour to discuss it.

The document was stamped *Top Secret* and originated from Vice Minister of War Yoshijirō Umezu in Sendai. Its title was: *Arrangements for Non-Chinese Natives in the Japanese Empire of Manchukuo in the Event of an Outbreak of Hostilities with the Republic of China.*

It made for alarming reading. The first section detailed how, in the event of hostilities, Manchukuo would be placed under martial law. City curfews would be introduced where necessary. Chinese courts would be abolished. Civilians of any race or political affiliation would be tried by Japanese military tribunals, with local agencies, including the police, summoned as needed.

Rodzaevsky scribbled in the margin: '*Treated as everyone else.*'

Foreigners serving the Japanese cause—members of the Asano Brigade, MIA personnel, covert operatives, and captured volunteers—would be subject to the Imperial Code and tried under courts-martial conditions. There would be no appeals. Sentences would be swiftly executed.

Another note: '*Few survivors.*'

Further clauses banned drug use by military personnel—especially opium—on pain of death. The Kenpeitai were declared subordinate to the Tokumu Kikan and would henceforth report directly to them. Rodzaevsky privately doubted the practicality of such bans. If enforced, they would cripple half the MIA. More personally, it signalled the end of Nakamura's profitable side arrangements.

The next section addressed the status of aliens. Russians, the largest group, would be permitted to leave—but only to the USSR, and only if they possessed valid passports. BREM was to assist with these departures. This rule extended to other Soviet citizens, including Ukrainians, as well as Western Europeans employed by Standard Oil. The latter were free to leave voluntarily. Stateless former Russians and Koreans, however, were to remain in situ—even if the territory changed hands.

Rodzaevsky doubted many Russians would take the offer. Returning to the USSR was not an option—Stalin would almost certainly have them executed as spies or Trotskyites.

Those already pledged to fight for Japan would be armed and organised into defensive militias, assigned to hold territory rather than reclaim it. The rest—anyone sixteen or older—would be forcibly conscripted the moment conflict broke out.

There it was—buried in the middle of the report. Rodzaevsky read it twice. He looked up. Matkovsky had reached the same passage and he nodded.

Japan had no intention of attacking the USSR. It would only defend itself in the north.

The title of the document had been suggestive—but this was confirmation. Tokyo's war planners were focused not on Soviet territory, but on the south: the Republic of China. Despite years of anti-communist rhetoric, Japan's military priorities lay in conquest and occupation across the Yangtze, not a strike against Stalin. Rodzaevsky felt both relief and resentment. The cause he had championed—the great northern crusade—was no longer on the table. His role, and that of his fellow émigrés, had just been downgraded from vanguard to expendable auxiliaries.

He looked up. Matkovsky had reached the same passage and nodded.

The report then addressed potential flashpoints. If the USSR attempted to exploit the situation, two groups—the VFP and Semenov's Cossacks—would be expected to support Japanese efforts. Their failure to reconcile would carry serious consequences.

Rodzaevsky clenched his jaw. His VFP recruiters had been canvassing in Cossack territory. Several brawls had erupted, and young party members had returned bloodied but emboldened. Worse, in Nazi circles, Semenov was viewed as the more legitimate White Russian leader.

The final pages addressed economic strategy: the nationalisation of food production, mining, and steel under a new five-year plan, and renewed exploration for oil.

Miyake returned.

He demanded the report remain secret until Tokyo authorised its implementation. Semenov, he added, had already agreed to these terms.

That Semenov had been approached stung. But this was not the time to sulk.

Both men agreed to the secrecy clause and were invited to ask questions.

Matkovsky spoke first.

'There is no timeline for events. Could you elaborate?'

Miyake looked at him levelly.

'Such decisions are made at High Command level. I do not have that information—and even if I did, I would not share it. For today's purposes, assume the timeline is imminent.'

'What do you mean by imminent?'

'I speak unofficially, but I believe it means months—not years.'

Rodzaevsky scribbled *Imminent (неизбежный)* on the document's margins, then asked,

'The VFP is treated the same as all other groups—even though we've been your staunchest ally?'

'That may be true, but this report is from Tokyo. I have no say in it. Besides, you gain something unique: the support of what may become the greatest power of the twentieth century—the Land of the Rising Sun. Your membership will grow, likely into the many tens of thousands, as you offer protection others cannot.'

    Rodzaevsky and Matkovsky were driven back to their respective offices by the relief driver. He asked if the VFP had a safe in which the document could be locked. Rodzaevsky said it did. He later summoned Chen and considered locking the report away—before deciding he would reread it overnight.

    He never did. By morning, he was preoccupied with his upcoming time with Baoqi. The document remained in his briefcase.

    Chen faced a difficult decision: whether to use the hidden radio and risk compromising Ms Liu, or wait. He chose the slower, safer option, praying that 'imminent' did not mean within the week.

    While Rodzaevsky was with Baoqi, Chen discreetly photographed each page, hid the film beneath the bench, and turned the screw to the correct position.

    The reactions from other interested parties were predictable. Mao was elated and issued orders for full mobilisation of the Red Army. At the time, significant wrangling continued over how the Communist 1st Route Army, the 8th Route Army, and the 4th Rote Army might be incorporated—at least nominally—into divisions of the NRA. All, ultimately, would report to Chiang Kai-shek. This development pushed that discussion forward.

    Stalin's reaction was equally enthusiastic, though tempered by characteristic caution. The intelligence appeared to originate from the highest levels in Tokyo—raising the possibility that Zhou Enlai's source extended beyond Manchuria. Stalin's first step was to send Zhou a direct message requesting confirmation that this was the same informant and that the material was reliable. Zhou responded without delay, affirming both.

    Stalin next contacted his most valuable agent in Tokyo, Richard Sorge. Sorge reported that discussions were underway concerning Germany's growing reluctance to continue supplying arms to the Republic of China. Though not a direct confirmation of Chen's intelligence, it was telling. It signalled that Germany—Japan's new ally—

was preparing to disengage from its relationship with Chiang Kai-shek and move towards closer alignment with Japanese military policy. This shift strongly indicated that Japan's focus remained on subjugating China, rather than launching immediate aggression against the USSR.

With these two independent corroborations—Zhou's confirmation from within Manchukuo, and Sorge's strategic insight from Tokyo—Stalin judged the overall picture credible. The man with the pipe made his decision accordingly.

He summoned Beria, requesting a list of available human assets with knowledge of China to assist in the analysis. Beria's reply was blunt: none. He had already eliminated them as suspected Japanese spies.

For Chiang Kai-shek, the news was devastating. He had watched helplessly as Japan encroached steadily upon northern Chinese territory, particularly Hebei Province, establishing puppet regimes and eroding Nationalist control. In a desperate bid to forestall further conflict, he had already signed the secret He–Umezu Agreement in 1935—a pact requiring the KMT's regular forces to withdraw from Hebei altogether.

In that region now stood only a nominally independent army—roughly 100,000—under the command of Feng Yuxiang, the veteran Zhili warlord. Though Feng had once opposed Chiang in 1930, his 29th Route Army had been reformed in Shanxi and now stood as an uneasy ally. Chiang convened his generals. Together, they pored grimly over the map.

While the Soviets were preparing to offer military assistance under Stalin's Zed Programme and the groundwork was being laid for a Sino–Soviet Non-Aggression Pact, the situation in the far west of China was rapidly deteriorating. In Xinjiang Province, Mahmut Muhiti—Commander-in-Chief of the Nationalist 6th Uyghur Division in Kashgar—had grown resentful of Soviet puppet governor Sheng Shicai's growing dominance in Ürümqi. Anticipating a trap, Muhiti fled across the border into India. In his absence, a group of Uyghur officers declared an independent administration and launched a rebellion.

All Soviet advisers, along with suspected pro-Soviet officials, were executed. The NKVD retaliated swiftly. 400 Uyghur students studying at the University of Tashkent were rounded up. No questions were asked about their politics or religion. Every one of them was executed within a single day. The Soviet Consul-General in Ürümqi was recalled to Moscow—and shot.

Soviet aircraft bombed the city of Yarkand. Along the border with Xinjiang, a large troop build-up commenced. Though it remained a proxy war for now, the conflict cast a long shadow over prospects for a National Front. Chiang feared abandonment. German arms were dwindling. Soviet arms, though promised, had not arrived. The rebellion in the west was hushed up; the wider public remained unaware.

Two weeks later, Chen began to question his own judgement. Something was wrong.

He and Rodzaevsky were being followed. It was not paranoia, but a hardened instinct. The subtle cues that seasoned operatives learn to trust: a car lingering too long behind them, a shadow that appeared outside Nakamura's when they parked. He never sensed it when alone. That led him to the obvious conclusion—it was Rodzaevsky who was being watched.

If surveillance was indeed underway, it was being executed by experts. That meant one of two possibilities: the Japanese, or the NKVD.

On his next trip to the love nest, Chen turned the screw on the bench to the right, signalling that the drop-off was compromised. He stopped examining the briefcase entirely.

Then, without warning, Lydia summoned Kostya with a cold expression and tear-streaked cheeks. An envelope lay on the table. She gestured for him to open it.

Inside were photographs.

They showed him and Baoqi, arriving and departing separately from their secret rendezvous, one particularly damning image of Baoqi at the Cabaret Fantasia, and two more of Nakamura's Barber Shop.

'You had better explain yourself. Who is this woman? And how did you meet her?'

'Her name is Ms Tao. I met her at the Cabaret Fantasia. She works there as a cocktail waitress.'

Lydia jabbed a finger at the photographs.

'And this is where you meet?'

There was no point denying it.

'And who pays for this sordid arrangement?'

Kostya sighed.

'Tell me—why would a young Chinese woman find you so attractive?'

Another sigh.

'And this picture of a barber's shop—is it a brothel?'

He told a half-truth. He debated whether to confess to an affair—or something worse.

'Yes, it is. But I go there only for business—with the proprietor.'

'In Nakhalova? The sleaziest part of the city?'

'It's hard to explain, but—'

'Shut up and listen to me.'

Lydia's voice trembled, but her tone was firm.

'Konstantin Rodzaevsky, you are a fool. The cheating I could almost forgive. God knows, I've had nothing in that department since Yuri died. But this? This is unforgivable. You've humiliated my family. You've endangered my safety. You've made yourself a target for blackmail. There were weeks when your allowance barely paid for food and rent, while you were screwing some tart. Judging by the pictures, an expensive one. I don't even know if any of what you've told me is true.'

'I'm sorry. What can I say?'

'Nothing. Your suitcase is in the other room—packed for tonight. Go find a hotel. Tomorrow, I won't be here. Collect the rest of your things and leave. I want a divorce.'

Rodzaevsky retrieved the suitcase. Head bowed, he left.

In the days that followed, Chen noted unsettling developments. Rodzaevsky, once enthralled by Baoqi, was now unable to see her. She had vanished. There was no sign of her outside the Cabaret Fantasia.

A message reached Chen via the grocery store: Baoqi had been extracted to the safe house. Later, he learned that she had been given a choice. She could keep her money and return to civilian life—dangerous, but hers. Or she could give it up, travel to Yan'an, and embrace communism.

She had taken several hours to decide. In the end, she chose to leave for her hometown.

The day after Lydia's outburst, Rodzaevsky told his staff he would be taking a short leave. He summoned Chen and instructed him to drive to a rental agency. At his home, they loaded boxes into the car. He handed Chen a card with an address in Chinese.

After two trips, the move was complete.

The third destination was a legal office. Chen found it odd—until he saw the sign: *Criminal Cases, Bail Bonds, and Matrimonial Affairs.*

The final stop was in Pristan. An art supply shop. They picked up a Russian woman—Neolina Yalisheva—who greeted Chen in fluent Chinese. A friend from church, she said. She was helping Konstantin set up his new residence.

Chen suspected his employer might not be capable of living alone.

On 8 July 1937, as Chen walked home, a headline caught his eye in a Russian newspaper: *Skirmish Between Chinese and Japanese Troops at the Marco Polo Bridge.*

He knew the bridge—called *Lúgōu Qiáo* (卢沟桥) in Chinese. Named by Marco Polo himself, it was no ordinary landmark. In the days that followed, as he scanned newspapers while waiting for Rodzaevsky, it became clear that ceasefire negotiations had failed.

By 25 July, full-scale combat had broken out, though no declaration of war had yet been issued. On 9 August, Japanese forces attacked Shanghai.

The Second Sino–Japanese War had begun—known in China as the War of Resistance Against Japanese Aggression.

The conflict would escalate into the wider war that would soon engulf the world.

Chen felt vindicated. Yet his thoughts turned, with heavy dread, to the safety of Daxia and Weidong.

He did not yet know that the most consequential piece of intelligence—the one that would change the course of his life—was still to come.

Mark Oulton

Postscript

The report discussed in Chapter 28, entitled:

Kwantung Army Epidemic Prevention and Water Purification Department—Unit 731 (Pingfang/Harbin) and Chemical Weapons Section—Unit 516 (Qiqihar), did become a reality.

Here is a brief summary from my book, *The Dead Microphones*, which explains what happened later.

'Apart from biological experimentation within Unit 731 and other related units, the biological agents were also released on the Chinese public. One experiment was to infect the inmates with *Yersinia pestis*, which causes pneumonic and bubonic plague, as well as typhus. The sickest were kept alive so their blood could be transfused to infect others, while the least sick were shot. The final step for the last batch of infected prisoners was to expose them to vast quantities of fleas and their bites. The fleas were then packed in dust and inserted into bombs. On 4 October 1940, the bombs were dropped over Quzhou in Zhejiang Province. At least 2,000 civilians died from the ensuing plague, and another 1,000 in nearby Yiwu. Another attack using anthrax killed around 6,000 people in the same area. In a further example, more than 1,000 wells were contaminated in order to study cholera and typhus. The estimates are around 30,000 dead—many after the Japanese had surrendered.

Another shocking part of Unit 731 is that no one was ever prosecuted by the Allies for the crimes. There is documentary evidence in the museum that hints at the reason why, in the form of a US report dated June, reference *WAR 99277*, from the Legal Section of SCAP (Supreme Command Allied Powers) to WDSCA (War Department Special Staff Civil Affairs Division):

1. The reports and files of the Legal Services Section on Ishii and his co-workers are based on anonymous letters, hearsay affidavits and rumours. The Legal Section interrogations to date, of the numerous persons concerned with the BW (Biological Warfare) project in China, do not reveal sufficient evidence to support war crime charges. The

alleged victims are of unknown identity. Unconfirmed allegations are to the effect that criminals, farmers, women and children were used for BW experimental purposes. The Japanese Communist Party alleges that: "Ishii BKA (Bacterial War Army) conducted experiments on captured Americans in Mukden and that simultaneously, research along similar lines was conducted in Tokyo and Kyoto."

2. None of Ishii's subordinates are charged or held as war crime suspects, nor is there sufficient evidence on file against them…

3. None of our Allies to date have filed war crimes charges against Ishii or any of his associates.

4. Neither Ishii nor his associates are included among major Japanese war criminals awaiting trial…'

There were both American and British POWs at Unit 731, and even more in other units. Although never proven, part of the Japanese interest in Unit 731 was the bacteriological reaction of different ethnic groups, and they would have made convenient test subjects. The American government and its allies essentially turned a blind eye in order to secure intelligence on BW, and never brought charges. Many of the Unit 731 personnel returned to academic life in Japan. Twelve members of Unit 731, captured by the Russians, were put on trial in Khabarovsk in 1949. They received light sentences relative to the crimes—between two- and twenty-five-years' imprisonment—presumably having cooperated with the Russians. They were later repatriated to Japan.'

Supplementary Notes

Uniform Insignia and Military Rank (1929-1937)

Although the Chinese Red Army initially embraced a flat, egalitarian command structure, the integration of defecting Nationalist units—accustomed to rigid hierarchies—necessitated a partial adoption of formal ranks and insignia. By 1929, officers were sometimes issued horizontal bars, coloured lapel tabs, or red stars, particularly in areas where captured factories could produce standardised uniforms. These symbols helped instil discipline in a rapidly expanding force made up of both volunteers and reluctant conscripts.

However, this system remained uneven and ideologically contentious. In 1937, shortly after the formation of the Second United Front with the Nationalists, the Red Army formally abolished all rank insignia in favour of political titles and collective leadership—a decision that would remain in place until the later standardisation under the People's Liberation Army in 1955.

Understanding Pinyin Tone Marks

In Mandarin Chinese, each syllable is pronounced with a tone. This novel uses *pinyin*, the Romanised spelling system for Mandarin, and includes **tone marks** to help readers pronounce names and terms more accurately. There are **four tones**, plus a neutral tone. Their shapes can be remembered like this:

- First tone (¯) — high and level (e.g. mā)
- Second tone (´) — rising, like asking a question (e.g. má)
- Third tone (ˇ) — dipping then rising (e.g. mǎ)
- Fourth tone (`) — sharp and falling (e.g. mà)
- Neutral tone — light and unstressed, no mark (e.g. ma)

Examples from the novel:

- *Máo Zédōng* – First and second tones: high and rising
- *Báijiǔ* – Second and third tones: rising and dipping
- *Lǔgǒu Qiáo* – Three third tones: dipping, dipping, dipping (Marco Polo Bridge)
- *Yìwū* – Fourth and first tones: falling and level
- *Mántou* – Third tone followed by a neutral tone: dipping then light

These marks distinguish words that otherwise look identical in Roman letters. For example, *mā, má, mǎ,* and *mà* are have different meanings in Chinese.

Manzhouli Day and the Neon Swastika

Manzhouli Day, as described in the novel, is fictional. However, the giant neon-lit swastika mounted above the Russian Fascist Party (RFP) offices in Manzhouli, approximately three kilometres from the Russian border, did exist. The sign was visible to incoming travellers and remained illuminated day and night, serving as a declaration of the RFP's ideological alignment and its role in the Japanese-backed regime in Manchukuo.

Others

The following is fictitious: Peasants' Improvement Society. The publication, *The Motherland*, did not exist although there were several similar ones that did.

Although Suichuan was captured in 1928, the disposition of the battle forces is entirely speculation.

When Mao approached Nanchang in 1930, there is no evidence that *USS Luzon* and *USS Oahu* were docked but these two vessels are real.

The name Radio and Intelligence Communications Group known as the 'Pigeons' is fabricated, but the structures described are similar to those that were developed.

The spy school and sparrows established in Ningdu in 1931 by Li Kenong is a fabrication but the Russian sparrow school at Kazan certainly existed.

There is no evidence that an attempt was made to kidnap Rodzaevsky in Harbin in 1936.

There is no evidence that Rodzaevsky was involved in the selection of people for Unit 731.

In the 1930's, the Japanese couldn't find the oil they hoped for in Manchuria. It was there as shale oil and the massive Daqing oilfield was discovered in 1959.

Mark Oulton

List of Fictitious Characters (in alphabetical order)

Anna Kvaratskhelia, Bai (Teke), Bei Xiansheng (Mr Bei), Cadet Ma, Cai, Chen Fengbao, Chen Minghe (aka Feng Shaogong), Chen Weidong, Chen Yinghui, Consul-General André Fournier, Consul-General Jean-François Monteux, Dmitri Smirnov, Egor Konstantin Orlov (though Yao Wenxun is real), Géraldine Fournier, Great-Uncle Huang, Hu Chengong, Lei Tian Long, Levan Kvaratskhelia, Li (Teke), Lieutenant Colonel Oleg Alekseev, Lieutenant Ding, Lieutenant Wang Zheng, Luo, Lao Chen, Lao Shu, Ms Li, Ms Liu, One-eyed Gu, Pascal Allard, Peng Gangchao, Philippe Chastain, Raymond Camus, Ruan Daxia, Second Lieutenant Bai Jun, Senior Cadet Pan, Tang Baolin, Wei Haoyu, Wang Brothers (Teke), Wang Lisun, Xu (Teke), Xiao Huang, Xiong Hehua, Yamato Takahama, Ye Jingsheng.

The remaining characters all existed, although, their words and actions are at the discretion and imagination of the author. The exception is from Mao's thoughts on guerrilla warfare, in Chapter 13, although that was not written down until 1930.

List of Acronyms (in alphabetical order)

BREM – Bureau of Russian Émigré Affairs in Manchukuo. Russian: *Бюро русских эмигрантов в Маньчжурской империи*. 1934–1946.

CCP – Chinese Communist Party (CCP). Chinese: 中国共产党. 1921–present.

CER – China Eastern Railway. Chinese: 中國東省鐵路, Russian: *Китайско-Восточная железная дорога*. 1897–1945 (then renamed).

Comintern – Communist International. Russian: *Коминтерн*, Chinese: 共产国际. 1919–1943.

CSR – Chinese Soviet Republic. Chinese: 中華蘇維埃共和國. 1931–1934.

GRU – Soviet Army Intelligence. Russian: *Главное*

разведывательное управление. 1918–1992.

KMT – Kuomintang National Party (KMT) / Guomindang (GMT), also known as the Chung-kuo Kuomintang. Chinese: 中国國民黨. 1919–present (from 1949 in Taiwan).

Komsomol – All-Union Leninist Young Communist League. Russian: *Всесоюзный ленинский коммунистический союз молодёжи*. 1918–1991.

MIA – Manchukuo Imperial Army. Japanese: まんしゅうこく, Chinese: 滿洲國軍. 1932–1945.

NFPA – National Federation of Peasants' Associations. Chinese: 中华全国农民协会. 1927–1964.

NKVD – The USSR People's Commissariat for Internal Affairs. Russian: *Народный комиссариа́т вну́тренних дел*. 1934–1946.

NRA – National Revolutionary Army. Chinese: 國民革命軍. 1924 (8)–1949.

OGPU – USSR Secret Service and Police. Russian: *Объединённое государственное политическое управление*. 1923–1934 (then absorbed into the NKVD).

RFO – Russian Fascist Organisation. Russian: *Русская фашистская организация*. 1925–1931. Precursor to the RFP.

RFP – Russian Fascist Party. Russian: *Российская фашистская партия*. 1931–1943.

RSFSR – Russian Soviet Federative Socialist Republic. *Российская Советская Федеративная Социалистическая Республика*. 1918-1922.

SIGINT – Signals Intelligence.

Teke – First intelligence service of the CCP. Chinese: 中央特科. 1928–1935.

TK – *Tokumu Kikan*, Special Intelligence Organisation of the Japanese Army. Japanese: とくむきかん. 1919–1945.

VFP – All-Russian Fascist Party. Russian: *всероссийская фашистская партия*. Created from a merger of the RFP and VFO in 1933.

VFO – All-Russian Fascist Organisation. Rival organisation to the RFP based in the USA. Russian: *всероссийская фашистская организация*. 1933–1939.

Acknowledgments

This novel could not have been written without the help of Dr David Ian Chambers, who taught Chinese politics and modern history at Bristol University (1981-1987). He then joined the British Foreign and Commonwealth Office (FCO), later serving as a member of Her Majesty's Diplomatic Service in London, Hong Kong, Beijing, and Bangkok. His knowledge of early Chinese communist SIGINT is, in my opinion, peerless.

Similarly, Dr Matthew Rothwell's work was an inspiration to me, particularly on the early years of the CCP. He is the host of the podcast *People's History of Ideas* (peopleshistoryofideas.com) and the author of *Transpacific Revolutionaries; The Chinese Revolution in Latin America* and several articles on global Maoism.

I would like to thank my great Australian friend, Dave Lambert. He spent more than a decade working in China before returning to Adelaide and helped me proof this novel. I have been the fortunate beneficiary of his accomplished accipitrid eye for detail (in English and Chinese).

Finally, I would never have completed this book without Jeff Gee. His knowledge of the history and politics of this period in Chinese history is extraordinary and accomplished.

About the Author

Mark Oulton is a world traveller and astute observer of international culture. Born in the UK, he was moved around the world as a child due to his father's work in education and overseas development. He spent his formative years in Syria, Kenya,

Malawi, and Nepal, as well as being educated in the UK from the age of twelve. As an adult, he lived in the UK for many years, working for the largest private company in the world and then as a company director in Bristol, UK, in agriculture and related trading and marketing. He then worked in the US for seven years before finally settling in China in 2015. He speaks French, passable Mandarin Chinese, and several other languages poorly. His most recent work as Global Market Research Manager for a leading Swiss corporation took him to every corner of the globe. He also writes about topical issues such as sustainability in agriculture, as well as the plastics and aluminium industries.

When not writing, his hobbies include cooking, painting, cycling, and gardening.

Exclusive Excerpt from Red Spy in Harbin: Book Two – The Middle Years

Chen had been told by a porter in Beijing that the journey would last around five hours, including two stops for water and one for coal. Every adult had purchased hot water from platform vendors, dispensed from enormous steel urns, and mixed it in their flasks with a few precious tea leaves—most tea now came from the south, firmly in Nationalist hands. Each passenger carried with them bags of steamed buns (*mántou* – 馒头), better when warm but still filling when cold, along with hard-boiled eggs and pickled vegetables.

Chen glanced at his fellow passengers seated on the hard wooden benches. Most were men, but in one corner sat a well-dressed young woman with two children—perhaps six and eight years old. He could not begin to imagine what circumstances had compelled a family like that to travel this line.

The man sitting opposite him seemed eager to talk and stank of *báijiǔ* (白酒), the fiery liquor favoured in the north. Chen answered cautiously. The man turned out to be a trader from Shandong, claiming he still had access to one of the few surviving tea gardens in the north. He had both Japanese and Chinese clients and made no attempt to conceal that the war had proved highly profitable.

When Chen asked what lay beyond the heavily guarded railway line, the trader lowered his voice and pointed through the window.

'Think of it like a lake,' he said, 'with bridges and roads across it owned by the Japanese. But outside the railway—in the lake itself—live the communist guerrillas. They control most of the territory. The Japanese will occasionally make sorties, of course.'

He gestured to a village in the distance, smoke curling from its rooftops.

'That one will say the communists just left.'

He pointed to another hamlet nearby.

'That one will claim they haven't seen a communist in months.'

After weeks of massaged newspaper reports in Harbin, this was the first tangible evidence Chen had encountered of a spirited and effective resistance from his comrades.

There was little time for further conversation. The man soon nodded off and began to snore. The rhythmic clatter of wheels over track lulled Chen into a fitful slumber of his own.

He was jolted awake by a sound that wrenched him upright—harsh, metallic gunfire. The unmistakable chatter of a machine gun.

Heart pounding, he peered through the window. There was no visible aggressor—only a deep, thundering roar that chilled his blood. He had seen before what bombing raids could do—he remembered the carnage at the Battle of the Xiang River, where so many communists had died.

He leapt to his feet, shouting for the passengers to get down. Some obeyed, others were too slow. The aircraft strafed the train with terrifying accuracy. A woman screamed and threw a blanket over her two children. Bullets ripped through the wooden walls. A man too slow to duck was nearly decapitated by a flying shard of glass.

The assault lasted perhaps five minutes. Chen called again for everyone to stay down. Then the train's own machine guns opened fire. There were explosions—louder, more concussive. But somehow, his carriage remained intact. The train ground to a halt.

Chen, though no expert on aircraft, deduced that the attackers had switched to cannons—targeting the engine or the rails themselves. From where he lay, he caught a glimpse of a plane banking away, its wing marked by a white sun on a field of blue—the insignia of the Republic of China Air Force.

There was no third wave.

The carriage was a butcher's shop. Blood pooled on the floor and soaked into the wood. Flesh and blood streaked the walls. The screams of the injured filled the air. The two children survived under the blanket. Their mother had not. A passenger helped them out before they saw her body.

The air reeked of fresh blood—and vomit. Chen could not bear it. He retrieved his coat and climbed the embankment, collapsing against a frozen boulder. He felt nothing—not the cold, not the wind, not the wet bite of snow through his trousers.

Japanese soldiers who had been aboard the train were now returning from the forests. Chen realised they had been trained to leap from the moving train at the first sound of gunfire. They were regrouping.

The engine had been obliterated, a twisted frame of molten metal. The forward gun posts were annihilated. And with a surge of grief, Chen recognised the brutal irony—Chiang Kai-shek's air force had killed more Chinese than Japanese. This was the reality of modern warfare: blind, impersonal, indifferent to sides.

His thoughts turned to the aircraft. They had been fast, modern, and well-armed. Could they have been Soviet-made?

Reinforcements arrived from a nearby blockhouse. The troops began to clear the dead, dragging bodies into two forward carriages. But Chen's greatest horror awaited in the remains of the first-class carriage—reserved for Japanese officers. It had caught fire, perhaps from a broken stove. The officers had burned alive.

Not even the enemy deserved that.

Soldiers began dismantling what remained of the most damaged cars, tearing wood into splinters for a makeshift fire. The warmth, however, was not shared with the Chinese passengers. Fuel for their stoves had run out, and the cold settled over them like a curse.

Mark Oulton

Printed in Dunstable, United Kingdom